The Narrow Seas

A Novel of Viking Age England

Book Eleven of The Norsemen Saga

James L. Nelson

Fore Topsail Press
64 Ash Point Road
Harpswell, Maine 04079

To my beloved Felicity Fern Lockard,
Darling granddaughter,
A new generation of Viking Princess.

The Narrow Seas:

Those seas over which the King of England claimed sovereignty from the earliest days of England's emergence as a maritime power. They were the two seas which lay between England and France (the English Channel) and England and the Netherlands (the southern North Sea).

Oxford Companion to Ships and the Sea

The Viking Longship

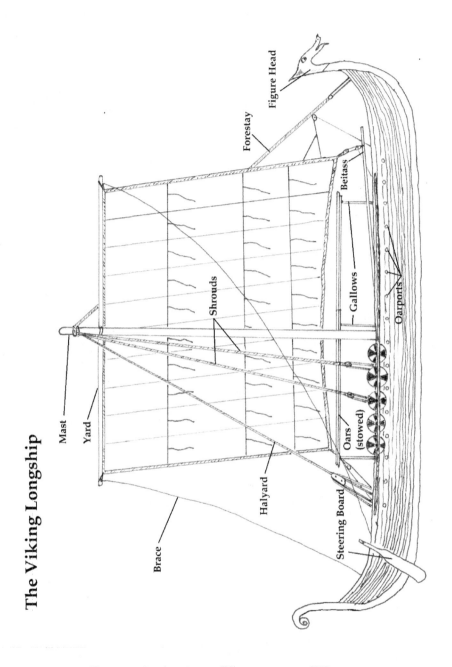

Mast · Yard · Brace · Halyard · Shrouds · Forestay · Figure Head · Beitass · Gallows · Oars (stowed) · Steering Board · Oarports

For terminology, see Glossary, page 372

Prologue

The Saga of Thorgrim Night Wolf

There was a man named Thorgrim Ulfsson. He was the son of Ulf of the Battle Song, who was a renowned warrior with many exploits to his name. As a young man, Thorgrim went raiding with a jarl named Ornolf Hrafnsson, and Thorgrim, like his father Ulf, achieved many things and won great fame and riches for himself. When he grew older, he and Ornolf returned to East Agder, in Vik in the country of Norway, where they were from. Thorgrim purchased a farm there, and he met with much success as a farmer, just as he had in his raiding, since he was smart and hardworking.

Thorgrim was known then as Night Wolf, since he would often grow bad-tempered as the darkness came on, and it was thought that on such nights he would take on the form of a wolf and travel the countryside. Men knew to avoid him when he was having the wolf dreams, but otherwise, he was well-liked and respected, and men sought his council on many things.

Ornolf, too, thought very highly of Thorgrim and offered Thorgrim his beloved daughter Hallbera's hand in marriage. This union was very agreeable, both to Thorgrim and to Hallbera, and they were wed and were very happy in their marriage. Hallbera bore Thorgrim three children: a son named Odd and another named Harald, and a daughter named Hild. The sons were handsome and strong, and Hild was fair and of kindly temperament, like her mother.

Now, Ornolf was known as Ornolf the Restless, because he was never content to remain at home, but rather was always eager to sail to distant lands and to raid there, despite having as much wealth as a man might want. He often implored Thorgrim Ulfsson to go raiding once again, but Thorgrim was content on his farm and did not wish to leave his family, and thus he rebuffed his father-in-law's requests.

A few years after the birth of Hild, however, when Hallbera was no longer a young woman, she died giving birth to a daughter, though the daughter lived and was named Hallbera after her mother. Thorgrim Night Wolf was greatly distraught with the death of his beloved wife, and so when Ornolf next asked him to go raiding, he accepted, since now his farm seemed to bring him only grief. His first son, Odd was a grown man by then, with a farm and a family of his own, but his younger son, Harald, was fifteen years of age and ready to go raiding with his father. So Thorgrim brought the boy with him, while Hallbera the Younger went to live with Odd on his farm.

Ornolf's ship was called *Red Dragon* and aboard her he and Thorgrim and their men sailed to Ireland where they raided many churches and villages and had many adventures. Though they meant to return home after one season, the fates intervened and they remained in that land for two years. Ornolf the Restless was killed fighting at a place called Vík-ló, but he made a good death and was much mourned.

Sometime after Ornolf's death, when Thorgrim was at sea with his fleet of ships (for during his time in Ireland many others joined with him because he was known as a lucky man and a skilled warrior) a great storm arose and blew Thorgrim's ships across the sea to Engla-land. There they continued to raid had much success, gathered even greater riches. Despite his good fortune and reputation, Thorgrim Ulfsson's heart longed to return to his home in East Agder. He was no longer a young man, and the many wounds he had suffered gave his considerable pain. He wished to give up the life of raiding and take his ease at home, but the gods willed otherwise.

And though Thorgrim did not know it, there was little peace to be had in East Agder, or all of Vik, in those days. That part of Norway was ruled by a king named Halfdan Gudrødson, who was known as Halfdan the Black. Though Halfdan had ruled for a full twenty-five years, and had seen his kingdom and his wealth grow threefold in that time, he was a greedy and ambitious man and wished to bring even more of the country under his rule.

The farm that Thorgrim had left behind continued to prosper under Odd's direction, but Halfdan wished to have the farm for his own, so he decreed that Thorgrim owed taxes and tribute that had not been paid and said that Thorgrim must surely be dead as he had been gone so long from that country. For those reasons, Halfdan declared, he would take Thorgrim's farm for his own.

Odd, however, did not believe that his father was dead, and he knew that the taxes and tributes had been paid to King Halfdan and so he would not allow Halfdan to take Thorgrim's farm unjustly. Odd's neighbors likewise did not wish to see the king take a man's land with no reason and they joined Odd in his fight against Halfdan. When Odd was captured by the king and beaten almost to death his neighbors contrived to free him and secret him away, which made Halfdan very angry, and made him vow vengeance on all of them.

None of this was known to Thorgrim Night Wolf, who was then still in Engla-land at a place called Hamtun, where he and his men had built a *longphort*. There he had fought with the king in that part of the country, which was called Wessex, and Thorgrim had taken many captives for himself. Thorgrim had demanded ransom for the captives, which the king agreed to pay, and Thorgrim was determined, more than ever, that once the ransom was paid he would sail to his home in Norway and allow nothing to stop him.

Here is what happened.

Chapter One

Now answer me, Much-wise, this that I ask,
and fain would learn from thy lips:
who here doth rule, and hold in power
The wealth and wondrous halls?

Day-Spring and Menglod
The Poetic Edda

The sky was thick with cloud, and the rain was coming down in sheets. It buffeted the squalid fishing village — now a *longphort* — as well as the larger town of Hamtun across the water, and all of the south coast of Engla-land, it seemed. Maybe the entire world, as far as anyone could tell. The open ground between the hovels closest to the river and the river itself, which was damp earth in the best of times, was a field of mud now, interspersed with great puddles that danced and rippled in the downpour.

Thorgrim Night Wolf stood under the edge of the tent, a massive affair made from one of the ship's sails spread over a stout frame. He stood just back from the stream of water coming off the bolt rope and looked out over the soaked ground.

Good day to take a man's head off...

This village where they had come ashore was on the south side of a wide river the English called the River Terstan, or so they had been told by Geldwine, the Saxon fisherman they had taken as their pilot. It was a sorry place, a cluster of a few dozen wattle-and-daub-built thatched huts, a couple of wooden docks extending out from the shore, a church with a stunted, square tower. There were fishing boats pulled up on the banks and nets spread out on the shore to dry, Thorgrim guessed, though how anything was supposed to dry in that miserable country he could not imagine.

The Northmen had been a few weeks at this place, landing here after doing battle with an English fleet that had surprised them on the river. Thorgrim and his men reckoned it a victory of sorts, seeing that the English had retreated, but the Northmen had paid a heavy blood price for that dubious honor.

They tied their ships to the docks and pulled them up on the muddy banks, putting the water between them and the Wessex army to the north. They found the village deserted, which was hardly a surprise. When a fleet of longships appeared off an undefended town, the folk rarely stayed to welcome the newcomers.

Thorgrim stared for a moment at the mud and the growing puddles, then sighed, pulled his hood over his head, and stepped out into the rain. The hood and the cloak he wore over his mail shirt were still damp from the last time he had ventured out from under the tent. He knew they would never actually be dry until the sun came out, which he assumed it had to do eventually, but at least the wool garments spared him the irritation of having the rain falling on his head and his shoulders.

He crossed the open ground, heading for the river's shore, the mud pulling at his soft shoes. He stopped for a moment and looked behind him, running his eyes over the walls that made up the longphort. When they realized they would be in that place for more than just a few days, they had fortified it against an attack from the landward side. They had pulled down a half dozen houses, depriving any attackers of the cover the structures might have provided, and used the timbers to build a crude half-circle wall, running from shoreline to shoreline and enclosing that part of the river bank they meant to defend.

Thorgrim watched the sentries on the walls moving slowly back and forth, no doubt miserable in the rain and waiting for their watches to end. There were more men under the tents, some gaming, some tending to weapons. He knew there were men sleeping in the small huts that had been left standing within the confines of the walls.

Time for some entertainment...

"Harald! Louis! With me!" he shouted and, a moment later, his son ducked out from under the tent. Harald was sixteen and not quite as tall as Thorgrim (though Thorgrim was of no great height), but he was powerfully built and considerably more filled out than he had been when they sailed from Vik several years before. His hair was blond, like his mother's, and braided behind, and his beard, such that it was, was blond as well.

He tromped through the mud and the rain toward Thorgrim. Like Thorgrim he wore a mail shirt, but he wore no cloak over it, and the polished iron links, wet with the rain, shone in the muted light. At his side he carried the sword Oak Cleaver, a magnificent Ulfberht blade that had belonged to his grandfather, Ornolf the Restless.

Harald stopped a few feet from where Thorgrim stood, his expression serious, the rain running in streams down his face and hair.

"Today?" he asked.

"Today," Thorgrim said.

A moment later, Louis de Roumois joined them. Louis was a Frank, though he had been a runaway apostolate from the monastery at Glendalough when he had been taken prisoner by Thorgrim's war band. He had traveled with them ever since, fought in many battles alongside Thorgrim and his men. For that he was given his freedom, but still he remained with them. Like Thorgrim, he wanted only to get back to his home, and knowing that Thorgrim would have to cross to Frankia, or at least Frisia, to get there, Louis figured staying with the Northmen was his shortest route.

"Yes, Thorgrim?" Louis asked as he approached. In his time with them Louis had picked up the Northmen's language to an admirable degree. "Why must you drag me out in this miserable rain?"

It was a reasonable question, but Thorgrim was not sure he would bother with an answer. He did not particularly like Louis, and had meant to kill him on various occasions, but had always been stopped by the Irishwoman, Failend, who had been Louis's lover once, and then Thorgrim's.

Still, Thorgrim had come to have a grudging respect for the Frank. Louis was bold and skilled in battle, and sensible in council. What's more, he seemed to have a better grasp on the complex politics swirling around them in the kingdom of Wessex, better than Thorgrim or any Northman could hope for. Not that Thorgrim cared in the least about the politics, but he understood it might have an effect on ransom payments, which he cared about very much.

"Time to keep my promise to this king of Wessex," Thorgrim said. He had heard the king's name, several times, but he could not begin to pronounce it.

Louis frowned. "One more day, perhaps?" he asked.

"No," Thorgrim said. He looked back at the big tent and he could see the crew of his own ship, *Sea Hammer*, getting reluctantly to their feet, strapping on swords, and wrapping cloaks around their shoulders and heads. They knew what Thorgrim was about, and knew they would be expected to join him.

"Sea Hammers, to me!" Thorgrim called, and the men ducked out from under the tent and came stomping through the mud in his direction. He turned and continued down toward the water. All of the ships had been secured to the shore or the docks, save for *Sea Hammer*, which was anchored by the stern fifty feet from the bank with a cable run from her bow to a heavy stake driven into the earth. The prisoners were housed aboard her, and they were easier to guard out on the water like that.

Thorgrim stopped by the stake jutting up out of the mud and looked toward the bow of his ship, blinking the rain out of his eyes. Gudrid, who, with a few others had remained aboard to guard the prisoners, was standing on the foredeck, leaning over the side, and looking ashore. Thorgrim waved an arm as if beckoning him and Gudrid waved back, then disappeared aft.

"Take up that cable," Thorgrim said, nodding toward the rope tied to the stake. "Pull her in."

A dozen of *Sea Hammer*'s crew grabbed onto the cable and began to heave as Gudrid and his men eased the anchor line off the stern and the ship was hauled bodily toward the bank. Soon the bow came to a stop in the shallow water, as close to shore as it was going to get, and the men made the rope fast to the stake once more.

Gudrid leaned over the side. "All of them?" he asked.

"Yes, all of them," Thorgrim said. There was a lesson to be learned here, and Thorgrim wanted to be sure it was learned well.

Two of Thorgrim's men came over *Sea Hammer*'s side and landed in the waist-high water, spears in their hands, and the first of the prisoners came after them. There were fourteen in total and they varied greatly in appearance, from young and fit to old and corpulent. They did, however, have several things in common. They were all wealthy, all men of great importance in Wessex. They were all dressed in torn and filthy clothing that had once been the finest of tunics and leggings. They all wore expressions of anger and fear.

They had been taken at Winchester, while Thorgrim and a handful of his men, imprisoned and condemned to burn at the stake, were trying to escape from that town. The Northmen had managed to get free and over the wall when these West Saxons had come riding out in pursuit. They were the nobles of the shire, what the English called ealdormen, and they had ridden forth to impress their king and for the fun of cutting the escaping heathens down. They had ridden right into an ambush that Louis and Bergthor had set for them.

Now they waded ashore as the spearmen of *Sea Hammer* formed a loose cordon around them, though the prisoners did not look quite up to making any bold attempt at escape. They had been a week aboard the ship, drinking water and eating dried fish and bread, not the sort of fare they were accustomed to in their great halls. They had slept on the deck under a tent spread over the yard and used a wooden bucket as their privy. They had not been mistreated in any way, but the sustained terror and the boredom and the unaccustomed hardship had taken any fight right out of them.

Thorgrim led the way back up the shore. Most of the Northmen had come out from under the tent now, or from the huts, because they, too, were bored and this offered some potential entertainment. Someone had taken the stump they used for cutting kindling and set it up in the open, and now the men made a broad half-circle around it.

When he reached the stump Thorgrim gestured for the prisoners to stand in a loose line facing the others. Bergthor stepped up to Thorgrim's side, his expression cheery as ever, if a bit worried as well.

"You're going to do this thing?" he asked.

"Yes," Thorgrim said.

The two men had known each other of old, and their fleets had blundered into one another a few weeks before. They had joined forces, and though Bergthor was ostensibly Thorgrim's equal in command, he generally deferred to Thorgrim, as most men did.

"But...not all of them?" Bergthor asked.

"No," Thorgrim said. "Just one. I want the others to watch. If we set them free, I want them to fear us, to know we're men of our word."

Bergthor nodded and said nothing more. Thorgrim turned to Harald.

"Harald, tell these sorry bastards that I gave their king one week to deliver their ransoms, and that one week is at an end."

Harald nodded and spoke to the assembled men, translating his father's words. In the short time that they had been in Engla-land, Harald had picked up enough of the English tongue to communicate tolerably well. He seemed to have a surprising ability with language. That had only become clear upon his learning Irish in order to pursue an Irish girl with whom he was smitten, and English was much closer to their native Norse than that. In truth, even Thorgrim could understand an occasional word or two of English.

As Harald spoke, Thorgrim watched the prisoners' faces. He could see traces of renewed alarm, but for the most part, their looks did not change. This announcement would come as no surprise. If they had not guessed at first why they were being brought ashore, the chopping block would certainly have tipped them off.

Harald stopped and turned back to Thorgrim.

"Tell them I promised if the ransom was not here in a week, I would send their heads back to the king," Thorgrim said. "And now I mean to do that."

Louis stepped up as Harald was speaking the words. "Is this the best path, Thorgrim?" he asked, speaking softly. "Sure, it would be better to give it some more time."

"No," Thorgrim said. "If they think we're weak, we'll get nothing. But I'll show some of that mercy you Christ-men are always going on about. I'll just kill one, not the whole lot."

"Merciful, indeed," Louis said. "And of course, there's no ransom to be had for dead men."

Thorgrim nodded. "That's right." He turned to Harald. "Tell them I mean to send one man's head back to their king. Ask them if any wish to volunteer."

Harald called out the words and Thorgrim watched their faces. Glances back and forth along the line, or eyes downcast, feet shuffling. Then one man pressed his lips together and took a step forward. He was older than most, but well-built and had a noble bearing about him. That, and the fact that he had the guts to step up to die for the others, suggested to Thorgrim that he was one of the chief men of the area. Probably the one the king would least like to lose, which made him more valuable than most.

"Boldly done," Thorgrim said. "But I think we'll hold onto that one for now." He pointed to a man three over from the volunteer, a younger man, more frightened looking, with less of the air of a leader about him. He wore a silk tunic that had probably been a fine garment when he rode from Winchester, and leggings so shredded they were hardly worth keeping on.

"We'll have that one," Thorgrim said. Three of the Sea Hammers stepped over to the chosen man, took him by the arms and pulled him out of line. He made some sound of protest, his fear turned to confusion, then disbelief and panic as he was all but dragged forward.

They pulled him over to the chopping block, pushed him down to his knees, and quickly bound his hands behind his back. He looked up at Thorgrim, rain streaming down his blanched face. He spoke, the words coming loud and fast.

"He says…" Harald began, but Thorgrim held up his hand.

"It doesn't matter what he says." Thorgrim pulled his sword, Iron-tooth, from its scabbard and stepped around until he was sideways to the kneeling man. He nodded and two of those who had dragged the man over pushed his head down onto the chopping block. The Saxon was still yelling something though his head remained pressed to the wood. Thorgrim lifted the sword over his shoulder.

"Lord Thorgrim!"

The voice came from the wall, one of the sentries who was standing watch. "Lord Thorgrim!"

Thorgrim frowned with annoyance. He lowered the sword and turned. "Yes?"

"Message from the tower, Lord! Men coming!" Thorgrim had positioned men as lookouts in the tower of the small church. It was not terribly high, but it was the highest point around. They were instructed to send word to the wall if they saw anything of note.

"Men?" Thorgrim called.

"Yes, Lord! They say riders…a dozen or so. With shields and banners. And two carts. Heading here, by their looks!"

Thorgrim nodded. He looked down at the man on his knees, his head still pressed to the chopping block.

"Harald," he said. "Tell this one he might be the luckiest bastard in all of Engla-land."

Chapter Two

Now answer me, Much-wise, this that I ask,
and fain would learn from thy lips:
what is that gate called? Ne'er among gods
was more fearful barrier found.

Day-Spring and Menglod
The Poetic Edda

Lucky the young Saxon lord might have been, but Thorgrim knew his luck could be short lived, that he might have earned only a reprieve, not a pardon. That would depend on what exactly was coming their way. Of course, it did look promising. A dozen men in mail with banners flying would not be sent to escort carts bearing dried fish.

He ordered the prisoners moved under the tent and climbed up the ladder to the top of the wall with Harald right behind. Starri Deathless was already there. His two axes were hanging from his belt, which suggested he was hoping for a fight, but his tunic was still on, which meant he did not really think he would get one.

"Night Wolf!" he said as Thorgrim approached. He nodded toward the riders and the carts. They were visible from the wall now, just approaching the edge of the little village, coming down the one road that led in and out. "I think they'll attack us, I can feel it."

"Hmm, I fear not." Thorgrim knew that Starri did not think so either. He and Starri and the others had nearly been killed a dozen times in their fight on the river and in their recent foray to Winchester, and that delighted Starri Deathless as much as a man could be delighted. But it also made the forced idleness of the past few weeks even harder to bear. He was hoping for relief, but he would not get it from this party approaching.

They waited in silence as the carts made their laborious way down the muddy road, the riders moving slowly so as not to leave the oxen behind. Thorgrim could see more details now: the bright armor and helmets, the fresh-painted shields, the horses clad in armor of their own. Wealthy and powerful men.

Finally, the riders came to a stop twenty feet from the wall and the three men in the lead removed their helmets and looked up. Two of them Thorgrim recognized, or at least thought he did.

"We know these men, don't we?" he said to Harald.

"Yes," Harald said. "The younger man is the Frank who came before. The older one also came before. Leofric is his name, I think. The other one, with the big moustache, I do not know."

Thorgrim nodded. The young man, the Frank, spoke up, a short burst of words. Thorgrim turned to Harald.

"He reminds us he is Felix from the court of Æthelwulf, king of Wessex," Harald said, "and he bids you good day.'"

"Tell him good day," Thorgrim said and Harald translated the words. Felix and the older man, Leofric, nodded. The third man remained motionless, staring up at them.

Once again Felix spoke in his soft, almost musical Frankish accent. When he was done, Harald said, "Felix says he has the ransom and hopes you did not cut the prisoners' heads off yet. He says if not, best open the gate so they might come in."

Thorgrim stared down at them a moment, then looked over the other armed men and the carts. No trickery that he could see, and he could not imagine how there might be.

"Very well," Thorgrim said. "Tell him to hold a moment."

He and Harald climbed back down the ladder and Thorgrim ordered the gate cleared away. It was not actually a gate, per se, just a gap in the wall that had been piled up with shorter baulks of timber and sundry other debris. As a gang of men pulled that debris away, others stood ready with spears and shields and axes in the unlikely event that Felix had more men lying in wait to storm the longphort.

Soon the way was clear and Felix and Leofric and the third man came riding through, with the other mounted warriors following behind and the carts rolling in behind them. Once they were well inside Thorgrim ordered some of the timbers put back across the opening in the wall, just enough to discourage anyone hoping to rush the gap.

Bergthor stepped up to Thorgrim's side as Felix started talking again. "He says the ransom is here," Harald said, "on the carts. One hundred pounds of silver for every man who is still alive."

Thorgrim did not answer. Rather he stepped over to the first cart and pulled the heavy cloth cover back to reveal a series of iron-bound boxes of various sizes. He opened the lid of the first one. Inside, the pile of silver gleamed dull under the overcast sky. Coins and ingots and brooches and rings and arm rings, silver in every possible configuration.

He turned back to Felix. "Your prisoners are unhurt," he said. "Once I'm sure we have the silver agreed upon you may take them and go." He noticed that Felix had brought no horses for the prisoners, and supposed he intended to carry them back in the carts. It was a humiliating way to travel, but Thorgrim suspected that neither Felix nor his king were much pleased with the stupid way these men had let themselves be taken for ransom.

He looked over at his own men who were watching the proceedings with eager expressions. He called to four of them, men who had been with him a long time, men whom he trusted to make a survey of the ransom and judge that it was all there. He then instructed Bergthor to find four of his men to join them. It would not do to have only men from one camp do the counting. That was how ugly disputes began.

Now Felix was talking again. Thorgrim turned to Harald.

"He says while the men are counting, might we get out of the rain. He says he has business he wishes to discuss."

Thorgrim frowned. *Business?* He could not imagine what business they might have. It had been Thorgrim's intention to load the silver aboard the ships and be gone on the next tide. The last thing he wished to do was remain in this place and do business with men who had tried to burn him alive.

On the other hand, it would not hurt to hear the man out, nor was Thorgrim any more eager than Felix to stand about in the downpour waiting as fourteen hundred pounds of silver was counted.

"Very well," Thorgrim said. "Come with me. Bergthor, you had best join us. Harald, get Louis and join us as well." He crossed the muddy ground to one of the small huts within the walls and pushed open the door. The house consisted of a single room and a loft, with a bed in one corner and an oak table near the hearth where a low fire burned, belching smoke and adding to the odors of wet wool and cooked meat.

A half dozen men sat around the table, drinking and eating, but they stood when Thorgrim entered and grabbed up their shields and cloaks and spears and left the hut to their chiefs. Thorgrim shed his cloak and stood for a moment in front of the fire, letting what little warmth it was creating wash over him. Finally, he turned and gestured toward the table.

"Sit," he said. Felix sat on the bench facing him, and Thorgrim saw that the other man, the one with the moustache, had come as well, and he sat next to Felix. He was a big man, bigger than Felix by far, with the hard face of a warrior, a short goatee and an impressive moustache that swelled off his upper lip and dipped down either side of his mouth. Bergthor sat on the bench facing them.

The door opened again and Harald stepped in with Louis right behind him. Thorgrim gestured to the bench on which Bergthor sat and Harald and Louis sat as well. Thorgrim found a stool and took his place at the end of the table. He picked up one of the cups the other men had abandoned, looked into it, found it was full of ale, and drained it. He set it down again and looked up. Felix and Louis were eyeing one another and their enmity was not hidden.

Felix spoke a few words in Frankish, sharp and harsh sounding. Louis cocked an eyebrow in response and spoke a few words back, to which Felix replied in the same ugly tone.

"What does he say?" Thorgrim asked Louis.

"He tells me how much he admires me, and the bold way we all made our escape from Winchester," Louis said. Thorgrim did not press him further. He doubted that he would get anything more enlightening from the man.

The two of them, Louis and Felix, shared some history, that was clear. It had to go back to Frankia: whatever it was ran deeper than a chance meeting in Winchester, where Felix had ordered Louis removed from the prison in which they had all been held.

Until that moment, Thorgrim had not really cared enough to ask, but now he saw that the connection between the two might be of some importance. It was why he had asked Louis to this meeting. If nothing else, his presence seemed to unsettle Felix, and that was for the good.

Thorgrim turned to Felix. "The other man, the old man, he's not joining us?"

"No," Felix said, after the words had been translated. "I asked that he watch the counting. Silver can go missing when it's counted. This is Grifo," he said, gesturing toward the big man beside him. "He's part of the king's hearth-guard and he gives good council."

Thorgrim looked at the man. He did not have the look of a counselor, but Thorgrim nodded a greeting and Grifo nodded back, then stared past Thorgrim into the fire.

"Very well," Thorgrim said. "We're out of the rain. State your business."

Harald translated and Felix nodded as he did, then Felix turned to Thorgrim and began to speak. He spoke for some time, and when he was done, Harald began. "Felix says the king is making...I didn't understand the word, but it seems to mean a voyage or a trip...to the city of Rome."

Thorgrim nodded. *Rome...* He knew roughly where Rome was, somewhere far off to the east. The Romans had built all those extraordinary roads in Engla-land, and the magnificent buildings that were now mostly in ruins. They had created all that and then, for some reason, had left and abandoned all the good work they had done.

"He means to cross the sea, the narrow seas, to Frankia," Harald continued. "That's why all the ships are here, the ships we did battle with, and all the warriors who were aboard them."

Thorgrim nodded again. He waited for more, but apparently that was all Felix had said, because Harald asked a question and Felix answered with another lengthy reply.

"Felix says that us being here is a problem," Harald continued. "They don't want to fight their way past us, not with the king and his household on board. There will be women and children on many of the ships. And they don't want to leave the county unprotected with us still here."

Thorgrim's face remained expressionless as he considered the words. Felix was being unusually candid for a man in talks with his enemy and it made Thorgrim suspicious and wary.

"He says they don't have to sail from here, they could sail from Lunden," Harald continued, "but it would be difficult, and the king is impatient."

"Very well," Thorgrim said. "What does he want? Is he asking that we leave?"

Felix started in again, even before Harald could translate. When he was done, Harald just stared at him for a moment, as if he was not certain he had heard correctly. He asked a question and Felix answered, then Harald turned to Thorgrim.

"Felix says the king wishes for us to sail in company with him. To Frankia. As warriors. Protection."

Thorgrim frowned. He looked at Felix who met his gaze with a face that betrayed no expression. He looked back at Harald. "Does this Frankish bastard think we'll swear an oath to the king of Wessex?" Thorgrim asked.

"No," Harald said. "He says they'll pay us for our service. We need only see them safe across the narrow seas to Frankia, no more."

Thorgrim was not sure what to say to that, but Louis apparently was. "Now see here, Thorgrim, before we agree to anything, we had best…" he began, but Thorgrim held up his hand to stop him. He had been watching the big man, Grifo, who had been staring into the fire this whole time, showing no apparent interest or understanding of the goings on.

"I think this is a trap," Thorgrim said, his eyes on Grifo's face. "I think these dogs are lying. We have their silver; we need nothing more from them. We'll cut their throats now and be done with it."

He saw it then, just the faintest reaction on the man's face, the slightest twitch of an eyelid. Grifo's discipline was impressive indeed, but it was not perfect.

Both Bergthor and Louis started in at once, reacting to Thorgrim's words, but Thorgrim spoke over them. "Watch what you say. That one, Grifo, speaks our language, and I'd wager that's why he's here."

With that Grifo looked Thorgrim in the eye. He did not speak, his expression did not change. He just looked at Thorgrim for the length of five heartbeats, then looked down at the fire again. Thorgrim turned back to Harald.

"Ask Felix what the king will pay us for his protection," he said and Harald translated the words.

"He says that can be negotiated," Harald said. "Today he wants only to know if we are open to such an arrangement."

Thorgrim looked at the others. He could see this proposal had taken them as much by surprise as it had him, and no one could form an immediate opinion on the wisdom of such a thing.

"Ask him when we would sail, if we agreed to this," Thorgrim said. Harald turned to Felix.

"Two weeks' time," Harald said when Felix had answered.

Thorgrim was silent for a moment. His first impulse was to laugh at the notion and give Felix a swift kick for suggesting such a thing. But when he thought about it, he realized that this should not be dismissed out of hand. There was much to consider here.

"Tell Felix to return the day after tomorrow," Thorgrim said. "We'll give him our answer then." When that was settled, they stood and filed back out into the rain, which thankfully had tapered off to a heavy mist. The ox carts were empty, the various iron boxes carried off to the big tent. Gellir, one of the men Thorgrim had picked for the counting, stepped up as he approached.

"We emptied each box, Lord Thorgrim," he said. "All fourteen of them. They were all full of silver, no iron or anything to try and trick us. We didn't weigh the lot, but it seemed right. We can weigh it all if you wish, but it would take some time."

"No, that's good what you've done." Thorgrim did not care for the tedium of weighing it all out. If there were fourteen iron boxes full of silver, that was good enough for him. "Go fetch the prisoners."

A moment later they arrived, a line of dirty, angry men in shredded clothing, men trying to cling to what little bit of dignity they had left. Their appearance was in sharp contrast to that of the men who had come for them, Felix and Grifo and Leofric and the other men-at-arms in their gleaming armor, fine wool capes draped over their shoulders. Nor did Felix seem much inclined to ease their discomfort. He greeted them with a curt nod and spoke one brief sentence, which prompted a chorus of protests from the men.

"Felix says they're to ride in the carts," Harald explained. "And they want to know why horses were not brought for them, and clothing as well."

Thorgrim could not help but smile. The king, apparently, was going to make these men pay with their dignity for the aggravation they had caused. He watched with amusement as the now-freed prisoners climbed slowly and grudgingly into the back of the carts, seating themselves on the rough boards, while the men at arms and Felix and Grifo and Leofric mounted their fine horses. The carters snapped their whips and the oxen began to walk as the riders led the way through the gap in the wall that had again been opened for them.

Thorgrim crossed the muddy ground to the big tent under which many of the men were huddled, Bergthor at his side. The iron boxes of silver had been stacked there against the longphort's makeshift wall.

"Can you believe this Felix fellow?" Bergthor asked. "Asks if he can hire us like farmhands…he's just trying to trick us into not sacking Winchester, but he don't fool me. The man has balls, I'll give him that."

"He does," Thorgrim agreed. "Time enough tomorrow to work that out. Right now, I think we best divide up this silver, let every man have his share and be done with it. Less chance for trouble that way, I think."

"I suppose you're right," Bergthor said. He glanced over at the fourteen boxes stacked against the wall.

"No easy task, dividing all that among…what? Five hundred men?" Thorgrim said. "Do you have a man who can do it?"

"Well, I have this fellow Ofeig who has a head for that sort of thing," Bergthor said.

"Good," Thorgrim said. "Set him to it, and I'll have one of my men help him out, and we'll get this all divided up. That'll raise men's spirits despite the rain, I can tell you."

He smiled at Bergthor's uncertain look, then walked off. He found Gudrid and told him to help Bergthor's man with the division and found Harald and told him to keep an eye on the whole undertaking, and to call him if anything seemed amiss. He found Louis at the far end of the tent and told him to follow.

They returned to the small hut which was once again vacated for Thorgrim's use, and he and Louis sat by the fire. Thorgrim poured cups of ale and took a long drink, and then he spoke.

"Tell me about this fellow Felix," he said.

Louis shrugged as Thorgrim knew he would, because that was Louis's response to nearly everything. "He's a Frank," Louis said. "So I would expect you to think that he's a liar and a thief."

"Is he?" Thorgrim asked. "You don't seem to have a very high opinion of him. Or him of you."

Louis nodded and considered the question. "He serves the king of West Frankia. Charles the Bald. He's Charles's man entirely."

That surprised Thorgrim. "I thought he serves this king of Wessex."

"He does," Louis said. "He was sent by Charles to help in Æthelwulf's court. But I suspect the real reason he was sent was to be a pair of eyes for Charles. I have no doubt that everything that's done in Wessex is reported to Paris."

"I see…" Thorgrim said. "But why do you two hate each other? I thought you were a good and loyal Frank like him."

Louis sighed. He looked down at the table for a moment, and then up at Thorgrim. "I've told you some of my story," he said. "Do you want to hear more?"

Thorgrim did recall Louis telling him some bits of how he had come to be where he was when they had taken him prisoner in Ireland, but he had not cared enough to remember any of it. Now, however, the tale seemed to have some relevance, so he said, "Yes, tell me."

"My father was Hincmar, le duc de Roumois," Louis said. "Duc…it's a noble title…like…like a jarl, I suppose. But higher, I think. A very important man, good friend of the king. I had… have…an older brother, Eberhard, who of course was in line to inherit the title. Me, I was the captain of my father's horse guard, a *chevalier*. A soldier. We protected the country. Mostly by killing the damned Northmen, who were like a plague."

"Yes, like a plague," Thorgrim agreed. That explained Louis's skill with sword and shield, his unflinching courage in battle, a thing that Thorgrim was willing to grudgingly acknowledge.

"When my father died my brother became le duc de Roumois, and he was welcome to it. Even if I had a right to the title, I wouldn't have wanted it. I loved the life of a chevalier, and the folk of Roumois loved me. Why shouldn't they? I protected them from their enemies, and I saw that my men didn't abuse them, as soldiers so often do. Being duc would have driven me mad.

"But my brother, he wanted very much to be le duc de Roumois, and he was frightened of his own shadow. So he got it in his head that I meant to take his place, that I'd use my soldiers and the love of the folk to put myself in his seat. As if I would ever want such a thing."

"Why didn't he just have you killed?" Thorgrim asked. "It's what most men would have done."

"I don't know to be honest," Louis said. "Maybe he was afraid that the people would turn on him. Or, more likely, that the king would be displeased. Or maybe he was just too much of a coward even to have someone else do it. Whatever the reason, he disbanded my troop of horse, arrested my officers, and had me sent off to Glendalough to become a priest and spend my days praying in exile."

Thorgrim took a drink of ale. This all made sense, and explained how a Frankish warrior had come to be captured running from a monastery in Ireland. "You didn't care to be a priest and pray all day?"

"I did not."

"But this still doesn't explain why Felix hates you," Thorgrim said.

"Ah, yes, Felix," Louis said, as if remembering the original subject. "Felix and I knew one another in Frankia. My father and I went frequently to court, and I knew Felix there. Not well, but well enough. We liked one another, actually. But my brother told tales in court about my treachery after he shipped me off. Tales about how I had tried to take his place. As a way of justifying what he had done. They believed him, of course. He was…is…le duc de Roumois, after all. So, in the eyes of Felix and the king and all the court in Paris I'm a traitor and a criminal. And then I arrive in Winchester in the company of heathen raiders, and you can imagine how well that was received. It just proved the rumors true, in Felix's eyes."

"Yes, I can imagine," Thorgrim said. He took another sip of ale and thought about all that. "Here's what I don't understand," he said at last. "The only thing you seem to care about is getting back to Frankia. But I reckon they'll behead you, or worse, as soon as you get there." He waited for Louis to shrug, which he did.

"Stupid, I know," Louis said. "Most of what I do is stupid. I'm ruled by many things…my pride, mostly, or my cock…but not my brain. Still, I'm a Frank, and I belong in Frankia. And I have been wronged, and I want vengeance, or I want to die fighting for it. Either is better than sitting in a foreign land and stewing in my anger."

Thorgrim looked at the young man for a moment. Louis was about the same age as his oldest son, Odd, and as manly and brave as he could ever hope a son to be. Louis would rather die with a sword in his hand than suffer the wrong that had been done him. Thorgrim could respect that.

"You'd make a good Northman," Thorgrim said.

Louis smiled. "I suppose that's the highest compliment I can hope from you, so I will accept it. Thank you."

"So what of Felix's offer?" Thorgrim asked. "Should we trust him?"

"No, you should not trust him," Louis said. "But that doesn't mean you shouldn't take him up on it. It's true that King Æthelwulf means to cross the narrow seas to Frankia. I learned that in Winchester. We know their ships are here just as Felix said. We fought them. And it makes sense that they can't leave with enemies lurking at the gates. I don't see how Felix was lying about any of that."

"You think they would actually pay us silver to protect them going across the sea?"

"I think kings pay you heathens tribute all the time, just so you'll go away," Louis said. "This is no different, except they're asking a little more of you. If you insist on being paid before you sail then they can't cheat you. And the best part, of course, is that you mean to cross the narrow seas anyway. Now you get silver for doing it."

"You make a good argument for me accepting Felix's offer," Thorgrim said. "And it just happens that it would get you back to Frankia, which is exactly what you want."

Louis smiled. "It does work out well for me, but it works out well for you, too. And for Felix and Æthelwulf. Sometimes it seems that everyone gets what they want."

"Sometimes it seems that way," Thorgrim agreed. "And that's when you know the gods are toying with you."

Chapter Three

*Wherefore shouldst thou not show thy name
Except thou have cause of strife with thy foemen?*

Greybeard and Thor
The Poetic Edda

The wagon came rolling and jolting out of the hills to the north, down the road to the market town of Rykene. The town was three or four miles inland from Fevik on the coast of Norway. Three or four miles as the raven flies, much farther as the weary oxen plods.

The road from Rykene to Fevik was twisted and often impassable, but Rykene was pressed against a wide river, the Nidelva, which gave the town easy access to the sea. That made it a good place from which to move the bounty of the north country to other markets far beyond.

If there was wealth to be had from selling to those markets, the folk who drove the wagon seemed to have none of it. The driver was an older man, his long beard mostly white, his back hunched as he sat on the seat, reins in hand. His hair was stringy and unkempt, his face and hands smudged with ash. His wife sat at this side, and though her hair was still black, the lines on her face showed her to be near her husband's age. Like her husband she seemed worn down by decades of hard work and worry.

Their wagon rolled along on iron-rimmed wheels fashioned from wooden boards, which, like the wagon itself, had gone gray from age, save for those places where repairs had been made with fresh, new-cut planks. Two horses pulled the load. They were short and stocky and well past their prime, but still strong enough and able.

The wagon bed was full to the top, its load covered by a heavy tarpaulin, and sitting at the back of the bed was another couple, younger than the driver and his wife. Like the older couple they wore rough woolen clothing in browns and dull greens — tunic and dress, cloaks and hoods — and they, too, appeared worn from hard living.

The road was deeply rutted, but it had not rained in some time, and the ruts stood as dry ridges of dark earth and not the impenetrable mud that they could become. That was good, because there was a tolerable amount of traffic in and out of Rykene that time of year. Men and women on foot, some carrying loads, some driving livestock, riders and carts and wagons, they were all coming and going along that nondescript way.

The summer was over, the first hints of the changing season were making themselves known: a chill in the morning air, a bit of color in the foliage. The people within traveling distance of the market town who had goods to sell were eager to sell them now, and buy what they would need to get them through the long winter, when travel was not nearly so manageable, and the sea routes to the other markets were shut down by storms and ice.

The road had been running downhill but began to flatten out as the wagon neared the river. The town, which consisted of a score of wood frame homes and shops with steep thatched roofs and a temple standing proud on a prominent hill, lay just ahead, huddled against the northern bank. The older couple driving the wagon caught glimpses of the masts of the knarrs and other vessels along the waterfront that had worked their way up the river to load with cargo.

"Here we are," the old man called back, tugging on the reins to bring the tired horses to a stop. Behind him the younger man grunted and hopped down from the back of the wagon, then reached up and helped his wife down as well. Once she was on the ground, the young man stretched to work the stiffness out of his muscles.

"How do you fare, Torfi?" the older asked.

"Sore," the younger man said. "Too much sitting. But I'm fine." Under his tunic, across his back, he felt the dull ache of the lacerations that had mostly, if not entirely, healed. But he also felt strength in his arms and legs that had not been there for some time, and that was encouraging.

"Me, too," the older man said, and with a grunt of effort, he climbed down from the seat, then reached up to help his wife down. "I'll lead these miserable beasts in from here."

He walked forward, reins in hand, and when he reached the horses' heads he scratched their necks and said soft words in their ears. Torfi and his wife walked around the wagon and joined him. A few people passed by on foot, and a cart maneuvered around them. Torfi looked at each person as carefully as he dared, searching for some reaction, but no one even looked his way.

"Is there always so much trade carried on here, do you think?" Torfi asked. The words were not whispered, but neither were they spoken loudly.

"I think not," the older man said. "This time of year, people are anxious to get their business done."

"Good," Torfi said. "That's good."

The older man nodded. They had discussed this before. The more people in Rykene the better, for a variety of reasons.

"Are you ready to go on?" the wife of the older man said to Torfi. "Are you strong enough?"

There was genuine concern in her voice, and Torfi found it irritating. He knew he shouldn't, but he did, though he managed to hide it.

"He'll tell you he's fine," Torfi's wife spoke up. "Even if the Valkyrie were lifting him dead from the battlefield he'd say he was perfectly fine."

That brought smiles to the others' faces. The older man turned and gave the reins a gentle pull, and with a creak and a groan the wagon rolled forward again.

They passed the temple, and the road widened as it ran between the cluster of buildings that made up Rykene. They passed blacksmiths working in their shops and woodworkers and bakers. Where the road ended a few hundred yards ahead they saw the river and the cluster of ships and boats tied up there. They glanced right and left, looking for any sign of danger, but found themselves ignored on all sides.

A road ran along the river shore, separating those buildings closest to the river from the water's edge, a road that was the heart of the market town. Dozens, hundreds of people were making their way on foot or pushing barrows or leading horses or oxen pulling carts. Had it not been so wide, the road would have seemed impossibly crowded.

On the river side, wharves thrust out into the water where boats were tied two and three deep. On the shore side, the road was lined with rows of temporary stalls; wood frames lashed together and draped with heavy sailcloth. Most were occupied by various merchants and farmers and fishmongers, but some were standing empty.

The older man walked the horses up to the closest stall, where a thin fellow in a tunic that was once red, but had faded to something less than that, was selling combs.

"Are there stalls for rent?" the older man asked.

"Some are." The thin man leaned over his table and pointed up the wide street. "End of this row, at the tavern. A fat man named Kalf, you should find him there. He's the one rents the stalls. And a tight bugger he is, too."

"Thanks, friend," the older man said. He gestured to the others, tugged the reins again, and led the way up the road.

They found Kalf where the comb merchant had indicated, sitting at a small table outside a tavern, picking at the remnants of a slab of pork ribs. He was indeed fat, and he had not spent lavishly on his clothing or appearance.

"Kalf?" the older man asked.

"Perhaps," the fat man said. "Why do you care?"

"My name is Olaf. This is Torfi. And our wives. We were told we could rent a stall from you."

Kalf squinted as he regarded them, as if squinting would provide greater insight into their words. "I've not seen you around here before," he said. "Where are you from?"

"Nævesdal, to the north," Olaf said.

Kalf grunted. "Never heard of it."

"Few have," Olaf said.

"Why do you want a stall? What do you have to sell?"

"Lamb skins, mostly," Olaf said. "And reindeer. Some pelts. Fox. Hare."

Kalf grunted again. "Why'd you come to Rykene? No markets closer to…whatever miserable village you're from?"

"Bigger market here. More goods to trade. And silver. Reckoned it was worth a try."

Kalf nodded toward Torfi. "This one ever talk?"

"When I have something to say." Torfi had been trying to keep his mouth shut, but could do so no longer. "You always ask such a lot of questions?"

"Only of them I don't know," Kalf said. "Strangers. Not fond of strangers."

"Why's that?" Olaf asked, looking around. "This is a market town. Must be new faces all the time."

"That's a fact. And it means an honest merchant like me don't know who he's dealing with. And all the horse shit that's been stirred up as of late."

Olaf shook his head. "In Nævesdal we've heard no word of any trouble."

"Ha!" Kalf laughed. He glanced left and right, but there was no one within earshot. "Well, then, yours must truly be some sheep-buggering little dung heap of a town, if Halfdan the Black ain't been by to make your life a misery."

"Halfdan? King Halfdan?"

"So he styles himself," Kalf said. "He's been on a rampage. Or was. Seems some folk to the south got a belly full of his greedy ways and stood up to him. Fat lot of good it did them. He crushed them like bugs. And then made us all pay for their crimes with extra tariffs."

"Who was that?" Olaf asked. "Who stood up to him?"

"As I hear it, one was Odd Thorgrimson. Son of Thorgrim Night Wolf. Who was son of Ulf of the Battle Song. Odd was grandson of that old buggerer Ornolf the Restless, too," Kalf said, and when he said "that old buggerer" there was humor and admiration, not malice, in his words.

"He *was* grandson?" Olaf asked. "This Odd, he's dead?"

Kalf shrugged. "Some say he is. Some say he escaped. If he ain't dead Halfdan certainly wants him that way. Had those bastards in his house guard searching everywhere. They were at it for weeks before they gave it up." Then the fat man's tone changed, as if he realized he'd been tricked, and he said, "Now who's asked a rutting lot of questions?"

Olaf's next question concerned the price of the stall, a query more to Kalf's liking, and soon, transaction complete, they led the wagon back behind the empty lean-to they had rented. Torfi climbed up on the wagon and unlashed the tarp and pulled it back, revealing the stack of lambskins and other pelts underneath. They pulled out the component parts of a trestle table and set it up and began to stack the furs on top.

"This Odd Thorgrimson, he must have had a goodly number of men with him to take on King Halfdan that way," Olaf said in a conversational way. "And for Halfdan to consider him a real threat."

"Wouldn't know," Torfi said. "But I'd have to think you're right."

"The affairs of kings, it's none of our business," Olaf's wife said. "And I'm happy for it."

"Me, too," Torfi's wife said. "If I knew there was trouble waiting here in Rykene I don't think I would have come."

"We don't know there's trouble," Torfi said. "Kalf said something about Halfdan giving up. I don't know what he meant, but I hope it means the trouble's passed."

"Trouble's not gone, friend," said the man in the stall next to them, a cheesemaker with various wheels and lumps and blocks of yellow and white and marbled cheese on display. "It might have left for a while, but it will be back, you can count on it."

"Halfdan?" Olaf asked.

"Halfdan," the man said. "Where are you from, that you haven't heard of these troubles?"

"Nævesdal, to the north," Olaf said.

"Must be well to the north, to stay out of Halfdan's way," the cheese merchant said. "I'm Bodvar. I have a farm a few miles to the south." He extended a hand and shook those of his four new neighbors.

"I'm Olaf," Olaf said. "My wife, Vigdis. This is Torfi and his wife, Gudrun. We came down for the market and, once our pelts are sold and the gods allow, we'll return home, and be glad for it."

"A good choice," Bodvar said. "Most around here think the troubles are not over yet."

"What do people think might happen?" Gudrun asked. "Kalf said something about Halfdan giving up. But we still don't really know what anyone is talking about."

"Here's the tale as I heard it," Bodvar said. "Down south, in Fevik, there was this fellow Odd Thorgrimson. He's son to Thorgrim Night Wolf, whose name is pretty well-known. This Thorgrim, he went a'viking a few years back and hasn't been seen since. Most reckon he's dead. Anyway, Halfdan, he's always looking to get richer, more powerful. He tried to take Thorgrim's farm, or some say Odd's farm, and Odd, he raised an army and fought back. But Halfdan put him down."

"Killed him?" Gudrun asked, but before Bodvar could reply a thick-set woman with a jug in one hand, a loaf of bread in the other, stepped up and set her burden down on Bodvar's table.

"You watch your mouth, husband," she said in a harsh whisper, her eyes moving left and right. "You've no idea who's listening. Or who you're talking to."

"Ha!" Bodvar laughed. "This is my wife, Valgerd, and a nervous one she is."

The others nodded their greetings. Torfi considered the stout woman. She looked to be many things—pragmatic, humorless—but nervous was not one of them.

"We want no trouble, forgive us," Olaf said. "We've come down for the market. We've heard nothing of these things Bodvar was telling us."

"Well, you'll hear stories aplenty, I'll warrant, while you're here," Valgerd said. "Some say Halfdan killed Odd. Some say Odd drove Halfdan into hiding. Others say Odd came riding in on Odin's six-legged horse. It's all nonsense. No one knows the truth of any of it."

Someone knows the truth, Torfi thought, though he said only, "I see."

Bodvar was about to continue when a gaggle of buyers approached his stall and his wife forcefully redirected his attention their way. There was no lack of business to be had at Rykene, it seemed, and soon Vigdis and Gudrun were selling lambskins and pelts even as Olaf and Torfi were still pulling them from the back of the wagon and loading them onto the table.

All through the day people examined their wares, haggling and handing over silver, mostly, but also other things of value — wine and meat and cloth — in exchange for skins and furs. And all the while, the four who had come from Nævesdal examined the customers and searched the crowd of people who flowed up and down the street.

They looked for any who seemed overly curious, or who seemed to be scrutinizing the people rather than the goods they sold, but they saw nothing beyond buyers looking to buy and sellers eager to sell and sailors looking for diversion and, occasionally, men they took to be the chief men of the town who walked with small retinues of armed men and seemed pleased by the sight of the crowded market.

Evening came at last and the sellers in the stalls began to put their remaining goods away for the night. Various lanterns and torches appeared along the street, throwing patches of uncertain light here and there. Olaf and Torfi and their wives began to load the lambskins and pelts back into the wagon. When that was done, Torfi pulled a few stones out from the wagon bed and arranged them in a circle and kindled a fire. Soon it was burning bright, and the women set two chickens they had traded for a fox fur onto a spit and began roasting them over the flames.

Next, Olaf pulled four stools out from the wagon and set them around the fire. The four of them sat, enjoying the smell of the cooking meat and the warmth of the flames that gave some relief from the early fall chill.

"It was a good day," Vigdis said. "A good choice to come to this town."

"It was," Olaf said.

"A good day," Torfi agreed. "More than half our skins and pelts gone in one day."

They sat in silence for a while, then Gudrun stood and found four cups and filled them with ale from a jug and passed them around. They drank and made desultory conversation and stared into the fire. A little while later, Gudrun declared the chickens done and they tucked into the birds with ready appetites.

Evening had turned to night by the time they finished their meal. Torfi stoked up the fire so they might enjoy its warmth a bit longer, then he stood and stretched and ambled off to the far side of the wagon. He stopped there and looked out into the dark, away from the fire, and let his eyes adjust until the road and the buildings and the ships seemed to resolve out of the night.

He stood very still and listened. He heard the creaking of the hulls against the wharves and the lap of water. He heard a soft breeze blowing through the buildings and the sound of voices, far off. He heard an owl, and the rustle of some little creature nearby. But he heard nothing that alarmed him, nothing to cause any concern.

For a few moments more he remained where he was, looking, listening, then he turned slowly and walked back to the fire and sat down on his stool. He picked up a stick and poked at the burning logs and the fire flared and burned with renewed enthusiasm.

"It seems no one has any interest in four sheep herders from Nævesdal," he said at last. He spoke very softly, so that his words would not be heard beyond the fire ring.

"I thought the same," Olaf said. "All today. And no one seems to be paying attention now?"

"No," Torfi said. "Not that I could see."

They were quiet for a moment, and then Gudrun said, "We heard the same story from several mouths. Halfdan was searching for the fugitives, a thorough search, but now he's given up. Gone back to Grømstad."

"That seems to be the tale people tell," Olaf said. "But I wonder. Has Halfdan really given up?"

"He'll never give up," Torfi said. "He may have stopped looking for now, but he'll never give up. Still, I'd wager he'll make peace, if it's in his best interest."

The others nodded at that.

"We came here that we might learn something," Olaf said. "Did we? Do we think it's best if we return to Nævesdal, or might we move farther afield?"

That was met with silence at first. It was the one big question facing them now, and none seemed too eager to commit to an answer.

"I think perhaps there might be markets to the south," Torfi said at last. "If we continue south we might find a welcome. If we travel with care."

Again, the others nodded.

"So, will we spend another day in Rykene?" Olaf asked.

"We paid two day's rent on the stall," Vigdis said. "I doubt that skinflint Kalf will give us our money back."

The others smiled.

"Another day, then," Torfi said. "Another day to keep eyes and ears open, and if we still feel the way is clear then we continue on."

The others muttered agreement.

They talked a bit more, about this and that, and then Vigdis stood and announced she was ready for bed, and the others stood and said the same. The stools were moved aside and water thrown on the dying fire and the four of them climbed up into the back of the wagon, each couple to either side.

"It was more comfortable last night," Olaf said. The night before, and every night since leaving Nævesdal, they had slept on a thick bed of lamb skins. But now, after a brisk day in the market, the bed was not nearly so thick.

"The price of success, I fear," Torfi said. He lay down on the pelts that were left, and they were enough for his own comfort anyway. Gudrun sat next to him and spread a blanket over the two of them, then laid down as well. She pressed herself against him and he shuffled closer to her. He meant to put his arm around her and pull her close, but before he did, he reached out to the side of the wagon and pushed his fingers down through the furs until his fingertips brushed the thing they were searching for. He paused for a moment, gently stroking the object, the talisman.

It was a sword. Blood-letter, the sword of Ulf of the Battle Song.

The sword of Odd Thorgrimson.

His sword.

Chapter Four

The same year a great army of heathens came with three hundred and fifty ships to the mouth of the river Thames....

Asser's Life of King Alfred

The witan, the council of ealdormen and the archbishop and bishops and the more prominent thegns in Wessex, were the men who the king was willing and sometimes actually interested in listening to. Felix tried not to smile as they came filing past.

He found it amusing on many levels. The witan made their way into the chamber adjacent to the throne room, to which they had been summoned, maneuvering as they approached the door like horse soldiers on a battlefield vying for the most advantageous position. No one wanted to be first. No one wanted to be last. No one wanted to enter beside a man whose status was much less or much greater than his own.

Many of these men Felix had seen just a few days before as they climbed, sore and weary, humiliated and angry, down from the back of the carts. They blamed Felix for that business and either scowled at him now or avoided looking at him altogether.

They were not entirely wrong to blame him. In fact, they were not wrong at all. He had made those arrangements himself, his own petty revenge for the awkward situation in which they had put Æthelwulf and himself.

Felix was not what one might call lighthearted, but he still found the whole thing terribly amusing.

I should thank those fools, really, he thought as he smiled and nodded to each, whether they scowled at him or not. Because of them he had been forced to consider the Northmen's presence more closely, to visit their encampment and to negotiate with them. Riding to

32

Hamtun had given him time to mull over their predicament and wonder how the king and his entourage might put to sea with an enemy ensconced right across the river. It was then that he hit on the idea of paying the heathens to change sides.

It took two days' travel with the slow-moving oxen to get from Winchester to the Northmen's camp in the sorry little town called Gillingas, across the water from Hamtun. In that time Felix was able to examine his idea, to look at it from various angles and probe it for flaws and weaknesses.

The biggest unknown, of course, was the heathens themselves. Felix had no notion as to whether or not he could work with them in the same way he could with civilized men, so he held off on any final judgement until he could observe them firsthand. To his surprise, the savage Northmen were more reasonable than he would ever have expected, which he found most encouraging. Now it was time to see if the Englishmen could be reasonable as well.

There was a boy standing at Felix's side, joining him in watching the witan parade past. "These men seem very angry with you," he said, his voice soft and almost musical. Felix looked down and smiled. Alfred, King Æthelwulf's seven-year-old son. Felix liked Alfred and recognized him as a bright boy, brighter than his older brothers, if not as robust. He would be making the pilgrimage to Rome with his father, the boy's second time to the Holy City.

"They do seem angry with me," Felix agreed. "Why do you think that is?"

"Because you made them ride in the ox carts," Alfred said matter-of-factly.

"That could well be," Felix said. "Have they been complaining to your father?"

"I don't think so," Alfred said. "But I heard them talking amongst themselves. They said you are a Frankish sod…sood…"

"Sodomite?" Felix supplied.

"Yes," Alfred said. "What's that?"

"Someone who is feared, yet respected," Felix said. "But you should not use that word yourself."

Alfred soaked up words like butter on warm bread, and Felix knew he had to be careful. He did not want young Alfred to get into trouble, and certainly did not want him banished from his company. The boy was the best pair of eyes and ears that Felix had at court.

At length, the last of the king's council had filed into the room and taken a seat at one of the tables that sat perpendicular to the head table. There was no jockeying for those seats: each was carefully assigned in order of every man's importance, which generally meant his wealth, though position in the church hierarchy or the length of one's relationship to the king played a part as well.

Æthelwulf, of course, was seated at the head table, with his oldest son Æthelbald to his right and his second son Æthelberht, to his left. Alfred, too young to be at the table, was consigned to a chair against the wall, and from there he would observe everything.

Felix nodded to the guards who flanked the doors and the men closed them as Felix walked around the perimeter of the room to take his place next to a man named Swithun, the Bishop of Winchester, who was seated next to Æthelbald at the head table. Felix set down the various scrolls and parchments he carried and settled himself in the big oak chair.

He glanced toward the back of the room to make certain that the two priests who were ordered to act as scribes were ready. They were at their tall desks, quills poised, so he turned to Æthelwulf and said, "At your pleasure, Your Highness."

"Very well." Æthelwulf turned to Swithun. "Bishop, please lead us in prayer. We surely need the Lord's guidance at this time."

"Of course, my Lord Majesty." Swithun launched into a prayer that was heavy on the presumption that God would guide King Æthelwulf's hand in smiting his godless foes. When he was done, Æthelwulf lifted his bowed head and ran his eyes around the room.

"Lords, thank you for coming," he said. "Trying times, as you know. We needs must sail for Frankia, but the damned heathens are still across the river from Hamtun, and they don't seem much inclined to leave."

"That surprises me," said an ealdorman named Eanwulf. "They are much richer now than they were just a week before. Is that not enough to induce them to go away?" Eanwulf was the most influential of Æthelwulf's ealdormen, and not one of the fools who had been ransomed, so he felt free to offer that not-so-subtle slight.

"Apparently not," said Æthelbald. "We've had men watching them, and there's nothing to suggest they're making ready to get underway."

There was silence for a moment as the council waited for someone to offer some thought or insight. There were two sorts of men, Felix knew, who would be willing to speak up just then: the king's old friends — wealthy, important men who did not fear his wrath — and the young and bold ones who hoped to gain Æthelwulf's notice. It was one of the latter who spoke next.

"I say we attack on the morrow, or the next day," came a voice from the back of the room. It was a young thegn named Drefan who, as Felix understood it, had good reason to want to slaughter the Northmen, or at least try. Drefan's head had apparently been on the block, and had the ransom arrived just moments later than it did, Thorgrim would have separated that head from Drefan's body.

We must take this one with us across the seas, Felix thought. *He might be the luckiest bastard in Engla-land.*

"We have the men-at-arms now," Drefan continued, "and the heathens are weak after our king did such great slaughter in the Battle of the River Itchen. I council that we attack directly."

Felix looked around. There seemed to be little enthusiasm for that suggestion. King Æthelwulf's ships had indeed done great slaughter during their fight on the River Itchen, but it had been at the cost of considerable English blood spilled. The king himself had been wounded, which had necessitated their retreat before a complete victory could be won. None of the council seemed eager to repeat that brutal day.

"We might fight the heathens and we might win," said Leofric, who sat near the head of the table, as was his due. He was one of the men who did not fear the king, at least not so much to keep from speaking his mind. "But it would be a bloody business, and it's not what's most important just now. The most important thing is to see his majesty gets safe to Frankia and thus to the Holy City."

Heads nodded at Leofric's words. Each of the ealdormen and thegns had brought their own men-at-arms with them, but that did not mean they wished to see them lost fighting the heathens. Soldiers were not easily come by.

"We could say damn the heathens and sail from Londun," offered Ealdorman Egbert, who sat directly across from Leofric. "That way is clear enough."

More silence as that suggestion was considered, though it was hardly a clever idea, or new. Sailing from Londun was one of the obvious choices, and it offered many obvious drawbacks.

"A damned great expense," Æthelwulf said at last, voicing the biggest concern of both him and the others, who would be expected to pay for such a venture. "Our ships are at Hamtun. We'd have to get new ones. And the entire court would have to travel to Londun. No small distance."

That was met with muttered agreement, followed by another bout of uncertain silence. Felix sat through it, and sat through a few more nonsensical suggestions and statements of the obvious before he judged the time was right to make his initial thrust.

"Sire," he said, leaning forward and looking over at Æthelwulf, "if I may be so bold, I have had a thought that might be just the way forward."

"Please, yes, go ahead," Æthelwulf said. "No one else seems to have any damned ideas."

Felix stood and looked around the room, amused by the variety of expressions he saw looking back at him: curiosity, loathing, uncertainty, boredom. But he was not really addressing all of the men here. Most of the younger thegns did not matter, nor did the men who had been taken by the heathens for ransom, since they had fallen out of the king's favor. There was only a handful, such as Leofric and Egbert and Eanwulf and the king's sons, whom he had to convince.

"Lords, we are all aware of our situation," he began. "The king's fleet has been collected at Hamtun, we are all but ready to sail to Frankia, but the heathens stand in our way. We have little hope of their leaving, and even if they do, it's likely they'll be lurking in the Soluente, and we'll find ourselves fighting them there.

"Now, I have no doubt we would beat them again, as we did the last time, but the risks are too great. We'll have women and children with us this time, and priests and the archbishop. Not to mention the gifts and treasure we bring for the journey to the Holy City."

He paused and let those words sink in. He looked around the tables. He saw more curiosity now, more interest in what he was saying.

"Leaving from Londun is not viable, we know that. So here is what I have in mind: we sail from Hamtun as planned, and the heathens sail in our company. We hire them, like house guards, if you will, to escort the king's ships across the narrow seas."

Silence followed those words, but Felix did not continue because he knew that the crash of voices would come, and an instant later it did. Nearly every man in the room began to speak at once, most in tones of outrage, some incredulous, some amused. It went on like that for nearly a minute before the king raised his hands and called for silence.

"Well, Felix, you've taken us by surprise, I would say," Æthelwulf announced, when the last of the voices had died away.

"It's outrageous! The very thought!" thundered an ealdorman named Godric, one of the men who had been ransomed by the heathens. "As if we could ever trust those vipers!"

"Are we certain they can't be trusted?" Felix asked. "They did keep their word concerning the hostages." He knew Godric would not care to have the witan reminded of that, and he could see on the man's face that he was right.

"Did they?" one of the thegns called from the end of the table. "They nearly cut Drefan's head off."

That was met with another chorus of shouts and protests. Felix held up his hands, and when it was reasonably quiet again, he spoke.

"I have no wish to defend the heathens. I loathe them as much as any man," he said. "But the fact is that their leader, Thorgrim, gave us one week to deliver the ransom, and it was a week and a day when I arrived with it. What's more, he said he would kill all the prisoners, but I have it on good authority that he intended to kill only one that day."

And the most useless one, at that, he thought.

"But really, Felix, do you think we can bargain with these people?" Eanwulf asked

"It's hardly unknown to pay the heathens tribute, rather than do battle with them," Felix said. "It's been done often enough. In Frankia King Charles has even paid one band of Northmen to fight another. Not so different than what I'm proposing."

Before Eanwulf could reply to that, Leofric chimed in. "As it happens, I've dealt with this Thorgrim before. Back in Devonshire. I won't say that he's a man of honor, since I'm not sure that can be said of a heathen. But I will say that he kept his word when he gave it."

"Exactly," Felix continued. "I think if we meet Thorgrim's price, we can trust him to see the king's fleet across the seas. Whatever price we agree upon, we pay him half of that on our departure and half when we reach Frankia. That gives him a reason not to betray us, or to just sail off. And when we get to Frankia, I have no doubt that my lord King Charles will agree to pay most or all of the balance."

"Ha!" Byrnhorn snorted. "I know Charles of old, and I know he's a tight-fisted one. You really think he'll pay a tribute that he had no part in agreeing to?"

Felix thought about that for a moment. "No," he said at last. "Most likely he'll have the heathens put to the sword. In which case it's no dishonor to us. We owe nothing, and there's a good chance we can recover the tribute we paid on sailing."

Heads nodded at that and Felix could sense a growing appreciation for the wisdom of his plan.

"This is all well and good," Æthelbald said, "but is it likely the heathens will oblige us?"

"My guess is that they will, Lord," Felix said, which was not actually true. He did not have to guess. He knew for a fact that the heathens would oblige, because he had already struck a deal with them.

The offer had been made in the smoke-filled hut in the heathen's camp. Felix had returned the following day, as Thorgrim instructed, to hear the answer. He brought Grifo with him, in part for protection on the road and in part because Grifo could speak the Northmen's language. It was why he had brought Grifo the first time, but Thorgrim had guessed the truth of the thing and so guarded his tongue, which made Grifo less useful. Still, Felix wanted his own man there to be sure there were no misunderstandings based on poor translation.

They met in the same smoky hut with the same men from Thorgrim's camp, including Louis, who Felix was not happy to see. Louis was a traitor, an enemy of Charles's court, and the moment he set foot in Frankia he would be escorted to the executioner's block. But worse, as far as the negotiations went, he was also a Frank and a noble who understood the politics of the Frankish court. Louis knew Charles and knew Felix and he would not be as easily duped as an ignorant heathen like Thorgrim would be.

But in the end, and despite Louis's presence, the negotiations had gone as well as Felix dared hope.

"Tell me what you want, and what you'll offer." Thorgrim spoke through the young, yellow-haired man named Harald, whom Felix suspected was Thorgrim's son.

"We want to cross the narrow seas to Frankia," Felix said. This had all been laid out the day before, but Thorgrim, apparently, wanted to be clear, which was fine. "We'll have women and children with us. We want to sail from here unmolested and we want you to sail in our company. We want you to defend the king's ships against any attack."

"Attack?" Thorgrim said. "We promise to leave you in peace, and if anyone else attacks you, we fight in your defense?"

"Yes," Felix said.

"For instance," Thorgrim continued, "if you're attacked by a fleet of Northmen, we're to protect you?"

"Yes," Felix said. "And please don't tell me that Northmen don't ever do battle with fellow Northmen."

When that was translated, Thorgrim smiled. "No, I won't tell you that," he said, but even as Harald was translating, the fat one named Bergthor began to speak. He spoke to Thorgrim and he spoke in a hushed and emphatic tone.

Felix looked at Harald, but it was clear that Harald had no intention of translating this exchange. He looked at Grifo.

"The fat one says he can't believe that Thorgrim is even thinking of doing this," Grifo said. He spoke Frankish, his native tongue, which, as far as Felix knew, none of the others, save Louis, could speak.

Thorgrim spoke next, his tone not so insistent.

"Thorgrim tells Bergthor they should at least hear us out, hear our offer," Grifo said.

Then the fat one said something else, stood abruptly and left the hut.

"He says he's heard all he needs to hear," Grifo said.

Interesting..., Felix thought, though it was not clear how this might be of use, or if it would be a problem. He turned to Thorgrim and Thorgrim gave him a raised eyebrow, then spoke.

"Thorgrim says, what will you pay us to keep you safe?" Harald said.

"Ten pounds of silver for each of your ships," Felix said, and once again Thorgrim smiled on hearing the translation.

"One hundred pounds of silver for each of our ships, paid before we sail," Thorgrim said by way of his son.

"The king is a wealthy man," Felix said, "put he just paid you fourteen hundred pounds of silver. His treasury is near empty."

Thorgrim listened to the translation, then spoke. Harald turned to Felix. "Thorgrim says he thinks the rich fools who were taken prisoner paid the silver, not the king. He says one hundred pounds of silver for each ship."

Felix nodded. *Clever man*, he thought. "Twenty pounds of silver for each ship," he countered.

"Forty," Thorgrim said.

"Agreed," Felix said. "But only half when we sail. You'll get the other half when we are safe in Frankia."

"Do you not trust us?" Harald translated Thorgrim's words.

"No more than you trust us," Felix said. "Which is to say, not much at all." And on hearing that translated, Thorgrim smiled once again and stuck out his hand and he and Felix shook on the deal. It was done.

But Felix told the witan none of that. He had no wish for any of them, especially the king, to know that he had negotiated with the heathens of his own accord. Neither had he wanted to make his proposal to the witan unless he was certain the heathens would agree. If the witan rejected the idea, there would be no harm in going back on his word to Thorgrim.

"I propose we offer the heathens one hundred pounds of silver for each of their ships," Felix said next, and once again the room exploded in outrage.

"Lords, lords, please!" Æthelwulf called over the voices of the witan and one by one the men fell silent. The sound had nearly died away when Byrnhorn's voice filled the room.

"One hundred pounds of silver? That's madness!" he shouted, and his words were met with nods and shouts of agreement.

"I have to agree that seems a bit much," said Leofric, always the voice of reason.

"Perhaps it is," said Felix. "Mind you, I have every hope to get it back once we reach Frankia, and King Charles...sees to the situation."

"That is if the damned heathens don't sail off with it," Byrnhorn said, to more general agreement.

"My lords," Æthelwulf said, "what say you to this? We offer the heathens forty pounds of silver for each of their ships, with half to be paid when we sail and the other half to be paid on reaching Frankia. Then, if they do sail off, it's with no great fortune."

Heads were nodding at that, since it was the king's suggestion, and because it seemed quite reasonable compared to Felix's offer.

"Are we agreed then?" Æthelwulf asked. "We'll approach the heathens, see if they'll agree to our terms?"

The witan nodded their agreement, and voiced their assent. Æthelwulf looked at Felix. "Felix, you'll ride to the heathens' camp, see about making the arrangements?"

"I will, Lord Majesty," Felix said. "You may count on me."

Chapter Five

Sore shame 'twould be to wet my burden,
in wading thus thro' the water toward thee
Those mocking words would I pay thee, mannikin,
could I but reach yon side of the sound now.

Greybeard and Thor
The Poetic Edda

Bergthor was not a happy man. He was not happy when he stormed out of the hut where Felix was laying out his plans, and he was not happy when Thorgrim finally left the hut himself and ordered the gap in the wall opened so Felix and Grifo could leave. He was not happy when he confronted Thorgrim a few hours later, after having poured a fair amount of mead down his throat.

"Thorgrim!" he called, slogging through the mud to the table where Thorgrim sat under the tent, the remains of a meal spread out in front of him. Harald and Brand sat near him, and Gudrid and Hall and few others. Louis, as was his wont, sat by himself, some distance away.

"Bergthor," Thorgrim said. "Come, have a cup with me." He watched as Bergthor approached, tried to gauge what the man might do. Was he coming to talk, to plead, to fight? Thorgrim preferred it was none of those things. He would be happy if Bergthor would just drink with him and let all of this pass, but he did not think that would happen.

He could see Bergthor's anger as the man approached, his desire for confrontation, bolstered by drink. Bergthor stopped at the edge of the table and stared at Thorgrim and Thorgrim looked back at him, keeping his face expressionless. Bergthor was angry enough to fight, but he was not drunk enough to draw a sword on Thorgrim Night Wolf.

Thorgrim was the first to look away, reaching over and taking up a pitcher of ale and filling a nearby cup. "Sit, Bergthor," he said. "Sit and talk to me."

With that Bergthor seemed to sag, like a sail that had lost its wind. He dropped on the bench across the table from Thorgrim, picked up the cup, and drained it in one swallow. Thorgrim filled it again. He was glad to see the fight was out of the man. Thorgrim of twenty years earlier would have provoked Bergthor into drawing his sword and then killed him, but he was not that man anymore.

"Do you actually trust that son on a bitch, that Felix?" Bergthor asked after taking a more judicious drink from his cup. "He's a Frank, by all the gods, and he's in the employ of the King of Wessex. Could a man be less worthy of trust?"

"I trust him, yes," Thorgrim said. "I trust him to do what's in his own best interest, the same as I trust any man. And it would seem that his interest is to get this king to Frankia. And that's easier done by not fighting us. Or anyone. And the best way to avoid a fight is to do what he's doing, which is to pay us to not fight, or to fight anyone else who threatens his king."

Bergthor scowled, looked down into his cup, and considered that. He had never been the sharpest blade in the smithy and the drink was not helping.

"I think he'll double-cross you, you'll see."

Thorgrim almost shrugged but he caught himself. The last thing he meant to do was pick up a Frankish habit. "I don't see how. Either he brings us twenty pounds of silver for every ship, or he doesn't. If he doesn't, the deal's off. And they'll pay the price for that."

Bergthor fell silent again, his eyes on the table. He took another drink and set down his cup. He frowned and looked up at Thorgrim. "I thought we'd thrown in together. Thought we had joined forces, you see? Thought we were going raiding. Winchester, it's still ripe for plucking. There's lots of wealth to be had, all over this country."

Ah, there it is... Thorgrim thought. Bergthor was not a lucky man. He and his men had not had good fortune thus far. But he reckoned that his luck had changed when he met up with Thorgrim Night

Wolf. He reckoned this was a partnership that would bring wealth and fame to him and his crews.

"We were well met, Bergthor," Thorgrim said. "I'm happy we crossed paths, and I have you to thank for the ransoms we received. But I'm trying to get home, you know that. I was trying when we met, and I still am. My men wanted to come with you to Winchester, so I agreed. But now I'm heading back to Vik, and if no man wants to join me, I'll sail *Sea Hammer* there single-handed."

Bergthor was silent for some time, drinking his ale, looking down at the table. Finally, he looked up at Thorgrim. "Your men wanted to come to Winchester," he said. "Maybe they want to stay in Wessex, join us in raiding. Do they all want to sail for home?"

Thorgrim considered that. He did not know. He had taken it for granted that they did, but, in truth, he did not know.

"I don't know," he admitted. "But on the morrow, I'll ask."

So the next day, after *dagmál*, the time of breaking the night's fast, Thorgrim called all of the men of the longphort together. The rain had stopped and there were even bits of blue sky showing where the clouds were breaking up, so Thorgrim ordered one of the tables brought out from under the tent, and he and Bergthor climbed up on top so they could look out over the assembled crews.

"All right you men, listen up," he said, and the buzz of hundreds of conversations faded away. He ran his eyes over the men looking up at him: many, many faces that he knew so well, many others, Bergthor's men, whom he hardly knew at all. He had assumed that his men, at least, were as eager as he was to get back to their homes. But Bergthor's words had made him realize that perhaps they were not.

"I think word has pretty well gotten out as to what our plans are," Thorgrim continued. "In case there's any confusion, the king of Wessex means to sail to Frankia within a fortnight of now. And he'll pay us forty pounds of silver for every ship so that we won't attack them when they do, and for us to sail with them and see no one else attacks them either. That's it."

He paused while the men considered that and the volume of discussion rose again. Though he had never officially announced his intentions, since he was not in the habit of discussing or debating his plans, he doubted that any of them were surprised. In a crowded longphort word spread like the most virulent disease.

"Now, I mean to cross to Frankia and then sail for Norway," Thorgrim continued. "And nothing will stop me, short of the gods striking me down. Any man of my ships' crews, or any of Bergthor's, is welcome to come with me and get their share of the silver the English pay. Any man who doesn't is welcome to do as he wishes."

Those words prompted more discussion among the crowd, then one of the men, one of Bergthor's men, shouted, "What's to stop us from taking the silver and plundering the English ships anyway?"

"I am," Thorgrim said. "If I take the English silver and give my word I'll offer protection, then I'll offer protection. Any man who wants to break his word has to go through me and my men first. And that holds until we reach Frankia, or until the English go back on their word."

The men were quiet for a moment, as if surprised by what Thorgrim had said, as if surprised that he meant to keep his promise to Englishmen. Then Bergthor spoke.

"You men who came with me, we meant to keep raiding. That was our plan. There's still lots of plunder to be had on these shores, and I still mean to lead you in taking it. Thorgrim, he's set on sailing for home, but he gives any of his men leave to join us if you want. The choice is yours."

"I say we keep on and fill our ships with English silver and gold!" another of Bergthor's men shouted, and that was met with enthusiastic cheering from many of those gathered around.

Thorgrim watched the men as they yelled. It was Bergthor's men who were joining in; his own stood silent, or looked around in curiosity. Like himself, most of the men who manned his ships had been years from home and they were done with raiding.

In the time they had been together, on the coast of Ireland and Engla-land, they had all won and lost several fortunes. But their luck had been good of late, and each man was considerably more wealthy than he had been only a short while before. None of them cared to tempt the gods further. Better to take what they had and make for home.

"No man has to answer now," Thorgrim said. "We sail in fourteen days, or thereabouts, and you each have until then to make up your minds." With that he hopped down from the table, his feet sinking in the still-muddy ground. The impact sent a wave of sharp pain pulsing out from the spear wound he had received during the fight on the river, a wound that was just now healing up. He gritted his teeth and cursed himself for a fool for not remembering that such a jump was ill-advised.

"Night Wolf!" Starri Deathless came hurrying over, and he had an odd look on his face, part agitation, part concern. "I'm worried, Night Wolf, about what you said."

"What of it?" Thorgrim asked as the pain subsided.

"Well, this plan of yours," Starri said. "You mean to protect the English?"

"I do."

"But...shouldn't we be fighting them? Not protecting them?"

"We'll protect them, unless we need to fight them," Thorgrim assured him. "I mean to be ready for whatever comes."

"A man like you, you can't just go home to die in your bed," Starri said.

"I can if the gods will allow it," Thorgrim said. "But I doubt they will."

In truth, Thorgrim hoped there would be no more fighting. He had had his fill of it, something that Starri would never understand. Unfortunately, what Thorgrim hoped for, he found he did not often get.

"I think there's every chance that the English or the Franks will betray us," he said. "And so yes, there'll be fighting."

Starri smiled. "I'm glad to hear it, Night Wolf. It's why I stay with you, you know."

"I know," Thorgrim said. Starri was berserker and, for him, battle was life's blood, the reason for existence, what drink or sex were to other men. Starri believed that the gods favored Thorgrim, and because they loved him they would always lead him to battle. In Starri's mind, fighting was a gift, and death in battle the greatest gift of all.

"Don't you want to go home, Starri?" Thorgrim asked. "Buy a farm, get a wife? Enjoy your wealth?" He was teasing the man, but he knew Starri would not realize that. Thorgrim did not actually know where home for Starri was, or if such a place even existed, short of Valhalla.

"What wealth, Night Wolf?"

"The plunder you've got. The silver and gold. I know for a fact you were given at least three pounds of silver only yesterday."

"Oh," Starri said. "I suppose I was." Starri gave no more thought to silver than he did to the bread and porridge he ate at dagmál. "Now, what by all the gods did I do with it?"

"In any event," Thorgrim said, "we sail in fourteen days. You have until then to decide what you'll do."

Two weeks. That was how long Thorgrim gave Starri and the rest to choose the course they would follow, but it did not take any of them that long to decide. Thorgrim doubted that they spent even the remainder of the morning considering the question.

Of the five hundred or so men in the longphort, thirty of Thorgrim's men elected to join Bergthor's and continue raiding. A dozen of Bergthor's men opted to come with Thorgrim and sail for Frankia and then home.

Thorgrim hoped that would be an end to it, that they would all just bide their time and then part ways. But he knew it would not be like that. It would not be that simple.

Men were like the weather. At first, they seemed unpredictable, as if you could never guess what was coming. But after years of observation, of noting this or that, of being aware of what conditions led to what outcomes, one could start to make predictions. Of course, there were always surprises, breaks in the pattern, twists that one did not see coming. But for the most part, when a storm was brewing, Thorgrim could see it well in advance.

And what he saw now he did not like. Two camps of men, one intent on leaving, one intent on staying, stuck together on a small plot of land. Two camps with little shared history and quite a lot of time on their hands and ample drink. Thorgrim could see the clouds building.

The day after announcing his intentions to the collected crews he called his captains together. They met in the hut: Hardbein, captain of *Fox*, Halldor who commanded *Black Wing*, Asmund, master of *Oak Heart*, and Harald who was once again in command of *Dragon*. *Blood Hawk* had been Godi Unundarson's ship, but Godi was feasting with the gods now, having stood like a boulder against breaking seas, fighting their enemies at Winchester so the others might escape. Thorgrim had given command to Gudrid, who had proven himself a good man and a good sailor.

He himself held command of *Sea Hammer*, largest of the fleet. Six ships, a tolerably strong fleet, and six ship masters. Thorgrim asked Bergthor to join them as well.

The others were already assembled when Bergthor arrived. "One of your men said you wished me to be here?" he said as came into the hut. His tone was not hostile, not like the day before, but it was also far from friendly.

"Yes," Thorgrim said. "I'm meeting with my captains. About what needs must be done. I thought you should join us."

"Why?" Bergthor asked. "It's no business of mine."

"No, it's not," Thorgrim agreed. He felt his temper flare, never a good thing. "But as long as you and your men are still here, I thought it would be for the best."

Thorgrim had hoped Bergthor and his men would leave the longphort once the two of them had decided to part ways. He had no authority over Bergthor's fleet, of course; he could not order them to go. Bergthor's crews had done as much as Thorgrim's to build the walls and protect that spot of ground. So, if they were going to remain, Thorgrim figured it would help if Bergthor was privy to his plans.

Once Bergthor had settled on a bench, Thorgrim turned to his captains. "I don't want your crews sitting around and drinking all day," he said, getting right to the heart of the matter. "That will not end well. We'll be crossing the narrows seas. If we're lucky, it's a day or two out of sight of land. If not, a week or more. We need the ships to be ready. What state are they in?"

One by one the masters described the state of their ships. They had already been working on them, repairing damage inflicted by the battle and the usual ravages of time and the sea. Stove-in planks were being replaced, rotten planks were being replaced, rigging was being freshly tarred, sails were being patched and reinforced, new deck boards cut, ironwork scrapped and painted. Each of the captains understood the dangers of the open sea, and the dangers of idle men, and they were doing their best to guard against both.

"We'll send out foraging parties soon," Thorgrim said. "Gather up what food we can from the country hereabouts."

"What?" Bergthor asked. "Your Wessex friends, they're not bringing us food and drink?"

They're not bringing you *one miserable thing, silver included,* Thorgrim thought, but he said simply, "No, they're not."

The meeting went on for some while longer, then the men went off to see about their various tasks and Bergthor went off to see about something. What that was, Thorgrim had no notion. Drinking. Eating. However he and his men meant to pass their time. Thorgrim did not care, as long as it did not interfere with his own men's work.

And so it went, as one day dragged into another. Thorgrim's men worked on their ships at the south end of the longphort and Bergthor's men migrated to the north end of the longphort, where they roasted oxen they scavenged from the countryside and drank ale and mead they scavenged and, on occasion, came to watch and comment on the work that Thorgrim's men were doing.

Thorgrim marked the days and set guards to keep the two camps apart as best they could. He sent out men on horseback to round up cattle and sheep and had them slaughtered and salted down. He punished those men, his and Bergthor's, who came at one another with fists or knives or swords, but happily these incidents were few. He felt the tension rising, day by day, and hoped the violence would not get out of hand before the English arrived, ready to sail.

They almost made it.

It was just shy of two weeks after he and Bergthor agreed to part ways that it all fell apart, and it fell apart over a pig.

It was not a large pig, no more than a month or so old, and no one was quite sure where the animal had come from. That was the problem. It came charging into Thorgrim's camp in a blind terror, careening from tent to table. Three of Thorgrim's men lunged for it as it raced past, and, to the delight of the others, ended up face down in the omnipresent mud.

Starri Deathless was sitting nearby, and he watched with amusement as the young swine eluded its would-be captors. Then he stood and tugged his tunic up over his head and snatched up his two axes, his usual precursor to battle. The man was bored, ready for action, and this seemed to be the best he was going to get.

He moved quickly, darting around a fire pit and vaulting over a bench to get himself in the path of the charging pig. Starri was thin and wiry. He could move with astounding speed and he could change directions as quick as a squirrel. But so could the pig, and it darted aside when it saw Starri in its path and raced off in another direction.

A crowd was forming now, men who were also bored and, having witnessed the others' humiliation, were ready to at least watch the fun if not join in. They called for Starri to chase after the pig, but Starri remained where he was. Rather than charge off in the animal's wake he took one of his axes, cocked it over his shoulder, and threw.

The weapon tumbled through the air, end over end in a flawless arc, and landed ten feet in front of the running pig. A great moan of disappointment went up from the onlookers at Starri's having missed. But Thorgrim, who had come out of the hut on hearing the commotion, understood that they had it wrong. If Starri had meant to kill the pig with his thrown ax, he would have killed the pig. What he did was a diversionary tactic.

Sure enough, when the ax landed in the pig's path, the pig veered off to his right, running away from that new threat. Starri shifted his position, three quick sideways strides, crab-like, and the second ax was up. The pig seemed to be charging toward a knot of men when Starri let the ax go. Men flinched as the iron blade flew in their direction but the spinning weapon missed them by a foot and drove into the ground just ahead of the pig, who altered course hard to starboard.

This time Starri ran forward, toward the animal, in a line to intercept. The two had closed to ten feet when the pig turned to its right, but even as it did Starri leapt to his left, matching the pig's move. Five feet, four, and the pig jerked to the left, but too late. Starri was there and his foot came down on the pig's flank, rolling it on its side and holding it pinned to the ground, squealing and thrashing.

The men cheered and applauded and Thorgrim joined them. He thought of his older son, Odd, who entertained his household by wrestling massive pigs to the ground.

I'll see him again, soon, Thorgrim thought. *My boy, Odd…I'll see him again.*

Then the cheering tapered off and another voice, ugly and coarse, cut through the buzz of talk. "Thank you for catching our pig, Starri Deathless. We'll take it now."

Thorgrim had not seen them approach, two dozen of Bergthor's men. They carried axes and spears and swords. The one who had spoken was a man called Steindor who commanded *Raven*, Bergthor's second largest ship. He was a big, humorless man with a bead that fell halfway down his chest.

"Your pig?" Starri looked down at the pig, as if surprised to see it there. "It seems to be under my foot, not yours."

Steindor turned and nodded to the two men next to him and they advanced on Starri. Steindor said, "So it is. And now it will go on our spit."

Starri smiled a simpleton's smile, as if he did not quite understand what was happening. He let his arms drop to his sides and stood there, rangy and loose. "I guess I'd hoped to eat this pig myself," he said.

"Hope all you want," said one of the approaching men. He reached out, intent on taking the pig, and Thorgrim thought, *That's a mistake...*

What happened next happened too fast for any eye to follow, entirely. Starri lifted his leg and the pig bolted away. One of Steindor's men shouted in surprise and fury and then Starri's leg came up at him and his fist swung sideways at the other man. There seemed to be a blur of arms and legs and then both of Steindor's men were on the ground, both bleeding profusely from their noses and mouths.

Well, thank the gods he didn't have his axes, Thorgrim thought, as he hurried forward to put himself between Starri and the men behind him and Steindor and his rapidly advancing band. More men were rushing over from Bergthor's end of the longphort, and others coming up from where Thorgrim's ships were pulled up at the water's edge.

"Hold, hold, hold!" Thorgrim shoved his way through the men. Starri and Steindor were feet apart and Thorgrim pushed himself between the two of them.

"That bastard'll pay for that!" Steindor shouted. His sword was in his hand and he used it to point past Thorgrim's shoulder at Starri behind him. Thorgrim caught a movement in the corner of his eye. He shifted to his left and slammed into Starri as Starri was lunging forward, knocking him aside as he did.

"Go back to your camp, Steindor," Thorgrim said. "Your business is done here."

"My business is done when I kill that madman," Steindor said, pointing at Starri again.

"Yes, Night Wolf, the man has to kill me!" Starri shouted. "It's the only thing the gods will allow! One of you bastards get my axes!"

Then Bergthor was there, pushing through the press of his own men. "Steindor, what by all the gods is going on here?" he shouted as he broke through at last, standing at Steindor's side, but looking at Thorgrim.

"These whores' sons stole a pig, belongs to us," Steindor said, his eyes never leaving Starri.

"A pig?" Bergthor said, incredulous. "This is about a pig?"

"Yes, and I'm going to gut the pig!" Starri shouted. "Gut the pig! The pig with the beard, there! And I'll eat his black heart!"

With that both sides erupted in shouting and waving weapons and Thorgrim felt the two mobs, his and Bergthor's, start to press closer. He could feel the breaking point come nearer, the moment when the storm would open up. And then a voice called out from the longphort wall.

"Riders! Thorgrim! Riders!" It was Gudrid, standing above the break that served as a gate, yelling through cupped hands.

Thorgrim felt the tension drop away, as if every man there had set down a heavy load. He looked up at the wall. Gudrid was waving and shouting.

"I'll come," Thorgrim called. He looked over at Starri. Four men had their hands on him, not restraining him exactly, but ready to if need be. He looked over at Steindor. The man had taken a step back, his sword held low at his side, Bergthor's hand on his shoulder. The moment had passed, the fog of violence whisked away.

Without a word Thorgrim headed for the wall, Harald behind him. He climbed the ladder to the top where Gudrid was standing. He looked out over the road that led to the longphort.

"Where are the riders?" Thorgrim asked.

"No riders," Gudrid said. "I lied. Seemed like the others needed some distracting. I apologize."

Thorgrim gave a faint smile. "Well done. It did the trick. For now." He turned around and looked out over the longphort and the river beyond. He frowned and squinted.

"Do you see a boat out there?" he asked.

"I see it," Harald said. "It's Hall, coming back."

Every morning Thorgrim sent a boat out to keep an eye on the English fleet tied up in the river to the south of them. That morning

Hall had been put in charge of the boat. His orders were to not return until sunset. Unless he had something to report. And here it was, not yet noon, and he was coming back.

"Maybe the English will save us from ourselves after all," Thorgrim said.

Chapter Six

A.D. 854. King Æthelwulf registered a tenth of his land over all his kingdom for the honor of God and for his own everlasting salvation.

Anglo Saxon Chronicle

Hall drove the boat up onto the mud and met Thorgrim in the middle of the camp. He arrived with the news that Thorgrim hoped he would bring: the vanguard of King Æthelwulf's entourage had arrived at Hamptun and was already loading supplies aboard their ships. That was enough to drive away any anger left in the longphort over the Battle of the Pig.

Despite the arrival of the king's men on the nearby River Itchen, they heard nothing from them until the following day. At first light Thorgrim sent his scout boat out as usual, but it returned soon after dagmál, and with it another, larger boat with bright painted strakes and pulled by eight oars on each side. Colorful flags flew at the bow and stern and Thorgrim saw the glint of sunlight off metal, spear points or helmets or the like.

Some of that glinting had better be silver, he thought, as the West Saxons approached. *And a lot of it.*

The two boats pulled up in the mud and Thorgrim's men climbed out of the smaller one and men-at-arms clad in mail and helmets, with swords at their side, climbed out of the larger. They stood in a loose line as Felix slid out after them and waded ashore through knee-high water. Behind him, and looming over him, came Grifo, in a bright mail shirt.

"Thorgrim!" Felix said, and he actually seemed to be smiling, just a bit.

"Felix," Thorgrim said. "You have silver for us?" Harald, standing at Thorgrim's side, began to translate, but Grifo beat him to it.

Felix answered, and Harald, unwilling to let Grifo beat him again, said quickly, "He says he does. Twenty pounds of silver for every ship."

Thorgrim was about to answer when he saw Bergthor approaching from the north end of the longphort with four men spread out behind him as if they were making a leisurely charge at a shield wall. Thorgrim folded his arms and waited until the men were closer. He saw that one was Steindor, who commanded Bergthor's second largest ship and who, though he did not know it, had nearly died at Starri's hands in the dispute over the pig. The others were the captains of Bergthor's other ships. Thorgrim could not recall their names.

This is not a good thing, Thorgrim thought. He had no notion of what Bergthor wanted, or what he would say, but he knew it would be a complication, whatever it was.

"Thorgrim," Bergthor said, and nodded to the others. "Felix."

"What is it, Bergthor?" Thorgrim asked.

"We've been talking." Bergthor indicated the men behind him. "We changed our minds. We'll sail with you."

Thorgrim frowned and Grifo quietly translated the words, then Felix spoke.

"Felix says he thought all of you were sailing from this place to Frankia," Grifo said.

"Tell him we are," Bergthor said. "Tell him we want our twenty pounds of silver for each ship, and we'll sail with them and protect them. Tell him it's dangerous at sea."

Thorgrim stood in silence, looking at Bergthor, considering this. Finally, he spoke. "You can take the silver, Bergthor. You can sail with us. It's no matter to me. But heed this — if you mean to attack this West Saxon fleet, you'll have to get through me and my men first."

"I wouldn't betray you, Thorgrim Ulfsson, or go back on my word," Bergthor assured him. "Us..." he gestured again at the men behind him, "...we just saw this was the best course."

Thorgrim scowled. Grifo translated the exchange and Felix answered again.

"Felix says the deal was that all you heathens leave here," Grifo said. "When you escort us across the narrow seas, you get another twenty pounds of silver. But you have to leave this place, all of you."

"There, you see, Thorgrim?" Bergthor said. "If you don't let us sail with you, it's you who's breaking his word."

Thorgrim stared at Bergthor for a long moment, long enough for Bergthor to start fidgeting in discomfort. He did not know what game the man was playing, but whatever it was, it was probably none too subtle, because Bergthor was not a subtle or clever fellow. So he would let Bergthor sail with them, and he would keep a weather eye out, and the moment Bergthor drifted off course he would stamp him like vermin. Thorgrim turned to Felix.

"Tell your men to get the silver out of the boat and bring it up to the tent," he said. "We'll count it out now."

The counting and dividing and distributing took the rest of the day. Twenty pounds of silver for each of Thorgrim's six ships, twenty pounds for each of Bergthor's five. Once the silver had been delivered and Thorgrim was satisfied that it was all there, Felix took his leave. He left them with assurances that they would sail in two days' time. He told Thorgrim that word would be sent.

The next day, and the day after that, were spent getting the ships off the mud and into deeper water, taking each alongside the one questionable wharf and loading it with food and drink, with the weapons and tents and gear that had been in use ashore, and then bringing each ship to anchor. Rigging was set taut, sails bent on yards, shields arranged in shield racks. The scout boat went downriver each day, and each day returned to report that the English were doing much the same thing as the Northmen, though in considerably greater confusion.

Two days after Felix delivered the silver, the fine-painted boat pulled upriver once again, this time with Grifo in the stern. It pulled alongside *Sea Hammer*, which was riding at anchor, and Grifo climbed aboard.

"What news?" Thorgrim asked, meeting the man amidships.

"The height of the tide will be near noontime," Grifo said. "The king's fleet will sail then, and you'll sail behind them."

Thorgrim nodded. By "sail" Grifo meant "row." There was not a breath of wind just then. But at least the current would be sweeping them seaward, and that would make the pulling easy. He looked over *Sea Hammer*'s side, downriver. The boat that had delivered Grifo was fifty feet away and rowing back toward the English camp.

"Your boat has left you," Thorgrim said.

"It has," Grifo said. "I sail with you. Those were Felix's instructions."

Thorgrim felt a flash of anger. He did not need a spy in his midst. "He said nothing about that to me. He does not instruct me."

"Maybe not," Grifo admitted. "But you need not fear. I won't sink your ship, or set it on fire. Like the old saying goes, we're all in the same boat."

Thorgrim scowled but said nothing. It was not worth the trouble to argue, and what's more, he might well get as much information from Grifo as Grifo hoped to get from him.

"Don't expect to eat our food," was all he said, then turned and walked aft. Vali was sitting near the break of the afterdeck and Thorgrim said, "Go ahead. Two notes. Make them good."

Vali nodded, stood, and lifted a long horn to his lips. He took a deep breath and blew a note, deep and loud, then breathed again and blew another. It was the signal Thorgrim had arranged a few days earlier, and it told all captains to raise their anchors and follow *Sea Hammer* downriver.

Forward, Hall and Bjorn and a dozen others were heaving in on the anchor rode, a strong cable made of braided seal skin, while the rest of the ship's crew took the oars down from the gallows and handed them along to the rowers on the sea chests.

Hall turned and shouted aft. "We're right over the anchor now, Lord Thorgrim!"

Thorgrim looked down the length of the ship. The last of the rowers was in place, oars run out of the row ports and held straight out over the water as if *Sea Hammer* was a cormorant, drying its wings.

"Bring it in!" Thorgrim stepped aft and rested his hands on the tiller. Forward the men at the anchor rode heaved away and Thorgrim felt the ship's bow swing as the anchor lifted from the mud and the current took hold.

"Give way!" he shouted. The oars came down with an easy symmetry and the rowers pulled and the drifting motion of the ship turned to a deliberate forward thrust. He pushed the tiller to one side and *Sea Hammer* began a slow, sweeping turn until she was broadside to the current, and then continued to turn until her bow was pointing downstream.

Thorgrim kept an eye on the rest of the fleet as his own ship moved through one hundred and eighty degrees of turn. The other vessels had oars run out and anchors hove in, and a few were already underway. Harald, of course, in command of *Dragon*, was one of them. Thorgrim suspected that the boy had the anchor hove short and the rowers in place an hour ago. Harald could not stand to be second in anything; he would have been underway even before *Sea Hammer* if he had not been certain that would meet with his father's unambiguous disapproval.

"Pull easy," Thorgrim called to the rowers, and Onund, who was seated at the stroke oar position, set an easy pace. The tide and current were with them, sweeping them downstream, and for the time being the rowers needed only to keep the ship moving a little faster than the current so that the steering board would bite.

They were still making for the mouth of the River Itchen when the first of the English ships appeared, emerging from behind the riverbank with its cluster of thatched houses and the ruins of some Roman building and wall. It was a vessel of war, long and sleek, almost the equal of the ships that the Northmen built. Bright banners flew from the masthead, and a huge wooden cross was suspended halfway up the mast. The oars rose and fell with a steady, well-disciplined rhythm. Thorgrim wondered if that was the king's ship, but he guessed not. He suspected the king would remain near the middle of the English fleet.

"Back water!" he called to the rowers, and on the next stroke they reversed direction, pushing the oars, rather than pulling, the backward thrust holding *Sea Hammer* steady against the current. He leaned over the side and looked at the fleet aft. The other captains had seen what he was doing and were also backing their oars, holding their places in the river, allowing the West Saxons to get clear before coming in astern of them.

Two more of Æthelwulf's ships followed the first, and then the fourth appeared, largest thus far, with boldly painted strakes of red and blue and banners flying from the masthead and the yardarms and a cross not just on the mast but on the stem and sternpost as well.

"That's the king's ship," Grifo said. He had come aft and was standing at the edge of the afterdeck, though he had sense enough not to climb up and stand at Thorgrim's side.

"How well manned is it?" Thorgrim asked.

"He's got the best rowers, and a master who knows the waters between here and Frankia like it was the pond by his great hall," Grifo said.

"Men-at-arms?" Thorgrim asked. "Is he well protected.?"

"Well enough," Grifo said. "Enough to fight off any heathens with a mind to attack." He might have meant the words as a warning or a threat, but he spoke them with little conviction, as if they were not true, or he did not think Thorgrim needed to be warned.

They watched as the king's ship turned downriver and two more large ships followed astern.

"That's it," Grifo said. "Those five ships, that's all the king's fleet," and no sooner had he finished than Starri Deathless, perched as usual at the masthead, called down, "That's the last of these miserable English bastards, Night Wolf!"

Grifo looked up, curious, then looked at Thorgrim. "Who's that?" he asked.

"Starri," Thorgrim said. "He's called Starri Deathless."

"Kind of a strange one, isn't he?"

"He's not like most men, I'll grant you," Thorgrim said. "Good man in a fight. Don't provoke him. It won't go well."

"I'll remember that," Grifo said.

Thorgrim said nothing more. He looked to starboard. *Dragon* was there, as he had ordered her be, and to larboard *Fox*, also as he had ordered, but a few of Bergthor's ships had also come up with them, which was not as planned. Felix had said the Northmen's ships should follow astern, and Thorgrim had set down exactly the order in which they would do that.

Leading Thorgrim's fleet would be the smaller ships, *Dragon*, under Harald's command, and astern of her, *Fox*. Harald thought he had been given the lead because of his bold fighting during the battle with the English fleet months before; Thorgrim was certain that the boy assumed as much. And certainly, Harald's brave action had gained the young man considerable reputation. But it was not why Thorgrim put him at the head of the fleet. Not at all.

Coming upriver, Thorgrim had placed the smaller ships at the back of the fleet, thinking they were less likely to meet the brunt of any attack there. But he had been wrong. When the West Saxons launched their ambush, the attack had come from astern, and the smaller ships had been mauled before the larger ones could turn and come to their aid. He would not make that mistake again.

"Harald!" he yelled across the water and his son, standing at *Dragon*'s tiller, waved in response.

"Go ahead!" Thorgrim pointed forward, past *Sea Hammer*'s bow. "Take your position!"

Harald waved again. Thorgrim heard him give a command and with the next stroke his rowers switched from backing their oars to pulling ahead and *Dragon* shot forward, following the English ships downriver. The rowers did their job well, pulling together with a steady rhythm. Thorgrim was happy to see it, mostly for their sake. Harald would not go easy on them if they had made a mess of it under his father's eyes.

Thorgrim turned to larboard. *Fox* was there, holding her position about a hundred feet away, Hardbein standing aft at the tiller. "Take your place astern of *Dragon*!" he called and Hardbein waved and *Fox* moved forward, drawing up to take position off *Dragon*'s larboard quarter.

"Now, where's this bastard going?" Grifo asked, nodding over the starboard side. One of Bergthor's ships was also drawing ahead, passing by *Sea Hammer*, drawing up on *Dragon*'s starboard side, opposite *Fox* but farther off.

Stupid whore's son, Thorgrim thought. He had arranged his own fleet carefully, but had not told Bergthor what to do with his, other than instructing him to keep his ships back. *Oak Heart* was bringing up the rear of Thorgrim's fleet, and he had told Bergthor to keep all of his ships astern of her.

"He'll keep clear, if he knows what's good for him," Thorgrim said, then called to his own rowers and they, too, began to pull. Thorgrim felt the ship underfoot surge ahead, a good feeling. They were moving now, their bow pointed west, or near enough.

You better not make a hash of this, Bergthor, or by all the gods I'll rip your throat out, Thorgrim thought but he kept him mouth shut and tried to keep his mind on East Agder, and home.

Harald Thorgrimson's eyes were everywhere: on the rowers, on the ships ahead, on the banks of the river. He meant to follow his orders exactly. He did not intend to make any mistakes of any description, or to let any of his crew do so. He would not allow himself to be found wanting in any way. His father, he knew, would accept no excuses, and neither would he.

He was back in command of *Dragon*. She was the smallest of his father's ships, she and *Fox*, but she was his command, his responsibility. His father had taken her away from him (unjustly, Harald still felt) when he decided that Harald had been irresponsible in going after a whale and killing it single-handedly. Or mostly single-handedly. Sure, Thorgrim had been happy enough to feast on whale meat, but he had still taken Harald's command from him.

But that was all in the past. Herjolf, who had been given the ship, proved to be a disaster. Thorgrim had somehow discovered that it was he, Harald, who led the men during the fight on the river, and he had restored Harald's command because of it.

And now, honor upon honor, Harald had been tasked with leading the entire fleet. It was not favoritism, he knew that. If anything, his father was likely to be harder on him than on any of the others. No, he was certain it was because of his bold action during the fight with the West Saxons. And he meant to be deserving of the honor done him.

He looked ahead, past the bow. The current was swinging them a little to larboard and he adjusted the steering board to compensate. He could see they were starting to overtake the last of the English ships, and that would not do. "Pull easy!" he shouted and watched as, with the next stroke, the men eased their pace.

He glanced off to starboard, where he expected to see only the riverbank but instead saw one of Bergthor's ships, two hundred feet away and drawing abeam of *Dragon*.

"You whore's son, what do you think you're doing?" Harald said out loud. He had made a point of learning the names of all of Bergthor's ships and their captains, so he knew the ship was called *Wind Rider* and it was commanded by a man named Mar whom Harald had never particularly liked. *Wind Rider* was not the largest of Bergthor's ships, but she was not the smallest either. She was bigger, certainly, than *Dragon*.

Harald felt a sudden panic wash over him. *Why is this son of a bitch here?* he wondered. Had his father suddenly decided that he, Harald, was not to be trusted taking the lead for the fleet, and had sent a more experienced man in his stead?

"No," Harald said out loud, the better to reassure himself. Even if his father wanted someone else at the head of the fleet, he wouldn't have sent one of Bergthor's ships. He would have sent Asmund, in *Oak Heart*, or Gudrid in *Blood Hawk*, or he would have come himself.

Harald leaned over the rail and looked aft at *Sea Hammer* in their wake, as if he might find some answer there. She was directly astern and a few hundred feet behind, exactly where she had been, not reacting one way or another to *Wind Rider*'s charging out of line.

He looked back at *Wind Rider* and pressed his lips together. He did not know what to do, and that frightened him more than anything, because it meant he might do the wrong thing. His friend, Brand, was pulling the second oar forward, larboard side, and Harald longed to ask him for an opinion. And he might have, if he could have done so in private, but he knew better than to show any uncertainty in front of the others.

He pushed the tiller over a bit, edging *Dragon* closer to *Wind Rider*. His eyes were on Mar at *Wind Rider*'s tiller, but Mar was looking ahead, ignoring him. The two ships were nearly abeam of one another now.

What by all the gods is he thinking? Harald wondered. He could see *Wind Rider* was pulling ahead, the rowers digging in just a bit harder than *Dragon*'s. Trying to overtake them, but not obviously so.

He wanted to call out, to challenge them, but he was afraid that doing so would make him look weak or uncertain. And he was afraid that remaining silent would also make him look weak and uncertain, or would allow a simple misunderstanding to turn his role as fleet leader into a complete debacle.

"Mar! Mar! What are you doing!" he shouted, before he had even made a decision to shout at all, as if some part of him not controlled by his brain had decided that yelling was the correct approach.

Mar looked over and waved, and though it was too far to see for certain, it looked as if he smiled as well.

Harald frowned and felt the anger starting to boil. "What are you doing?" he called again. "You were ordered to stay back!"

This time Mar responded, but either he did not have Harald's strength of voice or he did not put much effort into it, because Harald could hear only a few words of Mar's reply. He thought he heard "too slow" and "fat Saxons," but that was all. He realized that

Wind Rider, two hundred feet off the starboard side, had now pulled ahead of *Dragon*.

"You men, pick up the pace!" he called forward and Arnor, who was pulling the stroke oar, leaned into it harder and the rest followed suite and *Dragon* began moving faster through the water. Harald looked forward. The rear-most West Saxon ship was five hundred feet ahead, not close, but also not terribly far. The English were moving slow, no doubt keeping pace with the king's ship ahead. Rowing as they were, *Dragon* would overtake them soon enough, and that was the last thing that Harald wanted to do.

He pressed his lips together and tried to think, but nothing came. He tried to imagine what his father would do, but nothing came of that exercise either. He looked over at *Wind Rider*. She was ahead of *Dragon* now, and had altered course to larboard a bit, on a heading to cross *Dragon*'s bow, or to get right in front of her. Or to drive into the West Saxon ship ahead.

"Hel take that bastard!" Harald said. It was not tolerable. None of those possibilities were tolerable. Time to act. His father might forgive a wrong decision, but he would not forgive indecision, or worse, something he perceived as cowardice.

"Pull harder! Double time!" Harald saw the men at the oars, who were facing aft, craning around, trying to see what was going on, but Arnor picked up the pace and without a word the others followed along and *Dragon* surged forward.

Harald leaned over the side and looked astern. *Sea Hammer* was in their wake, the distance between them opening up, and Harald wondered if his father could even see what was happening, or if *Dragon* was blocking his view. In any case, he was too far back to do anything. Even *Fox* had fallen well astern. It was up to him and *Dragon* now.

He looked forward again. The men at *Wind Rider*'s oars were pulling harder, the ship's pace quick through the water. She was still heading downriver but angling to larboard as well, and it was clear she was heading toward the West Saxon ship. Harald could not imagine what they were doing, but whatever it was, they could not be allowed to do it. There was no longer any doubt in his mind, no hesitation.

"Pick it up! Faster!" he shouted, and once again the rowers leaned farther forward, pulled back with greater power. Stroke on stroke, he saw faces growing red, sweat standing out on foreheads and running down cheeks as *Dragon* charged ahead.

Men on *Wind Rider* were yelling now. Harald could hear their voices drifting over the water, and he could see they were yelling at the West Saxon ship, not him. He could see arms waving, and the West Saxons were shouting back, as if they were arguing about who should yield to whom.

Mar, you dumb bastard, the Saxons don't speak your tongue, Harald thought. *Dragon* was directly astern of *Wind Rider*, coming right at her sternpost. No one aboard *Wind Rider* would be able to see the ship astern unless they leaned over the side and looked aft, and no one seemed to be doing that.

Ahead, *Wind Rider* had drawn even with the West Saxon ship, the gap between the two vessels a couple hundred feet, no more. And that distance was closing as *Wind Rider* kept veering stubbornly to larboard and the Saxon ship, just as stubborn, maintained her heading. They would hit unless one or the other changed course, and neither seemed willing to do so.

Harald looked at his men pulling at the oars. He opened his mouth to call for them to pull harder still, then shut it again. They could not pull harder. Every man who had been standing idle was now doubling up on an oar, and together they were all putting everything they had into it. He looked to starboard. The shoreline seemed to be flying past, as if they were on a galloping horse and not a longship under oar.

He looked forward again. A hundred feet between the two ships, the gap closing fast. *Wind Rider* was a dozen strokes from slamming into the side of the West Saxon ship. Harald pushed the tiller away and watched *Dragon*'s bow turn to larboard as well, just a bit. He was no longer questioning his actions, no longer doubting, no longer even thinking much about what he had to do. He could see it clearly, and nothing would stop him.

The rowers pulled again and then again, a chorus of grunts and groans coming from the packed men, the thole pins creaking, the fabric of the ship working with the strain. Fifty feet beyond the bow the men aboard *Wave Rider* had seen them coming and Harald could hear the shouts, could see Mar leaning over the side and waving them away. Harald pulled the tiller toward him and *Dragon* began to turn to starboard again.

"You men on the starboard side, get ready to run in your oars on my word!" Harald saw a few men look up at him, their eyes wide with strain, but most were looking down, putting everything they had into their stroke, and he could only hope they heard.

Another twenty feet. Harald pressed his lips together. The West Saxon ship was just to larboard, *Wind Rider* to starboard. Mar was turning, swinging away from the West Saxon, trying to keep clear.

Too late, Harald thought.

"Now! Starboard oars in! Now, now, quick!" he shouted, cursing himself for waiting too long, for forgetting that tired men would not move as fast. But there was nothing for it. All along the starboard side the men stopped pulling and ran the long oars inboard. *Dragon* surged up along *Wind Rider*'s side, her bow running right over the aftermost of *Wind Rider*'s oars, snapping them like twigs. Along with those, four of *Dragon*'s oars bent and snapped, the rowers failing to move fast enough.

The crew of *Wind Rider* was shouting, cursing, waving arms as *Dragon* continued to drive down her side, breaking the oars off nearly flush with the ship, ripping the shields out of the shield rack along the sheer strake. *Dragon*'s bow slammed into *Wind Rider* amidships, her heavy oak stem connecting with *Wind Rider*'s thin strakes and Harald had no doubt as to who got the worst of that exchange. Then *Dragon* bounced off and the rowers on the larboard side took another stoke and the two ships hit again in a shuddering collision.

"You idiot! You idiot! What are you doing?" The voice seemed to come from some place at Harald's side. He looked to his right. *Dragon*'s stern was up with *Wind Rider*'s and he and Mar were no more than twenty feet apart. Mar was red-faced and shouting and waving his arms.

"Keep clear!" Harald shouted back. "You...all of Bergthor's ships...are to keep to the back of the fleet!" He looked forward. "Larboard side, hold your oars!" All along the larboard side the blades of the oars lifted dripping from the river. The two ships were drifting apart, thirty feet separating them now, and Mar was still shouting.

"You bastard! I'll cut your heart out!"

"You know where to find me!" Harald shouted back, but he was losing interest in Mar. With half their oars snapped short, *Wind Rider* would not be overtaking anyone. Harald leaned over the side and looked astern. *Fox* was still a quarter mile back and *Sea Hammer* even farther, but they were catching up. The West Saxon fleet was still making its way downriver, as if nothing had happened.

"Starboard, run out your oars," Harald ordered, and when they did, he called, "Give way, all." Together the two banks of oars came down and the men pulled and *Dragon* began to move again.

"Pull easy." Harald saw the relief on the men's faces as they leaned back, their stroke steady and slow. He looked off to starboard and astern. *Wind Rider* was sideways in the river as the current swirled her along. He could see oars being passed across the deck, half the undamaged oars from the starboard side handed across to larboard. The shattered remnants of a dozen oars were floating in the space between the two ships.

I'm sure we'll speak later, Harald thought as he watched the ship drift away. He had introduced Mar to his ship, *Dragon*. Next the man could meet Oak Cleaver, his sword.

Chapter Seven

In the Land of the Slain
I warred and stirred up
Princes to strife without peace.

Greybeard and Thor
The Poetic Edda

Skorri Thorbrandsson knew that he was a man possessed. Beyond that, he was not sure what he was.

He had been King Halfdan the Black's *sœlumadr*, his overseer, for the lands north of Grømstad. It was a good office, and Skorri had done it well. It was the sort of position from which a man could wring a lot of wealth, and it was a fine stepping stone to bigger things, as long as one remained in the king's favor. Which Skorri had. Until he had not.

But he was not sure. After Halfdan had captured the rebel Odd Thorgrimson, he had set out with his army on a tour of the lands of which Skorri was overseer. Halfdan meant to demonstrate to the landowners, the *hauldar* there, what became of men who defied their king. It was an effective lesson, until Odd had escaped, aided by the traitors Onund Jonsson and Amundi Thorsteinsson. When that happened, Halfdan sent Skorri and Skorri's handpicked men to bring them back.

Skorri promised Halfdan that he would not fail, but in fact, he did, or at least, he had failed thus far. He chased Odd and the others by land and by sea until his boat was wrecked against a granite ledge and half the men with him drowned. He continued to chase the traitors, and even caught them, but by then they had been reinforced, their numbers too great for Skorri's diminished band, and so they had escaped again.

From that moment on, Skorri had felt like a man hanging from a rope, his feet unable to touch the ground, his hands unable to grasp anything of substance.

He knew better than to return to Halfdan and admit failure. Halfdan the Black did not countenance failure in any form. Skorri would not return to Halfdan's hall until he could bring Odd with him, in chains and alive. Halfdan would not be happy with a corpse, not at all. If corpses were to be made, Halfdan would do it himself.

Skorri tried to make this clear to his king. When the fugitives escaped by boat, Skorri sent his man Alf to tell Halfdan, and to assure him that he, Skorri, and the others would hunt them down. Alf was not pleased to be sent on that task, and Skorri never heard from the man again.

It was possible that Alf delivered the message and was told by Halfdan to remain with the army. Or he might have delivered the message and been killed by Halfdan in a rage. Or he might have deserted out of fear and never delivered the message at all. Skorri did not know which it was, but he was not optimistic.

After having caught Odd and then lost him again, Skorri sent another of his men, a warrior named Kollsvein, off to Halfdan's camp with the news. He instructed Kollsvein to tell Halfdan that they had nearly captured the traitor, and would continue hunting him until they did or died in the attempt. He told Kollsvein to return with word from King Halfdan. But like Alf, Kollsvein never came back.

The various fates that might have befallen Alf might have befallen Kollsvein as well. Skorri did not know what had become of the man and so he did not know if Halfdan ever got the message, or if he understood that Skorri and his men were still loyal to their king, and still on the hunt, or if Halfdan thought they had all turned traitor as well. He did not know if he was still Halfdan's man, or if he was an outlaw like Odd. But he was not going to send yet another messenger, and so, he had no way of finding out.

Skorri Thorbrandsson could almost feel his arms and legs flailing helplessly in thin air.

He pounded his fist on the table in frustration, which made the others in the farmhouse start and look over at him, but Skorri ignored them. Kolbein Thordarson opened his mouth to ask what was wrong, and then, thinking better of it, closed his mouth and looked away.

There were five men there beside himself, five out of the twenty-five or so he now commanded. They sat in the main room of a small farmhouse Skorri had taken as his own. The rest were out searching, if they had not run off.

There was only one other room in the house and it was a sleeping chamber, which Skorri had claimed. The farmer and his wife and three children had been banished to one of the outbuildings, and allowed back into the farmhouse only to cook for Skorri and his men, or to clean or to tend the fire. They had voiced no complaints, which was a very good choice on their part.

The fire in the hearth was stoked up high against the chill of the night, and it was hissing and popping and crackling loudly, so loud that Skorri did not hear the sound of the hooves until the riders were very close, likely just a few dozen yards away. The six men inside the house heard them at the same time, and as one they leapt to their feet and drew their swords. Skorri half turned and glared at Kolbein, who stared at the door. Kolbein managed to ignore Skorri's glare for a brief moment, but no more.

"I was about to post the guard..." Kolbein said, looking at Skorri, and then quickly shifted his eyes away as they heard footsteps approaching.

In truth, annoyed as he was by Kolbein's negligence, Skorri did not think these new arrivals were a genuine threat. If Halfdan was sending men to kill him, or if Odd or his compatriots had managed to gather warriors and courage enough to take the offensive, they would not simply walk up to the front door. They would be more discreet than that.

The latch on the door lifted and the door swung open and Valgard Arason, Skorri's second-in-command, came striding in, his leggings and shoes and the end of his cape splattered with mud. He looked at Kolbein and the others, who stood with their swords at the ready.

"Put your sword down, Kolbein," Valgard said. "I promise I won't kill you, at least not tonight."

Without a word, Kolbein and the other men returned their blades to their scabbards. Valgard stepped further into the house and the dozen men behind followed him in. They made directly for the fire, where they held their hands over the flames or snatched up the food and drink spread out on the table. All except Valgard, who stepped over to where Skorri stood waiting.

"Well?" Skorri asked.

Valgard shook his head. "No luck. We swept all through the country north of here. Vifil Helgason's farm was deserted, not even a goat or a chicken. We searched the farms beyond, and then went up into the hills. No one has seen the fugitives; no one heard a thing about them."

Skorri felt the fury building but he fought it down. "No one heard a thing…" he said. "Or were they just lying to you? You believed their lying words?"

Valgard nodded. "They were lying, no doubt. Some, anyway. At least, they were lying about hearing word of Odd and the others. Of course, they had heard something. There are rumors all over Agder. But if someone had actually seen them…or had real knowledge of them…that's harder to hide. If they were lying about that, I would have seen it."

Skorri looked hard at Valgard, but Valgard did not flinch or look away. He just looked at Skorri with a face that said nothing, a face half-hidden by a wild and unkempt beard and long, matted hair.

"Sometimes people are good liars," Skorri said. "Sometimes they need to be encouraged to tell the truth."

"Oh, I know that," Valgard said. "And those I was not certain about, I encouraged them. I gave them plenty of encouragement."

Skorri nodded as he considered Valgard's blank expression. He had seen Valgard give similar encouragement in the past, and he understood that the man knew how to get what he wanted out of people. It was why he had sent Valgard north, to the country where the fugitives had most likely fled. He had others searching to the south and along the coast, but he did not think Odd and the others had gone there.

"Sit," Skorri said, gesturing to a bench beside the table. He felt the initial anger draining away, and in its place a desire to forge ahead. This, Skorri knew, was one of the qualities that set him above other men. He did not wallow in anger or jealously; he pushed it aside and moved on. "Eat, drink, and tell me more about what you found."

Valgard grunted and pulled off his mud-splattered cape and tossed it aside. He sat on the bench and drank deep from a wooden cup filled with the farmer's miserable ale, then tore a chunk off the loaf of coarse brown bread. Skorri waited as Valgard chewed and swallowed and drank again.

"We went first to Vifil's farm, as you said to do," he began at last. Vifil Helgason was one of the landholders who had joined with Odd in rising up against Halfdan. When Skorri had caught up with Odd and Amundi Thorsteinsson again, after their escape, it was Vifil and his men who had protected them. It made sense that the fugitives would have gone to Vifil's home, but it also made sense that they would know better than to remain there.

"Nothing?" Skorri asked.

Valgard was chewing again, so he shook his head until he swallowed. "Nothing. No people, no livestock. Most of the stores were gone, but we managed to take some things for our use."

"Did you burn the farm?"

"No," Valgard said. "I don't think Halfdan much cares for burning valuable farms."

Skorri nodded. Halfdan loved vengeance, but he loved power and wealth far more. Better that Vifil's farm be preserved so that it could be given as a reward to a man who swore an oath to Halfdan. Better that vengeance be directed at the persons of Vifil and Odd and the others, and not at their property.

Valgard continued with his tale, explaining how they had ridden north in a great circle, checking the coastal villages to make certain no strangers had found passage by sea. They had visited the market town of Rykene and beyond, searching every farm and every village they could find. He told how they had explored paths in the woods and sheepherder's cottages, how they had found signs that men had been at some of those places, but nothing to suggest that those men had been the ones they sought.

They had continued up into the hills, to Nævesdal and a bit beyond, before coming south to meet up with Skorri again. They had been gone a week and a half and had found nothing of any significance.

Skorri felt the anger growing again, despite himself. He never thought that the others would find anything, but he had felt certain that Valgard would. He had based all his hopes on that assumption, and now the floor was collapsing under him.

"They must be moving," Skorri said. "They must be shifting their hiding places, maybe going from one village to another. You had no word of travelers, strangers on the roads?"

"No," Valgard said. "We spoke to some sheepherders who were moving with their flocks. Some sailors and merchants in Rykene, who were traveling, of course, and fishermen in other villages. We heard about some sheepherders from Nævesdal bringing skins to market. That was all."

"Sheepherders…from Nævesdal?" Skorri asked. This tugged at his mind, for no reason that he could think of.

"Yes," Valgard said, who seemed to share none of Skorri's concerns. "A farmer told us about them. They had passed a day or so before us. Just two sheepherders and their wives, taking a wagon to market."

Skorri frowned. "To market where?"

"Rykene, the farmer thought, but he didn't know for certain. It didn't seem of much importance."

No, it wouldn't… But for some reason it stood out to Skorri, like something that just didn't fit quite right.

"Sheepherders and their wives…so who was left tending the flock?"

Valgard shrugged as he chewed and swallowed a chunk of pork. "Don't know. I'm a warrior, not some miserable sheep buggerer. I know nothing of such things."

Skorri, however, did know of such things, having grown up on a farm until age fourteen when he had taken his father's horse and the few weapons he had and rode off to seek his fortune. And he knew that farmers and sheepherders might go to a local market day if they happened to have some surplus to sell, which was not often, but traveling some distance, by wagon, that seemed strange. There were a dozen reasons why it might not be, but still it seemed strange.

"Did you learn anything more of these people?" Skorri asked. "Two couples, you said?"

"Two," Valgard said, giving more thought to his words as he seemed to sense Skorri's growing interest. "The farmer who told me of them, he didn't say much more than that. I don't think he thought much about them. An older man and a younger man and their wives in some broken-down wagon."

*An older man and a younger man…*Skorri thought. *Amundi Thorsteinsson and his bitch of a wife? And Odd Thorgrimson and…what was that whore's name? Signy?*

He had no reason to think it was them, save for a feeling in his gut, but his gut had been right often enough. It was a month or more since Odd had slipped away from him, time enough for a strong young man like him to heal, even from the horrific wounds Halfdan had doled out. Time enough for him to come out of hiding and make his way back to his own people.

But not openly. He was a wanted man, and the ad hoc army he had assembled had melted away. Halfdan ruled again, without question, and Odd would know that the king was hunting for him.

No, if Odd were to return, he would do so in a hidden way. He would try to attract no notice, to appear as unremarkable as a man could be. Like a sheepherder, for instance. A sheepherder come to a market town, where he could keep his eyes and ears open, see how things lay, and if it seemed safe enough, continue on to his own country.

It was a thin reed Skorri was grasping at, and he knew it. Still, unless the other men out searching to the south and along the coast came back with something more definitive, it was all he had.

"You and your men, you take your rest," Skorri said. "You've earned it. Then tomorrow, we are on the hunt again."

Chapter Eight

Why should'st thou stretch
O'er the sound and smite me?
No reason have we for wrath.

Greybeard and Thor
The Poetic Edda

Thorgrim was furious. It was a free-floating, directionless fury, mostly because he did not know at whom he should rightly direct his anger.

He had seen the thing play out from *Sea Hammer*'s afterdeck, had seen Bergthor's ship move down the line of his own vessels, watched as it passed *Sea Hammer* and *Fox* and then even Harald's ship, *Dragon*, which he had directed would take the lead. The fury had started mounting then. It was a simple order — Bergthor's ships to stay back behind Thorgrim's fleet — and this dumb bastard could not even follow that direction.

Thorgrim could see it all well enough from his place on deck, but that did not stop Starri Deathless, clinging to the top of the mast, from narrating every bit of the action. "That son of a bitch, Bergthor's man, oh, he's pulling like he's being chased by wolves!" Starri shouted down from aloft, to Thorgrim's mounting irritation. "Do you see that, Night Wolf? What's he about?"

Thorgrim did see it, and he was not the only one. Grifo was still standing nearby, just forward of where Thorgrim stood at the tiller. He was leaning over the side and watching Bergthor's ship closing with the rearmost of the West Saxons. A moment of that and he wheeled around, facing Thorgrim, and though Thorgrim did not look at him, he sensed the man's fury.

Go ahead, say something, Thorgrim thought. *Make some accusation…it will do me good to put a sword through you….* But Grifo, apparently, had sense enough to keep his mouth shut, and he turned and looked forward again without uttering a word.

Thorgrim had considered driving *Sea Hammer* ahead, inserting himself into the mess he could see developing, but he knew better. That would only add to the confusion, make the whole thing an even greater debacle. For all he knew, the crew of Bergthor's ship had decided to go off on their own, were taking their twenty pounds of silver and heading for the open sea. And that was fine. Preferable, even.

But it did not happen that way. Bergthor's ship closed with the Saxon fleet, and Harald, seemingly on purpose, slammed into it, snapping half their oars. The whole thing was a great, festering, sea-borne shit-pile and it made Thorgrim furious: furious with Harald, furious with Bergthor and his incompetent men, furious with the gods who made him endure such idiocy.

"Ha!" Starri called down. "That boy of yours, Night Wolf! A bold move! It's that, or he doesn't know how to steer a ship! Either way, he took care of Bergthor's fools!"

And there was nothing Thorgrim could do about it. But happily, it seemed there was nothing he needed to do. Bergthor's ship was drifting off toward the southern bank of the river. *Dragon* and *Fox* were still where they were supposed to be and the West Saxon fleet seemed not to have been bothered at all.

Thorgrim made himself take a deep breath. He let it out and took another. It helped, but not much. He looked astern. The errant ship was falling farther behind, half her oars now gone. The rest of his ships were still where they were supposed to be, and Bergthor's well back. No one else seemed to be getting out of line.

They continued on in that way for the bulk of the day, the three fleets — the king's, Thorgrim's, and Bergthor's — pulling their way downriver toward the sea. The tide turned in the late afternoon and the rowing became more difficult and the pace slowed considerably. As the sun was dropping toward the western horizon they came to the place where the river (or inlet, perhaps, Thorgrim was not sure) widened to more than two miles across and then branched off east and west, with a great island like a low, ragged wall right ahead. To the southeast, framed by headlands, Thorgrim saw the open ocean.

The English fleet, leading the way, steered off to the east, keeping close by the northern shoreline. They pulled seaward for some time, then bore off to larboard, making for a long stretch of beach on the mainland. It was the same beach, Thorgrim realized, on which Harald had hauled out the whale he had so recklessly hunted and killed. It seemed an impossibly long time ago, though Thorgrim knew it was just a month past, maybe a bit more. No signs of the massive carcass remained that he could see.

The English fleet spread out as they approached the shore, the ships running one after another up onto the shingle, their crews pulling in the oars, climbing over the side into the waist-high water and heaving the vessels farther up. The king's ship — massive, ornate and stately — found its place in the center of the rest, and once all the English ships were ashore Thorgrim's fleet began landing on the downstream side, with Harald in *Dragon* taking the lead.

"Give way! Double time!" Thorgrim shouted after *Fox* went up on the beach. He pushed the tiller over and directed *Sea Hammer* to the place just beyond where the smaller ship had landed. *Sea Hammer* was making good way when her bow ran up onto the shingle with a loud crunching sound and the men ran the oars inboard and stacked them on the gallows.

By the time they were done Thorgrim had Iron-tooth buckled around his waist and his shield slung over his back. "Starri, come with me," he said because he knew Starri would come in any event. "Hall, Bjorn, Onund, with me." Grifo pushed himself off the side of the ship where he was leaning and took a step in Thorgrim's direction. "Not you," Thorgrim said. "This does not concern you."

He made his way forward, intending to jump over the rail near the bow and land on the beach, and not in the water, and thus avoid soaking his shoes and leggings. But before he did he remembered the wound in his side, and how much the impact with the beach was going to hurt, so he went over the rail amidships instead, where the leap was considerably shorter. He landed in knee-high water, teeth clenched, and waded ashore with his four armed men at his back.

Twenty feet up the beach he stopped and looked north and south along the shoreline. The English ships were all grounded, their bows run up on the gravel, men already carrying tents and cooking gear and food and barrels ashore, setting up an instant, if temporary, king's court right there on the water's edge.

His own fleet was mostly ashore as well, only *Blood Hawk* and *Oak Heart* were still making for the beach. Bergthor had been ordered to bring his ships in farther down the beach from Thorgrim's. And once again, Bergthor was not doing as he had been ordered.

That miserable bastard…I'll rip his throat out, Thorgrim thought. Bergthor's ships were beaching on the far side of the English fleet, putting the English between the two fleets of Northmen, not where they wanted to be and not where Thorgrim wanted them.

He turned and marched along the beach, which was swarming with dozens of English men-at-arms and servants and courtiers, who stood hurriedly aside for them as they approached. He passed the king's ship where an awning had already been set up in the stern. He smelled something cooking on board, heard musicians playing softly. Two hundred feet beyond he reached the place where Bergthor's *Wave Splitter* was pulled up on the shore.

"Thorgrim!" Bergthor was standing in *Wave Splitter*'s bow, leaning on the sheer strake, smiling down with his usual jovial expression.

Thorgrim stopped and looked up at him, arms folded.

"A good day's row, eh?" Bergthor continued.

Thorgrim did not reply.

"Here, you wait there, I'll come," Bergthor said, tone slightly uncertain now. He walked aft and called to a few of his men, and then he jumped over the side into the shallow water. Behind him, five of his people followed. They splashed ashore, trudging up the shingle to where Thorgrim waited.

"My man Mar, in *Wind Rider*, he made a mess of things, no doubt," Bergthor said. "I gave him an earful when we passed him, you better believe."

Thorgrim stared at Bergthor long enough for the man to start growing uncomfortable. "What was he doing?" Thorgrim asked at last. "What did he think he was doing?"

Bergthor shrugged. "Don't know," he said. He was trying to sound sincere, but there was a false note in his voice. "Mar, he ain't one for following orders too close."

Again, Thorgrim was silent for a moment. "You see that he follows orders from now on. You see that all of your men do." He nodded toward Bergthor's ships, lined up along the beach. "This isn't where I told you to come ashore."

Bergthor bristled at that. "What rutting difference does it make where I come ashore?"

"It's not what I told you to do. That's the difference."

Bergthor frowned and his eyebrows drew together. "This —" he gestured toward his ships, "— is not your fleet. And I'm not your oath-man."

"You can go your way, you and your men," Thorgrim said. "But if you're with us, you do what I say." He had not been happy with Bergthor's sudden change of plan, his decision to join in sailing with the English, and he was less happy about it now. Less happy and more suspicious.

"I do what you say, huh?" Bergthor said. "You seem awfully eager to please your Saxon lords here."

Now it was Thorgrim's turn to frown. He rested his hand on Iron-tooth's hilt and took a step forward. He saw the defiance on Bergthor's face crumble before he had even completed the step.

"I mean," Bergthor said, "I don't know why those Saxon pukes should be telling Thorgrim Night Wolf what to do. You should tell them."

"I've got no love for the Saxons," Thorgrim said. "But I took their silver for the promise I'd protect them. So I'll protect them. You made the same bargain. I just hope you don't have anything else in mind."

"No," Bergthor said. "No, of course not. Like you said, as long as them English don't betray us, we won't betray them. Right?"

Thorgrim looked at Bergthor for a long moment, saw the hints of uncertainty and concern on his face. *You're playing some game, aren't you?* he thought.

"As long as no one betrays us, we don't betray them," Thorgrim agreed. He turned and walked back in the direction he had come, past the line of English ships, where tents were already rising on the shingle and fires burning in pits on the beach. Felix was waiting to intercept them, as Thorgrim suspected he would be, Grifo standing beside him. Grifo, Felix's eyes and ears on *Sea Hammer*, would no doubt have relayed everything that had taken place aboard.

Thorgrim was not in the mood for this, but neither was he able to avoid it.

"Thorgrim," Felix said as he approached. He was not smiling.

Thorgrim stopped, looked Felix in the eye. "Yes?" he said. It sounded like a challenge.

Felix spoke. Grifo translated.

"Felix asks what happened on the river? He says it looked as if your ship tried to run into one of the king's ships."

"Not my ship," Thorgrim said. "Bergthor's ship. My ship was the one that fended them off. Protected them. Like I gave my word we would do."

Grifo translated. Felix looked as if he was not sure what to say to that. Finally, he spoke.

"Felix says he trusts that won't happen again," Grifo said.

"It won't," Thorgrim said. "But tell Felix to see that the king's guards are ready tonight. Not standing in a shield wall or any fool thing like that. Just see they're under arms and on alert."

Grifo translated, and the look of concern deepened on Felix's face as he did. "Why should they be ready?" Grifo translated. "Do you expect trouble?"

"No," Thorgrim said. "But tonight, Bergthor's men will be drinking the way Northmen drink, or so I'd guess. And sometimes blood can spill when they do." In fact, Thorgrim had the notion that Bergthor was looking for trouble. Why, he did not know. Nor did he care. He just knew that Bergthor and his men would need a good beating down.

"Just see that the English don't spill any of that blood," Thorgrim added, "unless they have no choice."

He left Felix there and returned to *Sea Hammer* and the other ships. His men had managed to find enough driftwood to build a large fire, and down by the water's edge others were turning a couple of sheep into sides of mutton for roasting. A barrel had been stove in and cups and horns were rapidly filling and draining.

Thorgrim turned to Hall. "Get the captains together, meet me by *Sea Hammer*," he said, and then he turned and walked down to where his ship rested in the shingle. A few minutes later the captains of the other ships were assembled. They were curious, he could see it on their faces, save for Harald, who looked uncertain. Thorgrim realized he had not spoken to the boy since they had come ashore. Harald would not know if his father was pleased with him for fending off Bergthor's ship or angry with him for the collision.

"What happened out there, Harald?" Thorgrim demanded.

"Ahh…" Harald began, unsure what to say.

Didn't you guess I would ask this? Thorgrim wondered. *How can you not have an answer ready?*

"Mar…" Harald went on, "he's the captain of *Wind Rider*…he came pulling past us, as you saw. Even though you said that *Dragon* was to take the lead. I didn't know what he was about. I thought maybe he was just going off on his own, and I figured he could do that if he wanted. But then it seemed like he would run into the king's ship, and I knew that would be a bad thing. I knew you wouldn't want that. So I hit him instead. Broke his oars on the larboard side."

Thorgrim nodded. "Good. But tell me, did it look as if Mar meant to hit the king's ship? Was he doing it on purpose?"

"Well, he saw the English ship, I know that for certain. He was yelling at them. Like he wanted them to give way to him. Not that they could understand him. But it was Mar who changed course and nearly hit the English. The English never changed course at all."

"So, it was no accident," Thorgrim said.

"No," Harald said. "It was no accident."

"Very well." Thorgrim turned to the others. "I don't know what Bergthor's about, but he's up to something. Nothing good. You all make sure your men keep sober tonight, or near enough. My guess is we'll have work to do before we sail again."

Asmund nodded in the direction of the English camp rising from the shingle. "Don't know when that will be," he said. "Looks like they're building a bloody city over there."

"Yeah, I don't care to go through this horseshit every time we come ashore for the night," Halldor said. "We best get to crossing the narrow seas soon."

"We'll be on blue water quick enough," Thorgrim said. "At least most of us." There followed a bit more discussion in that regard, general preparations for the crossing, and then the captains took their leave.

"Harald, hold a moment," Thorgrim said as his son turned to walk away.

"Yes?"

Thorgrim started to speak, but paused, struck suddenly by his son's appearance. He was a good five inches taller than he had been when they sailed three years earlier, and probably two stone heavier, but all of it muscle, it seemed, and a broadening in the chest and shoulders. His hair was bit darker now, still tied in a plait down his back, and he sported blond wisps on his jawline that could be construed as a beard.

Good-looking boy… Thorgrim thought. *Strong boy.* And then he realized Harald was waiting for him to speak.

"What do you think the weather will be tomorrow?" Thorgrim asked.

Harald's eyebrows came together, just slightly. Whatever he had expected Thorgrim to say, it was not that.

"The weather? Well…." He thought for a moment. "Around here it seems we get rain, and then when it clears up, we'll get a good breeze for a day or so, westerly mostly, and then a few days of calm. We had the rain not long ago, and the wind. It was calm today, and I'd guess calm tomorrow."

Thorgrim nodded. *Good for you, taking note of these things. Learning.* It was the sign of a genuine sailor, and a genuine leader.

"I think you're right," Thorgrim said. "So it looks like the poor bastards on our ships' crews are rowing again on the morrow, at least part of the day."

Harald gave a smile. "Looks like," he said. It drove Harald crazy, Thorgrim knew, to stand idle, or what he considered idle, while other men strained at the oars, and that was to his credit. But a ship's master had to see all and be ready for anything. He could not be stuck behind an oar. And so Harald took his place on the afterdeck and acted as a master should, and that was also to his credit.

He would come to learn, Thorgrim knew, that the responsibility of command was a much greater burden than the dumb animal labor of pulling an oar, as hard as that work might be.

The two of them walked back to where the fire was blazing on the beach, the air filled with the smell of driftwood smoke and the now-roasting sheep, turning on iron spits. They drank ale and spoke of ships and farming and East Agder and Odd and Hild and little Hallbera. They ate mutton and Thorgrim watched his men and saw that they were drinking ale, but not pouring it down their throats with abandon, so they would not be sprawled out and insensible come the dark hours of the night.

The same was not necessarily true of Bergthor's men. Thorgrim and the others could hear them on the far side of the English camp, shouting and singing and laughing. They heard curses as fights broke out and the occasional scream as someone claimed victory, someone suffered defeat.

It was well after dark, and Bergthor's men were still at it, when they heard the voices of the West Saxons speaking in loud protest. Or at least it seemed to Thorgrim that that was what he was hearing.

"Harald," he said, "what are they saying?" The voices were getting louder and more emphatic. Some of Thorgrim's men were on their feet, some snatching up weapons. It was not clear what was happening, but it sounded as if there might soon be fighting involved.

"I'm not sure…" Harald said. "I thought I heard something about 'get back to your camp'. And one of Bergthor's men, or someone speaking our tongue, calling someone a whore's son."

Thorgrim stood and looked north toward where the English were, but he could see nothing save for the silhouettes of men in the light of the fires.

"Should we go?" Asmund had his sword in hand, and a dozen of his men were standing behind him.

"No, hold a minute." Thorgrim raised his hand. They listened a bit more. More shouts, some words that Thorgrim recognized, some he did not. Nothing beyond that. He guessed that Felix had heeded his words, that the English soldiers were standing ready, and that Bergthor's men did not feel much inspired to cause any great trouble. At least not with sober and well-armed warriors. Soon the sounds of the encounter faded away, and only the sounds of Bergthor's men's revelry were left.

Finally, that too faded away. Thorgrim's men drifted off to sleep, leaving Thorgrim to sit and stare into the last of the flames burning down in the fire pit. Quiet fell over the long stretch of shingle beach until at last there was only the sound of the waves lapping the shore, and the crunch of the ships' bows as they lifted and fell, ever so slightly, and the collective snores of hundreds of men.

Thorgrim leaned back and looked up at the great sweep of stars overhead. He breathed in the smell of the wood smoke, a comforting smell, and the faint smell of roast meat and the brackish water fifty feet away. He could hear the sound of insects in the tall grass and some sort of night birds.

Peaceful, he thought. It was nice. Quiet and soothing. It made him sorry to think that soon he would have to pick up a stick and beat this hornet's nest into a frenzy of violence. But there was nothing else to be done. Beat it he must.

Chapter Nine

Fain would I now put trust in thy faith
Wert thou not wont to betray me.

Greybeard and Thor
The Poetic Edda

Thorgrim remained seated by the fire for some time longer, then he stood and stretched his arms and his back.

"It's time," he said. He walked over to where Harald was sleeping and nudged the boy with his toe. Harald shifted, groaned, and sat up.

"It's time," Thorgrim said. "Get your men, and wake the other captains. Tell them to get their men and gather here." For a moment Harald just stared, uncomprehending, and then he nodded and got to his feet and stumbled off.

"What is it, Night Wolf?"

Thorgrim turned. Starri was there, as if he had resolved out of the night. His tunic was still on, but he had his two axes thrust in his belt and he had an eager look on his face.

"Time to see about Bergthor and that lot," Thorgrim said.

"That's what I thought," Starri said. "Well, I'm with you."

"I'm glad of it," Thorgrim said. "But those —" he pointed at Starri's battle axes, "— will have to stay here."

"What?" Starri asked, as if Thorgrim had spoken in some foreign tongue.

"Fear not, you'll be well armed," Thorgrim said.

Starri frowned, but he drew the axes from his belt and dropped them by the edge of the fire pit.

When the rest of the men were assembled, Thorgrim ordered a dozen empty barrels be collected. Then, as men hurried off into the dark to see to that, Thorgrim gathered his captains together and explained what he intended to do.

Soon the men returned, rolling the barrels into the firelight near where he stood. Thorgrim picked up Starri's axes and handed them to the two men standing closest to him.

"Cut those hoops away," he ordered, and the men chopped down on the wooden hoops that held the barrel staves in place. One after another they fell away until at last the dozen barrels were no more than a dozen piles of staves.

"Very well, you men, listen to me," Thorgrim said loud enough for all around him on the quiet beach to hear. "These barrel staves are your weapons tonight. We won't draw blood unless we must, you hear me? Now each of you, gather with your captains and let's be on our way." He picked up a barrel stave and felt the weight and balance in his hand. He nodded his approval. An effective weapon.

Grifo was standing near the edge of the fire pit, looking around, unsure as to what was happening or what he should do. Thorgrim caught his eye and nodded. "You, come with me," he said and without a word Grifo stepped toward him, snatching up a barrel stave as he did.

Thorgrim led the way along the beach, the path illuminated by the stars and the glow of the West Saxons' fires. There were guards posted near the English ships, half asleep at that late hour, but they straightened at the approach of this large host of Northmen. Thorgrim saw spears coming level, heard swords drawn from sheaths.

They were nearly up to the king's ship before someone confronted them, stepped into Thorgrim's path, a dozen spearmen at his back. They were all in mail, all wearing helmets that gleamed in the faint light. The man in front spoke, a few brusque words.

"He says 'what's your business?'" Grifo translated.

"Do you know him?" Thorgrim asked.

"I do," Grifo said. "He's Osred, captain of the king's guard."

"Tell him we're going to speak with the others. The other Northmen. This is not his concern."

Grifo turned to Osred. He spoke, translating Thorgrim's words, or so Thorgrim assumed, and, it seemed, adding a few of his own. Whatever he said seemed to work, and when he was done Osred scowled, threw a glance at Thorgrim and the men behind him, then stepped aside and gestured for his men to do the same.

Thorgrim pushed past and continued down the beach. They came at last to Bergthor's camp, if such it could be called. The fires were burning down and in their light Thorgrim saw bodies heaped on the ground. It looked like the aftermath of some terrific battle, though in this instance he knew the battle had been with ale and mead, and Bergthor's men, apparently, had lost.

He stopped and waved his men down toward Bergthor's *Wave Splitter*. Asmund was behind him and Thorgrim gestured for him and *Oak Heart*'s crew to continue on. They paraded past, moving toward the next ship run up on the beach, and the only sound they made was the crunching of their soft shoes in the gravel. Behind them came Gudrid with *Blood Hawk*'s crew, and they continued on as well.

"Night Wolf! Night Wolf!" Starri Deathless appeared at his side, speaking in an emphatic whisper. He had two barrel staves thrust in his belt where his two axes had been.

"What, Starri?"

"Well, all the men have barrel staves. And you have a barrel stave. And I have barrel staves. But you have your sword as well. And the others have their edged weapons. Why am I the only one who only has barrel staves?"

"Because I don't want anyone to get killed, and I don't trust you to not kill anyone," Thorgrim said.

"Oh," Starri said, and he paused to think about that. Then he opened his mouth to speak again but before he could another voice from the dark interrupted him.

"Thor's arse! What by all the gods is going on here!" The voice was close by, and it nearly made Thorgrim jump in surprise. Bergthor came stumbling up, his hair and beard a tangle. "Thorgrim? What are you doing?"

"That's what I want to ask you," Thorgrim said. "What are you doing?"

"What...what do you mean?" Bergthor looked around as if he might find an answer somewhere on the beach. Behind him two more of his men came stumbling up and then more behind them. Thorgrim could hear men aboard the ship stirring as well.

"I mean I want to know what you're doing," Thorgrim said. "You're up to something, changing your mind about joining us, sending Mar to run into that English ship…don't tell me you didn't send him…" he added as Bergthor made to protest. "Now, goading the Saxons here on the beach. What's it about?"

Bergthor scowled, and Thorgrim could see the indecision on his face. Then his expression softened and he took a step closer. "See here, Thorgrim, I know you're a man of honor," he said, his tone conspiratorial. "You give your word and you don't go back on it. And that's how a man should be.

"But you said yourself, if the English betray us, then we owe them nothing. If, for instance, they attack us, then we can fight back and we can plunder them good. And they have a lot of silver and gold and such with them, you know that. So…I provoke them, they fight, we owe them nothing. We're free to cut them down and take their silver. And it's no stain on your honor. Nothing you did."

Thorgrim nodded. It made sense. It made sense that Bergthor would come up with something like that. And Bergthor no doubt thought himself very clever for doing so.

"Good plan, Bergthor, well thought out," Thorgrim said. "But I can't let you do it. No doubt you think me a fool, but I'm not going to let you play your tricks on these Saxons."

Bergthor frowned. Behind him his men were pushing closer, listening to this exchange. Thorgrim saw the ugly looks on their faces as well.

"I told you before, Thorgrim Ulfsson, I'm not your oath-man. I don't take my orders from you."

"I'm not here to order you, Bergthor. I'm here to stop you from goading the English."

"Are you?" Bergthor said. He had clearly poured quite a bit of courage down his throat, and his men gathering at his back were further bolstering his resolve. "And how do you mean to do that?"

"I'm going to burn your oars," Thorgrim said.

That gave Bergthor pause. His eyebrows came together and the look on his face was almost comical. "What?"

"My men and I, we're going to take all the oars off your ships and we're going to burn them. And then when the Saxon fleet leaves on the morrow, and we leave with them, you all will stay here. Cutting down trees to make new oars, would be my guess."

Once again Bergthor's expression changed, this time a wide grin spreading across his face. "Ha!" he shouted. "There's a good joke, Thorgrim!"

"Stand aside, Bergthor," Thorgrim said.

"What?"

"Stand aside. We're going on your ship. To get your oars."

And again, Bergthor's face changed, the look of amusement turning to one of rage. "I'll have your heart out first!" he shouted, taking a step back and drawing his sword.

Huh… Thorgrim had doubted the man would have the courage to pull a weapon. He would not have done so had he been sober, Thorgrim was certain of that. *So be it.*

"Bastard!" Bergthor swung the blade with a powerful backhand stroke, but Thorgrim leaned back and the tip passed his chest with inches to spare. The momentum carried Bergthor around and Thorgrim swatted him on the side of the head with the barrel stave he held in his hand, making him stumble.

"Ow, son of a bitch!" Bergthor cried, catching himself and straightening. He drew back and lunged for Thorgrim's belly. Thorgrim knocked the blade aside with the barrel stave, then brought the oak board up hard under Bergthor's chin. Bergthor staggered back, and that seemed to shake his watching men from their collective stupors.

With a great communal shout of outrage Bergthor's crew surged forward, cursing, yelling, drawing swords and hefting spears and axes. Thorgrim swiveled sideways to see that his own men were ready to meet them, but all he saw was Starri Deathless right beside him, a massive grin on his face. Starri reached down and pulled the barrel staves from his belt with the same motion Thorgrim had seen him draw the axes a hundred times. He shrieked—a terrifying, unearthly sound—and raced forward, the barrel staves held over his head.

The closest of Bergthor's men came at Starri with a sword held horizontal, and he thrust and slashed as Starri raced toward him. Starri leapt up as the blade came at his belly and kicked it aside. He brought both staves down on the man's head like he was beating a drum and the man crumpled under them. Starri landed on the falling man with both feet, driving him the last few inches to the ground, and flailed out left and right, hitting another of Bergthor's men in the gut, a third in the side of the head, doubling them over.

Thorgrim could spare no more attention to Starri Deathless. Bergthor was back up, coming at him again, blood smeared on his left cheek and running into his beard, his eyes wild. He held his sword in front of him, a more cautious stance, waiting for Thorgrim to make a move.

Behind Bergthor, Thorgrim saw his other men plunging into the fight, barrel staves rising and falling: Louis de Roumois lunging, parrying and reposting with the oak shaft as if it were the finest of Frankish blades. Grifo hacking left and right. Hall swinging his stave two-handed in a wide arc. Thorgrim heard the sharp sound of wood on iron and steel, the dull thud of oak on skulls and shoulders and arms, the grunts and curses of men being struck.

I have no time for this, Thorgrim thought, suddenly irritated that Bergthor was forcing him to play this game. He lunged at Bergthor with the barrel stave, making Bergthor step back and parry the thrust. But Bergthor's blade found only air as Thorgrim jerked the stave out of the way, bringing it back over his shoulder and swinging it around with a powerful sweeping blow.

The flat wood caught Bergthor on the side of the head and sent him sprawling sideways, the sword flying from his grip, a grunt escaping his mouth as he crumpled to the shingle.

Bergthor's men fell back in the face of this surprising and savage attack, and Thorgrim stepped forward in pursuit. He saw an axe raised high, its target Vali, who was fighting a man with a spear. Thorgrim smacked the axe man's hand hard with the stave, sending the axe spinning off into the dark. The man whirled around in surprise, looked Thorgrim in the eye, and Thorgrim swatted him hard on the side of the head. The blow knocked him to his knees, then Thorgrim drove a foot into his chest and sent him flying into the man behind him.

Thorgrim looked around for the next one to take on, but there was no one there. He saw more fighting going on closer to the water, shadows struggling in the dark, but it was only a few men here and there. The bulk of it seemed to be over. He cocked his head and listened. He heard fighting in other places along the beach, his men with the crews of Bergthor's other ships, but that, too, seemed to be tapering off. There had not been much fight in Bergthor's tired and drunken men to begin with, and what fight there was Thorgrim's men had quickly beaten clean out of them.

From somewhere ahead in the dark Thorgrim heard a louder scuffling, shouts of protest, a yell of pained outrage, and he had a good notion of what it was. He limped off in the direction of the sound, his wound aching, and found Hall and Louis de Roumois and a few others cursing, struggling, restraining Starri Deathless, who was flailing and lashing out with his legs and barrel staves. At the men's feet lay three others, bloody and cowering. One was trying desperately to crawl away.

"You bastards! You bastards!" Starri shouted, twisting in the men's grip. "By the wrath of all the gods, I'm just hitting them with sticks!"

"Enough, Starri, it's done," Thorgrim said, and at the sound of Thorgrim's voice Starri immediately stopped thrashing and the men released him.

"That was excellent, Night Wolf!" Starri said enthusiastically. "I can't tell you him much I enjoyed this! Them with real weapons, me with sticks, it really evens things out, makes the fight go on much longer. I think I'll fight with sticks alone from now on."

"I'm sure your enemies would be grateful if you did," Thorgrim said. "Now, if you're done beating these poor bastards we have work to do."

"Certainly, Night Wolf, certainly." Starri stepped forward, gave the crawling man one last good kick in the side, then slipped the barrel staves back into his belt. Thorgrim looked around. He could make out the faces of the men closest to him, and saw the dark shapes of others farther off.

Hall was standing to his left. "Get a dozen men or so, go aboard the ship here and get the oars off. Bring them to the fire pit up there." He pointed to a point of light farther up the beach where the last of a bonfire was burning down. He turned to Louis de Roumois, who was standing to his right. "Get the rest of our men and set them as guards over Bergthor and his crew, to see that none of them tries anything heroic."

Louis looked around him. There were men lying at his feet, and others scattered around the beach. "I don't think they have much heroics left in them," he said. "If they ever did."

"All the better," Thorgrim said. He left the Sea Hammers to that task and walked down the beach, toward Bergthor's other ships. Thorgrim's men had outnumbered Bergthor's to begin with, and at least a third of Bergthor's men had been too drunk to even stir at the sound of the fighting. The others had mostly been asleep and were taken by surprise, so the struggle had not been overly long or involved.

Thorgrim stopped at the first of Bergthor's ships, the one he had sent Asmund to take. The defeated crew sat sullenly under guard, with some bloody noses and scalps among them, and a few broken hands and arms, but nothing worse than that.

A dozen of Asmund's men were already aboard and passing the oars down to others standing on the beach. Thorgrim left them to it and moved on. By the time he arrived at the second ship, Gudrid's men were already making their way toward the bonfire carrying stacks of oars on their shoulders.

The last ship in the line had been Harald's responsibility, along with Hardbein and the crew of *Fox*. They were working by the light of a few torches, taking the last of the oars down off the side of the ship when Thorgrim arrived. The crew of the ship, Bergthor's men, were sitting or lying on the beach, circled by guards from Harald and Hardbein's crews.

"Harald," Thorgrim called as he stepped close. Harald turned and smiled a bit and nodded.

"Father," he said. There was thick streak of blood running down the side of his face and dying his blond beard a brownish red.

"You're wounded," Thorgrim said, nodding toward Harald's scalp. Harald touched the wound and then looked at the wet blood on his fingertips. He frowned a bit, as if just realizing he had been cut.

"It's a small thing," he said. "A lucky stroke. But you're limping. Where you hurt?"

Before Thorgrim could answer, a voice called out, angry and bitter, from the cluster of men sitting on the beach. "There he is, Thorgrim Night Pup. Traitor to his people."

Thorgrim looked over. Steindor sat on the ground, legs drawn up in front of him. In the torchlight Thorgrim could see the blood streaking his face, and one eye already swollen shut. He must have put up quite a fight.

"You're a coward, Night Pup," Steindor said. Brand, who was standing close by, took two steps toward the man and hit him hard on the back of the head with his barrel stave, but the blow seemed to have little effect. "Why don't you stop playing with wooden swords and come fight me with a man's weapon?"

Brand wound up to hit the man again and Harald took a step in Steindor's direction, but Thorgrim held up a hand and said, "That's enough." He looked at Steindor who was making to rise. "I'm going to burn your oars, Steindor. One more word from you and I'll burn your ship as well, with you on it."

He paused, waiting for Steindor to speak. He saw the uncertainty on the man's face, defiance wrestling with prudence. And then prudence seemed to prevail and he shut his mouth and sat once more.

Thorgrim turned back to Harald. "I'm not hurt," he said. "Just the wound I had before. Once you get these oars over to the bonfire, you can pull your men back, let these sorry bastards be. They'll have plenty to sleep off."

Harald nodded and Thorgrim left him to it. By the time he was halfway back to the fire pit, the dying flames had been rekindled with a crisscross of ash oars, dry and well-seasoned, that caught easily and burned with gusto. The flames were already reaching ten feet into the air as more of the confiscated sweeps were added to the pile, and a stream of men carried the rest on their shoulders along the beach. They reminded Thorgrim of a line of ants moving crumbs from a loaf of bread dropped on the ground.

He stopped twenty feet short of the fire, and even at that distance the flames were hot on his face and hands. *Now here is something I have never done before*, he thought. He had never in his long and varied life ever put a ship's oar into the flames, and here he was burning dozens of them. He figured that would satisfy him, doubted he would feel the urge to ever do that again.

For a long moment he looked into the flames and his mind went back over the time he had spent a'viking in Ireland and Engla-land. He had done many things in those years that he had never done before. But the joy of new experiences, he knew, was the realm of young men, enthusiastic men, and he was neither of those things.

Tomorrow we head across the narrow sea. He felt a pang of trepidation even as the words formed in his mind. An hour earlier, Bergthor had also thought he was crossing the narrow seas on the morrow, but he had been wrong. Bergthor was not motivated like Thorgrim was. For

Bergthor, the last two years of his life had not been entirely directed toward arriving at this place, as unpredictable as it might have been.

Thorgrim frowned and rested his hand on the butt of the barrel stave thrust in his belt. *If the gods try to stop me this time I swear on my father's grave I'll take this stick and beat the lot of them bloody.*

Chapter Ten

Truly I ween that my words are spoken:
Too slow art thou in thy traveling.

Greybeard and Thor
The Poetic Edda

The pile of burning oars grew taller and the flames mounted in height to ten, then fifteen, then twenty feet. Thorgrim stared into the fire. His hand rested on the end of his barrel stave. His mind was with the gods.

What do they play at? he wondered. There was a time when he was sure that he knew what pleased the gods, and knew a great deal more besides. But he was older now, and experience had demonstrated, again and again, that he actually knew very little indeed.

He sighed. Here was one thing at least that he did know. Whatever it was that pleased the gods, his threatening to beat them with a barrel stave was not numbered among it.

He turned to his right. Starri Deathless was there, though he had not seen or heard the man approach. "Starri, come with me," he said, and Starri nodded, wordless, and followed him down the beach to where *Sea Hammer* was pulled up onto the shingle.

Five sheep, the last of the mutton on the hoof, were staked out near the fire pit that Thorgrim's men had dug. Thorgrim looked them over and chose the biggest and most blemish free. He pulled the stake out of the ground and led the animal down toward the water. Starri, who had gone aboard *Sea Hammer*, dropped to the beach from the ship's side. He had a big wooden bowl in his hands and a wolfskin over his shoulders, with the wolf's head draped over his own. He fell in beside Thorgrim as they made their way to the water's edge.

Neither man spoke as they led the sheep into knee-deep surf, but the animal was less sanguine about the goings on, bleating and pulling against the rope around its neck. Starri straddled the beast as if he meant to ride it, holding it tight between his knees. Thorgrim dropped the rope and pulled the seax from the sheath that hung horizontal from his belt.

"Njord, I make this sacrifice to you," Thorgrim said, "that you might bring my ships and my men safe across the narrow seas, and carry us on the wind you command back to our homes."

Starri grabbed the sheep under the chin and pulled its head back, and with a quick and powerful swipe of the blade, Thorgrim opened its throat so fast that the animal made no sound at all. It kicked in its death throws and twisted between Starri's legs, and then it went limp as the blood flowed dark from its rent throat into the water washing around their feet.

Starri let the blood flow for a few heartbeats, no more, then stuck the wooden bowl under the animal's open throat and let the remainder of the blood fill the vessel. He handed the bowl to Thorgrim, grabbed the sheep's back by the wool, and with one deft motion swung it up and around his back and draped it over his shoulders.

Thorgrim led the way back through the surf to the beach and around to *Sea Hammer*'s bow. He handed the bowl back to Starri and drew Iron-tooth from its scabbard. He dipped the tip of the blade into the sheep's blood and flicked a stream of it at the ship, then another and another. In the light of the burning oars, which now illuminated a good stretch of the beach, he saw the lines of fresh blood gleaming against the dark wood. Once again he asked Njord to bring his ships and men safely home.

That done, he moved on to *Oak Heart*, the next of his ships. Once again, he flicked streams of blood across the ship's bow and called for Njord's blessing on the voyage. Ship by ship he moved along the beach until each of the vessels had been thus anointed. Then he and Starri crossed back to the massive fire roaring in the pit on the beach.

Twenty feet from the edge of the flames they stopped. "Are we to partake as well?" Starri asked.

"No," Thorgrim said. "Give it all to the gods."

Starri nodded. He grabbed the sheep draped around his neck and held it straight up over his head. He let out a howl, an unearthly sound, a language that only he and the gods could understand, and then he moved toward the fire. Thorgrim saw the last drops of blood spilling from the throat of the limp beast.

Sheep held high, Starri walked right up to the fire's edge, though how he could endure the heat Thorgrim could not imagine. Starri cocked his arms and threw the sacrifice into the flames. For an instant, Thorgrim could see its outline, black against the red and yellow inferno. And then, with a great surge of heat and light and a whoosh of flame, the fire took the carcass and whisked it off to Njord.

Starri retreated from the edge of the fire pit, walking backwards until he was at Thorgrim's side. Thorgrim saw that his face was black from the soot and his wispy beard seemed to have been singed. There was a scattering of dark holes in his tunic where sparks had burned through, and Thorgrim imagined they must have burned his flesh as well, but he seemed not to have noticed.

"The gods were pleased with that," Starri said. "Did you see how eagerly they took the sacrifice? They were pleased."

"Good," Thorgrim said. He would not question Starri's insight in that regard. Starri, he knew, thought that it was he, Thorgrim, who was favored by the gods. But Thorgrim felt certain that Starri was the one to whom the gods spoke.

Yet they toy with us both, he thought. *I want only to reach my home, and Starri wants only to die in a bloody fight, and again and again the gods dangle it in front of us, then jerk it away…*

It was a fool's game, trying to guess what the gods were about, but in this instance Thorgrim had to admit Starri seemed to be right—the gods had been pleased with his sacrifice, insignificant as it might have been.

He watched the fire for a bit more, then found his bed and slept for the brief remainder of the night. He woke to clear skies with high, white clouds, and no wind to speak of, just as he and Harald had predicted.

The early morning air was filled with the smell of cooking as the English and the Northmen prepared to end the night's fast, and with the sound of the king's men breaking down and stowing away the elaborate camp they had established. Thorgrim climbed down from *Sea Hammer* and strode up the beach to a place where he could see all the ships pulled up on shore and all the varied activity going on.

The fire pit in which they had burned the oars was mounded high with black, charred wood, and wisps of smoke were still rising from the debris. Bergthor's fleet lay beyond that, but Thorgrim could see nothing going on there, no one stirring, no sign of life. Bergthor's men would not be much motivated to roust themselves. Most of them would have aching heads, and more than a few would have aching bruises from beatings with barrel staves. Some even had lacerations and broken bones that would need tending.

Even if they do stir themselves, they'll be going nowhere today, Thorgrim thought. Bergthor and his men would not be leaving that beach until they made new oars or until the wind filled in, and neither of those things were likely to happen before the sun went down again.

The same was not true of Thorgrim's ships, of course, and by the end of dagmál they were ready to get underway, though the English were not. For most of the morning hours the Northmen waited as the king and his extensive entourage made ready for sea, stowing away the tents and cooking gear and barrels and crates and tables and all manner of things they had brought onto the beach for the movable court.

The sun was approaching midday by the time Felix and his guards came by *Sea Hammer*. Thorgrim and a few others were sitting on driftwood logs near the bow, drinking ale for want of anything better to do. Harald was there as well, having come by to report *Dragon* ready for sea. That done, Harald had remained, because, Thorgrim knew, he was afraid that something important might happen without him.

Grifo was still aboard *Sea Hammer* when Felix arrived, but he hopped over the side and joined Thorgrim and the rest on the beach. Felix looked up at *Sea Hammer* and then over at the other ships, and then he spoke.

"Felix says the English will be getting underway soon," Grifo said.

"Good," Thorgrim said. "I was afraid they'd set their camp back up for their midday meal."

Grifo did not bother translating that, and Felix continued. "He says you and your ships should get underway once all the English ships are clear. Follow astern, like you did coming down the river."

"Tell him, 'Very well,'" Thorgrim said, but Felix apparently did not think his instructions required a response, because he continued speaking.

"Felix asks if the other ships, Bergthor's ships, will be sailing with us," Grifo said.

"No," Thorgrim said. "Their oars got burned up in a fire."

Grifo translated. Felix nodded, though he and the others had to be fully aware of the situation already. The West Saxons had watched the Northmen's internecine battle, and Grifo had no doubt reported everything. Thorgrim wondered if they would demand that Bergthor and his men return the silver, with all the complications and spilled blood that that would entail.

If they did, it was their affair. Thorgrim was done with Bergthor, and he had seen to it that Bergthor was done with him.

But Felix made no mention of the silver, which did not surprise Thorgrim. It was not a priority for him. It was clear that Felix's chief concern, for whatever reason, was to get the king and his court to Frankia. Besides, it was not Felix's silver that had been handed to the Northmen.

For a moment Felix remained where he was, silent, looking out at the water, as if struggling to make a decision. Then he turned to Thorgrim and spoke.

"He says we should go with him," Harald said, beating Grifo to the translation.

Thorgrim considered asking Felix where they were going and why, but instead, he just stood, as did Harald and the other men sitting on the driftwood logs. Felix spoke again, and this time Grifo beat Harald to it.

"Felix says, 'just Thorgrim.'"

Thorgrim met Felix's eyes. "And Harald," he said. Grifo translated. Thorgrim saw on Felix's face the debate going on in his head. Then the Frank shrugged.

"Felix says, 'fine,'" Grifo said.

Felix turned and led the way, Grifo, Thorgrim, and Harald trailing behind, and the guards who were there to keep Felix safe from the heathens taking up the rear. They crunched along the beach and Thorgrim considered that last exchange. He was not sure why he had insisted that Harald come with them. It was a reflexive act, no thought put into it. Part of it certainly was that he did not want Grifo to be the only one there who could translate his and Felix's words. But it was more than that.

It's time for the boy to become a leader, Thorgrim thought. That, he realized, was why he had insisted that Harald join them. He had taught his son a great deal about fighting and seamanship and commanding a ship's crew. Now it was time to bring Harald into the other worlds of leadership: how to deal with friends, how to deal with enemies, how to deal with those who might be both at once.

Thorgrim had no idea what Felix wanted, but if it was important enough that it had to take place in private, then it was something he wanted Harald to be part of.

They came at last to the king's ship, pulled up on the shore, dozens of men swarming around it and handing gear up to more men aboard. Thorgrim ran his eyes over the vessel. It was a lovely thing, there was no doubt, well-built of oak with a high curved prow on which was mounted a massive cross with a carving of the Christ-god nailed to it, arms outstretched, painted blood dripping from the hands, feet and side.

Like Odin, Thorgrim thought. Odin had hung from a tree for nine days to learn of other worlds and to understand the runes. Thorgrim wondered if the Christ-god had done the same, for the same reasons. He guessed not.

"This way," Grifo said and they followed Felix along the side of the ship to where a stout, elaborately painted ladder was leaning against the side. Felix led the way up the ladder and onto the deck.

The ship was about the same size as *Sea Hammer*, though there were fewer rowing stations. The after end was taken up by a table and a number of seats, all well-upholstered, and roofed over with a richly embroidered awning above. There was a carpet on the deck as well, and stacks of blankets and furs. A ship fit for a king.

"What say you, Harald," Thorgrim said. "Should I fit *Sea Hammer* out this way?"

Harald smiled. "You'd never want to go ashore if you did."

Thorgrim guessed he was probably right. The king of Wessex, however, did not seem to feel the same way, since he was not yet aboard. There was still one tent set up on shore, the largest and finest, and Thorgrim guessed the king and his court were still there, since there was no one save for servants and crew aboard the king's ship.

Felix led the way aft, under the awning, to the large table lashed to the deck. There were several vellum scrolls laying on the polished oak top. Felix picked one up and held it in his hands.

"The master of this ship, and the masters of the others, they have all made the voyage to Frankia many times," Felix said. "They know the way well. You need only follow them. But I thought it might be helpful for you to see this anyway." With that he laid the scroll on the table and unrolled it, placing little iron statues of sundry beasts on the corners to hold it down.

Thorgrim and Harald leaned over the table and looked at the scroll, but Thorgrim could make no sense of what he was seeing. Various irregular shapes in blue, other irregular shapes that had been left uncolored, a scattering of pictures of men and beasts and sea creatures, and over it all the writing that the English and the Frankish used. A series of curved lines at regular intervals ran across the scroll, side to side.

Felix spoke, pointing at the vellum, and Grifo translated.

"This is a drawing of the world," Grifo said. "Or the world known to the Romans."

Felix pointed to an odd-shaped patch of white in the upper left corner. It looked like a salamander. Or, more accurately, a salamander that had been stepped on.

"That's Engla-land, where we are," Grifo translated after Felix spoke.

Thorgrim's eyebrows came together. He could not make sense of what Grifo was saying. He was standing on the shore of Engla-land at that very moment, and the dead salamander looked nothing like what he was seeing. He glanced up at Harald. Harald was leaning over, studying the drawing, and frowning deeply.

Felix moved his finger to a spot just below the salamander and spoke again.

"That's Frankia," Grifo said. Felix continued to speak, and his finger traced a circle and then came down on the spot it had been before. "That's all Frankia, but there is where we are bound. Paris."

Thorgrim shook his head. This was making no sense at all to him. He had traveled throughout his home country, had been to Ireland, Engla-land, even Frankia and Frisia in his younger days and he had never seen anything that looked like what he was seeing now.

He looked up at Harald, wondering if Harald was any more enlightened than he was. His son was still frowning, but before Thorgrim could speak, his expression went through a striking change, like the sun breaking through clouds. His mouth fell open and his eyebrows came together and he leaned back and cocked his head.

"So...this is a picture of the world? As if...we were birds, high above, looking down?" he asked.

Grifo translated and Felix answered

"Yes," Grifo said. "That's it. Flying very, very high above. High enough to see half the world."

Harald leaned farther over the vellum. He put his finger on various spots. "Engla-land?" he asked. "And Ireland? And Frankia?"

"Yes," Grifo said when Felix had answered.

Harald smiled broadly. He seemed to be delighted with this. "You see, Father?" he asked. "You understand what this is?"

"Yes..." Thorgrim answered, but in truth he was not entirely sure he did. He certainly was not experiencing it in the profound way that Harald was, and that led him to believe there was something he was missing. He turned to Grifo. "Where did this come from?"

"It comes from the work of a Roman," Grifo said, translating Felix's answer. "A man named Ptolemy."

Roman, Thorgrim thought. The same men who had built those roads, and the buildings that must have once been so fine. They seemed like some race of minor gods with the things they could do.

"What is this?" Harald pointed to a patch of blue.

"That's an inland sea," Grifo translated. "It's called the Mediterranean." Harald just nodded, and stared at it, seemingly in wonder.

"Mediterranean..." he said thoughtfully, shaking his head.

Thorgrim was starting to lose patience. It was interesting, to a degree, but seemed to have little bearing on what they were about. "Ask Felix why he's showing us this," he said.

Grifo asked and Felix answered. "He says he wants you to know where you're bound. In case your ships get parted from the West Saxons'." Grifo put a finger on the vellum, on the place Felix had identified as Frankia, at a point where an irregular line met what Thorgrim guessed was supposed to be the narrow seas.

"This is the mouth of the River Seine," Grifo said. "In Frankia. Where we are bound, Paris, is down that river. You can see the river is all but due south of us here." Grifo shifted his finger and placed it on Engla-land. "So if we're parted, you can sail south and you should reach the river."

Thorgrim nodded. "Very well," he said. He straightened, half turned to leave, when Harald said to Grifo, "And our country? The North Country? Where is that?"

Thorgrim might have been ready to get back to *Sea Hammer*, but Harald, it seemed, could not be pulled from the scroll spread out on the table. He turned to Felix, asking questions in English, and each answer was followed by another question, until Thorgrim thought they might spend the next week standing there. They were interrupted at last by a servant in a fine linen tunic and a hat with an absurdly large feather jutting aft, one of the king's household men.

"He says the king is ready to come aboard," Grifo said. "Time to repair to our ships."

Thorgrim was in no way disappointed to hear it. He and Harald and Grifo climbed back down to the beach and retraced their steps back toward *Sea Hammer*.

"Felix might have just told us to sail south if we got separated," Thorgrim said. "Don't know why the Frankish dog had to waste our time like that."

"Waste our time?" Harald said, as if Thorgrim had said the most ridiculous thing imaginable. "It's so much better to see it in that way, don't you think? To have in your mind what these lands look like?"

"They don't look like that," Thorgrim protested. "White and blue. Flat."

"No," Harald said. "But don't you see what a great thing that is, that drawing of the entire world? What a wonder it is?"

"No," Thorgrim said. He looked at Harald, who was still seemingly in rapture from this experience.

"Well, I thought it was like…nothing I've ever seen," he said, and said no more.

They reached *Sea Hammer* and Thorgrim gave his last instructions to Harald and the other captains who were there. Soon after, the first of the West Saxon ships was pushed into the water and, under oar, backed away from the long beach. The others followed suit, one after another, until the last of the fleet was heading southeast, the open sea beyond their bows.

Next came *Dragon*, first of Thorgrim's fleet, under Harald's eager command, pushing off the shingle and pulling after the English ships, followed by *Fox* and *Blood Hawk*.

Oak Heart and *Sea Hammer* were the last to get underway. Thorgrim stood on *Sea Hammer*'s afterdeck, his hand on the tiller, eyes on the rowers, their oars held straight up. He heard the grunts of the men under the bow heaving the ship into the water, the crunch of their shoes in the gravel. *Sea Hammer* slipped astern and Thorgrim felt the ship's bow dip and bob a bit, her forefoot free of the ground, and the men on the beach swung themselves up over the rail.

"Ship oars! Back stroke!" Thorgrim called and the oars were run out the row ports and the men pushed against the shafts and *Sea Hammer* moved stern-first away from the shore. Thorgrim looked to the north. Bergthor's ships were still run up on the beach, but now he saw men milling about, some watching Thorgrim's fleet pulling away, others tending to fires or moving listlessly here and there.

They had made no move to interfere, had actually had no interactions with the English or Thorgrim's men at all. And that was fine as far as Thorgrim was concerned. He was happy to leave Bergthor there, to waste not a moment more in thinking about the man. He wondered if they would ever meet again, but he did not think so. For that to happen, they would both have to make it back to Vik alive, and those chances seemed slight.

He looked over the starboard side. *Sea Hammer* was well clear of *Oak Heart*; he could turn now without hitting the other ship. "Starboard, hold your oars! Larboard, give way!" The starboard oars came down into the water and stayed there, the larboard oars pulled, and *Sea Hammer* turned neatly around until her bow, like those of the other ships, was pointed toward the open sea.

"Give way, all!" Thorgrim called. They were headed to sea and Bergthor was behind him and Thorgrim never looked back.

The English fleet set the pace, and they set a thankfully easy pace, as there was every indication that the men would be rowing all day. Their heading was roughly south, crossing the same water that Thorgrim and his ships had passed weeks earlier, where Harald had launched his boneheaded attack on the whale, where they had met up with Bergthor's ships.

He looked to the west. He knew that the land just off the starboard side, which he had suspected was a massive island, was indeed an island. And he knew the coast beyond that island continued on in a roughly east-west line. He knew that because they had come from that direction.

Thorgrim turned and looked to the east and a bit astern of *Sea Hammer*. A massive headland blocked his view of the rest of the coastline, but he knew now, or at least believed, that it continued easterly before trending off toward the north. And that belief was based on the scroll that Felix had just shown him.

Maybe there is something worthwhile in that, he thought. For many months now, after having been blown across the sea from Ireland to the shores of Engla-land, Thorgrim had had only the vaguest notion of where he was, of what the lands around him looked like. As far as getting home, his intention was to sail east until he reached Frankia or Frisia, and then follow the coastline north. That certainly would have led him back to the North Country. But now, he had in his head a truer understanding of the contours of the land and the seas.

A Roman drew that... Thorgrim thought next. That was what Felix had said. Or at least, the scroll was based on something a Roman had done, a picture of the world as the Romans knew it. But the picture had not shown his own country, the lands of the Danes and the Swedes and the Norwegians, and Thorgrim guessed that was because this Roman fellow knew nothing about those places.

I guess the Romans were never there, in the north countries. Which would explain why they had no roads like they had in Engla-land. And that was too bad. They could use roads such as those in Norway.

He shook his head and pushed such pointless thoughts aside. He had more important things to think on now. He had the English fleet to get safely across the narrow seas. He had his silver to collect in Frankia and his ships to take north. He had his home to return to. And there were still many, many miles to go before he reached that place.

Chapter Eleven

To my boar now bear the ale of memory
So shall he tell forth all this tale
When the third morn comes and with Angantyr
He shall trace back the mighty men of their race.

The Lay of Hyndla

The market at Rykene was just as busy the following day, and the four sheepherders from Nævesdal spent all of it in their stall, selling their pelts and lambskins, keeping just enough for them to still have a bed of sorts. They heard more tales of Odd Thorgimson and the rebellion he had led. They heard nothing about King Halfdan still searching for the man, or any indication that there might be trouble lying in wait on the way south.

They spent one more night sleeping by the harbor, listening to the sounds in the dark and anything that smacked of danger, but they heard only the creak of the ships, the lap of the water, the laughter of the men in the taverns. The next morning, just after sunrise, they were moving again, but that was no hardship. It was what they were accustom to. They had been moving almost nonstop for the past month and more, since they had abandoned the comforts of Vifil's farm.

Six weeks had passed since Amundi Thorsteinsson and Onund Jonsson had conspired to free Odd from Halfdan the Black, to free him before Halfdan finished torturing Odd to death under the eyes of all the people who had followed Odd into rebellion. The pair had managed the task, but just barely; Odd was near death when they took him from the tent in Halfdan's camp, and getting him away all but finished the job. They fled in an old fishing boat they had stolen, sailed it right into a gale with Skorri Thorbrandsson in pursuit and in their wake.

They managed to get ashore while Skorri and his men wrecked on a granite ledge. They moved inland, all but certain that Skorri was dead, but on that count they were wrong. Skorri had lived, and he continued to hunt them, and would have taken them all prisoner if Vifil Helgason, one of those who had followed Odd, had not arrived with his men under arms.

Odd Thorgrimson was young and strong and he came from good stock, but he was within sight of death by the time they carried him off to Vifil's farm. When they arrived at last, through the storm-lashed night, they laid him out by the hearth and Signy fed him broth and tended to him and cleaned and dressed the terrible lacerations on his back.

Despite that relief he was soon burning with fever and tossing under the furs they had piled on him and muttering in his febrile dreams. It seemed likely, that first night in Vifil's hall, that Odd would die just when he was finally safe.

But he did not. A day and a half later the fever broke and Odd's strength began to fill in again like a flood tide coming into a shallow bay. Soon he was sitting up and conversing and eating like a man who had been nearing starvation. And then he was standing and walking with help, and then with no help at all, even wandering around the grounds beyond Vifil's hall. And that was a good thing, because it was clear to everyone that he could not stay.

Skorri was Halfdan's man, which meant that he had all the king's resources to use in hunting down the fugitives. He might not have had enough men to defeat Vifil and the others when he met them on the road, but he would soon enough, and he would know where to look for them. Odd could not stay, and neither could Amundi or Onund Jonsson or any of those who had helped Odd escape. Neither could Vifil or any of his household. When Skorri returned with an overwhelming force, which he undoubtedly would, they had to all be long gone.

They packed what they could in Vifil's various wagons and carts and on his horses and they headed north—Vifil and his family and his men and his servants, Odd, Onund, Amundi, all of them—and one by one they went their separate ways, which they reckoned would make them harder to find. Vifil and his chief men remained with Odd and Amundi and their wives, bringing them to a sheepherder's hovel far up in the hills where Vifil sent his flock in the summers. There they paused once more to gather their strength.

But even there they knew they could not remain. Skorri would be unrelenting in his search, and, unlikely as it was that he would find them in that remote place, it was still too great a risk. So Vifil and his men rode off in one direction, and Odd, Amundi, Signy and Alfdis headed in another. They traveled in the wagon Vifil had given them, a tired old vehicle with horses to match, but one that would attract little notice. They dressed like poor farmers in clothes they had purchased from actual poor farmers they had met on the way. They camped in the woods and rolled through tiny villages where the people made a hard living from the land and the forest and did not ask questions of strangers, and were not apt to cooperate with haughty men from the king's house guard.

It was not long before the hunters came. Odd and the others learned from people they met in their travels of mounted warriors, well-armed and arrogant, who swept into the villages looking for fugitives from the king's justice. It seemed, from what they heard, that the king's men were not entirely certain who they were looking for—a couple of men, a few dozen men, men with their wives and servants. They asked about strangers, anyone who stood out, which did not mean a couple of farmers and their wives in a decrepit wagon. Odd and the rest seemed to raise no suspicions as they kept on the move.

There were close calls, to be sure. They arrived in a small village on the Nidelva River well upstream of Rykene only to learn that the searchers, whom they thought to be long gone, had just left that very morning. Once they had sheltered in the woods off the road as five mounted warriors came riding past. They could not tell if the warriors were the king's men or not, but it seemed unlikely that such men would have any business in that country other than seeking out Halfdan's enemies.

For weeks, they continued on in their nomadic way, and for all their difficulties Odd found enough food and shelter and, thanks to all the time they spent in hiding, sufficient rest that his strength quickly returned. The seeping wounds on his back closed up into ugly pink ridges of skin and then began to fade into scars that he would carry for life, but other than that he started to feel like the man he had been before he became Halfdan's prisoner.

And then, it seemed, the searchers were gone.

Days passed with no sign of them, and no word from the people they spoke with in their travels that any mounted warriors had been through the area for some time. Skorri, or whomever Halfdan had sent to run them down, could have no certain knowledge of where they had gone, and so it stood to reason that he would eventually conclude they had not gone north. In which case they would search elsewhere. Or they would give up looking.

Odd did not think that Halfdan would ever give up entirely. But neither did he think the king would continue to waste his time and treasure fruitlessly hunting. Halfdan could be patient when patience was called for. It was quite possible that he would return to his great hall at Grømstad and wait for the fugitives to show themselves.

"We should go south," Odd said one morning as the four of them were gathered around the fire. They had run the wagon up into a clearing in the woods for the night, and now, with dawn just past, they were watching an increasingly agitated Signy, who did not like to be watched, make the morning porridge.

"South?" Amundi asked.

"South. Not Fevik, or any place we're likely to be recognized. But we should make our way south. See what we can see, listen to what the folk are saying."

"Why?" Alfdis asked.

"Because we can't keep hiding out here until we're dead," Odd said. "We need to find out what Halfdan's up to, if we're to have any hope of returning to our old lives."

"Returning to our old lives?" Alfdis said. "What chance is there of that?"

"I don't know," Odd said. "Some, I suppose. In any event, I think we should find out if there's a chance. I'd like to stop running. I'd like to see my children again. I suspect you would, too."

"And how do we find that out, find out what Halfdan's up to?" Amundi asked. It was a question Odd was ready to answer because he had been thinking this through for the past few days, ever since those first indications that the searchers had left that part of the country.

"We go to a market town," he said. "That's where we'll meet folk from all over Agder. And farther. That's how we'll find out how things lay."

"If we show up in some town, strangers asking questions, we'll have the king's men on us before we've unhitched the horses," Alfdis said.

"That's why we go to a *market* town," Odd said. "Market towns are filled with strangers. And I doubt we'll have to ask many questions at all. You know how people love to talk. All we need do is listen, and I'll wager we'll hear all we need to hear."

They discussed it some more, and none of the others could find fault in Odd's plan. They would pick a town where they were less likely to meet any who knew them, though there seemed to be little chance of their being recognized. Odd had lost a lot of weight; he was thin and drawn. His normally neat hair and beard had grown long and matted, and with the application of charred wood crushed into a powder he turned it from light brown to near black. Soot on his face, and ragged and patched clothing, made him look considerably more like a poor laborer than the well-to-do farmer and warrior that he was. Or had been.

The others applied similar disguises, and soon they were rolling south, buying lamb skins and furs along the way to serve as their goods to sell when they arrived in Rykene, the market town on which they decided.

They spent two days there, two days of success both in selling and gathering information, and then headed south again.

The road from Rykene started out decent enough, as wide as two wagons and generally smooth, but it grew worse as they continued on. Rykene was a port town, connected to the world by the river Nidelva, and no one seemed to worry too much about travel overland. Soon the ruts and washed-out sections began to appear, and the way narrowed down to a single wagon's breadth, which was not too great a problem, since there was little traffic save for those on foot, and they were not many. But on those few occasions when they did meet another cart or wagon coming north, it required some negotiation to find a place where the two might pass abreast.

Soon they found themselves in open and deserted country. "It's been some years since I've traveled this way," Amundi said. "You might know it better than me, Odd. But I do believe this road will fetch up with another that runs between Fevik and Grefstad."

"I think that's right," Odd said. He walked beside the wagon now. Since they had left Rykene, he had alternated between walking and riding, trying to build his strength back up, but not driving himself to exhaustion. "A few more miles and we'll meet the Fevik road. East will take us to Fevik, west to Grefstad. And I reckon that road's not as miserable as this goat track."

There was no discussion as to which direction they would go. Odd's farm was in Fevik, and there was no place in Norway he was more likely to be recognized. Even Grefstad was a bit of a risk, though he had been there on only a few occasions. Their chief hope was that the search had been called off, and that was what they meant to discover.

They rolled through a stretch of forest that ran close to the road and Odd stepped behind the wagon and found Blood-letter where it was hidden under the blankets and few remaining furs. He could not carry the sword—no hard-scrabble farmer would own such a weapon—but he set it in the back of the wagon in such a way that it remained hidden, yet he could snatch it up quickly if need be.

But, happily, there was no need. They passed out of the stand of woods, and the countryside opened up in front of them, rolling away downhill, a landscape of still-green fields and granite outcroppings and stands of trees here and there. A few miles beyond they saw what appeared to be a cluster of buildings, smoke rising in thin trails, nearly straight up into the still air.

"What village is that?" Alfdis asked. She was riding on the wagon, sitting beside Amundi, who was driving.

"Not a village, I don't think," Odd said. "If I remember right, that's where this road joins the Fevik road. There's an inn there, a few houses. That's about it."

"We'll water the horses there, if we can," Amundi said. "And find some food for ourselves. But let's not tarry long." On that the others agreed.

The closer they drew to the crossroads the better the road became, and by the time they reached the inn and the few houses clustered around, they were able to drive the wagon at a reasonable pace. The inn, they found, was a respectable size, built of rough-hewn wooden planks and a thick sod roof. A well stood in the yard and stables on the side and the grounds all around it were well trampled.

They found a water trough and Odd and Amundi unhitched the horses and led them over to it while Signy and Alfdis went into the inn itself. It was not long before the women returned carrying a ham and a block of cheese wrapped in course cloth.

"We spoke with the innkeeper and his wife," Signy reported in a low voice, "and they did not seem much interested in anything more than our silver."

"Three others as well," Alfdis said. "Men. Travelers, I should think. Drinking by the hearth. They seemed more interested in us than the innkeeper was."

"They're men," Signy said. "Their interest is all between their legs."

When the horses had drunk their fill, Odd led them back to the wagon. He was hitching them up again when three men stepped out of the dark interior of the inn and into the bright midday sun.

"Here are the three we told you about," Signy said in a low voice. Odd glanced at them, long enough to take them in, not so long as to suggest interest or concern.

The man in front was not tall, but he was big, with a wide chest and ample gut. Not a man one would call fat. Burly was a better word. He wore a faded blue tunic crisscrossed with black streaks, and leggings that sported patches in several places. On his head was a wide wool cap, red in color, that draped down over one side, a truly impressive garment.

He wore no shoes, and indeed it would have taken quite a bit of leather to cover his big, splayed feet. His face was all but perfectly round, covered in a dark beard and split by a wide smile. It was the sort of smile that might have been genuine, or might have been completely fabricated. It was hard to tell.

The men behind him, flanking him on either side, were thinner, taller, and dressed much like he was. There was something deferential in the way they stood in his wake. It was clear who was in charge.

"Well, now, good day to you, my lords!" the burly man said, and though he did not speak overly loud, there was power in his voice. And humor as well, which made what might have been a threatening posture seem less so. But that did not make Odd any less suspicious. Quite the opposite.

"Good day," Amundi said, turning toward the man as Odd turned away, stepping to where the horses blocked the man's view of him. Amundi's farm was in Vik, bordering Thorgrim's, and he was less likely than Odd to be recognized in this country.

"Lovely wagon you have there. Lovely." The man ambled closer, his eyes moving over the battered vehicle, his two companions following behind. Odd glanced over the horses' backs at the three men as they approached. Knives on leather belts, but no other weapons that he could see. They did not seem to be warriors of any sort, but they looked like hard men, none the less.

"It's a wagon," Amundi said. "A bed and four wheels that seem in no danger of falling off."

"Ha!" The man laughed with seemingly genuine mirth. "Now, I have to guess that such folk as you are bound away for Fevik, am I right?"

"No, not Fevik," Signy said. Odd knew his wife and he knew she was less patient than Amundi, less willing to put up with nonsense.

"No? Where to, then?" the man asked.

"Not Fevik," Signy said.

"Well, that works out fine, do you see!" the burly man replied. "My friends and I, we're going to not Fevik as well, aren't we?" He turned and looked behind him and the two men nodded.

"Well, we wish you joy in your travels," Signy said as she put the meat and cheese in the back of the wagon and hid it under a blanket.

Odd thought about Blood-letter, hidden there as well, wondered how quickly he could get around behind the wagon and snatch it up.

"Here's my worry," the man said, taking another step toward them. "My friends and me, we're not the walking sort, do you see? And we have no horses. But you have this lovely wagon, and all that room in the back of it, and it seems a shame to be rolling around with all that room and the three of us made to walk like beggars or such."

"A shame indeed," Signy said. "But we're not going to Fevik."

"And neither are we, like I said!" the man exclaimed.

"I'm sorry," Amundi said, sounding more conciliatory that Signy did. "The horses are near death as it is. And you're…not the lightest of loads, it would seem. It's why we're walking as well."

The burly man frowned. "As you will, then," he said.

It took a few moments more to get the horses hitched again, but when they were set Amundi took the reins and led them down the road, with the others walking beside the wagon so they would not appear to have been lying. Odd kept his eyes forward and down, and the grinding of the wagon's wooden wheels on the hard-packed road muffled all other sounds. For that reason, it was not until they had walked a good quarter mile or so before Odd realized that the burly man and his companions were walking with them, ten feet behind the wagon.

"Hold up!" Odd said, the first words he had spoken since the three men appeared. He held up a hand and Amundi stopped the horses. The men following behind stopped as well, and Odd turned and addressed them.

"We can't carry you in the wagon. We told you that."

The big man spread his hands as if shocked that he had been misunderstood. "Yes, you told us, my lord. That's why we're walking."

Odd glared at him but did not respond. For a moment they just looked at one another, Odd's expression blank, the burly man's face split in his dumb grin.

"Very well, then," Odd said at last, gesturing toward the road ahead. "Walk."

"What? Ahead of you?" the man said. "There may be bandits lying in wait. No, no, we'll let you go first, brave men such as yourselves."

Odd looked at him for a moment more, but the big man folded his arms and did not stop smiling and did not move.

This is ridiculous, Odd thought. The man looked as if he would stand there and die of thirst before he would yield, and Odd had neither the power nor the authority to make him walk ahead. So, without another word, Odd turned and continued up the road, with Amundi beside him, leading the horses.

They walked in silence, Odd and his people and the three unwelcome fellow travelers, and Odd tried to imagine who the three might be. They did not look like Halfdan's men, not at all. Halfdan's men would be fitted out like warriors and mounted.

Robbers, perhaps? Bandits who lurked around the crossroads looking for likely travelers to rob? That seemed more likely, but if so, then they were not very discriminating thieves. Odd's party did not look as if they had anything worth taking. Even the horses and wagon were pretty worthless.

Have they guessed who we are? Odd wondered next. If they had, then they might be looking to take them all prisoner, sell them to Halfdan. That could be lucrative, indeed.

He considered the meat and cheese in the back of the wagon. If he were to step back there and cut off a slice of meat, it would raise no suspicions, and it would give him a chance to pull Blood-letter before the strangers could make a move. With sword in hand he could hold those three off long enough for Amundi to pull his own sword, which was also hidden in the back of the wagon. Together they could probably defeat three men armed only with knives.

Odd slowed his pace a bit, letting the wagon draw ahead. He was thinking of how he would move casually around the back when the burly man's voice came booming out, making Odd jump in surprise.

"Here, now!" the man said, and Odd could hear his footsteps coming up behind. "It's rude, you know, us keeping your company and never introducing ourselves!" He drew abreast of Odd and Odd saw he was still smiling. "My name is Bragi! Bragi Shipslayer! Now there's a name you've heard, I trust."

Odd was still not sure what the man was about, or exactly how he should react, but it was clear that there would be no ignoring him.

"Bragi Shipslayer…" he said. "No, I don't think I know the name."

"No?" Bragi said, half turning toward his two companions who were still just behind him. "Do you hear that, boys? He's never heard of me."

"Can't imagine," said one of the men.

"Must not be from anywhere near here," said the other.

"Must not." Bragi turned back to Odd and Amundi. "Let me introduce my fellows, here. This is Huginn," he said, pointing to the man on the right, "and this is Muninn."

Odd half turned and nodded his greeting. Huginn and Muninn were the names of Odin's ravens, and Odd doubted anyone's mother had given them to her sons. Nor did those two look like brothers. He wondered at their real names.

"And what's your name, my friend?" Bragi asked. "Where are you from?"

"I'm Torfi," Odd said. "My wife, Gudrun. That's Olaf and his wife, Vigdis. We come from Nævesdal."

"Nævesdal? Never heard of it. Is it on the sea?" Bragi asked.

"No. Far from it."

"Oh, well that explains how you've never heard of Bragi Shipslayer, the greatest sailor who has ever set out from this land or any other!"

"We're sheepherders, we know little of the sea," Odd said, and thought, *Sailors…*

That fit very neatly with his impression of the men; the bare feet, the odd gait he had noticed, the streaks of black on their clothing which on closer look he saw were the marks left by tarred ropes. Indeed, the men smelled powerfully of pine tar and linseed oil. And while most sailors whom Odd had known traveled better armed than these three, still the knives were very much tools of that trade.

"Sheepherders! Well, more's the pity!" Bragi said. "But you look a fine young man. If you ever want to give up that miserable existence, rolling about with sheep, and want to be a sailor, just let me know and I'll put you to work."

"Do you have a ship?" Amundi asked.

"At this moment, I do not," Bragi said. "Ships are like women, you know. One moment you have a fine one, and the next she's sunk, or run up on a ledge. The ship, that is, not the woman. Well, women too, I suppose. Anyway, no, I am without a ship just now. Hoped to get to Fevik and find one there, but when we saw what fine traveling companions you would be, we reckoned we'd come with you."

"And ride in our wagon?" Signy asked.

"If the offer is made," Bragi said.

"It is not," Signy said.

"Fine, then, we can walk. Great thing about this country, any direction you walk, you come to the sea eventually."

They continued for a while in silence, but Odd suspected that Bragi was not one to suffer silence for long, and he was right.

"And you fine people, where are you bound?" he asked.

"Grefstad," Odd said.

"Grefstad? Miserable place," Bragi said.

"You know it?"

"No, never been there," Bragi said. "But it must be miserable. What? A dozen miserable huts, far from the sea? Am I right? What, by all the gods, would take you there?"

"We hope to sell the rest of our skins," Amundi offered.

"You come all the way from...what was it? Neverdown? Just to sell some lambskins? Can't you sell lambskins where you come from?"

"Everyone has lambskins to sell there," Amundi said. "You ask a lot of questions, Bragi Shipslayer."

Bragi shrugged. "I'm curious. Smart fellows like me, we're curious. Isn't that right?" he said over his shoulder to the two men following behind.

"Curious," said Huginn.

"Yeah, curious," said Muninn.

"And a man whose seen all the lands I've seen, and all the things on the sea, if he's curious, like me, he can learn far more than most men. I could tell you tales of...well, let me tell you of this one time when...Huginn and Muninn, they can tell you the truth of this, they were there..."

The words flowed into one of Odd's ears and left unimpeded out the other, as his mind raced and his senses were tuned to everything beyond Bragi's blathering. That was why, even over the sound of Bragi's voice and the creak of the wagon's wheels, he heard the hoofbeats, far off.

"Hold a moment, Olaf," he said. He nearly said Amundi but caught himself before he did. Amundi pulled the horses to a stop and everyone stood in silence.

"Riders coming," Bragi said. With all other noise gone the sound of the horses was clear, and it was clear they were not far off.

"Riding fast," Amundi said. They could hear that as well. The beasts were not at a full gallop, but they were not just walking either. They were moving at a pace that would maximize speed and distance.

"You look worried, my friends," Bragi said. "Is there a reason you should be worried?"

"No," Odd said. "Unless its bandits or such. But now we have you, our new friends, to help us fight."

"Ha!" Bragi said. "No, I don't think so. If you'd shared your wagon, then perhaps we would join you, but now, any fight you have is your own. Come along, boys." That last was directed at Huginn and Muninn.

The road was bordered with tall grass, with clumps of high brush and trees scattered around. Bragi turned and ambled off into the brush, his two companions at his heels. In a moment the three of them were lost from sight, leaving Odd and the rest standing on the road, listening to the sound of the horses, which were closing fast.

Chapter Twelve

Jealousy, that's what it was. It was thin-fingered envy that nabbed you,
stealing away my delight, Nightingale, out of the broom!
Sour as my soul had become, you could fill it with honeying sweetness,
lilting it into my ears, lifting it into my heart.

Alcuin

It was known as the Great Room and it was very much that. Marble floors in black and white checkers around the perimeter with inlaid mosaics taking up the middle portion. Walls of carefully fitted stone blocks, rendered smooth and square and adorned with marble details, rose up to a ceiling thirty feet above.

Overhead, every flat surface of the ceiling was covered with frescoes of Biblical scenes, images of heaven, and portraits of the long-dead patriarchs of the family that ruled Roumois, and it was all held in place by an intricate lattice-work of elaborately carved beams.

The room might have been part of a cathedral, or a king's palace, but it was not. It was in le Château de Roumois, home of Eberhard, le duc de Roumois, and generations before him. A hundred men could have comfortably occupied the room, and forty could sit at the massive polished oak table that ran down the center of the space, but Eberhard was there alone, save for his two oldest companions: rage and fear.

The letter was laid out on the table in front of him. It was from Felix, late of the court of King Charles, now of the court of Æthelwulf of Wessex. It was dated a month past. It was the very worst sort of news. But it was not, Eberhard had to admit, entirely unexpected. The exact circumstances that Felix spelled out were not something he could have foreseen, to be sure, but he had been expecting something like this for a long time.

My Dear Eberhard... the letter began. It was written in Felix's neat hand, the words translated into his precise Latin.

Eberhard had known Felix nearly all his life, since he had been old enough to travel with his father to the king's court in Paris. Felix was seven or eight years his senior, though being as competent, gracious, and worldly as he was, he had always seemed much older. They had been friendly, if not friends, per se. The same had been true with Felix and Eberhard's younger brother, Louis, friendly, if not friends.

But that was a long time ago. Not so long in years, perhaps, but long in the great upheavals of life.

I have news from the Court of Wessex, news that will surprise and, I fear, not please you... Felix's letter continued.

> *We recently captured a band of heathen raiders who were attempting to sneak into the king's court, and I was shocked to find among their numbers your very own brother, Louis, who had apparently fled from the monastery at Glendalough and joined with those godless killers. Louis was in my custody and it was my intention to return him to Frankia for trial, but through the incompetence of the Englishmen guarding him, he managed to escape and flee back to the company of the heathens, where he is beyond my reach.*
>
> *As distressing as this news may be, there is yet good that may come of it. The presence of the heathens in question have thus far prevented the sailing of King Æthelwulf's fleet to the court of Charles, a Royal embassy of which I know you are aware. To remove this obstacle I have arranged for tribute to be paid to the heathens in exchange for their accompanying the king's fleet across the narrow seas to Paris, and I have no doubt that Louis will sail in their company. Thus, your brother will be delivered unto your hands, and in the company of heathens, which will render him beyond question an enemy of the King of Frankia and all civilized men. Thus, you will need no further reason to deal with him in a manner that will best guarantee the safety of the people of Roumois...*

Damn you, Felix, Eberhard thought. The man had a gift, Eberhard had to admit, a great skill when it came to making the most disastrous situation seem like some grand opportunity, and for making his own part in any such disaster seem like it had nothing to do with him at all. It was a skill that had brought Felix to the heights he enjoyed in two royal courts, but he did not fool Eberhard. Felix had allowed Louis to escape through some blunder of his own making, and now he had arranged for heathens to bring his brother back to Frankia. It was all an unfathomable nightmare.

"Damn it!" Eberhard said and pounded his fist on the table.

This is what you get, you coward! he thought, words he would never speak out loud. He was alone in the Great Room, but there were ears in le Château de Roumois, as there were in every palace, and he did not want those ears hearing such a thing from anyone, least of all himself.

But he could not stop from thinking them.

Why…why didn't I kill that little bastard? Eberhard thought next. When their father, Hincmar, le duc de Roumois, had died, Eberhard, the eldest son, had taken his title and his place, as was right. Louis, then in command of the horse guards, had never questioned that succession. Still, Eberhard feared his brother.

For years, Louis and his dashing chevaliers had kept the people of Roumois mostly safe from the depredations of the heathen Northmen, and the people loved him for it. He commanded the respect and loyalty of the chevaliers and all the men-at-arms of Roumois. Louis might have had no immediate ambitions to become duke, but that could change, and if it did, he was well positioned to rise up against his brother.

Having Louis killed was the obvious thing to do, and Eberhard had certainly considered it, but in the end chose not to. Careful as he might be, the people of Roumois would certainly suspect him of being behind his brother's death, which would cause Eberhard to lose favor with them. He was not terribly concerned about that—the people had no authority over him—but King Charles would be displeased as well, and that he could not afford.

And, he had to admit, at least to himself, at least in his darker moments, that the thought of committing fratricide frightened him.

So instead, he packed Louis off to the monastery in Glendalough, in Ireland, at the edge of the civilized world, and he sent enough annual tribute to secure the abbot's assurance that Louis would not be leaving his life of holy contemplation. He dissolved the horse guard and arrested Louis's second-in-command, a man named Ranulf, and the captains below him as well.

Eberhard never really spoke about Louis after that. To the few who asked, he told them how their father, on his deathbed, had begged Louis to abandon the rough and sinful life of a soldier and turn to God instead, and how Louis had tearfully agreed. It was an unlikely story to be sure, but few men were in a position to question le duc de Roumois, and those who were did not really care.

Felix alone, on a few occasions, had dropped hints that he understood the truth of the matter, and suggested that Eberhard had made the right decision.

So Louis sailed off to the west, and Eberhard continued to cement his rule in Roumois and ingratiate himself in Charles's court in Paris. Still, Eberhard could not shake the notion that he should have had his brother killed, that he could not afford the risk of his remaining alive. The months became a year and then two, and still the fear and suspicion grew a little stronger, a little more prevalent.

It was just after that first year had passed that Louis began to appear to him. Late at night, in the dark of his bed chamber—Louis standing by his bed in his mail shirt, a sword in his hand, the blade dripping blood. Louis sitting on one of the chairs by the wall, legs crossed, smiling that wry half smile of his. And Eberhard screamed and kicked at the bedclothes until his servants came racing into the room, and by then, Louis was gone.

The appearances were dreams, no more, or so Eberhard hoped. But they did tell him one thing: disloyalty was honeycombing his rule and he had to do something about it. He knew that the palace was riddled with traitors, men and women still loyal to Louis. And the fountainhead of that treason had to be Ranulf, the old campaigner who had taught Louis the ways of the soldier.

Ranulf was still in prison, but as long as he lived he was a threat, so Eberhard ordered him killed, and ordered that his head be brought to him for confirmation. Two days later, the captain of the house guard did just that, holding the severed head up for display, dull eyes open wide, blood dried on the hacked stump of a neck. Eberhard forced himself to not vomit as he nodded in approval, though after more than a year in prison, more than a year's emaciation and growth of beard, Eberhard barely recognized the man.

Ranulf's death sated Eberhard, at least for a while, but soon the fear reasserted itself. Servants and officers of his guard became objects of suspicion, so Eberhard ordered them questioned under torture, and if that questioning revealed disloyalty of any kind, they followed Ranulf to the headsman's block. Yet even that, Eberhard realized, was not enough to keep his dukedom safe. He was snipping at the branches when he should have been severing the root, which was Louis himself.

Through discreet inquiries he found an assassin, a man who could be counted on to see that Eberhard's problems were solved at long last and for good. He gave the man a quantity of gold and sent him off to Glendalough. And that was the last that Eberhard had ever heard of him. He might have run off with the money; he might have been killed in any of the hundreds of ways a man could be killed between Frankia and Ireland; but whatever happened, Eberhard received no word of his brother's death, no word of Louis whatsoever. Until now.

Eberhard pounded his fist on the table again, but not so hard or emphatic this time. He felt the rage dissipating, like a stab of pain that fades away, like a cramped muscle that begins to unwind. He could not simply wallow in his fear, he had to act, had to plan. He was ruler of Roumois, its people, villages, churches, roads, and waterways. He had things to do.

He stood and took a few steps away from the table, paced back and forth a half dozen times, then turned toward the door. "Hildirik!" he called, because he knew that his secretary would be just on the other side of the door, likely with his ear pressed to the wood, waiting, listening.

There was a moment's pause—Hildirik pretending that he was not standing poised and ready to enter—and then the door swung open and the secretary poked his head in. He was old, how old, no one knew, well-informed and easily frightened, just what Eberhard wanted in a man who was seeing to his affairs.

"*Monsieur le Duc?*" Hildirik asked.

"What do we have today?"

"Ah…" Hildirik said. He took another step into the room and shut the door. In his arms he held a number of scrolls and parchments, wax and Eberhard's seal, all the tools of pending business. "We have a few matters, my lord," he said.

Eberhard sighed and sat again. He gathered up Felix's letter and set it face down beside him, because he did not want Hildirik to see it. He did not entirely trust the man. Hildirik had served Eberhard's father, had been part of the household for as long as anyone could remember, but he seemed to have no loyalty to any man, only to Roumois itself. Still, he was valuable, and knew everything that went on in the dukedom, so Eberhard had decided to let him live. For now.

Hildirik stepped over, laid his load on the table, and picked up the topmost parchment.

"A dispute, my lord, over a parcel of land at Fontanelle…" Hildirik began, and Eberhard settled back to endure the tedium that was his day-to-day life, administering Roumois, its petty squabbles between neighbors, its threats real and imagined.

They made it through a little more than half of Hildirik's documents and other concerns before Eberhard had had enough.

"I think we're done now, Hildirik," Eberhard said, pushing his chair away from the table and getting to his feet.

"Yes, my lord." Hildirik knew better than to protest, but he did clear his throat and add, "One last thing, my lord?"

"Yes?"

"I just wish to report, my lord, that Mariwig's guard is assembled and they're awaiting word. And the carriages and the rest of the train are all in order now."

"Very good." Eberhard glanced down at the letter from Felix, face down on the table. It was all of a piece. Word had come from Charles the Bald alerting Eberhard to the imminent arrival of King Æthelwulf of Wessex. Eberhard and all the lords under Charles's rule were expected to attend. To that end, Mariwig, the captain of the reconstituted horse guard and the foot soldiers as well, had been ordered to have his men ready to accompany Eberhard and his retinue to Paris.

It was not that the road was particularly dangerous, or that Eberhard needed that many men-at-arms to protect him. He had a personal bodyguard of twenty excellently trained men under the command of a captain named Otker whose loyalty was beyond question, and they could provide protection enough. It was more that a man such as Eberhard had to make a decent show of his arrival in Paris, and that required a display of numbers, foot soldiers in mail, mounted troops, banners flying.

As Eberhard's thoughts drifted along those lines, Hildirik stood silently by. Finally he spoke. "Would there be anything else, my lord? Or would you…"

"Is Mariwig loyal, do you think?" Eberhard asked.

"Mariwig?" Hildirik asked, surprised, apparently, by the question. "Yes, lord, I would say he's certainly loyal. I know there were…doubts about his brother, but Mariwig is a good man."

Eberhard nodded. The two of them, Mariwig and his brother, had been part of Louis's horse guard. They had come under suspicion, and they had been questioned. Mariwig's brother had failed to assuage those suspicions, failed badly enough that his head had been removed from his body.

Mariwig, however, had seemed more genuine in his response. He had been returned to duty intact, and his subsequent service and apparent dedication to his duke had earned him command of the chevaliers and of the three hundred or so men-at-arms who made up Eberhard's soldiers of foot.

"Good." Eberhard looked down at the letter again, thought for a moment, then made a decision. He looked up at Hildirik. "Is Mariwig nearby?"

"He's in the yard, my lord, overseeing the training of the men."

"Send for him," Eberhard said.

Hildirik bowed and hurried out of the Great Room. Eberhard sat, picked up Felix's letter once more and stared at it, seeing the words but not reading them, his mind wandering off to other thoughts. Soon, Hildirik returned with Mariwig following behind. The chevalier was dressed in a mail shirt and coarse wool trousers. His hair was damp and there was sheen of sweat on his face from the exertion of training the men under his command.

"My lord?" Mariwig said, bowing with a soldier's quick, mechanical motion. He was a tall man, and broad, with a face marked by pox and half covered by an unkempt black beard. An ugly man.

Eberhard found him slightly unnerving, a bit frightening. But he imagined an enemy would as well, and that was good.

"How are the men doing, Mariwig?" Eberhard asked.

"Not so bad, my lord," Mariwig said. "The new ones, they're a sorry lot, get worse each year, my lord, but I'll see they're whipped into useful men. The older hands, they're full ready for whatever's needed of them."

"Are they loyal?"

Mariwig frowned and his eyebrows came together. He clearly did not expect this question. "Loyal, my lord? Yes, they're loyal. Loyal as ever men were."

"Good," Eberhard said. "I need loyal men. I have word…it seems the king of Wessex has paid tribute to a band of Northmen to accompany his fleet across the narrow seas. It will bring the heathens right to our doorstep."

"Northmen, my lord? We've dealt with Northmen before, and—"

"Louis is with them," Eberhard cut him off.

"Louis, my lord? Your brother?" Eberhard saw the surprise on Mariwig's face, and that was good. It meant that word of Louis's arrival had not reached the court ahead of Felix's letter.

"Yes, my brother," Eberhard said. "It seems he's joined up with the Northmen. And he'll be coming here."

"Joined with Northmen, my lord?" Hildirik said. "Joined with the enemies of King Charles and God himself? Well, my lord, I think he'll find little welcome in Frankia."

"I should think not." Eberhard kept his eyes on Mariwig's lined and weather-beaten face, looking for some hint of how he was taking this news. Was he pleased? Suspicious? Angry? But Eberhard could read little in the chevalier's expression.

"What say you to this, Mariwig?" Eberhard asked.

"Well, my lord…" Mariwig seemed to be struggling to find the right words, aware, no doubt, of the importance this held for his duke. "I'd have to agree with Hildirik, my lord. If he weren't enemy enough before, joining with the heathens puts him at odds with the king and God. And all of Roumois. I should think the king will see about this."

"King Charles will see to punishing Louis for his transgressions, I have it on good authority," Eberhard said. "But the king has a great many things to see to. I might have asked Otker and his men to take care of this matter, but I'll need them by me when we go to Paris. So I want you and your men to be ready. Do you follow me?"

"Yes, my lord," Mariwig said, in that infuriating way that he had, that always left Eberhard wondering if he really did follow.

"If the king is too distracted by affairs of state to deal with this matter, I want to be certain that we can do so in his stead," Eberhard continued. "We…you and your men-at-arms…must see that Louis is…never a threat again. Do I make myself clear?"

"Yes, my lord," Mariwig said, and beside him Hildirik nodded vigorously.

Eberhard gave a hint of a smile, and for the first time since reading the letter from Felix, he felt a sense of calm tamping down the panic, just a bit. Of course, Louis would find no welcome in Frankia, any more than the heathens would. Felix's words had eluded to that fact. The Northmen would not be suffered to live. Once Æthelwulf was safe ashore, it would be the sword for the lot of them. And for Louis as well.

He had sent a man to Glendalough to deal with Louis once and for all, and nothing had come of that. But now God was giving him a second chance, delivering Louis right into his hands like the sacrificial ram in the thicket that he had given to Abraham. King Charles's men would deal with Louis, or his own men would, but either way Eberhard's problems would be solved at no cost and no blame to him.

"Good," Eberhard said. "Good."

Chapter Thirteen

To some grants he wealth, to his children war-fame
Word-skill to many, and wisdom to men
Fair winds to sea-farers, song-craft to skalds
And might of manhood to many a warrior.

The Lay of Hyndla
The Poetic Edda

Evening was coming on and the wind was beginning to fail. *Fox*'s sail collapsed, then rippled, snapped, and collapsed again. Harald broke off his discussion—an increasingly animated discussion— straightened, and looked around.

The last ship of the English fleet was a hundred yards or so ahead of *Fox*, where it had been all day. They had put out under oar from the gravelly beach, the wind being, as Harald and his father had predicted, all but nonexistent. Harald had taken his assigned station, leading his father's ships as they trailed behind the English, keeping a certain distance back from the wary Englishmen.

Behind *Fox*, Thorgrim's ships had spread out in a long line abreast, far enough apart that they could see as much ocean as possible, near enough that they could come together to bring all their strength to bear quickly if need be. They were there to provide protection, which meant seeing any threat as early as possible, and reacting to it quickly, and in force.

They had seen no threats, however, and not much of anything else. As they passed the big island off to the west, the English fleet turned south and headed out to the open water. Harald followed behind, and the rest of his father's ships followed behind him.

The king's ships set an easy pace, which was good, since it was not clear how long they might have to row, or if they would have to row clear across the narrow seas to Frankia. Harald rotated his men as best he could, but he had only eight more men than there were oars, so it was tricky to give them all an equal amount of work and rest. He forced himself to remain at the tiller, where a ship's master should be, as much as he longed to take a place on a sea chest and pull with the others.

The nearest land was about five miles astern when the breeze began to fill in. Just a little at first, a few puffs on Harald's cheek, enough to make him look out to windward to see if there was any indication that more was on the way. But even if there was, he could do nothing about it unless the English did first. Those were his father's orders: follow what the English did. If they rowed, the Northmen rowed. If they set sail, the Northmen would set sail.

The puffs of wind became more frequent, and finally evolved into something that might be called a breeze, and still the English stayed at the oars. Harald saw his men glancing out to windward, heard the low tones of muttering as they continued to pull at the oars despite the growing wind, enough to fill the ship's sail and relieve them of the tedium of rowing.

Harald gripped harder on the tiller. He cursed the English under his breath even as he considered ordering his men to stop their muttering. He had no intention of explaining to them why they were still rowing: if he did that, they might come to expect an explanation for every order, and it was their job to obey whether or not they knew the reason why. That was one of many things he had learned by watching his father in action.

He opened his mouth, ready to call for them to shut up, when the English ship ahead pulled in its oars. He let his men take two more strokes as he watched the English swing their yard athwartships and loosen sail, then called, "Rowers! Ship oars! Make ready to set sail!"

The men's sour looks turned to smiles even before the last words had passed Harald's lips. The oars came in and were quickly stacked, the yard swung around and the sail cast off.

"Hold!" Harald called, sharp and emphatic, as the enthusiastic men started hauling on the halyard. "You pull when I say, and not before. You hear me?"

Heads nodded, and the men looked sheepish as they stood waiting, hands on the rope. Beyond the bow the English sailors were still preparing to hoist their sail. If *Fox* had set hers then, they would have been right up the Saxon's stern before the Saxon had gathered way.

After what seemed to Harald to be a ridiculously long time, the English ship hoisted its yard, its red and white striped sail flapping and filling as the yard was braced around. The ship began to gather way and Harald called, "Very well! Haul away!"

Fox's yard rose up the mast and starboard and larboard men hauled the thick sheets aft.

"Larboard brace, haul away!" Harald shouted and overhead the yard pivoted around, its larboard end swinging aft, it's starboard end forward. The sail flogged and then filled and the ship heeled a bit under the pressure. Harald felt the vibration in the tiller, the great wooden beast stirring to life. He heard the note of the water running down her side as she gathered way.

Soon they were rolling along with eight knots of wind, enough to keep *Fox* heeled over a bit and moving about as fast as a horse at an easy trot. Beyond the bow the sea was dotted with the sails of the English fleet plowing along on their southerly heading. They were slow ships, and ponderous, and again and again Harald had to order *Fox*'s sheets eased away so that his more nimble vessel did not overtake them.

They continued on like that through the afternoon as Engla-land sank below the horizon astern, and soon there was nothing but the long, easy swells of the narrow seas to be seen in every direction. It was a glorious sight, and a little unnerving. It was more than two years now since Harald had left Vik with his father and grandfather, and in those years of raiding the coasts of Ireland and Engla-land he had spent only a little time beyond the sight of land.

The sun was starting to sink toward the west, off the starboard side, and Harald ordered a cup of ale for all hands, who had little enough to do with the ship under easy sail. He remained at the tiller as the barrel was broached and men dipped their cups. Soon after, Brand came ambling aft, two cups in his hands, and he handed one to Harald.

"I'll take this over rowing," Brand said, lifting his cup in salute.

"Me too," Harald said.

"Ha!" Brand said. "You're master of the ship! You don't row. You tell others to row."

Brand had joined Thorgrim's band in Ireland, but he and Harald had not really known one another until Thorgrim put Brand aboard *Fox* to augment that ship's crew. Since then, he and Harald had become good friends. They were of similar age, though physically they were quite different, almost opposites. Where Harald was stocky and thick of arm, Brand was more slight, more wiry and quick. His hair was brown to Harald's blond, though they both wore it in a long braid down the back. Brand's beard was thicker than Harald's not so impressive effort, but not by much.

"I would rather row than tell men to row," Harald said, and Brand smiled. Harald meant that sincerely, and Brand knew it. For Harald, the hardest part of leadership was ordering others to do things rather than doing them himself.

"Rowing is easy," Brand said. "Keeping command of this lot, that's hard."

Harald nodded. "There's a lot to think about. This morning I reckoned we'd be rowing all night. Figured we'd be in the middle of the narrow seas, well clear of land, during the dark hours. But if this breeze holds up, we might be approaching Frankia at night. That's not good."

"No," Brand agreed. "But lucky for us, the Saxons are going first. We just listen for the sound of their ships smashing on rocks and their men screaming in terror, and if we hear those things, we turn around."

"That's good advice," Harald said. "Maybe you should be master."

"Not for all the silver in Frankia would I be master!" Brand said. "I wasn't born to it, like you."

Born to it... Harald had never felt he was born to lead. His brother Odd, he was the natural leader, heir to the legacy of Ulf of the Battle Song and Thorgrim Night Wolf. But Odd had married and become a farmer, and had not gone raiding, and so Harald had taken up his father's mantle, though he wore it uncertainly. Most of the time he felt like a fraud.

They stood for a while in silence, enjoying the sun and the breeze and the motion of the ship under their feet. Finally, Harald spoke again.

"I saw the most amazing thing this morning. The Frank, Felix, showed it to me."

"What was that?"

"You've seen maps before, haven't you? A map of a certain kingdom, say, or of some section of country?"

"Yes," Brand said.

"Well, Felix showed me a map like that, but it was a map of the entire world. Or nearly. Ireland, Engla-land, Frankia, Frisia. A great sea...I forget what it was called...that I didn't know existed. It was...amazing."

Harald had been thinking about that map nearly every moment that his thoughts had not been occupied with driving *Fox*, and he was eager to tell Brand about it. Brand, he knew, would understand in a way that his father clearly did not. He and Brand had often talked about the wide world, and how they would like to see what was there, well beyond the parts they knew about, which they were sure were only a small part of the whole. They imagined what sights must be out there, what riches there were to be had, and how much they longed to drive their ship to those places.

"A map of the whole world?" Brand said. He frowned a bit as he considered that.

"Well, not the whole world. Our northern lands aren't on it. It was made by a Roman, that's what Felix said, and so it only shows the world that the Romans knew about. I guess they didn't know our country, but they knew about a whole lot else."

"Hmm..." Brand said, considering this information. "I guess it doesn't matter that our country's not on it. We already know about that."

"Exactly," Harald continued. "Think of it. A map of the world. A man who has that, he can know how to sail to places he might not even have known were there."

"Right now the only map we have is the one we keep in our heads," Brand said. "And that's all we know about the world. And for me, that's just our own country, really. We've been to Ireland and Engla-land, but I don't know how those lands are shaped, or where the coasts lead."

"I don't either," Harald said. "Or at least I didn't until I saw this map. I always reckoned on navigating by following a coastline, mostly. I know experienced men can read waves and the movement of birds and whales and such to find distant lands, but I don't have that art. And besides, it's not exactly reliable. We hear often enough about men going out to sea and never returning. Maybe they go right off the edge of the world, since they don't know where they're going. But with that map, if it was correct, we would know."

Brand shook his head. "It's an amazing thing. To get our hands on such a thing…"

"Yes, if that was possible…" Harald said, and as he thought it, a new idea, a sense of purpose, began to flicker in his head. "I wonder if it would be possible?"

Brand looked up and was about to speak when the sail collapsed in a flaw of wind, rippled, and then snapped full again. Harald stood straighter and looked out past *Fox*'s bow toward the English fleet. A moment before, the sails of those distant ships had seemed almost solid with the wind filling them, but now they were now flogging and twisting in the failing breeze.

"Is that the end of our wind?" Brand asked.

Harald looked to the west, the sun sinking lower. "Yes, I think it is," he said.

Brand sighed. "Back to the oars?"

"I don't know," Harald said. "That's for our Saxon friends to decide." In truth he was too distracted to care very much. The map, Felix's map, had been lodged in the back of his mind all day, but now having spoken of it out loud, having discussed it, it was no longer in the back of his mind. It was foremost.

He was sure that Brand understood. Harald had seen something that morning, and it was something that was going to change everything.

Chapter Fourteen

Come now, let ancient kinsmen be numbered,
Who is freeborn, who is gentleborn,
Choicest of all the men under Midgarth.

The Lay of Hyndla
The Poetic Edda

From where he stood by the wagon, Odd saw the riders a few hundred yards away, coming up over a hill and then disappearing from sight as the road dipped again.

"Let's keep moving, act like we have no concerns," he said, pulling the hood of his cape up over his head. "Whoever this is, let's hope they won't bother with a few poor sheepherders."

Amundi pulled his hood up as well, gave the reins a tug, and the horses moved grudgingly forward. They were just getting up to speed when the riders came around the bend fifty yards ahead and slowed at the sight of the wagon. There were five of them. Three were wearing mail, two wore leather armor. None held spears, which meant they were probably all armed with swords, which in turn meant they were warriors of some experience and not miserable bandits or the like. Plus, they were mounted, which lesser men would not have been.

This is not good, Odd thought, but kept his head down and trudged on and hoped that the disguises he and the others had adopted would be enough to hide them.

The riders had slowed from a trot to a walk, and finally they stopped completely. They waited on the road as the wagon rolled toward them, and Odd knew there was nothing he and Amundi and the women could do but continue on. Any other move would only make the situation worse.

They were twenty feet from the horsemen, who were standing in line abreast and blocking the road, when the rider in front called, "Hold up, there."

Amundi pulled the horses to a stop and he and Odd looked up at the man while still keeping their heads bowed a bit, their faces deep in their hoods. They did not want to look defiant, and they did not want to let the rider get a good look at them.

"Who are you?" the rider asked.

"We're sheepherders, me and Torfi and our wives," Amundi said.

"And who are you?"

"Olaf. Olaf Bjornson."

"'Olaf Bjornson'…" the man said, as if trying out the name. "And where are you going, Olaf Bjornson?"

"To market. Taking our lambskins to market."

"To market? Where?"

"Grefstad," Amundi said.

"Grefstad…" the rider repeated.

He's toying with us, the bastard. Odd looked down at the road again and pictured the man's face from the brief glimpse he had had of him. There was certainly something familiar about him.

Odd had encountered many of Halfdan's warriors during his time as a prisoner, but that time had all melded together into one feverish nightmare, and he could no longer be certain of anything or anyone he had seen. Still, it was more than likely that these were Halfdan's men, and the best that Odd and Amundi could hope for was that they would not be recognized in their sheepherders' attire and the changes wrought by the past weeks of hardship.

It was quiet for a moment, and Odd glanced up to see that the riders were talking in low voices amongst themselves. He felt his whole body tense, felt the sweat stand out on his back and his hands, and he asked the gods to hide them from these hunters, asked that the riders dismiss the four of them as not worthy of consideration and be on their way.

But the gods did not listen.

The conversation stopped and, as one, the five riders slid down from their horses. One of them took up the horses' reins and the other four walked slowly toward the wagon. Their swords were still sheathed, but their hands were resting on the pommels and they approached in a way that conveyed menace, and was meant to. They stopped in a semicircle facing the four people clustered near the wagon.

"Sheepherders?" the lead man said, addressing Odd. "From around here?"

"No," Amundi chimed in, "from up in…"

"I didn't ask you, 'Olaf Bjornson,' did I?" the warrior cut him off. He turned back to Odd. "From where?"

"Nævesdal." Odd kept his eyes down, which made him look submissive and helped to hide his face.

"These must be the ones Skorri sent us to look for," one of the men behind offered. "Two men, two women, pretending to be sheepherders."

"Ain't pretending, lord," Odd said, as meek as he could. "No cause for us to pretend."

"Oh?" the lead man said. He took two steps closer, so that he and Odd were just a foot apart, and he stared at Odd's face, his brows wrinkling in concentration. Odd looked down, avoiding his eyes, but the man reached out and jerked his hood off, then grabbed Odd under the chin and raised his head so they were looking right at one another. The man leaned in closer still, scrutinizing Odd's face. Then he let go of his chin and turned toward the others.

"Don't know for certain," he said. "Might be him. I never saw that whore's son right up close, and this one's a filthy, half-starved runt."

"Check his back," another of the men said. "That'll tell you. He could never hide what Halfdan did to him."

The leader nodded and turned back toward Odd. "Take your tunic off, you miserable turd."

"Take…my tunic off?" Odd said, playing dumb, playing for time, his mind grasping for any way out of this.

"Are you deaf? Take your tunic off, or by the gods I'll cut it off, and I won't be too careful doing it." His hand shifted from the pommel of his sword to the grip, and his fingers wrapped around it.

"Very well, very well," Odd said, holding his hands up as if warding off an attack. He grabbed the hem and realized as he did that there were only two choices now: die, or be taken prisoner. And he had no intention of being a prisoner, ever again.

Amundi and the women can get away, he thought as he slowly lifted the hem of his tunic. If he could hold the attention of these men for even a few moments it should be enough for the others to run off.

Of course, they never would. Amundi, Alfdis, Signy, they would choose to fight and die. But at least Odd could give them the chance and the choice to get away.

The hem of the tunic came up to his eyes and then in a sudden flourish, he pulled the garment over his head and brought it down over the head of the warrior facing him. Odd heard the muffled cry of surprise from under the cloth and the man's hands came up and clawed at the tunic that was smothering him.

As the man struggled, Odd lunged forward and grabbed the grip of his sword, then jumped back, pulling the sword free of the scabbard as he did. The warrior whipped the tunic off his head and threw it aside and his eyes went wide as he saw Odd standing there with his sword in hand.

Odd lunged straight at the man's gut, but the man was not too surprised to react. He twisted sideways as the point came at him and the blade bounced off his chainmail. He twisted back and grabbed for Odd's hand, hoping to pull the sword free, but Odd leapt clear, leaving him to grab at air.

Then everything seemed to go mad all at once. The three men behind shouted and drew their swords and charged forward. Odd shouted, "Amundi! Signy! Run!" Out of the corner of his eye he saw Amundi turn and run back down the road, but he knew full well the man was not fleeing, he was going for his sword, hidden in the wagon. Amundi was no more willing to be taken prisoner than Odd was.

"Take him alive!" the leader shouted as the three others stepped around him, swords held ready. "If we kill him, Skorri will kill us!"

Very well, then, Odd thought. This would make dying with a sword in his hand harder than he hoped. He took a step back, his eyes moving from one man to the other. The four were coming at him slowly, spreading out, encircling him as he tried to gauge which of them would make the first move.

The man to his right took a tentative step forward, stepping within the arc of Odd's sword stroke, and Odd whipped his blade around horizontally in a wild swing. The man leapt back, but not quick enough, and the point slashed through his leather armor and the flesh beneath, not enough to kill him, or even put him down, but enough to hurt, a lot, and slow him up, and that would help.

Good blade, Odd thought. He stepped back and then back again, eyes shifting side to side. The man whose sword he had taken now drew a seax and closed in with the rest. Where Amundi had gone, Odd did not know, but he hoped it was to run off with the women.

The man on Odd's left was moving now and Odd slashed at him and made him jump back and then, with the backstroke, slashed at the man beside him. That one did not jump back, but rather met Odd's blade with his own. The steel rang out as the swords hit. Odd felt the vibration up his arm and he knew that he did not have the strength he had enjoyed just a few months before. How long he could keep this up, he did not know.

The two blades were still pressed together when Halfdan's man pushed Odd's aside and lunged, but Odd parried the attack and stepped to his right. The wounded man was pressing a hand to his bleeding chest, and Odd swung his sword at him, hoping to finish him or drive him away. The man ducked and stumbled back and Odd moved to his right again and pressed his back against the wagon to stop any of his attackers from getting behind him.

They were closing in again, warily, and Odd's eyes were moving from one to the other when he saw, past them, Amundi stepping around the horses. He had grabbed his sword and come back around the wagon the far way so that he might hit Halfdan's men from behind. It would give him a second or two of surprise, which might make all the difference.

Smart man, Odd thought. The men facing Odd did not see Amundi, but unfortunately, the one holding the horses' reins did and he shouted a warning just as Amundi charged forward. The man on Odd's left half turned and saw the threat and broke off to meet the attack.

Amundi stopped in mid-stride, swung at the man, a powerful, two-handed crosscut, but Halfdan's warrior had his blade ready, met the blow, and turned it away. And that was all that Odd saw, because the three men facing him now stepped up as if driven by some invisible force.

Blades lunged and came sideways at him and he worked his sword left and right, parrying the blows, dodging the blows, driving the men back when he could. His arm ached and the sweat was coming in earnest, running into his eyes and making his grip slick on the sword's hilt. He knew he could not go on like that much longer. He took a wild swing at his attackers, then another, backhand, not even hoping to connect, just hoping to drive them back for a heartbeat or two, time in which he could breathe and wipe his eyes.

It worked, but just for an instant, and then they were moving forward again. Odd was bracing for the attack when he saw a flash of movement to his left, and though he knew better than to take his eyes off his enemies, he looked.

It was Bragi Shipslayer, and behind him, Huginn and Muninn, moving quick and noiselessly on their bare feet. Odd had absolutely no idea what they would do, or for whom they would fight, or if they would fight at all. But he did not wonder long.

Bragi grabbed the man on Odd's left by the shoulder and half spun him around. The man's mouth opened and his eyes went wide in surprise—he had neither seen nor heard Bragi coming—and then Bragi cocked his arm and drove his fist straight into the man's face, as powerful a punch as Odd had ever seen.

The warrior's nose seemed to disappear under the blow and the blood burst out like surf around Bragi's fist. Halfdan's man was lifted off his feet and tossed into the man beside him, the warrior holding the seax. The two of them staggered sideways and together they began to fall. Before they did, Bragi leapt forward, surprisingly nimble, and grabbed the man he had struck by the collar, jerked him upright and hit him again.

Huginn darted behind them and grabbed the wrist of the man holding the seax and twisted it back. The man shouted and dropped the short sword and Huginn drove his fist into that man's face, with similar, if less devastating, results than Bragi had delivered.

Muninn had run off to join with Amundi and now he and Amundi and Halfdan's warrior were circling around one another, looking for their chance to land some deadly blow.

All this Odd watched in stunned amazement, as did the fourth of Halfdan's men, the one Odd had wounded. Then, in the same instant, both Odd and the wounded men came back to the reality of the moment. They turned toward one another, their eyes met, and they lunged.

Odd was the slower of the two, but that was all right. As the other's blade came at him, he slapped it aside as he lunged, knocking the point out of line, then driving forward. The man's eyes went wide and Odd felt his sword point hit the man's boiled leather armor, hesitate for an instant then tear on through. The man's eyes went wider still and blood came out of his mouth as he doubled over. Odd pushed the blade in as far as his extended arm would allow, then pulled it back and let the man fall.

Amundi and Muninn and Halfdan's man were still engaged in their strange duel. Muninn had his knife in hand and the three of them were moving in circles, taking tentative swipes at one another, when Bragi let out a big sigh and shouted, "Oh, by all the gods, are you still dancing around like some kind of princess?"

The man Bragi had punched was sprawled out motionless on the ground, unconscious or dead. Bragi reached down and picked up his sword, then ambled over toward the three men. Muninn stepped back and lowered his knife as Bragi approached. Amundi stepped back as well, leaving Halfdan's man standing with his weapon raised and watching as Bragi walked straight at him, sword point dragging in the dirt.

Bragi stopped five feet from the man, just out of range of his sword. For an instant, the two stood motionless, looking at one another, each waiting for the other to make a move. Halfdan's man had his sword up in a stance that left him ready to attack or defend; the point of Bragi's sword was still in the dirt.

Suddenly, Bragi lifted his sword and flung it at Halfdan's man, his whole body twisting with the effort. The long blade spun as it flew and Halfdan's man lifted both his arms to fend it off. The sword hit his upraised arms and fell harmlessly to the ground, but by then Bragi was in full motion.

Halfdan's man lowered his arms just in time to see Bragi's fist coming straight at his face and he had no time to even begin to react. Bragi's fist hit with a horrible crushing sound and the man staggered back, and as he did, Bragi snatched the sword out of his hand.

The man was still reeling, hovering between falling and keeping his feet, when Bragi swung the sword up, grabbed the hilt with two hands, then chopped straight down. The sword struck the top of the man's head and just kept going, cleaving his skull in two, driving the man to his knees, his head now a confusion of blood and brains. Bragi let go of the sword, which remained embedded, and the man toppled onto his side, twitching a bit before he lay still.

"Come, Princess Muninn, dancing is over," Bragi said and he walked back toward Odd, who was leaning against the wagon and breathing hard.

"Not bad, Torfi," Bragi said, looking around at the bodies lying on the ground. "We watched some of that, you know. Very entertaining. You fight good. For a sheepherder, I mean. Surprisingly good, even. But sailors like us, well, we can't stand just watching a fight, you know. Got to join in."

Odd's breathing had settled enough for him to talk, and he said, "I thank you. But you could have joined in from the start, and not run off."

Bragi frowned and shook his head. "How could we join in when we didn't know which side was worth fighting for?"

"Well, I'm glad you thought it was us."

"Did we?" Bragi asked. "I'm not sure we did. I just know that miserable pukes like these, these fine fellows with their mail and horses and fancy swords, they're always worth fighting against." He kicked the supine body of the man he had punched first, but still the man did not react.

Odd thought it was possible Bragi had actually killed him with just two fist-blows to the face, a remarkable feat.

He looked at the man lying beside him, the one whose sword he had taken. That man was certainly dead, Huginn having apparently cut his throat with his sheath knife, though Odd had not seen him do it. The third man had died on Odd's blade.

Amundi joined them now, and Signy and Alfdis. "Thank you, Bragi Shipslayer," Amundi said. "I wish I could say we were handling these four just fine on our own, but we were not."

"Not with swords, you won't," Bragi said. He held up his fist, which was dark with drying blood. "Now here's a weapon that will lay any man low!"

"I don't know what these men wanted with us," Odd said, looking at the bodies on the road. "I guess they were looking to rob us."

"Of course they were, Torfi," Bragi said. "And I am the mother-goddess Frigg. But if it turns out someone sent these bastards to look for you, then he'll have a pretty good idea of where you are soon enough."

"Really?" Signy said, looking at the dead men sprawled at her feet. "I don't think these ones will be telling any tales."

"No," Bragi agreed. "But there was a fifth man, holding the horses."

With that the seven of them turned and looked down the road. Four of the horses had wandered into the field and were eating grass. The fifth horse, and the man who had been holding the reins, were gone.

"Oh, the cowardly bastard!" Signy said.

"You can't call a man a coward just because he runs from Bragi Shipslayer," Bragi said, as if explaining a well-known fact to a child. "Most men, their guts turn to water when they see my fists."

"I have no doubt," Signy said.

"See here," Amundi said, "Bragi's right. Halfdan will know soon enough where we are, so we had better get moving."

"Not on the road," Odd said. "Overland. But where to?" Grefstad was no longer an option, nor was any town. Towns were where Halfdan would be looking.

"Ragi Oleifsson's farm is to the south of here, I'm quite certain," Amundi said.

Odd shook his head. "I don't want to put Ragi and his house in danger."

"Ragi's been bored half to death since he gave up raiding," Amundi said. "He lusts for danger the way some men lust for women or drink."

"Or some men for both," Bragi offered.

Odd sighed and looked up and down the road. They could not spend the afternoon arguing the point. They had to hide, and the home of a loyal friend was clearly the best choice. Ragi's children were grown and his wife had passed, so he did not have to be concerned about them. As much as he might worry about the rest of Ragi's household, Odd knew he had to think about Signy and Alfdis as well.

"Very well," Odd said. "Let's get these dead ones hidden. The wagon, too. We have six horses, so we can ride south." He turned to Bragi. "We need four of the horses. You're welcome to the other two."

"Oh, isn't that fine!" Bragi said. "Now that you owe us a ride in the wagon, you decide to leave it behind. And kindly offer us two horses."

"You're more than welcome to the wagon," Amundi said. "And the team pulling it."

"Whoever is hunting for you, I think they'll be hunting for us as well," Bragi said, "after the fun we just had. I believe someone mentioned Halfdan? So we'll also take horses and get off the road. But there are three of us, so we'll take three horses. And if the women care to ride in our laps, they are quite welcome."

"Thank you," said Alfdis. "But I'll gouge my eyeballs out first."

"Suit yourself," Bragi said.

Odd stared at Bragi, still trying to reckon what the man was about, still finding no answers. But Bragi was not his biggest concern. They had to get moving, get off the road, get to some safe place. There was no time to haggle about horses and such.

"Very well," he said. "Help us with these dead ones and we'll be on our way."

Chapter Fifteen

His shaft he shook, his shield he brandished,
His steed he galloped, his sword he drew,
War he wakened, the field he reddened
The doomed he slew, and won him lands.

The Song of Rig
The Poetic Edda

"Has the wind left us?" Louis de Roumois asked. He had come aft when the sail stopped its twisting and snapping to hang limp and impotent in the failing breeze.

Thorgrim sat on the edge of the afterdeck, having given the tiller to Hall. He looked out to the west. The setting sun often took the wind down with it, so he was not surprised to see their fine progress come to a halt. "Yes," he said.

"So…oars?" Louis asked.

Thorgrim took his eyes from the horizon and looked at him. Louis had no understanding of ships and the sea, and even less interest. Far from relishing his time on shipboard, he had always seemed to merely tolerate it. He had certainly never asked about matters of seamanship before.

"If the English row, we row," Thorgrim said. "Why does it matter to you?"

Louis shrugged and did not answer, but he didn't have to. Thorgrim knew already. Louis was very eager to get to Frankia. His every effort since he had first stumbled into Thorgrim's company had been directed at getting back to Frankia.

Grifo was sitting on the aftermost sea chest, ten feet away, his long legs spread out before him. He wore a long moustache that melded into the goatee on his chin, and his expression always seemed to suggest a preternatural lack of interest in anything around him. "Better for you, I think, if we just float around here, chevalier," he said.

Louis turned, leaned against the side of the ship, and looked at his fellow Frank.

"Pray tell, why's that?" Louis asked.

"I don't think you're so welcome in Frankia," Grifo said. "I don't know what you did, but I do know that if you weren't with Thorgrim, Felix would have killed you by now. But you won't be with Thorgrim forever."

"I won't, and I thank God for that," Louis said.

"Is that why you're here?" Thorgrim asked Grifo. "To kill Louis when my back is turned?"

Grifo shrugged. "Do you care?"

"Not about Louis," Thorgrim said. "But no one kills anyone aboard my ship, except me. Remember that."

With the wind gone *Sea Hammer* started to roll in the long ocean swell. Thorgrim looked past the bow, past *Fox*, Harald's command, to the English fleet beyond. The closest ship was a mile or so away.

"Starri!" Thorgrim called to Starri Deathless, who was at the top of the mast, and getting quite a ride with the wallowing motion of the vessel.

"Yes, Night Wolf?" Starri called down.

"What are the English doing?"

There was a pause, and then Starri called, "Sitting and rolling, just like us!" Another pause, and then, "Hold! Looks like they're taking in their sails!"

Thorgrim looked over the water. His eyesight was nothing to brag about, not nearly as sharp as it once had been, but he could make out the various squares of striped and colored wool cloth that were the West Saxon's sails, and he could see they were coming down.

"You men," Thorgrim called, "stow the sail." Forward the men, who had been largely idle as *Sea Hammer* was driven by the wind, stood and cast off lines and eased the long yard down, swinging it fore and aft as they did.

"Starri, let me know what the English are about! Let me know if they start rowing!" Thorgrim called.

"So, why does Felix want to kill you?" Grifo asked Louis as if their conversation had not been interrupted.

"I don't know that he does," Louis said. "At least, he didn't until I embarrassed him by escaping. It's my brother who wants to kill me. Felix was just doing his bidding."

"Your brother must be an important man, if Felix will do his bidding."

"He's le duc de Roumois," Louis said. "And he's worried that I want to be le duc de Roumois."

"Do you?" Grifo asked.

"No," Louis said. "I'd rather be boiled alive. But my brother doesn't seem to believe that."

"He hasn't killed you yet, apparently," Grifo said.

"He sent me off to be a monk in Ireland. For me it was nearly the same thing. Felix certainly knew how my brother felt, so when he took me prisoner…when he discovered I had left Ireland…he meant to bring me back to Frankia. To give my brother another chance."

Grifo chuckled. "You mean to say that Felix had you prisoner, with plans to bring you back to Frankia to be killed? But you managed to escape, and now you're going back to Frankia anyway?" He shook his head in amusement.

"I guess my brother is the smart one in the family, and I'm the handsome one," Louis said. "But at least I'll die on Frankish soil."

"That you will," Grifo said. "If your brother has Felix's ear, then he has the king's ear. And he'll make certain the king sees you as an enemy as well." He shook his head. "I don't think you'll fare too well in Frankia."

"How about you?" Thorgrim asked Grifo. "Why do you serve Felix?"

"Felix has gold," Grifo said. "And silver. I'll serve a man with gold and silver."

"And how do you come to speak our tongue so well?" Thorgrim asked. They had been talking in the Northmen's language, and Grifo spoke it nearly as well as a man born to it.

"You Northmen, you have gold and silver, too. Some of you," Grifo said. "So I served with Northmen, long enough to learn the language. Now, I'm hired out to the West Saxons. Just like you, Thorgrim."

In his younger days Thorgrim might have taken grave offense at that suggestion, that he would be servant to an English king. He might have been on his feet with Iron-tooth in hand at that point in the conversation. But he was beyond that sort of thing now.

"I serve no one," he said. "But I do look after my men. If an English king wants to pay us in silver to do what we meant to do anyway, then I'm willing to take it."

"Even if it means turning on your own people?" Grifo asked.

"I don't turn on my own people," Thorgrim said.

"I'm not sure Bergthor would agree," Grifo said. "Bergthor, who's probably carving oars as we speak."

Thorgrim looked at Grifo for a long moment, trying to divine his game. Was he trying to provoke a fight? Testing to see how far Thorgrim might be pushed? Or was he just a contrary son of a whore?

"Bergthor and his people are not my people," Thorgrim said. "Anyway, I gave my word. And I'm more loyal to my word than I am to the likes of Bergthor. He knew that."

Grifo nodded. He made no reply.

"Night Wolf!" Starri called again from the masthead.

"Yes?"

"The English dogs have their oars out! Looks like they're starting to row!"

"There you go, Louis, your wish comes true," Thorgrim said, standing. "We'll row clear to Frankia. Maybe you should take an oar, you're so eager for this."

"I'd take an oar if it would get us there faster," Louis said. "But if I did try rowing, just the opposite would happen."

Forward, a half dozen of *Sea Hammer*'s men were just putting the final lashings on the sail. Now the rest of the crew stood slowly and grudgingly to their feet. They had heard Starri's words as clearly as Thorgrim had, and they understood what they meant. They were not happy about it, not in the least, but they knew better than to say anything, or even grumble audibly in Thorgrim's presence.

A few minutes later, the oars were run out and the men took up an easy stroke. *Sea Hammer* began to gather way and Thorgrim could see the rest of his fleet doing the same, the ships rising and falling on the long swells, rolling and pitching without the force of the wind to hold them steady.

They did not row for long. They had not covered half a mile before Starri called down again. "Night Wolf! The Saxons are all coming together! Like sheep with wolves nearby! What are they about?"

Thorgrim frowned. He climbed up on the sheer strake and held onto the backstay for support and looked out across the water. He could see that Starri was right; the English ships were all clustering together. In a few minutes, they would all bump up against one another in a great seaborne huddle.

"Gathering for the night," Grifo said. "They're going to all gather around the king's ship and lash themselves together. Lie there overnight. That way they won't get separated in the dark."

"You know that for certain?" Thorgrim asked.

"No," Grifo said. "No one said anything of the sort to me. But I've seen English ships do the like before."

Thorgrim nodded. It made sense. Too much danger of losing one another in the dark, too much chance of piling up on the shores of Frankia. Better to lie ahull through the night and continue on in the morning.

"Hold your oars," Thorgrim called forward from where he balanced on the sheer strake, and the rowers stopped their pulling and sat with the blades of their oars dragging in the water. *Sea Hammer* slowed in her headway and began to roll harder as she turned broadside to the seas. Thorgrim took a firmer grip on the backstay.

He looked past the bow. Grifo was right, he could see it. The English ships were all closing with one another, gathering like sheep with wolves nearby, just like Starri said.

Thorgrim smiled. *For once we are the guard dogs, and not the wolves,* he thought.

He looked out to larboard and starboard. His own fleet was stretched out over a couple of miles, which allowed them to see as much ocean as possible, and he wondered how he was supposed to gather them together. But even as he was looking at *Blood Hawk* off his starboard side, the ship turned, her oars rising and falling, her bow slowly pointing toward *Sea Hammer*. He looked to larboard. *Black Wing*, closest on that side, was also making for *Sea Hammer*. The other masters had apparently guessed what the Saxons were about, and they were doing the same.

It was an odd sort of reunion there in the middle of the deep water, the six ships of Thorgrim's fleet gathering together. Heavy rope fenders were draped over their sides to keep the ships from grinding against one another, lines were passed from ship to ship and made fast, insults and jibes flew like arrows from one crew to the other.

The sun was nearly at the horizon when *Dragon*, the last to join them, was made fast to their floating island, bobbing and rolling in the swells. Thorgrim ordered *náttmál*, the evening meal, served out and the men ate and drank and took their ease on their ships. Darkness spread over the water and he ordered each ship to light a lantern and run it up to the top of the mast. To the south he saw a cluster of lights, low down, and he knew that the English had done the same.

The men, he understood, had no great love of this situation. They did not care to be riding atop countless fathoms of water in the dark of night. They were certainly as fearless as men could be; he had seen each of them in the throes of bloody fighting, had seen them all stand up to spear and sword and ax. But this was different. Here were terrors that could not be met with sharp iron or steel. Here, strange creatures—demons, monsters, ghosts of drowned men—all lurked beneath the black water.

None of the men would say as much of course, none would express their fears out loud, but Thorgrim knew full well that they were all eager for dawn to come. Even hours of rowing were preferable to this.

Nor was Thorgrim immune to that feeling. He was beyond the point where any man or earthly circumstance could frighten him, but that did not mean he could not be frightened.

He called his captains together and they climbed from ship to ship until they were all gathered in *Sea Hammer*'s stern. He asked each in turn if there had been any problems during the day's voyage, but none were reported.

"Each of you set a lookout and we'll be able to see what's around us in every direction," Thorgrim said. "Though I don't reckon there'll be much to see. Come morning we do as we did today, that is, do whatever the English do. Follow them to Frankia. Or, if some enemy appears, join them in the fight. Questions?"

There were none, so the men took their leave and returned to their ships. Thorgrim pulled out his furs and laid them out on the deck. He thought of Failend as he did, lovely, tough little Failend. She would have done this for him, had she been there. She would have pressed her small frame against him under the furs and kept him warm, and if they had not been aboard a crowded ship she might have made love to him until they both were spent.

He felt a wave of sadness as he lay down, alone, on the fur bed and pulled a blanket over him. He wondered where she was, if she was safe. He had tried to rescue her, had nearly been burned at the stake in the attempt, him and nine of his men. Godi and Aud had died. Thorgrim knew he did not have to feel shame at having let her down. But he still did.

Sleep, he feared, would elude him, between thoughts of Failend and thoughts of what lurked beneath the keel. But it came at last; deep, disjointed, and restless.

He woke with the sky above just growing light, the ship still moving in its easy, undulating way. He lay still and listened. He heard the slap of water on the hull and the rustling of the rigging as it swayed with the roll and the creak of *Sea Hammer*'s hull and the hulls of the other ships tied up alongside.

And something else. Some sound, coming from far off. A strange, musical sound, in a language he did not think he had ever heard. Singing, but not actually singing. It was an unearthly sound and he wondered if it was the chanting of the ghosts of the deep, the voices of drowned men, or some other terrible thing.

He sat up fast and cocked an ear in the direction of the unsettling noise. It floated across the water from someplace beyond *Sea Hammer*'s side. Thorgrim felt a building sense of dread as he listened.

"Chanting," Louis said from where he sat leaning against the side of the ship, ten feet forward.

"What?" Thorgrim asked.

"Chanting," Louis said. "The English. They must be celebrating mass...worshipping their Christ God. A dawn service."

Thorgrim nodded.

"Did you think it was spirits?" Louis asked.

"Yes," Thorgrim said. "I hoped they had come and take you and all the Christ worshipers down to the bottom of the sea." He pushed the blanket off of him and stood, stretching his stiff joints and muscles and forcing himself to stand upright.

The very top edge of the sun was just starting to break the horizon to the east, throwing a slash of brilliant orange light across the dark blue of the ocean and the lighter gray-blue of the sky. The seas were still calm, with a long, easy swell from the south. There was no wind to speak of. All along *Sea Hammer*'s deck, and on the other ships of the fleet, men began to stir.

Thorgrim gave them a few minutes to shake off the sleep, then called, "Cast off! The lot of you, cast off!" in a voice loud enough to be heard throughout the fleet. "Get underway and take up the positions you had yesterday."

The men aboard *Sea Hammer*, still half awake at best, began to shuffle around the ship, handing down oars from the gallows and passing them along. Others scooped cups of water from a barrel and drank them down or urinated last night's ale over the side.

The sun inched above the horizon and the morning light spread quickly over the water. One by one the ships of the fleet cast off the ropes binding them to one another. The gaps between them widened as they drifted apart. Soon each was running out its oars.

Thorgrim took *Sea Hammer*'s tiller in hand as the ships began to draw farther away from one another, each moving to the station they had held the day before. Like the Northmen, the English were underway, their oars just visible as they rose and fell. Between them and *Sea Hammer*'s bow, Thorgrim saw *Dragon* pulling for the English fleet, Harald eager to get where he was supposed to be.

For an hour the sun climbed higher and Thorgrim's ships drew farther apart and the English continued in their ponderous way, both fleets driven by their oars, the air still as the grave.

"Night Wolf!" Starri called down from aloft.

Of course he's up there, Thorgrim thought. He had forgotten about Starri Deathless. He wondered if Starri had been up at the top of the mast all night.

"Yes?"

"I see ships, Night Wolf! Beyond the English fleet!" he called.

Ships... Thorgrim felt a jolt like a minor bolt of lightning shoot through him. *Enemies to us?*

He did not know, though Starri certainly thought they were. That much was clear. Thorgrim could hear the delight in the berserker's voice.

Chapter Sixteen

The seas shall rise in storms to heaven,
It shall sweep o'er the land, and the skies shall yield
In showers of snow, and biting blasts
At the Doom of the Powers, the gods of war.

The Vala's Shorter Soothsaying
The Poetic Edda

Thorgrim could make them out, but just barely. He was standing on the sheer strake all the way aft, with one hand on the backstay and the other on the sternpost for balance. He was looking out over the deep blue water in the direction that Starri indicated, northeast of *Sea Hammer* and the rest.

He squinted against the light of the rising sun and saw them then. To his eyes they seemed little more than dark slashes on the dark water, with tiny vertical marks that were their masts. Like his fleet, like the Saxon ships, they were being driven by oar. There seemed to be half a dozen or so, moving toward the English fleet.

Frisian pirates? Thorgrim wondered. They were close enough to Frisia to encounter the raiders who swarmed out of that low country and into the narrow seas. Not that it mattered all that much who they were. They were foes to be driven off, that was all but certain. The only other possibility—that they were a welcoming fleet sent by the King of Frankia to greet his West Saxon visitors—Thorgrim thought highly unlikely.

"Starri!" Thorgrim called aloft. "What do you make of them?"

"Five ships!" Starri called down. "Frisians, maybe! They have an evil look about them, and they're making for our Saxon friends! You best strap Iron-tooth on, Night Wolf, I think there'll be fighting to be done!"

Thorgrim pressed his lips together. Time and distance. These things were all about time and distance, and those were not in his favor now. The Saxon fleet lay between the strangers and Thorgrim's ships. As hard as the Sea Hammers and the other Northmen might row, the pirates would reach the Saxons before Thorgrim's fleet could reach the pirates. The Saxons would have to fight alone for some time before their hired guards could join them.

And if the Northmen did pull for all they were worth, they would be worn out by the time they got into the fight. That was not so grave a concern—once the fighting madness was on them it would little matter how tired the men were—but it was another thing to consider.

"Ho! Those brave Saxon dogs!" Starri called down from the masthead.

Thorgrim shifted his gaze. The English fleet had turned, not toward the attackers, but away, directly away, running in front of them, sheep before the wolves. That at least would help Thorgrim and the others get into the fight in time, but it did not bode well for their getting any help in the melee.

"Pull, double time!" Thorgrim called and the men at the oars leaned forward and dipped the blades and pulled back, then lifted and leaned forward again, their rhythm twice what it had been a moment before. *Sea Hammer* surged forward, and Thorgrim knew that in a moment or two the other ships of his fleet would note the increased pace and match it. But still they would not reach the attackers in time, not before they were in among the English ships.

Thorgrim nudged the tiller over a bit, swinging the ship's bow to point at the spot where he imagined *Sea Hammer* and the Frisians, if such they were, would meet. He looked back over his shoulder. He squinted and ran his eyes along the horizon, and felt the first bit of hope starting to bubble up.

The sky overhead was blue now, with the sun full up and the darkness swept clean away. On the western horizon he saw piles of white clouds, one on top of the other as if they had been stacked there. Thorgrim had spent enough time in those waters, and was a keen enough observer of such things, that he knew what that meant: wind. Not much at first, but enough, and soon.

He looked forward. The men were already growing red-faced as they pulled at the oars, but soon the breeze would fill in and drive the ship faster than even the most vigorous rowing could do. And that meant the sail had to be ready to set the moment the wind was on them.

"You men who are doubled up at the oars, get the sail cast off and the yard swung round! There's wind coming!"

A half dozen men moved amidships, standing on the sea chests to reach the yard. The night before, as the wind had failed them, the long spar had been turned fore and aft along the ship's centerline and rested on the gallows, the sail lashed tight along its length. Now they would have to unlash it, raise the yard, and turn it nearly vertical so it could be dipped under the shrouds that supported the mast before they could set the sail again.

Thorgrim looked to starboard, and then to larboard. His men would have the sail ready to set by the time the first puffs of wind hit them, but the masters of the other ships had not seen the signs on the horizon, did not know that a breeze was in the offing. The closest of them were half a mile away on either side, too far to see what *Sea Hammer* was doing and too far for Thorgrim to communicate with them.

So be it, Thorgrim thought. If the gods willed it, they would bring him the wind that would drive him into the fight, and that was about all he dared ask for.

He looked up at *Sea Hammer*'s yard still resting on the gallows. The gaskets had been cast off, the sail draping down in great folds, and hands were casting off the halyard and taking a strain. There was no need for Thorgrim to issue orders or say anything at all. These men had sailed many miles in each other's company; they knew what to do.

"Heave away!" Hall called and the men at the halyard pulled and slowly the massive yard rose off the gallows. Once it was high enough a few others grabbed onto the end of the yard and dipped it under the shrouds so it could ride athwartships.

"Lower it down!" Thorgrim called. "No wind yet."

The halyard was slacked away and the yard came down to a point just above the rowers' heads, and the men at the oars continued to bend their backs and pull hard. Thorgrim scanned the horizon ahead. The English fleet was still moving directly away from the Frisians, the Frisians coming up hard astern of them, and Harald aboard *Dragon* had altered course to make for the attackers, just as *Sea Hammer* had.

Then Thorgrim noticed something else. He squinted and strained to pick out the details aboard his son's ship, until at last he was certain. Harald, too, had swung his yard athwartships, ready to set sail. He had not done it because he saw *Sea Hammer* doing it. He had not had enough time. No, Harald must have seen the clouds to the southwest and, like his father, guessed that it meant wind in the offing.

Thorgrim smiled to himself. *Good boy*, he thought. *Now, I hope we're right.*

They pulled on, *Sea Hammer* driving up the long, smooth swells and racing down the far sides, the Frisian ships drawing noticeably closer. Thorgrim could see details now: the curved black prows, the water curling around their bows, the rows of shields on the sides, the banks of oars sweeping forward and aft. Five ships, as far as he could make out.

He grabbed the backstay with both hands and swung himself down to the afterdeck just as Starri came sliding down from aloft, hitting the sheer strake with both feet, bounding to the deck and hurrying aft.

"Night Wolf!" he called and he stepped up onto the afterdeck. His arms were starting to make those strange, jerky movements they made when a fight was in the offing, as if the madness, like a fast-moving infection, was creeping up his limbs. The split arrowhead he wore as a talisman around his deck was dancing against his chest. "Night Wolf, can't these whore's sons row faster than this?"

"No," Thorgrim said, and he was about to point out that the yard had been swung around, something Starri had apparently not noticed, but Starri was not listening. He was already beyond listening. He was starting to make little growling sounds deep in his throat and his arms were jerking even more rapidly. Then, in one quick motion, he pulled his tunic up over his head and tossed it aside.

Thorgrim turned and looked aft and hoped the breeze would come, and come soon. In the past Starri had always managed to hold himself together until battle was joined, but that did not mean he would always manage to do so.

Then Thorgrim felt it on his face: a cool breath, a waft of a breeze coming up from astern. He turned and looked forward. The sail, hanging in big folds from the yard, began to stir, not just slatting with the roll of the ship, but an actual wind-induced rustle.

Thorgrim fought the urge to send men to the halyard. There was still not enough wind to drive the ship faster than the oars could do, and setting the sail would only slow them down. But he felt the breeze on the back of his neck, felt it moving his hair, and he felt more and more confident that his prediction had been correct.

The men at the oars continued to pull and Thorgrim felt the wind building, and just as a few of the rowers looked up in realization that a breeze had come, he knew it was time to set sail.

"Oars in!" he shouted. "Hands to the halyard, sheets and braces!"

They had been waiting for this moment, this moment of blessed relief, since Thorgrim had ordered the yard squared. The oars came running in with an alacrity that Thorgrim wished accompanied his every order, and the men stacked them on the gallows and lashed them in place. More willing hands clapped onto the halyard and hauled away and the big yard rose horizontally up the mast. The sail flogged and twisted and folded as the yard went up; with a snap it filled, holding its rounded shape as the sheets were hauled aft.

Thorgrim felt the motion of the ship changing under him. She was no longer a ponderous thing driven by brute force through the water, but rather a living creature, lively and responsive, a wild and powerful beast. He smiled as he took the tiller from Vali and said, "Go and arm yourself."

Vali did not hesitate. And indeed, the others were already on their feet, pulling mail shirts over their heads, settling helmets in place, strapping sword belts around their waists and lifting shields from the racks on the sides of the ship. They had done well for themselves, these men, raiding in the past year or so, and thanks to their plundering they were all much better equipped than they had been when they first set sail from their homes. Thorgrim doubted one in five owned mail shirts or swords when they left the North country, but now nearly all did.

He looked out beyond the confines of the ship. Harald's sail was set and he, too, was driving for the Frisian ships, which were still pulling, unwaveringly, for the Saxon fleet. The Saxons in turn were still rowing directly away from the newcomers, and if they meant to turn and fight, they were showing no sign of it.

Cowardly dogs...Thorgrim thought, but that was all the thought he would spare for them. Either they would fight or they would not, but either way it would not change his own intentions in the least.

He looked off toward the other ships of his fleet, which were starting to fall behind as *Sea Hammer* was driven faster and faster by the growing breeze. He thought he could see them preparing to set sail, swinging their yards around athwartships, but he could not be sure. The Frisians seemed to be making no effort in that regard, but then there was no reason why they would. They would prefer to go into a fight under oar. What's more, they had no wind. *Sea Hammer* and *Dragon* were bringing the breeze up with them.

Thorgrim's left hand moved of its own volition to rest on Iron-tooth's hilt and he realized that his sword was not there. In the past, in circumstances such as this, Failend would have come to him with his sword and seax and mail shirt and helmet. He had come to expect it, he realized, and now he felt a flush of loss as he realized that he would never again enjoy that small, but welcome, gesture.

"Hall! Come take the tiller," he called forward and Hall hurried aft and up onto the afterdeck. Thorgrim hopped down and pulled his gear, wrapped in a wool blanket, out from under the deck. He unfolded the blanket and pulled the mail shirt free. He held it in his hands and frowned.

This was always a question. On shore, given a choice, he would always wear mail into a fight. He was no berserker, no Starri Deathless. He had little concern for his own life, but he did not court his death, out of habit if nothing else. But wearing mail in a sea fight was something else. He had seen plenty of men dragged under by the weight of their mail, had actually won a fight once when he and his opponent had gone overboard, his opponent clad in mail and Thorgrim not.

Being cut down by a sword or an ax was one thing; being dragged down to the black depths of the sea was something else entirely.

On the other hand…

He looked up. Five Frisian ships, and his crew and Harald's would grapple with them alone long before any of the others could get into the fight. How long they would be fighting five against two he did not know, but he guessed it would be some time. He nodded to himself and slipped the heavy iron-linked shirt over his head, strapped his sword belt around his waist and hung his shield over his back.

The wind was building, *Sea Hammer* was driving through the seas in a more determined way, as if eager to get into the fight. Thorgrim saw the other ships of his fleet hauling up their sails, but they were well astern now. The Frisians were still pushing for the Saxons ships as if they had not even seen the Northmen driving down on them.

Louis de Roumois, leaning against the starboard side, just forward of the afterdeck, was wearing mail and his sword strapped around his waist and looking out at the Frisian ships in the distance. He did not look eager or impatient or afraid, but rather contemplative. It was how he always looked before a fight. Thorgrim had been in battle with the man often enough to recognize it.

Grifo stood opposite Louis, on the larboard side. He, too, was wearing mail and a sword, along with a conical iron helmet, and he, too, seemed in a thoughtful mood. And Thorgrim could well imagine what he was thinking about.

"Grifo," he said and Grifo looked up at him. "Remember, no one kills Louis except the enemy or me."

"I'll try to remember," Grifo said. Louis looked at him, looked at Thorgrim, then turned his attention back to the Frisian ships a quarter mile past the bow.

Thorgrim looked at the ships as well. The largest of them was leading the pack, its oars pulling hard and with an admirable rhythm. The leader's ship, no doubt, the vessel driven by the captain of the fleet. That was the logical choice for the attack, the only choice.

He pushed the tiller over a bit so that *Sea Hammer*'s bow was aimed at the Frisian ship's beam. With the wind astern and building in strength, it gave *Sea Hammer* a great deal of maneuverability, and Thorgrim meant to use that to his advantage. He looked over at *Dragon*. She was off *Sea Hammer*'s starboard side and charging into the fight, but the smaller ship could not match *Sea Hammer*'s speed. Thorgrim and his men would have to go in alone, but there was nothing for it.

Only a couple hundred yards separated *Sea Hammer* from the big Frisian, close enough that Thorgrim could see movement on the Frisian's deck, men racing fore and aft, men looking at the Norseman's ship charging down on them. The Frisian's oars took a long stroke and lifted, dripping from the water, and hung there for a second, then disappeared into the ship. They could see that the time for rowing was past, the time for fighting had come.

Sea Hammer's bow was still pointed at the center of the Frisian ship, and Thorgrim adjusted his course as the Frisian slowed. The other ships in the Frisian fleet were still driving with their oars, but their speed had dropped off, their masters no doubt not wanting to leave their leader astern, and they were starting to bunch up behind the lead ship.

Thorgrim pressed his lips together. One hundred yards. *Sea Hammer* was moving fast now, and he called for hands to be ready to haul up the sail once the two ships made contact, and for others to stand ready with grappling hooks to bind the ships together.

Fifty yards and the Frisians were gathered in the center of their ship and Thorgrim saw shields on arms and swords and spears in hands. Arrows streaked across the gap of water and thumped into *Sea Hammer*'s sides and one passed clean through the sail. Thorgrim heard someone scream up towards the bow, the familiar sound of a battle wound, as an arrow found the target it wanted, but he could not see who it was.

Thirty yards and Thorgrim pulled the tiller toward him and *Sea Hammer* swung hard to starboard, away from the Frisian's midsection and toward her bow, the place where he had intended to hit all along.

"Stand ready!" he shouted. He saw the confusion on the Frisian's deck as they realized this enemy would not be boarding them where they thought they would. He saw men pointing and others running forward, stumbling as they did.

He gave the tiller one last tug, turning *Sea Hammer* so that her stem would deliver a glancing blow to the Frisian's bow. He gripped the wood hard as the two ships struck, a powerful impact that made the ship shudder under foot. The two vessels ground together as *Sea Hammer* stopped dead in the water and slewed the Frisian around, driving her into the ships astern. He heard the groaning and creaking of wood on wood and wondered if his bow or the Frisian's would cave in under the impact, if one ship or both would flood and sink in the next moment or two.

Hands hauled away at the clewlines and *Sea Hammer*'s sail was drawn up to the yard as the two ships rolled against one another. Then the sound of crushing strakes was rent by a scream, not of agony but of fighting madness as Starri Deathless vaulted off the sheer strake near the bow and flung himself into the press of Frisians who were just then making their way to the bow, or picking themselves up off the deck where the impact had flung them.

In an instant Starri was among them, his two axes whirling, the Frisian defenders falling around him, but he did not fight alone for long. In a breaking wave the Sea Hammers followed him over the side, leaping down onto the Frisian's deck wherever the two ships ground up against each other. The air was filled with the sound of iron on iron, swords and axes beating on wooden shields, the battle cries, curses, shouts, and screams of fighting men.

Thorgrim left the tiller and raced forward, Louis and Grifo just ahead of him. He saw one of the grappling hooks lying on the deck, forgotten, apparently, in the excitement. He picked it up in his right hand, the coil of walrus hide rope in his left, twirled it a few times, and then sent it flying over the water between the ships. He watched with satisfaction as it dropped over the Frisian's sheer strake and he pulled hard on the rope and felt the hook dig into some unseen part of the enemy's ship. He wrapped the end of the rope around one of *Sea Hammer*'s cleats and hurried forward again.

A few dozen of his men had already made the leap onto the Frisian ship, the rest were crowded against *Sea Hammer*'s side, looking for the chance to get across. In any other instance they would have stepped aside for Thorgrim, but now their blood was up and they had no thought for anything but joining the fight, no eyes for anything but the battle on the other ship.

Thorgrim leapt up on one of the sea chests, which gave him a view over the men's heads. Starri was among the Frisians, doling out bloody, frenzied death with two axes sweeping left and right, and his other men were pushing the Frisians back. He looked to his left, and to his surprise he saw another of the Frisians' ships driving hard for the point where *Sea Hammer* and the first Frisian were lashed to one another, another of the pirates charging into the fight.

"Sea Hammers!" Thorgrim called, his powerful voice cutting through the cacophony of battle. "Sea Hammers! With me!" Iron-tooth was in his hand, though he had no memory of drawing the weapon, and he pointed toward the ship coming up behind them and not fifty feet away. He jumped down from the sea chest and headed aft again, aft to where this second ship would foul in the line binding *Sea Hammer* to the first ship and stop dead.

He reached *Sea Hammer*'s afterdeck, climbed up and paused. The second Frisian ship had taken the last pull of their oars and the rowers were drawing them in as the momentum carried the ship over the last dozen yards that separated them. He looked behind him. Grifo and Louis were there, and the other men who had been waiting for their chance to board the first ship, now ready to pour over the side of this newcomer.

He looked back at the ship just as she hit. Her bow came driving into the space between *Sea Hammer* and the first Frisian ship. It struck the rope on the grapple that Thorgrim had thrown and made *Sea Hammer*'s stern swing into it, nearly knocking Thorgrim off his feet. But the timing, he could see, was perfect: the Frisians were just tossing their oars aside, just getting to their feet, not ready to meet the onslaught that was coming their way.

"Away! Away!" Thorgrim stepped up onto *Sea Hammer*'s sheer strake, thinking as he did of how Starri, or even Harald, would have simply jumped from there onto the Frisian's deck. How he himself would have done so once, but no more.

Instead, he stepped across to the Frisian's sheer strake and jumped from there, a shorter leap to the deck below, jumped right in the path of some bearded monster charging up at him with more rage than smarts or skill, mouth open, screaming, ax held over his head.

The ax came down in a powerful blow and Thorgrim took half a step to one side. The blade passed him by inches and sank itself deep into the deck. Powerful as the Frisian was—and he looked powerful indeed— he had driven the ax so far into the wood that he could not easily pull it free. He was still roaring and tugging on the handle when Thorgrim drove Iron-tooth right through the man's neck, the wicked, sharp blade passing easily through flesh and muscle and nearly severing the man's head.

The Frisian, blood erupting from his neck and his mouth and running down his beard, his eyes wide, remained standing for a brief moment, as if too surprised to fall dead. Thorgrim used that moment, with the Frisian like a wall between him and the rest, to swing his shield over his shoulder and onto his left arm. The ax-warrior wavered, blood pulsing and gushing from the severed artery. And then he was down and the rest were coming up and Thorgrim's own men were swarming over the side and pushing up beside him.

Thorgrim raised Iron-tooth and shouted, an involuntary sound, more of a howl, as the Frisians came on. He turned a spear point aside with his shield, lunging at the spearman as he ran. He felt the blade hit something, pulled it back, slashed out backhand in front of him. He saw a quick movement to his right and Louis de Roumois was there, his sword darting in, circling around an awkward parry, lunging and striking like a viper, moving in the well-trained and practiced way of a man who had learned the art from a sword master and not in the hack and slash of battle.

The Frisians were getting in each other's way, which was good, but they were doing so because there were a great many of them, which was not so good. An ax slashed down in front of Thorgrim and he stepped back and felt the blade strike his shield and, he was pretty certain, tear a section of its face away. He lunged, but the axman stepped back as well, clear of Iron-tooth's point.

Grifo was to his left now, sword in one hand, a seax in the other, shouting and slashing with his weapons, a less disciplined attack than Louis's but just as lethal. A spearman lunged through the pack, the point of his weapon driving for Grifo's gut, but Grifo knocked the shaft aside with the seax and lunged with the sword, finding the spearman's bowels instead.

The Frisian grunted, doubled over, staggered back, and Grifo took a step toward him, pushing the sword deeper. As he did, his foot came down in the great wash of blood that had come from the neck and mouth of Thorgrim's first victim. Grifo's eyes went wide with surprise as his feet came up from under him. He went down hard, like he had been hit with a battering ram, and Thorgrim felt the impact of the fall in his feet and legs.

Looming over Grifo, grinning and screaming in triumph, stood a massive Frisian who had pushed his way to the front. He drew a long, two-handed battle ax back over his head, and with a look of frenzied delight, swung it down like Grifo was cordwood to be split.

He moved too fast for Thorgrim to use his blade, so Thorgrim instead dropped to one knee and held his shield up over Grifo's supine body as if keeping the rain off of him. The ax blade bounced off the iron boss and struck a glancing blow to the shield, shattering the thin wood and catching on the shattered fragments, stopping an inch from Grifo's chest. Thorgrim twisted the wrecked shield and slashed sideways at the axman, cutting him across his shins, making him shriek and stagger back.

Then Thorgrim was on his feet again, the remains of the shield left on top of Grifo's chest, as he drove the sword home deep into the axman and sent him sprawling back into his shipmates. He slashed left and knocked a sword aside and reached down with his left hand. He felt Grifo take a hard grip and he jerked up, pulling the Frank to his feet as he parried the sword again.

"You Frankish bastard, you better be worth that trouble," Thorgrim said as he let go of Grifo's hand and pulled his seax from the scabbard across his belly. Grifo, in turn, let out a cry of rage and flung himself at the Frisians coming at them, slashing with sword and seax as if his very honor was at stake. There were dead men on the deck at their feet, Frisians and Thorgrim's men, and men who were gravely wounded, thrashing and clawing and shrieking.

Louis was still on his feet, surrounded, fighting defensively now, keeping the blades off of him rather than doling out much punishment to his attackers. Hall was in the thick of it as well, his face and beard covered in blood, his mail shirt hanging open with a great rent down the front. They were being pressed on all sides, and more Frisians were working their way around behind. A moment or two more and they would be surrounded.

Thorgrim could not see much through the press of fighting men, but he could see the masts of the other Frisian ships, coming up behind them, and he could picture the oarsmen pulling hard to get into the fight, the dozens and dozens of warriors who would soon be swarming aboard. He looked to his right, and he was surprised to see a sail, bellied out and full of wind, not thirty feet away. It had to be on the far side of the first Frisian ship they had struck, the one Starri and the others were aboard.

And then Thorgrim remembered.

Harald... Harald had seen the signs of wind, had set sail early. And with that thought, *Dragon* struck the Frisian ship with a force that sent them all, Frisians and Northmen, staggering from the impact.

Chapter Seventeen

Needs must I help the youthful hero
To hold the heritage after his fathers.

The Lay of Hyndla
The Poetic Edda

The crushing sound of ship on ship, *Dragon*'s bow against the side of the Frisian vessel, was loud even over the din of the fighting. *Dragon* was moving fast under her full sail, and she hit harder than Harald had quite expected. He staggered and nearly fell, despite gripping *Dragon*'s tiller and bracing for the collision. He was still recovering his stance when it occurred to him that he might have stove in the bow of his ship, or shattered the Frisian's side, in which case one or both ships would soon be heading for the bottom of the sea.

No matter. He had already thought this through, all of it. Let one or both ships sink: their preservation was not his goal.

He had worked by instinct at first, as they headed into the fight, the wolf's instinct, the bear's instinct. The ships of his father's fleet, spread out in a wide arc. The Frisian ships closing with the Saxons. Harald's eyes moved from one to the other, his mind assessing the situation somewhere below conscious thought. A look astern, the sight of the clouds piling up on the horizon, and he knew; wind was coming.

"You men, doubled up at the oars!" he shouted. "Get the sail cast off and the yard swung round!"

The men were surprised—they had not anticipated that order—but they hopped up to obey. As they did, Harald realized that he had given no consideration to that decision. He had not agonized over the rightness or wrongness of it, had not battered himself bloody with self-doubt. He had not wondered what his father would do, what he would think. He had just seen what needed doing and had ordered it done.

It was only then that the worry came rushing in like the tide. He turned slowly and looked off the larboard quarter, back to where *Sea Hammer* was leading the rest of the fleet. And he saw, to his profound relief, that his father had also ordered his ship's yard swung around, the sail loosened off.

The sight brought with it a new swirl of feelings. Relief, for one. He, Harald, might be wrong, but he would not be alone. And something else. Confidence. Confidence in the understanding that he had acted the way a leader should act. He had acted the way Thorgrim Night Wolf would act.

The first puffs of wind came soon after, but Harald knew they would not be enough to drive the ship, so he kept the men at the oars, and for once he felt no compulsion to join them at the task. Not because the work was onerous—he could pull an oar as easily as any man aboard, easier than most—but because he understood, in a way he had not understood before, that pulling an oar was not what he should be doing. He was master of the vessel. He was making the decisions for all of them. And that was a more important and more difficult task.

He could feel the breeze stirring his long, blond hair, lifting his braid a bit then setting it down, but still he kept the men at the oars because his gut told him that the wind had not filled in steadily enough. He started to look over his shoulder, back toward *Sea Hammer*, to see if his father had set sail yet, but he stopped himself. It did not matter. Thorgrim would set sail when it was time for *Sea Hammer* to do so. Harald would decide when it was time for *Dragon*.

The men were red-faced from rowing and sweat was starting to run down their brows and Harald could all but hear their thoughts: *Why are we still at the oars? Why doesn't he set the sail?* Harald wondered if any man would dare to voice the question, but none did.

The breeze continued to build, and soon it was rustling his hair, and he knew it had enough force to drive the ship. "Oars in!" he shouted. "Hands to the halyard, sheets and braces!"

There were grunts of effort, grunts of agreement, grunts of relief as the men slid the long oars in and handed them up to the gallows, then tailed onto the halyard, the sheets, and braces.

"Haul away!" Harald called and the yard rose up the mast as the men pulled with a will. The sail snapped and rippled and filled and *Dragon* heeled to the pressure. Harald pulled the tiller a bit toward him as the wind tried to drive the bow off, and *Dragon* came to life in the thrilling way of a wind-ship as it first starts to run before the breeze.

"Get your weapons ready! Let us go and slaughter these dogs!" Harald called, and try as he might to remain stoic, he could not keep the edge of anticipation from his voice.

The men pulled weapons from their sea chests; they pulled out helmets and mail; they took their shields down from the shield rack on the ship's side; and Harald finally allowed himself a glance astern. *Sea Hammer*'s sail was set and drawing as well, the ship heeling and pitching as she surged forward over the long rollers. Harald's eyes, young and sharp, even picked out the figure of Starri Deathless at the top of the mast

There is the happiest man on this ocean, Harald thought, and he suspected that he himself was likely a close second.

Brand, his mail shirt on, sword belt strapped around his waist, iron helmet on his head, came aft and took the tiller and Harald dug his own gear out from under the afterdeck. He considered whether to don his mail—not always the best choice in a sea fight—but decided it was worth the risk and so pulled it over his head.

He took his sword, Oak Cleaver, from the oilcloth and fur bundle in which it was wrapped and pulled the blade half-way out of the scabbard. In the morning sun it glinted and shone, with not a touch of rust or discoloration. It had been his grandfather's blade, the sword of Ornolf the Restless, a magnificent Frankish-made Ulfberht, and Harald treated it with the respect that such a weapon deserved.

He slid the blade back and buckled the belt around his waist. He adjusted the sword so it hung just right and repositioned the seax that was strapped horizontally across his front. With a nod to Brand, he stepped onto the afterdeck and took back the tiller.

Dragon was moving well now, the breeze growing stronger with the rising sun. Harald ran his eyes along the horizon, taking in what ships he could see. The English were still rowing as fast as they were able, directly away from the Frisians, and Harald frowned at the sight.

Dogs, he thought. *Cowards.* It seemed the English meant to allow the Northmen to lead the attack, and only turn and fight once the battle was well underway. Maybe wait until Thorgrim's men had things well in hand.

Dogs... Harald looked out toward the other ships in his father's fleet. They were finally swinging their yards around, casting off their sails. Only he and his father had seen the wind coming before it arrived. Only *Dragon* and *Sea Hammer* were already underway, and that meant that they would be the first into the fight, and would fight alone for as long as it took for the others to reach them. That thought gave Harald a profound sense of satisfaction and a deep thrill.

He looked at *Sea Hammer*, now off *Dragon*'s larboard beam and charging at the Frisians. The ship was half as long again as *Dragon* and commensurately faster and there was nothing Harald could do to change that. There was a time when Harald would have found that unbearably bothersome, would have called for minute and continuous adjustments of the sails, would have made the men shift positions in order to get the tiniest increase in speed. But he was over that now. Mostly.

"Take a pull in the starboard sheet!" he called. The men grabbed onto the thick rope, leaned into it, and once they had pulled it in a fathom or so, Harald called, "That's well! Make it fast!"

He looked past the bow toward the Frisian fleet. They were still rowing and Harald doubted they would bother to set sail. They were gaining on the English, which was their objective, and they would want to come into a fight under the power of their oars. It was the proper way to go into a fight. Unless you were desperately eager to get into it, as he was.

"Larboard sheet, sheet in a fathom more!" he called, unable to stop himself.

Most of the Frisian fleet was blocked by the sail so Harald crouched to see under the foot. The largest ship, no doubt the chieftain's command, was leading the rest into the fight, and Harald was certain that his father was setting a course to intercept it. *Dragon* would reach the battle moments behind *Sea Hammer*. But who should they attack?

Harald looked at the ship just astern of the Frisian leader. A big ship, bigger than *Dragon*, but not so big that Harald was hesitant to lay into it. The thirty men aboard *Dragon* should be equal to sixty Frisian pirates.

But perhaps it made more sense to join *Sea Hammer* in attacking the lead ship. Or perhaps he should drive *Dragon* between the second and third in the Frisian fleet, attack both at once. The Dragons didn't have to beat them all, just had to hold their own until the rest of Thorgrim's fleet came up.

Harald frowned and wanted to curse out loud. There was nothing he hated more than this, this inability to decide, this questioning every decision, this wavering. It drove him to madness, and it made him wonder if he could ever truly be a leader of men. His father did not suffer from such doubts. Thorgrim made a decision; he made it fast; and he did not question it.

And then Harald had a thought that struck him like a slap to the face, a thought that made him stand bolt upright again. Something that had never occurred to him until that moment.

Perhaps his father did, in fact, suffer the same self-doubts that he did.

He had seen his father dozens of times heading into battle like an image of Thor carved out of oak, looking as if he had not one doubt in the world. But who knew what was going on in his head? Harald realized that to anyone watching him at that moment, he, to, would appear expressionless and confident, despite his roiling uncertainty. Was it possible that his father felt the same?

I will ask him, Harald resolved. It was not the sort of thing he would usually ask his father, not the sort of thing he could generally find the courage to ask. It might seem as if he was questioning his father's leadership, or suggesting that he, Harald, was too lacking in confidence to be a captain.

I'll do it, by all the gods, I will. He would summon the courage to ask, because Harald Thorgrimson feared nothing, save for appearing to lack courage. That was what he had told himself many times.

With that insight and with that resolve, the choice of how to attack the Frisian ships seemed to appear before him as if a fog had lifted off the ocean.

"We're going for the big bastard, the one in the lead!" Harald called to the men who were gathered at the windward side. They were armed now, helmets and mail in place, and waiting only to get into the fight. "*Sea Hammer* will get to them first. We'll board on whatever side is left free."

He saw heads nodding and wondered if anyone would make objection, or offer their own opinion as to what they should do. But fore and aft, mouths remained shut, and Harald took considerable satisfaction in that. A few months earlier, these men might have felt free to offer their suggestions, but no more. And that was just as well. Harald, having spoken, was not going to change his mind now.

He crouched again and looked under the sail. *Sea Hammer* had drawn ahead of *Dragon* now, racing for the lead Frisian ship. The Frisian was still pulling for the English fleet as if they had not even seen the Northmen coming. Harald pulled the tiller toward him and eased *Dragon*'s bow off to starboard. It was a tricky business, judging where two moving ships would meet on the ocean, but Harald did not doubt his ability to bring *Dragon* to exactly the right spot.

He stood again, ran his eyes over the sail and then outboard at the other ships. The tiller vibrated in his hands as the water rushed past the rudder. He crouched and looked under the sail again, just as *Sea Hammer* ran right up along the Frisian's bow. Even over the sounds of the wind and the seas rushing down the side, he heard the crunch of hull on hull, the unmistakable wail of Starri Deathless's war cry, and a moment later, the clash of weapons and the shouts of fighting men.

Grappling hooks! Harald thought, with a sudden flash of panic, and cursed himself for an idiot. He needed to have grappling hooks ready. It would be a foolish thing to let *Dragon* drift clear of the enemy with half her men still on board.

"Get out those grappling hooks, stand ready to get 'em into the Frisian wherever you can!" Harald called forward, trying to sound as if he had meant to give that order at that moment all along. Men lifted up the deck boards and fished the hooks and their coils of rope out from the space underneath.

Harald looked under the sail. A hundred yards at most. *Sea Hammer* was lying against the Frisian's bow, grappled, no doubt, and Harald saw a surge of activity on board the two ships, but what exactly was happening he could not tell. A second Frisian ship was charging up now, driving to get between *Sea Hammer* and the lead, and Harald wondered if he should change his plans, go after the second ship instead.

No, no, no, he thought, forcing aside the question. *You made a decision, and that's it.*

The sound of fighting was louder now, and an image appeared in his mind of an ax coming down on him, slicing him through the neck from above, a disturbing and unbidden image that seemed to always appear just before combat. Of the countless brutal ways a man could die in battle, that one always seemed the most horrific to Harald, though he was not sure why, and try as he might, he could never stop it from appearing at such a moment.

He wondered if the gods were giving him a vision of his eventual death.

"Get ready!" he roared, hoping his voice would drive the image away, and it did, to a degree. They were close enough now that he could see the other ships around the edge of the sail. *Sea Hammer* was lying against the Frisian's starboard side. For Harald to bring *Dragon* around to her larboard side, he would have to cross her bows and then spin the ship around. Tricky, but he was sure they had momentum enough now to do it.

Dragon came charging down on the others, and Harald felt the excitement crackling through him. He wondered, as he sometimes did, if maybe he was half berserker himself. Any thought of axes and wounds were gone; now his mind was entirely on the fight ahead.

"Get ready to brace the yard, larboard tack, and do it fast, on my command!" he shouted. "Stand ready with those grappling hooks!"

Sea Hammer's bow and the Frisian's bow passed down *Dragon*'s larboard side, not forty feet off. Harald had a fleeting image of a mass of struggling men on the decks, weapons and shields flailing, but he was too consumed with judging speed and distance to see more than that. He gripped the tiller hard as the bows of the other ships passed beyond *Dragon*'s stern.

"Brace the yard! Brace the yard!" he shouted and hands hauled away on the starboard brace and let go the larboard. Overhead the big yard swung around and Harald pushed the tiller forward, using all the power of his arms and shoulders and legs. *Dragon* heeled hard to starboard as she turned, swinging around through one hundred and eighty degrees, going back the way she had come, except now the Frisian ship was directly in her path.

They hit with a crushing impact that sent Harald staggering. He felt himself tossed forward and the tiller slammed into his gut, but he was wearing his mail shirt and barely felt it. He pushed himself off and straightened. *Dragon* was pivoting on her bow, swinging into the

Frisian ship and his men already had their grappling hooks in her and were hauling them together.

Harald abandoned the tiller, grabbed up his shield and raced forward. He jumped onto the aftermost sea chest lashed to the deck and made his way forward, jumping from chest to chest, his eyes on the deck of the Frisian ship. He saw a knot of fighting men, and in the middle of it, Starri Deathless, flailing his axes, screaming, his bare chest and back and his scraggly beard coated in blood. He could make out other men of his father's crew in the press. He could not see his father among them.

His own men, the crew of *Dragon*, were already leaping over the sheer strake and onto the Frisian's deck. As much as Harald wanted to be the first of them into the fight, he knew that was not possible, not when he had been aft steering when they hit. So he paused and looked down the length of the Frisian ship, looking for the best place to go aboard.

Dragon's bow was grinding into the Frisian's side and most of his men were leaping over at that spot, into a crowded and chaotic fight. But the ship was still turning, her aft end swinging toward the Frisian, the gap between them closing. Toward the stern of the Frisian ship, Harald saw a great giant of a man, a long battle ax in one hand, a shield in the other, a thick fur draped over his mail shirt, his face half-hidden by his beard. The chieftain, Harald had no doubt, leader of these raiders. He was bellowing orders, urging the others forward, flailing his ax and shield at those few of Thorgrim's men who managed to break free from the fighting and come at him.

Harald turned and jumped back over the sea chests, one, two, three. There was still a wide gap between the ships, but he had a good sense for his own capacity for jumping and he reckoned they were close enough. He pulled Oak Cleaver and stepped up onto the shear strake. He cocked his leg and drove himself into the air, over the strip of water that separated the two ships.

It was only as his foot was leaving *Dragon*'s side that he recalled that he was wearing a mail shirt and helmet, carrying a shield and sword and seax, and so weighed considerably more at that moment that he normally did.

Oh, shit! he thought as he saw himself dropping, dropping, several feet short of the Frisian ship. He threw Oak Cleaver as he fell, saw it fall onto the Frisian's deck, then flailed out with his now empty hand.

His fingers caught the edge of the ship and clamped down, and he reached up with his shield arm and grabbed the sheer strake with that hand as well.

He hung there at arm's length against the side of the ship, his chest thumping against the planks as the vessel rolled. Then he sucked in his breath and hoisted himself up. The weight of his mail, his helmet, his now-wet shoes and leggings, made the task more difficult, but Harald was called Broadarm for a reason, and with a flex of his arms, his head came up over the edge of the Frisian's ship. He paused, looked up, and found himself staring into the eyes of the giant chieftain, who grinned at Harald as he brought his ax back over his head.

Here it is, Harald thought, the ax coming down on his neck, splitting him in two. The chieftain opened his mouth and bellowed and swung the ax in a powerful down stroke. Harald let go of the sheer strake with his right hand and pushed off, pivoting away on his left hand, which still held the side of the ship. The ax swept down and struck wood right where Harald's neck had been just a heartbeat before, shattering planks as it drove down through the edge of the ship.

Harald saw the ax twist as the chieftain jerked back on the handle, but before the giant could wrench it free, Harald swung back and clamped his hand down on the iron head, holding it fast. The chieftain roared louder still as he tugged on the weapon. Harald got his left arm over the edge of the ship, his right hand still holding the ax, and he swung his legs up and caught the top of the strake with his foot.

With a grunt and a twist of his leg, Harald heaved himself up and over the edge of the ship, tumbling to the deck like a fish dumped out of a net. The chieftain had taken a step back and pulled a massive sword from his scabbard, which he held over his head just as he had held the ax. Harald pushed himself up to a crouching position, wondering if that was the only way that the Frisian knew to use a weapon.

The sword came hacking down and Harald held the shield up over him, held it at an angle, so that the big man's blade glanced off. The chieftain shouted something in the Frisian tongue and staggered, off balance, and Harald could have killed him then and there if he had had a weapon in hand, which he did not. He reached out and grabbed the handle of the Frisian's battle ax and pulled it toward him, splintering the wood of the sheer strake and twisting the head free.

In one motion he stood and swung the ax horizontally, as if the Frisian was a tree and Harald was aiming to chop him down. But the giant was quicker than giants were wont to be, and he swung his shield and knocked the ax aside, and with his other arm raised the sword and slashed down again.

Once again Harald managed to get his shield up in time, but the Frisian's sword hit the face of the shield square on, driving Harald back. He felt his foot catch something—what he did not know—and he tripped, falling sideways. His shoulder hit the deck hard, sending a bolt of pain through his upper body, but he managed to keep his grip on the ax as he lay there, partially stunned.

Sprawled sideways, Harald could see nothing but the Frisian's calves and feet and the bottom edge of his long fur cloak, but his dulled brain remembered the long sword. He held the battered shield up over him then rolled forward, bringing the ax over and down and hacking it into the big Frisian's foot, the only part of the man he could reach.

The blade of the ax came down through the leather of the man's shoe and embedded itself in the deck as blood gushed out around it. The Frisian shrieked and stepped back, leaving the ax and the front half of his foot behind. Something hit Harald on the helmet and the shoulder and clattered on the deck and Harald realized it was the man's sword, dropped in the surprise and pain of having his foot severed in two.

Harald let go of the ax handle and pushed himself up, snatching the Frisian's sword off the deck as he did. He brought the weapon, heavy and awkward, up in front of him, ready to fend off an attack.

The Frisian was still bellowing with pain and rage, his face red, his eyes wide and fixed on Harald's. He reached around under his cloak and his hand came back gripping a short sword. He roared again and lunged forward just as Harald lunged at him.

The stump of the Frisian's foot struck the ax that was still embedded in the deck and the man began to fall forward, a look of surprise on his face. He took a furious slash at Harald, but Harald twisted clear and thrust, the point of his sword meeting the Frisian's chest as he fell. With the combined force of Harald's lunge and the

Frisian's momentum, the blade passed easily through the mail, through the man's chest, out his back, and through the fur cloak.

Harald released the grip of the sword and jumped back, clear of the falling body. The Frisian hit the deck with an impact Harald could feel, but incredibly, he was not yet dead. He slashed at Harald again, still roaring, but choking as well as blood erupted from his mouth. Harald took another step back, leaned down and snatched up Oak Cleaver. He lifted the sword straight up, ready to bring it down on the man, but the Frisian was motionless at last, blood pooling quickly around him.

The fight still surged across the deck. Harald turned, shield up, Oak Cleaver at the ready. His men and his father's men had fought their way aft, and they were driving the last of the Frisians ahead of them. Harald found himself in a press of fighting men, men with swords and axes and spears and shields. Brand was hacking at the man in front of him, sword against ax, shields rising and falling. Harald saw Hall as well, similarly engaged, and from somewhere behind, he heard Starri's wild war cries and the desperate shouts of the men fighting him.

A spear came sailing through the gap, the iron point striking Harald's shield with force enough to go partway through. Harald reached over the shield and brought Oak Cleaver down on the shaft, parting it like a twig, freeing his shield from the encumbrance. He swung the shield sideways, knocking it into the Frisian in front of him, following the blow with a thrust of his sword.

He looked out over the water. The rest of the Frisian fleet was coming up fast, the nearest ship just fifty feet from coming alongside *Dragon* and pouring her warriors into the battle. But there was nothing to be done about it, nothing but to stand and fight.

Just as Harald came to that conclusion, the Frisian ship turned hard to larboard, turned away from *Dragon*, away from the fight. Harald frowned in confusion, watching the ship alter course until he was looking at her stern, her rowers pulling her back the way she had come, her sail dropping from the yard as she came stern to the wind. He caught something on the edge of his vision: *Blood Hawk* was sweeping around the far side of the fighting ships, her big sail straining, her men standing at the ship's side, mail gleaming, weapons ready.

Harald looked behind him. The rest of Thorgrim's fleet had come up at last, their sails full and driving them along. The sight of them was enough, apparently, for the Frisian raiders. One by one their ships spun on their keels and headed off the way they had come, setting sail to the growing breeze, leaving their fellows to fight on alone.

Their fellows, however, seemed to have little stomach left for combat. Harald heard the sound of weapons hitting the deck and he looked inboard again. One by one the Frisians were throwing down their arms, standing back with angry and dejected looks, those who were still standing, and the fighting was suddenly over. From somewhere behind him, Harald heard cursing and thrashing and wailing and he knew that a number of his father's men were trying to restrain Starri Deathless in his frenzy.

Harald let his sword and shield hang at his side. He looked through the men crowding the deck of the Frisian ship, and past them to the second Frisian ship that had come into the fight. The battle on that deck was over as well, and Harald saw his father standing on the afterdeck, pointing and gesturing in his familiar way of giving orders. Harald felt a sense of relief flood over him, the release of a worry he was not even conscious of feeling.

He turned in the other direction, looked out over the open water. The English fleet, which Harald had all but forgotten about, had set their sails to the rising wind. If they had not, Harald doubted he would have been able to see them, because they were nearly to the horizon, standing on for Frankia, leaving the Northmen and the Frisians to do battle in their wake.

Chapter Eighteen

Death-barrier stands, the sacred gate,
On the plain 'fore the sacred doors;
Old is the lattice and few have learned
How it is closed on the latch.

The Sayings of Grimnir
The Poetic Edda

Skorri Thorbrandsson led the way, and three of his men rode just behind him. They were not moving fast because they had nowhere to go.

They were making their way south along the road to Grefstad. They were close enough to the village that they could see the trails of smoke rising from the smattering of buildings there, even if the rolling country hid the village itself from view.

The information that Valgard had brought, the story of four sheepherders, two men and two women traveling by wagon, was not much, but it was the first possible hint of Odd's location that Skorri had heard in weeks. It made him desperate to continue the hunt, but his men had been scattered and he needed them assembled again. So he had waited impatiently for them to gather back to the farmhouse he had commandeered, and then he led them east toward Grefstad and Fevik, putting them on what he guessed was the path Odd would travel.

Once they had covered some ground, he split them up again, sending them out in bands of five to further the search. He himself had remained behind, keeping three men with him, keeping to the road, moving slowly, remaining essentially in one location. If any of the hunting parties found anything, he did not want them to have to go searching for him.

As a result, he found himself once again waiting for news, and stewing and growing angrier and more frustrated as he did. He reined his horse to a stop and spun the animal around so he was facing the others.

"Vefrod, Osvif, ride into Grefstad and have a look around," he said. "Make certain that Hermund and that lot didn't miss anything."

Skorri had sent Hermund and four others to search Grefstad and then continue east. Hermund was no fool, and if he had not found the fugitives in Grefstad, then it probably meant they were not there, but Skorri could not stand this impotent waiting any longer. He had to do something, even if it was just sending more men out to search.

"As you wish," Vefrod said, and he and Osvif spurred their horses and rode off to the south, their trot building quickly to a gallop, because they knew that Skorri was in no mood to tolerate slackness of any sort.

Skorri turned his horse and watched them ride off until they disappeared over the crest of a hill, then continued along the road, the one man still with him following behind. He stared out over the country and let his thoughts run unchecked. He had five scouting parties out. They would report back before the sun went down, and if they found nothing then he would move them further east and try again. He was casting a net, pulling it in, and casting it once more. Eventually, Odd would get caught up in it.

Unless he didn't. There was, in truth, a dozen ways that Odd could elude him again, but Skorri did not want to think about that, so he did not.

They continued on, walking their horses, Skorri so caught up in his thoughts that his man behind him had to call his name three times before it registered. Skorri turned his horse again to face his lone guard.

"I think I hear horses coming." The man nodded down the road in the direction they were riding. Skorri turned back, cocking his ear to the sound, and he heard it as well: riders, getting closer, moving fast.

This could be anything, he told himself, and indeed it could, but still he could not check the mounting excitement he felt. It could be anything, but the chances were that it had to do with the hunt.

A half a mile away three riders came up over a hill and raced toward Skorri and his man, pounding down the road. As they drew closer Skorri felt increasingly certain that two of them, the two in the lead, were Vefrod and Osvif. Who the third man was he could not tell.

"Come." Skorri whipped his horse's reins and galloped toward the three men. They closed quickly and Skorri recognized the third rider now; it was a man named Thorlak, who had been with Hermund's hunting party. The fact that he was riding hard meant he had news that could not wait.

Skorri reined to a stop and the others reined up beside him. They were all breathing hard, all five men, but Thorlak most of all.

"We met him on the road, Skorri," Vefrod said. "He said he had news. We came immediately."

Skorri nodded and turned to Thorlak, who was gulping air. Skorri pressed his lips together and forced himself to wait for Thorlak to catch his breath enough to speak, and in a moment, he did.

"We found them, Skorri, on the road leading east from Grefstad," Thorlak gasped. "Odd and Amundi and the women...."

"Did you take them?" Skorri demanded. "Hermund and the others, are they holding those bastards prisoner?"

"No, Skorri," Thorlak said, shaking his head. "They're dead. All dead."

Skorri frowned. He wanted Odd and Amundi alive because he knew Halfdan wanted them alive. But if he had to bring corpses to the king, it was better than nothing.

"Is Hermund bringing the bodies here?" Skorri asked.

"Hermund is dead, as I told you," Thorlak said. "Hermund and the others in our scouting party, they're dead. Odd and Amundi, they live, and they've run off again."

Skorri felt his stomach tighten, he felt the fury rush through him like flames in a hayrick. He wanted to strike Thorlak down right there, just for saying what he had said, but again he forced an unnatural patience on himself and said, "Tell me what happened."

Thorlak nodded and Skorri saw the fear in the man's eyes and knew he was not hiding his anger as well as he thought he was.

"We were riding east, the five of us," Thorlak said, "when we met up with them coming west. A wagon and two men and two women, dressed like poor sheepherders, like we were told to look for. We stopped them and questioned them, but none of us could say for certain that it was Odd Thorgrimson, because we didn't know his features so well, and he seemed much changed. But still we were going to bring them to you when they pulled weapons and fought, and they did not fight like sheepherders."

"No, I'm sure they didn't," Skorri said, still keeping his fury in check. "But there were five of you. Against two men."

"Yes, and we bested them easily," Thorlak said. "Or nearly did. And then three more men, they came out of hiding, hiding in the tall grass beside the road, and they joined in with Odd and Amundi, and they so surprised us that they managed to kill the others."

"They killed the others. But you ran." It was a statement, not a question.

"I fought with the others, side by side," Thorlak protested, his face flushing red. "And would have died with them, but I reckoned I would serve you better by getting away and telling you what had happened. Bringing you word of Odd."

Skorri was not sure what to think of this. He did not care to hear about one of his men fleeing from a fight, but then Thorlak was not wrong to think it important that this news reached him.

"I couldn't stop them getting away," Thorlak continued, "but I reckoned I could learn where they were going. So I rode off a ways then went back on foot, hiding in the tall grass, so I could hear. And I heard them say they would leave the wagon and go overland to one of the traitor's farms, a man named Ragi Oleifsson. They said he has a farm to the south."

Skorri stared at Thorlak while the man squirmed under his gaze. He had a pretty good notion of what had really happened: Odd and the others had killed most of Hermund's hunting party, and Thorlak had raced off in terror. He had made it some distance down the road before he realized he could not return that way, tail between his legs, so he had doubled back in hopes of learning something valuable enough that it might temper Skorri's wrath.

And in that, luck had been with him. If he was telling the truth about what they said.

"Ragi Oleifsson..." Skorri repeated, mulling over the name.

"That was the name they spoke," Thorlak said.

Skorri nodded. Ragi Oleifsson was indeed one of the traitors, and he did have a farm south of Grefstad. As Halfdan's overseer Skorri had visited it several times. And that meant Thorlak was likely telling the truth. Skorri looked Thorlak in the eyes and held his gaze for a moment before speaking again.

"You had best not be lying, Thorlak," he said, and his voice was calm and left no room for doubt as to his seriousness. "If I find you're telling tales…you cannot imagine what pains you'll suffer."

"I'm not lying Skorri, I swear on the graves of my ancestors and all the gods of the land!" Thorlak protested. "If Odd and them go to Ragi's or not, I can't promise, but I swear to you I heard them say they meant to do that."

Skorri looked at the sun. There was not much daylight left, not enough for them to wait on the others to gather and then set off after the fugitives. He considered having Thorlak take him to the place where the fight had happened, but he realized there was no point. Thorlak said Odd and the others had taken off across country, but Skorri guessed that if he were to ride for Ragi's house over the roads, he might well get there first.

He turned to Vefrod. "Do you know where Ragi Oleifsson's farm is?"

"No."

"It doesn't matter. Valgard does. You wait here for him and the others to return. Tell Valgard I've gone to Ragi's farm and he's to lead the others there. Do not waste even the least bit of time. There's a wooded hill to the north of the farm that overlooks it. Look for us there. And come in silence."

"As you wish, Skorri," Vefrod said.

Skorri turned to the others. "With me," he said and he did not wait for a reply before putting the spurs to his horse's flanks.

Chapter Nineteen

Tell me this, All-wise, since thou art learned
In the ways of all beings, I ween:
How is the Sea, which is sailed of men
Named by the wights of all worlds?

The Wisdom of All-Wise
The Poetic Edda

Thorgrim stood on the afterdeck of the Frisian ship, calling orders, directing the fighting, when *Blood Hawk* came sweeping past in pursuit of the fleeing raiders.

"Gudrid!" he shouted, and Gudrid, standing at *Blood Hawk*'s helm one hundred feet away, turned in the direction of the hail.

"Leave them be! Let the bastards go!" Thorgrim shouted. Gudrid waved in acknowledgement. He called a few orders forward and *Blood Hawk*'s sail came rising up and the ship's headway fell off. A moment later the oars were run out and the longship closed with *Sea Hammer* and *Dragon* and their two captured Frisians.

Even as Gudrid was waving his acknowledgement, Thorgrim turned his eyes toward *Dragon*, which was lying alongside the larger Frisian ship. Harald had driven *Dragon* right into the fight with a determination that filled Thorgrim with pride. Pride, and an undercurrent of anxiety, a sensation that was still foreign to him, despite his and Harald's having been a'viking together for nearly three years.

Never before had Thorgrim gone into battle with anyone whose life he prized so dearly, whose death would be so devastating to him. Certainly, he had had friends he did not want to lose, and when they died, would mourn their passing. But he would also rejoice in their dying well and taking their place in Odin's feast hall.

If Harald was killed in battle, he would die well, too, of that Thorgrim was certain. His son was as brave and bold as any man Thorgrim had ever fought beside — often too bold for his own good. But knowing that the gods would look with favor on Harald's death brought Thorgrim little comfort. Losing his wife, Hallbera, was the most painful thing he had ever experienced, even in a lifetime of pain. Losing Harald as well would be more than he could bear. It was a strange and unsettling feeling.

And it was why Thorgrim pleaded with the gods, before every battle, to send the Valkyrie for him first.

But there, on the Frisian's deck, Oak Cleaver in hand, stood Harald, pointing with his sword and calling out orders in a manner that Thorgrim recognized was, whether Harald knew it or not, a very close imitation of himself. He smiled and turned back to his own concerns.

The rest of the fleet had headed off in pursuit of the Frisians, but on seeing *Blood Hawk* giving up the chase and joining *Sea Hammer*, they, too, left off that effort and closed with the rest. Soon all of Thorgrim's ships were clustered on that patch of ocean, lashed to one another, a floating, rolling island of wood. Men from the other ships clambered aboard the captured Frisian vessels and helped gather the prisoners in the bow of the big ship, tend to the wounded Northmen, and throw the dead, or mostly dead, Frisians over the side.

Thorgrim left them to it and climbed back aboard *Sea Hammer* and he called to the other captains to join him. One by one they made their way aboard and came aft. Harald, who had his own wounded to attend to, and who felt more compelled than the rest to personally supervise all goings-on on board his ship, was the last over.

"Boldly done, Harald," Gudrid said, slapping Harald on the back as he joined them in the stern of *Sea Hammer*. "And good seamanship, seeing that breeze coming. I'll own that I didn't see it myself, not until it was on us."

That was met with mumbled acknowledgements from the others, nodded heads.

"You got in there, into the fight, bold as can be," Asmund agreed. "Done your father proud."

"The boy has courage," Thorgrim agreed. "He gets it from his mother." That brought smiles all around, eased the tension somewhat. The other men were sincere in their compliments for

Harald, but Thorgrim understood there was more to it than that. They were humiliated by not getting into the fight themselves. Heaping praise on Harald served as a sort of penance for them.

"If the English had shown even a bit of the courage Harald did, it would have been a fine thing," Halldor said and that brought on more nodding, more mumbling.

"Cowardly dogs," said Starri Deathless, who was sitting on the deck aft, leaning against the side of the ship, the fighting madness now dissipated. He was a frightening thing to look on: still bare-chested, still swathed in blood, now dried, his two axes lying beside him. He looked like something from an ancient legend, or a fresh nightmare. "We should kill them all."

"We might yet," Thorgrim said. "But first they must pay what they owe."

"What do you mean for us to do now, Lord Thorgrim?" Gudrid asked.

"What we planned to do," Thorgrim said. "Sail to Frankia. Collect our fifty pounds of silver for every ship. Then sail for home."

This was met with mutters of agreement from the five captains present, and one cleared throat from Grifo, who had wandered aft and stood at the edge of the group.

"Something you want to say?" Thorgrim asked.

Grifo looked at the other captains and then at Thorgrim. "You mean to sail to Paris, still? Demand your silver?"

"I do," Thorgrim said. "The English weren't obliged to fight, not to my thinking. They paid us to fight for them. It was a cowardly thing, running off, but they had that choice. But they *are* obliged to give us our silver. Especially now."

Grifo raised an eyebrow, then frowned and nodded, but said nothing more.

"And what of these Frisian bastards?" Halldor asked, nodding toward the ship tied alongside. "What'll we do with them?"

"We best be rid of them," Thorgrim said. "They're of no use to us."

Thorgrim could think of several ways to rid him and his men of the Frisians, but he chose the one that seemed the most expedient, and the most helpful. To begin with, they searched the two Frisian ships, and the Frisians themselves, and stripped them of anything worth taking, which was not much. A few purses with smatterings of coins, some small chests with bits of silver, various weapons, many of which were tossed overboard as useless.

These are some pretty piss-poor raiders, Thorgrim thought as the pile of loot grew to a non-too-impressive height on *Sea Hammer*'s deck. *The ones we killed…we might have done them a favor.*

The ones they did not kill were standing in the forward end of the big Frisian ship, angry and apprehensive and no doubt thinking they were about to join their comrades in the afterlife. But Thorgrim had no interest in butchering unarmed men, even Frisians, and he did not think the gods would look with favor on such a thing. So he stepped from *Sea Hammer* onto the other ship and regarded the sorry lot of prisoners and called, "Do any of you speak my language?"

There was a moment of silence, and then one man raised a tentative hand. "Yes, I do."

"Good," Thorgrim said. "Tell these others to do as I say, and I might let you live." The Frisian translated the words and then nodded at Thorgrim, and Thorgrim said, "Tell them to take off their clothes, all of their clothes, and throw them overboard."

This was met with looks of surprise, and anger, but no words of protest, and the Frisians hardly hesitated before they began stripping off their worn and filthy clothes and tossing them over the side of the ship. Thorgrim watched with approval as behind him his men laughed and shouted insults which none of the Frisians, save the translator, would understand. But they certainly understood humiliation, and they knew they were tasting it now.

Once they were fully naked, some making a weak effort to hide themselves, some standing boldly in the open, Thorgrim said, "Now, all of you, get your wounded on board the other ship and you may go."

The Frisian translated and for a moment the others remained motionless, as if they did not understand. And then one by one they began to spread out across the deck, gathering up the wounded lying on the warm planks. There were, in truth, not too many, since Thorgrim's men had been quite liberal in deciding which of the wounded were bound to die and had thrown them overboard with those already dead.

Soon the Frisian ship was underway, her sail set, her naked crew hauling the sheets aft, eager, no doubt, to get clear before the mad Northman changed his mind. Thorgrim turned to his own men.

"Get our dead on board the Frisian ship," he said. "We'll make a pyre of it to send them on their way."

There were only three men dead from Thorgrim's crew and one from Harald's, not too high a price for such a desperate and uneven fight, brief though it might have been. The dead men were laid out on the deck of the Frisian ship, still wearing their mail and helmets, shields on their arms, swords and spears at their sides. The sail was cut free of the yard and torn into strips, and a few of the sea chests were smashed up and made into a pile and the whole thing was set on fire, stoked by the westerly breeze.

The decks of the Frisian ship had been well-soaked with the blood of friends and foe and Thorgrim figured that would serve well for the sort of blood sacrifice he might normally make on such an occasion. He said a few words, loud enough for his voice to carry over the water to the assembled fleet, and the men stood at the rails of their ships and looked on as the fire spread.

They watched the Frisian ship burn until the deck was engulfed, until the heat was hard to bear even across the water, and the drifting embers were beginning to threaten all the ships. Then Thorgrim ordered sails set and the fleet was soon underway again, following in the wake of the English fleet, now long over the horizon.

The weather continued fine, and the five ships plowed their straight wakes south with the sun hanging over their starboard sides. They kept in a tighter formation now, since there was no need to watch as much ocean as they could, with their charges having left them behind. The bigger ships, *Sea Hammer* and *Blood Hawk*, eased their sheets, spilling wind from their sails so they did not outpace the smaller vessels. Thorgrim knew Harald would find that irritating in the extreme, like a pebble in his shoe, and he took quiet amusement from it.

The sun was just past its high point for the day when the low, dark coast of Frankia appeared over the horizon and Thorgrim called Louis aft.

"There's Frankia," he said, nodding toward the horizon. "Welcome home. Are we making landfall in the right place?"

Louis shrugged. "How would I know? Get me ashore and I know every hill and valley for a hundred miles around, but out here, it all looks the same."

Thorgrim said nothing. He had not really expected Louis to recognize the coast. Even to a mariner, coastlines looked pretty much the same from this distance. But he figured they could not be too far off, and once they were closer in, he would find a fisherman or a coastal trader to set them right.

Grifo came ambling aft, moving so casually that it was clear he had something on his mind. Thorgrim wondered if, with Frankia so close, he would now try to put a knife in Louis. If that was his intent, he had missed his best opportunity during the battle.

But Grifo did not look like a man set on murder. Instead, he stopped near the break of the afterdeck and leaned against the side of the ship. He stared for a moment at the coastline rising up out of the sea, then turned and looked up at Thorgrim.

"You mean to go to Paris, Thorgrim?" he asked.

"Yes," Thorgrim said.

"And demand the silver owed you?"

"Yes."

Grifo nodded and looked down at the deck, considering this. Then he looked up again. "They won't pay, you know," he said. "They'll put you all to the sword."

"They can try," Thorgrim said.

Grifo gave a bit of a smile. "I'm quite serious. They never meant to pay you. They reckoned if you sailed to Paris, then they could kill the lot of you there and take back what they already paid. They want you to go to Paris. That's why I'm here. To encourage you to go."

Thorgrim looked long at Grifo, looked into his eyes. "You know this how?"

"I'm Felix's man," Grifo said. "Of course, I know what he was planning."

Thorgrim nodded. The other question, the more important question, was why was Grifo telling him this? Was it part of Felix's plan? A diversion of some sort? And then Thorgrim remembered Grifo lying on the deck, the battle ax coming down for his head. He remembered holding the shield over Grifo, turning certain, bloody death into a chance to fight on.

Grifo was a warrior; he was not the sort to thank anyone for such a thing as saving his life. But he was not the sort to forget such a debt either.

Thorgrim turned to Louis. "What do you think of this?"

"I would not be at all surprised if this was the truth," Louis said. "There's no pit of vipers more treacherous than the Frankish court. But...tell us honestly, Thorgrim...you didn't really think Felix would keep his word, did you?"

"No," Thorgrim said, and it was the truth. He had assumed from the beginning that Felix would betray him, and assumed, as well, that he would find a way to counter that betrayal. "But I still plan to get my silver. By some means."

"Paris is the seat of King Charles's power," Grifo said. "The defenses...the soldiers he has there...you and five ships' crews would have no chance against all that."

"I would welcome you to my home in Roumois," Louis said, "if you could resist plundering the countryside. But I don't think I'll be much welcome there."

"Seems none of us have many friends around here," Thorgrim said.

"No, we don't," Grifo said. "I know Louis's brother'll put a knife in Louis as soon as he shows himself in Roumois. He won't kill Louis personally, of course. He'll have someone else do it. Planning on me doing it, probably. But his brother won't be in Roumois. All the lords in West Frankia, they'll be at court to greet the King of Wessex. None would dare miss that. And they'll be there with their men-at-arms. Which is more reason why you'd stand little chance in that wolf's den."

"Of course..." Louis said, and his voice trailed off as he considered that. "I'm a fool. Of course, my brother will be in Paris."

"But your brother must know you're coming," Thorgrim said. "Felix had time enough to send word. He must have left someone behind with orders to give you a proper greeting."

"Most likely he did," Louis agreed. "But I had friends once in Roumois. I might still."

"You might," Thorgrim agreed, but he was skeptical. In all the time he had known Louis de Roumois, the Frank did not seem to attract friends. Rather, he attracted people who wished to kill him, Thorgrim included.

"My advice," Grifo said to Thorgrim. "Throw Louis overboard, let him swim from here. You sail for your homeland, and the Franks and the Saxons be damned."

"That's good advice," Thorgrim said. "But I think we'll take Louis home and see what greeting awaits us there."

"Not a pleasant one, I'd wager," Grifo said.

"Probably not," Thorgrim agreed. "But I won't sail without my silver."

Chapter Twenty

Why loiter I thus in darksome hiding,
in the folds of rugged hills,
nor follow seafaring as of old?

Saxo Grammaticus
The Danish History

The man's name was Gunthar and his clothes and his manner suggested he was the sort who might own a small farm, one big enough to employ a few farm hands, but not so big as to spare him the toil of working the fields besides them. He rode a horse, but it was no fine mount. Rather, it looked as if it might pull a plow one day, a wagon the next, or serve to carry a rider another. He looked like a man who had been riding hard for many miles.

It was well past sunset when he approached the village of Jumièges, nestled in a bend of the river Seine, in the region of Roumois. For some time, as he neared the town, he had been able to see the impressive towers of the abbey silhouetted against the evening sky. But now it was full dark and he saw only a few pinpricks of light where lanterns had been lit in the windows of the great stone building.

It was late summer in a year that had been dry and the road under the horse's hooves was hard and dusty. Gunthar felt the dust clinging to him, caked on by the perspiration that came from riding hard over many miles of such roads.

He was not riding hard now. He was trying to not look like a man in a hurry. He was trying to look like a weary traveler in search of a bed for the night. Since he was just that (among other things) it was not a hard part to play.

189

He saw light up ahead, a watch fire burning near the high gate in the ancient stone wall that surrounded the village. He took a deep breath and steeled himself, but he did not slow his pace. His horse's hooves made a steady, weary, clopping noise on the hard-packed road as he grew nearer. Soon he could see the men he expected to see. Two of them. He wondered if there were more, standing out of sight.

As he closed with the men he could see light glinting off the few bits of iron and copper on the leather armor they wore, and off bright-polished helmets. He could see them shuffling toward the center of the road, blocking his path. He did not alter his pace.

He was twenty feet away when one of the men spoke. "Halt! Down off your horse."

Gunthar nodded and slipped from the saddle and for a moment he thought his knees would buckle after having been mounted for so long. He felt the ache in his muscles, the sore, chaffed spots between his legs and on his ass.

"Who are you? What's your business?" the soldier asked, but Gunthar did not answer as he arched his back and stretched and groaned despite himself, like a man unafraid to be questioned. He looked the men up and down. They each wore the crimson-and-white sash that marked them as part of the house guards of le duc de Roumois. But they carried spears rather than swords, and wore leather rather than mail, which told Gunthar that they were not warriors of any great importance.

Which was hardly a surprise. The best of the house guard were off to Paris with Duke Eberhard. The most expendable were sent to far-flung towns such as Jumièges.

"My name's Gunthar, and I'm from Rouen," he said.

The guards stared at him, silent for a moment. "Long way from Rouen," one said at last. "What's your business here?"

"None," Gunthar said. "I'm on my way to Fontenelle to see my brother, who's ill. It's late, I'm looking for a bed for the night."

Once again the guards stared at him. Once again, they said nothing, but before Gunthar could break the silence, he was interrupted by the sound of footsteps, the soft swoosh of chainmail. Another figure stepped out through the gate and into the light of the watch fire. An older man, his beard gray, his face weathered. Unlike the two guards he was wearing a sword and mail.

"Who's this?" the man asked, after he had given Gunthar a long look through squinting eyes.

"Traveler," said one of the guards. "Says he's from Rouen, bound for Fontenelle."

"To see his brother," the other guard offered helpfully.

"What's this all about?" Gunthar asked. "I've been to Jumièges often enough, and there have never been guards at the gate." It was a question that any traveler might reasonably ask, though Gunthar was one of the few who actually did not need to inquire. He knew what it was all about. Probably more than the men questioning him.

"Duke's business, not yours," the older man said. "Lift up your cloak, there."

Gunthar nodded with an appropriately surly look, enough to show he was annoyed, not enough to evoke a response. He grabbed fistfuls of his cloak and held it out so the guard could see his tunic and belt, could see that he had no weapons. The guard could not see the short sword concealed under Gunthar's tunic, tied against his back.

While the man looked him up and down, the other guard poked through the sacks hanging from the saddle. A loaf of bread and cheese, a jug of poor wine, a spare shirt, a leather sack with a few coins, that was all the man was going to find. Gunthar heard the soft jingle as the guard helped himself to a few of the coins, and then turned back and joined them in the middle of the road.

"Where do you mean to stay?" the gray-bearded one asked.

"There's an inn. Les Armes du Duc. I've stayed there before."

The guard nodded as if the question was some sort of test and Gunthar had passed, but just barely. "Go on, then," he said, nodding toward the gate. "But you cause any trouble, and by God you'll wish you had stayed in Rouen."

Gunthar nodded. He resisted saying any of the many things that came to mind. Instead he grabbed his horse's reins and led the animal forward, past the guards, and through the gate into the village beyond. He had not lied when he said he had been to Jumièges. He had, many times. He knew the town well, and so had little trouble navigating the tangle of narrow streets, though they were dark and lit only by a bit of moonlight and the occasional lantern hung at a gate.

He had, however, lied about staying at Les Armes du Duc. In truth, he meant to stay at Le Coq d'Or, but he did want the guard to know as much, so he did not make his way there directly. Rather, he headed off in the direction of the first inn, moving like a man who was mostly certain of his way, but not entirely. He stopped on a few occasions to look around, as if trying to establish where he was, though in truth he was looking to catch anyone following in the shadows.

But there was no one that he could see, and the few times he caught movement behind turned out to be stray cats looking for a meal or a mate, so he moved on. Soon he reached the gate of Les Armes du Duc and once again paused, stretched, looked around him. Still no one to be seen. He continued on, past the inn, past the shops beside it, shuttered and dark, and on toward the place he actually meant to go.

Gunthar was weary indeed by the time he reached Le Coq d'Or, through another mile or so of dark, winding streets. The hour seemed very late to him, though he guessed it was not as late as he thought, judging from the light in the tavern windows and the noise of the people inside. He tried the door to the gate and found it unlatched, so he pushed it open and led his horse into the courtyard.

It was not a big space, maybe a hundred feet square, with stables off to one side and a fire burning in a pit in the center of the yard. A few boys were crouched around the fire and one stood and approached as Gunthar came through the gate.

"Get my horse in the stable, boy," Gunthar said, handing the reins to the young man. "See he's brushed well, mind, and give my bags to the innkeeper. And keep your hands out of them."

"Yes, sir," the boy said, nodding and leading the horse away. Gunthar trudged on, up the two granite steps in front of the tavern and through the heavy oak door.

The tavern room was just as he remembered, though it had been a few years. The low ceiling and heavy beams supporting it were black with soot; the fire in the big fireplace in the west wall was throwing its light around the place, illuminating the room in yellow and orange and leaving dark shadows where the light could not reach. A bar made up most of one wall, a smattering of mismatched tables and chairs filled the rest of the floor. The room was crowded, filled with travelers like Gunthar and local shopkeepers and tradesmen looking to drink away some of the little silver they managed to earn.

It took Gunthar a moment to find the man he was looking for. He and another man were sitting at a table, a table in the far end of the room, as far from the light of the fire as it could be and all but lost in the shadow. Gunthar had to look for a moment to be certain, but when he was, he pushed his way through the crowd and approached. He paused a few feet from the man's table and waited while the man took a pull from a tankard and then set it down. The other man sitting there shifted nervously, adjusting his position so as to allow him to move quicker, to draw some unseen weapon if need be.

"Gunthar," the first man said.

"Lothar," Gunthar replied. It was not the man's name, but it was the name by which he was currently known.

Lothar nodded to a chair and Gunthar sat heavily. "How fare you?" Lothar asked. "How fares your cousin?"

"I'm well," Gunthar said. "My cousin is well. He sent me here. He's in Paris now, with the duke. But you probably knew that."

Lothar nodded. He was an old man, but still lean and tough. He wore his whiskers in a goatee and moustache, and what hair he might have had on his head was shaved entirely clean. His skin was dark brown and deeply wrinkled, the result of a lifetime, a long lifetime, spent mostly outdoors, mostly campaigning. There was nothing of the soldier about his clothing, but his bearing, the calm strength he exuded, were entirely martial.

"I did not know Mariwig was in Paris," Lothar said, "but I guessed he was. If he wasn't, it would mean something was very wrong." Mariwig, Gunthar's cousin, would, of course, be with Duc Eberhard. He was the captain of the duke's household guard.

"Are you surprised to see me?" Gunthar picked up Lothar's tankard and helped himself to a mouthful of ale.

Lothar shrugged. "Something's afoot. There seem to be a damned lot of crimson-and-white sashes afield."

Gunthar set the tankard down and leaned closer, and in a low voice he said, "Word has reached Eberhard. Louis is on his way back."

For a moment Lothar just looked at him, and then he slowly closed his eyes and his whole body seemed to relax as if some great tension had been removed. Gunthar stared at the man, whose actual name was Ranulf, though he had not been known by that name for a long time. With his shaved scalp, his goatee, the extra years, and a certain leanness courtesy of the time he had spent in Eberhard's prison, he looked less like the Ranulf of old than did the convicted rapist whose head they had brought to Eberhard in Ranulf's stead.

Ranulf opened his eyes. "How? How is Louis making his way back? The abbot at that monastery would not have let him go. Felix would not have allowed that to happen."

"I don't know all the story," Gunthar said. "I only know that Louis has somehow fallen in with a band of Northmen, and it's with them that he's returning to Frankia. That was what Felix wrote to Eberhard, anyway."

Ranulf nodded as he considered that. When the old duke had died, there had been little resistance to Eberhard's exerting absolute control. Eberhard was, after all, the rightful heir to Roumois. And even after Louis was exiled, the house guard disbanded, and those close to Louis arrested, there had been little protest beyond grumblings and a few condemnations, spoken in hushed voices.

But Eberhard was not satisfied. He saw traitors in every corner, and the more brutally he tried to root them out, the more he inspired others to treason. The new duke tried to eradicate any influence that Louis might have had in Roumois, and instead managed to create a vast and unseen web of people who despised him, who were loyal to Louis alone, and who waited only for Louis's return.

Through his own effort, Eberhard had created the one thing he feared the most.

"When do they say Louis will arrive?" Ranulf asked.

"They said he would arrive with the king of Wessex. Him and the Northmen. But the English arrived two days ago, I'm told, and the Northmen and Louis were not with them. So far, we've heard nothing more."

Ranulf frowned. "There's danger here. Considerable danger," he said. "We dare not go too early. We dare not wait too long."

"But we can't stand idly by," Gunthar said. "We must act. We must make ready."

"Yes," Ranulf agreed. "Word must be spread, plans made."

"So when shall it start?" Gunthar asked, but before Ranulf could answer, the front door of the tavern crashed open, thrown with a force that no friendly soul would use. Gunthar and Ranulf and the other man were on their feet in an instant and turning to the sound.

The light from the fireplace fell across the figure in the door and Gunthar recognized him immediately: the old soldier from the gate, sash across his chest, sword in hand.

"Damn the bastard!" Gunthar said out loud.

The soldier stepped into the room, five steps, scanning the dim-lit place. Behind him, four more men in leather armor, spears in hand. The tavern room was silent. Men at other tables began to stand, to step aside, glaring at the duke's men.

"Sit, the lot of you, sit!" the old soldier called, and some did, spurred by the authority in his voice.

And some did not. Gunthar remained on his feet and his hand reached around under his tunic and his fingers wrapped around the hilt of the short sword hidden there.

"We don't want this fight, not yet," Ranulf said in a voice that only Gunthar and the other man at their table could hear. Gunthar took his eyes from the soldier and looked at Ranulf and Ranulf nodded toward the door at the back of the room. Gunthar looked in that direction, and even as he did, the door flew open and four more spearmen, red-and-crimson sashes across their chests, stepped into the crowded tavern room.

The old soldier was making his way across the room now, his eyes moving between Gunthar and Ranulf, his sword in hand. The men with him followed in his wake, their spears lowered a bit, but they were awkward weapons to wield in that confined space.

"Gunthar of Rouen," the soldier said. "I thought you sought lodging at Les Armes du Duc."

"No room at the inn," Gunthar said.

"Or was it that you came to talk to our friend Lothar, here?" the man-at-arms asked. "Lothar, whose real name is Ranulf, if I don't miss my guess."

Gunthar tightened his grip on the hilt of the short sword and pulled down to free the weapon, but before the blade was clear of the scabbard, the room seemed to blow apart. A big man, a smith by the look of him, snatched up a chair and swung it around in a wide arc at the old soldier's head. The duke's man dodged the blow and the chair slammed into two of the spearmen behind, sending them reeling.

"*Bâtard!*" the man-at-arms shouted and slashed his sword backhand at the smith.

Gunthar saw the blade bite deep in the man's arm, saw the blood spray, heard the man shriek as he staggered back.

If the old soldier had thought spears and sashes would be enough to cow the men in the tavern, he was quite mistaken. The spearmen were still staggering as the rest of the crowd leapt into the fray. A half dozen chairs were in motion now, beating the spearmen down to the floor, while their captain tried to keep the crowd back, slashing and cursing at the mob that surrounded him.

"Come!" Ranulf shouted, nodded toward the back door. He, too, had a sword in hand, as did the man with him, though where the weapons had come from, Gunthar did not know. Ranulf kicked over the table and they turned toward the back door, only to find the other four spearmen fighting their way towards them, across the room, spears leveled, three men writhing on the floor in their wake.

The man with Ranulf grabbed up a chair with his left hand and hurled it at the guards with surprising force and accuracy, hitting one hard in the chest and the face, making him stumble into the man beside him. In that instant of confusion, Gunthar and the other two were on them, swords swinging like scythes.

A spear came driving at Gunthar's gut, but he swatted the point away, stepped in, and thrust, the short sword a much better weapon for such close work. The point found the man's leather breastplate and did not hesitate as it drove through. Gunthar felt the blade deflect off bone as he put his considerable strength behind it, saw the man's eyes go wide, mouth open, saw the blood welling out of his throat, and he jerked the blade out again as the man stumbled and went down in front of him.

The second spearman had wisely dropped his clumsy weapon and grabbed Ranulf's wrist before Ranulf could run him through, and now the two were struggling for control of the blade. Gunthar hacked down on the soldier's arm, parting sleeve and flesh, a deep laceration, no more, but enough to make the man let go of Ranulf. The soldier staggered back, clutching his wounded arm, and Ranulf lunged and put him down with his sword-point through the man's throat.

Ranulf's friend was ten feet away, bleeding from a cut across his cheek, a spear wound that, had it been an inch to the right, would have ended his life. The spearman he had been fighting was not so lucky, and he lay screaming and kicking and clawing at the floor at the man's feet, until Ranulf's man put an end to that.

And suddenly it was quiet. Gunthar looked around the room. All the spearmen were down, and even the old soldier had finally been beaten to the floor, a half dozen smashed chairs and tables scattered around him. None of the men in the tavern had fled, or cowered in a corner, or aided the duke's guards. They had all jumped into the fight, and they had all fought to keep Ranulf out of the duke's hands.

"Gunthar, my friend," Ranulf said. "You ask when it shall start. I say, it just did."

Chapter Twenty-One

Sea 'tis named among men, Wide Ocean of gods, time against
Wanes call it flowing Wave,
Jötuns, Eel-home, elves, Water-stave,
By dwarves 'tis called the Deep.

The Wisdom of All-Wise
The Poetic Edda

They spent another night at sea, which was not to anyone's liking, least of all Thorgrim's, but there was nothing for it. The bloody fight, plundering the Frisians, sending the dead off in a proper way, took all of the morning hours and then some. The fleet made southing for a while with a fair breeze, but the wind failed them soon after they sighted land, so the sails were stowed and the oars taken down from the gallows by the grumbling crew.

They pulled through the afternoon, making barely discernable progress. The sea came on in long rollers, and rowing was akin to dragging a cart over hilly country. It was not a job that could be kept up forever, or even for the rest of the day.

"Let's hope we meet no more Frisian raiders," Grifo said. He was leaning on the side of the ship just forward of where Thorgrim stood at the tiller. He nodded toward the men at the oars, red-faced, sweating, their pace having slackened noticeably. "These poor bastards will collapse if they have to lift a weapon."

"You've got my leave to take an oar yourself," Thorgrim said, but Grifo smiled and shook his head.

"I'm a warrior, not a sailor," he said. "I wouldn't even know which end of the damned thing to hold."

Thorgrim did not reply, but he knew that Grifo was not wrong. The men were nearing exhaustion. That concerned him, though not due to any feelings of sympathy. Thorgrim Night Wolf was rarely motivated by sympathy. His concern stemmed from other considerations.

Foremost was the speed the fleet was making, which would only grow slower as the men grew wearier. At that pace they would be near enough to shore when darkness fell to be in real danger, but not near enough to reach any sort of safe harbor. Better to remain at sea, and far from land, than to go blundering around on a strange coast in the dark.

"Toss your oars!" Thorgrim called, loud enough for his men and the men aboard the other ships to hear. "This is as far as we go today."

Once again, the five vessels rafted up to one another, and once again the men ate and drank and bedded down with their ships rising and falling under them, boards and spars creaking, rigging slapping, water bubbling along the sides.

Thorgrim slept little. They were far enough from land that they stood little danger of being swept ashore in the dark, at least under normal circumstances, but he had no idea what sort of currents ran along this coast. Some unseen river in the sea could be pushing them silently toward their destruction, and so he was up and down all through the night, his ears straining for the sound of breakers, his eyes looking into the dark for glimpses of water breaking white.

He knew that Starri Deathless was awake as well, up at the top of the mast, watching, listening, and that gave him some comfort. Starri had preternatural senses, and he was terrified of dying at sea, because he did not believe the Valkyrie would come for a man who drowned, unless he drowned in the midst of battle, sinking into the depths with his weapon still clutched in his hand.

Starri's presence, however, did nothing to mitigate Thorgrim's other concerns about the spirits and strange, unearthly creatures that inhabited the black depths beneath *Sea Hammer*'s keel. But there was nothing he could do about that, save to ask for Thor and Odin's protection, which he did, and to try his best not to think about it, which he did as well.

The sun rose the following morning to reveal the shores of Frankia now noticeably closer, though still far enough off as to present no danger. The captains of the various ships roused their men, who stood groaning, stretching, and cursing. Thorgrim saw that most, like him, had not enjoyed a restful night. They ate dagmál and shipped their oars once again and together they bent their backs to them, driving the bows of their ships south, ever south.

Thorgrim looked to the west, and he saw the clouds forming as they had the day before, and soon the first puffs of breeze wafted over *Sea Hammer*'s deck. Thorgrim ordered the oars stowed and the sail set, and the other ships followed his lead. By the time the morning was half gone, the fleet was once again rolling along, driven by the wind alone, water foaming white around their bows.

The coast of Frankia rose quickly from the sea, and Thorgrim, standing on the sheer strake, one hand on the backstay for balance, ran his eyes along the dark line of land ahead. He could see they were sailing into some great, half-moon-shaped bay, the headlands marking the eastern and western ends barely visible, so great was that body of water. Somewhere along that coast, presumably, was the mouth of the River Seine, which would lead them to Louis's home in Roumois, and onto Paris and the silver which Thorgrim still intended to collect.

"Starri!" Thorgrim called aloft.

"Yes, Night Wolf?" Starri was back aloft, having come down only for dagmál and to relieve himself over the side, and he would not have bothered to come down for the latter if Thorgrim had not explicitly told him he was not to piss from the masthead.

"See anything?"

There was a pause as Starri took another look around, and then called down, "Nothing yet! Nothing you can't see from there!"

They stood on, the breeze carrying them closer in shore until the open water lay astern of them and the land stretched from their larboard beams to their starboard.

"Night Wolf!" Starri called down some time later. "I see some sails, off to the east! Small… might be fishing boats!"

Fishing boats, Thorgrim thought. *Perfect*. Fishermen were bound to know the coast thereabouts better than most other mariners did, and they were less likely to put up a fight. Thorgrim pushed *Sea Hammer*'s tiller away, swinging the ship more easterly until she was sailing in the direction that Starri indicated. It was not long before even Thorgrim, with his low height of eye and less-than-perfect vision, was able to see the fishing boats, or at least their gray sails, off in the distance.

They were running for all they were worth, as indeed would any Frankish vessel that encountered a wolf pack of Northmen's ships bearing down on them. There were about a dozen of them, scattering in different directions, each hoping, no doubt, that the raiders would go for their neighbor and not themselves. Thorgrim looked over the array of boats and fixed his eyes on the largest of them. Any one, he figured, would be as good as another, but perhaps the master of the largest ship would have the most knowledge of a wide swath of the coast.

He nudged the tiller over a bit, turning *Sea Hammer*'s bow until it was aimed just ahead of the desperate boat, and in *Sea Hammer*'s wake, like geese following the leader of the flock, the others turned as well. About a mile of water separated the Northmen and the Frankish fishing boat, and the longships, their sails full, covered the distance in little time.

A few hundred feet off the fishing boat's stern, Thorgrim saw furious activity on board, men working desperately at something, but what, Thorgrim could not tell.

"Starri, what by all the gods are they about on that boat?" he called aloft.

"Ha!" Starri laughed. "They're throwing their fish overboard!"

Thorgrim smiled at that. They were no doubt trying to lighten the boat, to get more speed out of it, as if throwing the fish in their hold over the side would make their awkward vessel fast enough to escape a sleek longship such as *Sea Hammer*.

And, of course, it did not. *Sea Hammer* was a couple ship lengths away when the fishermen abandoned their useless effort and stood, sullen-looking, watching fate swoop down on them, watching the approach of what they must have assumed was ruin, and likely death.

"Louis! Get back here!" Thorgrim shouted and Louis came ambling aft and stood at the break of the afterdeck. "Come up here, beside me," Thorgrim said. "You'll have to talk to these sorry bastards."

Louis nodded and climbed up onto the deck and Thorgrim called for the sail to be hauled up. The speed came off the ship quickly as the sail was brought up to the yard, and *Sea Hammer* slowed to a stop alongside the Frankish boat. A couple of grappling hooks flew across the gap between them, catching in the fishing boat's rail, and the two vessels were hauled up close together.

Thorgrim looked down at the fishermen huddled at the stern of their vessel. An old man and a woman about the same age and three young men. A family, perhaps, or a man and wife and some hired crew. The best way to get honest information from any man, Thorgrim knew, was to mete out fear and promise in the correct proportions. In this case, the fear was already taken care of. He could see that from the terror on their faces.

"What do I tell them?" Louis asked.

Before Thorgrim could answer, the old man took a step forward, and as he did, he reached around his back and pulled out a long knife, holding it as menacingly as he could, though his shaking hand made the point of the blade jerk up and down.

Thorgrim smiled. "I'll say this, the old bastard has balls," he said to Louis. "Now, tell him we are trying to get to…wherever it is we're trying to get to. Tell him they won't be harmed if he helps us, and there's silver for him. Tell him if they betray us, it will go hard on them. You can tell them who you are if you think it will do any good."

Louis nodded. He leaned over the rail and called down to the people on the fishing boat and rattled on in his Frankish tongue. Thorgrim thought he heard him say "Louis de Roumois," but Louis spoke so fast and his accent was so odd he could not be sure. Still, he saw the people on the fishing boat relax, and start to nod as Louis spoke.

When Louis was done, the old man started talking, waving his arms as the words came out, pointing here and there. Finally, after what seemed a ridiculously long time, he finished, and Louis straightened and turned.

"I told him who I am and he seemed pleased enough, but I'm not sure he believes me. I asked him how do we find the River Seine, which leads to Roumois. He said the mouth of the river is to the east, and he would show us if we like."

"Good," Thorgrim said.

"He said he would like the silver first, before he shows us the way," Louis said.

Thorgrim frowned at that. He reached into the purse hanging on his belt, pulled out a silver coin and held it up. It was a West Saxon coin, stamped with the head of the king they had just saved from the Frisians.

"Tell him I'm going to drop this coin," Thorgrim said to Louis. "Tell him if he is not aboard this ship by the time it hits the deck, I'll personally butcher him and everyone aboard his boat."

Louis turned and called down to the fisherman, and Thorgrim watched the confidence leave the man's face and the terror come rushing back in. He dropped the knife he was still holding and raced for the side of his boat, climbing over and onto *Sea Hammer* faster than Thorgrim would have thought possible. He half-tumbled onto *Sea Hammer*'s deck, pulled himself up, and looked aft at Thorgrim to see if he had made it in time.

Thorgrim nodded and put the coin back in his purse. "Tell him to come aft," he said to Louis.

A moment later, they were underway again, *Sea Hammer*'s sail billowing out, her bow rising and falling on the rollers, the rest of the fleet following astern, and the fishing boat left far astern. At the old man's direction, they turned further east, bracing their yards around and heeling to starboard and they ran before the breeze.

It was not long before Thorgrim saw a break in the coastline, an indent that might have been a smaller bay or might have been the mouth of a river. A few miles closer and it was clear they were looking at the mouth of a river. Louis assured him it was the River Seine, though Thorgrim suspected that Louis did not really know that for certain, that the old fisherman had told him as much.

But it soon seemed likely that Louis was right, that it was the Seine, given its size. The river's mouth, spread wide like welcoming arms, was nearly four miles across by Thorgrim's guess. He ordered the sails taken in and the oars shipped and once again the men sat on their sea chests and pulled with an easy stroke as the small fleet left the narrow seas astern for the embrace of the Frankish shores.

"Ask the old man if he knows the river," Thorgrim said and Louis asked the question and waited for the reply.

"He says he knows it well to just below Rouen, but not so well beyond that," Louis said.

"Is that a help to us?" Thorgrim asked.

"My home, le Château de Roumois, is downstream of Rouen, so yes, that's a help to us. The old man can pilot us right to the château."

Thorgrim nodded. "Tell him to do that."

The tide was flooding at first, carrying the ships into the mouth of the great river and beyond, where the banks closed in to a still-impressive mile distance between them. The land along the river's shores consisted of great swathes of meadow laying across low, rolling green hills. They saw farms along the banks and small clusters of houses and herds of cattle.

Nice country, Thorgrim thought. *It's no wonder Louis loves it so.*

The fleet continued down that wide, brown way cut through the fertile land, sweeping around great bends in the river that had them going north one moment, south the next. They saw riders on the shore, groups of men on horseback who would follow them for some distance and then ride off over the hills beyond the river.

After some time, Thorgrim turned the tiller over to Hall and sat down on the edge of the afterdeck. Grifo was sitting on a barrel just forward of that, watching the country slide by.

"I hope you're right, about all the men-at-arms hereabouts being off to Paris," Thorgrim said. "The whole countryside's alarmed by now. We won't be surprising anyone."

"No, you won't," Grifo agreed. "But I think there's naught but small villages along this part of the river. If there's an army waiting, we won't know it until we reach Louis's château."

"And when will that be?"

Grifo shrugged. "If I was on horseback, I could make a good guess, but on this damned ship I have no idea."

"Ask the old man, then," Thorgrim said, nodding toward the fisherman who stood a bit forward of the afterdeck. Once they had come into the river with the shores of Frankia closing in on them, Louis had ambled off forward. Now he stood amidships, leaning against the mast, watching the countryside as *Sea Hammer* was swept along. But the fisherman seemed to know the river as well as he claimed, and Grifo could translate, so Thorgrim let Louis be.

Grifo spoke a few words to the fisherman and the fisherman replied in his gruff Frankish.

"He says there's about thirty miles to go, but the tide is just turning and it will be slow going against it," Grifo translated.

Thorgrim nodded. He looked at the sun, which was well down in the west. He looked at the river and he could see that the current was against them, the tide having gone from flood to ebb. Now they would be fighting both the outgoing tide and the natural flow of the river and their progress would drop off to all but nothing.

"We'll stop for the night," Thorgrim announced. "Do you know of a suitable place?"

"I don't," Grifo said. "I've been along this part of the river a few times, but I don't know it well. I'm from Châtres. This isn't my country."

Thorgrim considered asking the old fisherman, and no doubt he would know of a place where they could beach the ships, but he was a fisherman, not a warrior. There were things, such as the defensibility of a place, that would not occur to him.

"Louis!" Thorgrim called forward, and Louis turned and looked aft. "Come back here."

Louis pushed himself off the mast and walked aft, treading carefully between the lines of men pulling oars, larboard and starboard.

Thorgrim turned his attention to the northern bank of the river, then looked inboard again as Louis approached. "Louis, the tide's turned. We'll stop for the night."

Louis nodded. "Of course."

His voice was even, but Thorgrim saw that his eyes were red, and tears were rolling down the man's face.

Chapter Twenty-Two

Here I stand and await thee!
Ne'er metest thou with sturdier
Hero since Hrungnir was slain.

Greybeard and Thor
The Poetic Edda

They pulled the dead men off the road and into the tall grass. Bragi and Huginn and Muninn relieved the corpses of their purses and arm rings and any other silver they could find. Odd and Amundi relieved them of their mail and swords and seaxes. The weapons were rolled in a blanket and tied to the saddle of one of the horses.

Odd took Blood-letter from where it was hidden in the wagon bed and strapped it on. They would be riding horses with saddles and bridles: there would be no pretending to be poor sheepherders now.

Bragi selected one of dead men's horses, not the best one, Odd noticed. Bragi did not strike Odd as the sort who would leave the best for others, so he suspected the sailor did not know horses well enough to choose the best. Bragi then instructed Huginn and Muninn to take the old nags that were pulling the wagon, and left the last three saddled mounts for Odd, Signy, Amundi, and Alfdis.

"Alfdis and I will ride together on this one," Amundi said, selecting one of the horses. "Odd, you and Signy each take a horse for yourself."

"No, no," Odd said. "Signy and I can share. You and Alfdis, you have your own horses."

"Oh, by all the gods!" Bragi exclaimed. "Shall we stand here and argue about who's the most polite until they come and kill us all?"

They settled the matter quickly after that, with Odd prevailing; it was agreed that he and Signy would share one mount, and Amundi and Alfdis would each have their own.

When the wagon was as well hidden as it could be, they headed out through the tall grass, south over the rolling hills toward the sea. They would have liked to ride at a flat-out gallop, put as much distance as they could between them and the hunters, but they were not entirely certain how far they had to go, and they did not want to blow the horses out by pushing them too hard for too long. Nor could Huginn and Muninn, riding on the broken-down nags of the wagon team, have possibly kept up with the fine stolen mounts the others rode. So they trotted and walked, trotted and walked, covering the hilly country as quickly as they could.

They had been walking for some time when Odd, with Signy squeezed into the saddle in front of him, found himself alongside Bragi Shipslayer. Odd was a good horseman, and he could see that Bragi was not, though Bragi was making quite an effort to hide that fact.

"Bragi," Odd said, "why do they call you 'shipslayer'? Are you a famous raider? A pirate of some sort?" He asked in part out of curiosity, in part to pass the time, and in part to get the measure of the man. It seemed they were stuck with Bragi and his companions for the time being, and so it was worth trying to plumb his depths.

"No, not a pirate," Bragi said. "And not one for going a'viking and all that raiding nonsense. I'm a sailor, was born a sailor, and I'm simply interested in carrying the goods of the world across the seas. Engla-land, Ireland, Frisia, Frankia, the lands to the east, I've sailed to all of them! And to places other men have never heard tell of. Seen things no man could imagine."

"But why 'shipslayer'?"

"Because no man has had more ships wrecked under their feet than I have!" Bragi said. "No man has stood on more decks and had more ships crumble under them than Bragi Shipslayer!"

"Is that something to be proud of?" Signy asked.

"Of course!" Bragi said, as if it was self-evident. "Why is it that I wreck ships? Because I drive them harder than any man! No one is so bold and daring in his shiphandling than me!"

"Maybe it would be worth being less daring and losing fewer ships," Odd suggested.

"Ha!" Bragi laughed. "That's what I would expect from a 'sheepherder' like you!"

They rode on in silence for a bit, Odd bracing for Bragi's next question, the one in which he asked who Odd truly was, and why those men—the king's men, it would seem—had stopped them and tried to take them prisoner. But Bragi did not ask, and when he started talking again, the subject was once more himself.

"Some ships' masters, they fear storms," Bragi continued. "And some fear rocks, or strong currents, or any of the thousand things that can kill a ship. But me? I fear nothing! I'll drive my ships through anything, and never give it a second thought. And if the gods have not taken me yet, I don't think they're likely to anytime soon."

"Hmm…" Odd said. It seemed like bad luck to him to even think such an arrogant thought about the gods, never mind speaking it out loud. But arrogance seemed to be as much a part of Bragi Shipslayer as his broad chest and massive beard, so Odd moved on to another thought.

"You have a ship now?"

"No, no," Bragi said. "I had one, a fine little knarr. Quick and handy. But the currents north of Fevik, and all those cursed shoals…. Well, anyway, the boys and me, we were off in search of a new ship. Maybe buy one, maybe get hired on as master of another."

"Is it hard for someone known as 'shipslayer' to find work driving ships?" Signy asked.

"Sometimes," Bragi said. "And sometimes men will hire me to bring their wives on a voyage, hoping I'll wreck my ship and drown them in the end."

"Do they, indeed?" Signy asked, but Odd did not care for the direction he could see this heading, so he changed the subject.

"Your men, Huginn and Muninn," he asked, "they're sailors?"

"Sailors to their very bowels," Bragi said. "Oh, I know they don't look like much, but they're good hands…have a real feel for seamanship, you know? And loyal. They stay with me because they know I'm a lucky man. Favored by the gods."

"I see," Odd said, though he was not sure he did. There was no way to know for certain how much of what Bragi Shipslayer said was true, and how much was a great steaming pile of manure. But in truth, it did not matter to Odd. Bragi was of no consequence to him, and he hoped he never would be.

The sun was starting to set when they spotted a small farm a mile or so off, so they climbed down from their horses and stretched and huddled together and discussed what they would do next.

"The fellow who owns this place, I'll wager he has good meat and ale," Bragi said, nodding toward the cluster of buildings: a decent sized hall and various outbuildings, all surrounded by a stockade fence. "Daughters, maybe. I say we seek out his hospitality for the night."

Odd shook his head. "We can't stop, not until we reach Ragi's farm. These people are strangers to us, and we don't need to put them in danger."

"Oh, I forgot," Bragi said, "the king's men are hunting you! But why would a king care so much about a couple of sheepherders? You still haven't told us. Did you bugger Halfdan's favorite ewe, Torfi Sheep-biter?"

"It's getting dark," Amundi said, ignoring Bragi. "And I'm not certain I can find Ragi's farm in the dark. Not traveling overland like this."

In the end it was decided they would stop and ask for help. Amundi and Alfdis, the least threatening of the party, approached the hall and made themselves known. After some discussion back and forth, and the gift of a dagger with gold worked into the hilt, taken off one of Halfdan's men, the farmer offered to let them rest by his hearth and then to escort them to Ragi's home, which he said he knew well and was not far.

It was full dark when they headed out again. The farmer, whose name was Hogni, and one of his men, led the way over the uneven ground with torches held aloft. It was slow going, but it was not far, as Hogni had said. He had just lit his third torch when they came up over a rise and saw a compound in a low place between the hills, with a great bonfire burning on the open ground outside a long, hump-roofed hall. Various buildings, scattered around the grounds, were enclosed by a great oval of a palisade fence. Smoke coming out of the hall's gable end suggested a fire burning vigorously in the hearth, as did the light around the frame of the door.

"Ragi's farm?" Odd asked in a low voice, leaning toward Amundi.

"Yes, I believe so," Amundi said. "I don't know it well, but this looks like what I recall."

They rode on, and as they approached the gate in the palisade, the farmer called out a pleasant greeting to a man looking out over the top. The man called back, then disappeared, and a moment later the gate swung open.

They continued into the compound as the door to the hall opened and Ragi stepped out into the night. The light from the bonfire fell on his face, which had seen many hard years and looked it. The troubles of the past year, the rebellion and King Halfdan's suppression of it, had cut deeper still, Odd could see. Despite that, Ragi was smiling, and he lifted his one hand in greeting.

"Hogni!" he called to the farmer who had led them south. "What brings you here at this hour?"

"These travelers," the farmer said, gesturing toward the people riding behind him. "They said they were friends of yours, which I did not believe, since no man could be friends with anyone so unpleasant as you. But I agreed to bring them anyway."

Ragi laughed. "You agreed because they paid you, no doubt! You would never do an act of kindness for free! Well, climb down and have some meat and ale while I see who these folk are who claim to be my friends."

The farmer Hogni swung down off his horse and the others did as well. With Odd's help Signy untangled herself from the saddle and slid to the ground and Odd followed behind. He felt the apprehension growing: he had no idea what greeting he would get. Ragi was a good man, loyal and bold, but much had happened since the two of them had last met, and Odd's presence here put Ragi and his entire household in great danger.

But there was nothing for it now, so Odd stepped forward, his hand extended, and said in a loud voice, "Ragi, it's me. Torfi Oddson. You remember me, right? It's been some time."

Ragi took Odd's hand and shook, but Odd saw the confusion in the man's face. The bonfire was illuminating them in strange, deep shadows, and Odd knew that, beyond the unfamiliar false name, he was much changed since Ragi had last seen him. Changed well beyond the thick, unkempt beard and long, tangled hair he now wore.

And then Ragi recognized him. His eyes went wide and his mouth dropped open and he stared, speechless. Then he grabbed Odd with his remaining hand, pulled him close, threw his arm around him and hugged him, so tight that Odd could smell the odor of wood smoke and roast meat and wool from Ragi's tunic.

They stood like that for a moment and Ragi said, low, in Odd's ear, "Oh, by the gods, I had thought to never see you again!" Then he released Odd and stepped back, looking over at Amundi. "And you, too, my old friend!" he shouted and hugged Amundi in the same manner, then stepped back again and addressed the lot of them. "Come in, come in! There's a fine fire burning, and food and drink!"

He led the way inside. There was indeed a great fire burning in the hearth that ran down the center of the hall, and a dozen of Ragi's men were seated on benches, drinking, while servants bustled around.

"Listen here!" Ragi called to the men by the fire. "You fine fellows remember my dear friend, Torfi Oddson, I'll warrant!" Ragi gestured toward the newcomers. The men on the benches raised their cups in greeting, but it was not at all clear to Odd that they did recognize him, though he had met them all and fought beside them. But that was just as well. He did not care to be recognized.

"Ragi, I don't think you know these fellows," Odd said, indicating Bragi and his men. "This is Bragi Shipslayer, who tells us he's the greatest sailor to ever stand on ship's a deck, and two of his crewmen, Huginn and Muninn."

"'Huginn and Muninn'?" Ragi said with a smile. "It's good to meet you. You may fly over to the fire and have some ale. And Bragi Shipslayer? I am Ragi Oleifsson, and while I might not be the greatest sailor to live, I've spent time enough at sea."

"Well, then, you're a good man as far as I'm concerned," Bragi said. "And let me say to my sheepherder friend here," he continued, turning to Odd and speaking more softly than was his wont. "If you're playing this game of 'Torfi Oddson' for my sake, you may as well stop, since I'm quite certain that you're the notorious Odd Thorgrimson. In fact, I'd wager Huginn and Muninn's lives on it."

Odd felt as if he had been punched in the gut. He frowned and was not sure how to react, what to say: deny it? Run a sword through Bragi? But Amundi stepped up before he could do anything.

"Now, why would you say that, Bragi Shipslayer?" he asked.

"Ha!" Bragi laughed. "Well, any fool can see neither of you are sheepherders, no matter how much sheep shit you roll around in! So, it makes a fellow wonder why four people would be traveling about in such disguises. Now, there's been a lot of talk in the past few months about this fugitive Odd Thorgrimson. Everywhere I go I hear of him. And lots of fancy fellows on horseback asking after him. So I had my suspicions. But that bloody little tussle we had on the road, that pretty much gave me my answer."

"Bloody tussle on the road?" Ragi asked. "Odd, have you been tugging on the king's beard again?"

"We met some of Halfdan's fellows," Amundi said. "It did not end well for them. And to be fair, we have Bragi here to thank for that. If not for him there's a good chance our corpses would be laid out in Halfdan's hall right now. So, Bragi, I reckon you've earned the truth. I'm Amundi Thorsteinsson. This is Odd Thorgrimson."

"And you've earned my hospitality!" Ragi slapped Bragi on the shoulder. "Come, have a seat, have some meat and ale!"

He led them over to the fire burning in the hearth and set them near the head of it, next to him, and gestured for the servants to bring refreshment. They ate and drank and told Ragi the tale of their fight on the road to Grefstad, and then Odd and Amundi told Ragi what had happened before that, the escape from Halfdan's camp, the hiding, the market at Rykene.

Ragi shook his head as he listened to the story. "We had no idea what had become of you," he said. "Halfdan's men were through here, of course, looking for you. Several times. Turned my farm upside down and plundered it like they were raiding some village in Frankia. Same with all the others here abouts. Since we stood up to Halfdan, he's been careful to let us know how easily he can crush us all if he cares to."

"He doesn't want us to forget how powerful he is," Amundi said.

"You're right," Ragi said. "He wants us to believe he's powerful. But I'm not sure he's proved it."

"How do you mean?"

"Well," Ragi said, "Halfdan has never done battle with us, never really done battle with us, save for his attack on Odd's farm. And that time we thrashed him bad. When we took his great hall at Grømstad, there was no battle. Odd gave himself up." Ragi looked at Odd and nodded. "Most selfless act I've ever seen," he continued. "You knew what Halfdan would do to you, how he would make an example of you. In the end it was worse than I would have imagined. Probably worse than you imagined. But you took it, just so Halfdan would let the rest of us go free. I can't say I was happy about your choice. I'm still not. But it was bold. You sacrificed everything for the rest of us, and none of us have forgotten that."

"I could do nothing else," Odd said. "I led you into that folly."

"We're not slaves," Ragi said, "despite what Halfdan thinks. You didn't command us to follow you. We followed because we thought you were right. We followed because Halfdan can't be allowed to think he can treat free men like they're his servants. We wanted to teach him a lesson. And we did. But I fear it's the wrong lesson. Now he thinks he can crush us at his will. I think he's wrong."

They fell silent for a moment, drinking and staring into the fire. Then Odd spoke again.

"I thank you for your words, Ragi. I appreciate them. But I'm still sorry for the trouble I led you all into."

"Don't be a fool," Ragi said. "The trouble didn't start with you. All of us, we've been chaffing for years under Halfdan. I think Halfdan's kept clear of you, mostly, because you're the son of Thorgrim Night Wolf, grandson of Ornolf the Restless. But they're gone now, and that made you fair game. Or at least your father's property, which Halfdan lusted after, became fair game. Isn't that right, Amundi?"

"That's right," Amundi said. "You sparked the fire, Odd, but the embers were burning long before."

"And as for me," Ragi said, "I was as grateful as a man could be once the fighting started. This farming? This is no life. I made a fortune in raiding, and lost this while doing it." He held up his left arm. The sleeve of his tunic slipped down, revealing the stump where his left hand had once lived.

"So, my raiding days were over, and all that was left was to sit around here smelling like pigs and cows and wishing I was fighting like a man. Or at least that was how it was before you led us to take up arms."

"I'll drink to that!" Bragi lifted his cup up high. "To feel alive, a man has to be fighting, or have a ship or a woman bucking under him!"

"You know it, friend!" Ragi said, lifting his cup in solidarity.

Odd stared into the flames and considered Ragi's words. He wasn't sure what to think about them. He had been carrying the guilt for having brought Halfdan's wrath down on his neighbors. It never occurred to him that they might welcome it, that they had been looking for a reason to fight.

"Well, I'm glad to hear those words," he said at last. "But what's next, I don't know. Me and Amundi, we were traveling from town to town, disguised…or so we thought…trying to get a sense for how things lay, to see if we had to go back into the high country and keep hiding out. It seemed like we were doing all right until Halfdan's men caught us on the road."

Ragi shook his head. "Not Halfdan's men, I don't think. As I understand it, Halfdan's gone back to Grømstad. He's given up looking for you. For now."

Odd and Amundi exchanged glances. "If those weren't Halfdan's men, I can't guess who they were," Amundi said. "They weren't bandits, that's for certain. They were looking for us. And they were mounted and well-armed."

"Skorri Thorbrandsson's men, maybe," Ragi said.

"Skorri?" Odd said. "Skorri is Halfdan's man."

Ragi held up his one hand in a gesture of uncertainty. "I only hear rumors, hiding out on my farm here with the women and the servants. Broddi!" That last he shouted toward his men seating along the hearth. A big man with a thick black beard stood and stepped over.

"Yes, Ragi?"

Ragi looked at Odd and Amundi. "Broddi here has been abroad of late; he brings me news of the great, wide world. Broddi, what is this you were telling me about Skorri and Halfdan?"

"Heard it in Fevik, Ragi," Broddi said. "A week or two back. They're saying that Skorri's left Halfdan's service, gone off on his own. I don't know why. Some think he's afraid of what Halfdan'll do to him for letting Odd here escape. Which makes sense. I wouldn't care to go back to Halfdan and tell him I let his prisoner get away."

"Skorri didn't exactly let Odd get away, but that's neither here nor there," Amundi said.

"Don't know about that," Broddi said. "I just heard rumors that Skorri's gone rogue, and he and his men are hunting for Odd. Maybe hoping to get back into Halfdan's favor by bringing Odd in. Oh, and I'm sure Halfdan wants you dead too, Amundi. I don't mean to give offense."

"No offense given," Amundi said. "I'm honored to think they're looking to butcher me as well. In fact, they nearly did."

"Well, whoever's hunting for us, they'll come looking soon," Odd said. "The horseman who got away, he won't know where we went, but he'll know we're close by. And you can bet Skorri or whoever it is will be making a thorough search. So we won't put you in any more danger than we already have, Ragi. We'll be off on the morrow at first light."

"Don't be ridiculous," Ragi said. "You're as safe here as anywhere. Safer, I should think. As for me and my men, we'd be happy for the chance to fight."

"We can't ask that of you," Amundi said, but Ragi stood and looked down the length of the hall and called to his men.

"You men, tell me, would you rather live safe as pig farmers or die like men?"

This was met with loud cheers and shouts, lifted cups and spilled ale and calls of "Die!" and "Let us die like men!"

Ragi sat again and smiled at Odd and Amundi. "There's your answer," he said.

"Ah, it's good to be with such men as these!" Bragi said, lifting his cup as well. "Women are fine and all, but a man needs the company of those who'll fight!"

"Tell my wife that," Odd said, "and she'll gut you like a fish."

"Ha! I don't doubt it!" Bragi said. "Spirited woman. If Halfdan kills you, I'll take her to sea with me."

"Very well, then, we'll die like men," Amundi said. "But perhaps the Norns will spin their threads a bit longer, and death will not come so soon."

"Not for us to know," Ragi said. "I just hope they let me take Halfdan down with me."

They drank to that, and then they drank to other things. And then they ate more of Ragi's fine fare and drank some more. Some of Ragi's men staggered off to sleep, some collapsed on the floor where they sat. Odd was soon looking for a way to extract himself, to make his excuse to stagger off to bed where Signy was already asleep, but Ragi did not seem to be slowing down in the least.

It was Amundi who saved him, or nearly did. "Ragi, you are the finest of hosts, but I must be off to bed," he said, setting his cup down on the bench.

"One more drink, Amundi, and then —" Ragi began, but he was cut off as the door flew open and Ragi's man, the one who had been standing guard by the gate, charged in, slammed the door, and barred it shut. The men by the hearth looked up as the guard turned, and in the light of the fire they could see that his face was red from having sprinted across the grounds.

"Men at the gate, Ragi!" he said. "They came in the dark, on foot. I didn't see them until they were right there!"

"Who?" Ragi asked.

"Don't know! I called out but they didn't reply, save for one who demanded I open the gate. Which I didn't."

"Good choice." Ragi stood. "But I can guess who this might be."

"Skorri?" Amundi said. "How could he possibly have found us here? So soon?"

There was shouting outside the hall and pounding on the door, and then a voice came loud through the thick oak. "Ragi Oleifsson! In the name of King Halfdan, open this door!"

Ragi looked over at Odd and Amundi and shot them a look of genuine amusement, a crooked smile and eyebrows raised. He took two steps toward the door. "In the name of King Halfdan?" he called back. "Who is this?"

"Skorri Thorbrandsson! I have thirty warriors with me, and we'll break down this door if you don't open it immediately! I know you have the fugitives in there! Send them out and we'll be on our way!"

Ragi looked over at the guard who had been on the wall. "Thirty armed warriors?"

"Seemed about that," the man said.

"Hmm…. I'm impressed." He turned back to the door. "Skorri! Do you really speak for Halfdan? I heard rumors that you left his service!"

There was a pause after that, and then Skorri called back, "I am the king's man, and I'm here on his business! This will not go well for you, Ragi, if you defy me!"

"Well, I have forty armed warriors!" Ragi shouted, which was about double the actual number. "And if you try to come through that door, things will not go well for you!"

The pounding on the door resumed, but Ragi ambled back toward the fire. His men were on their feet now, some with weapons drawn. None, Odd noted, looked terribly concerned.

"Well, my friends, it looks like the time has come," Ragi said and his men nodded and those holding weapons slipped them back into the scabbards. Others picked up the cups they had set down, drained them, and set them down again.

"Let's make ready," Ragi said next.

Without a word, and to Odd's surprise, the men all walked off in different directions as if they were heading to bed. A few moments later they assembled again. Some had bundles rolled up in blankets and lashed tight, others carried saddlebags filled to capacity, or sacks of cloth or leather. A few sat down on the benches again. Most continued to eat and drink.

The pounding on the door, which had stopped for a moment, now resumed, but just briefly, then Skorri shouted again. "Ragi! I am not a patient man! Send the fugitives out, or by the gods, I'll put your hall to the torch!"

Odd turned to Ragi. "I'm going out," he said, and pulled Blood-letter from its scabbard. "I'm happy to go and die, but I will not bring you and your men and the women with me. Throw open the door and I'll go out fighting. Die the way a man should die."

"I'm sure you'll have your chance, but not this night," Ragi said. "If you take one step toward that door, I'll kill you myself."

"Skorri's here for me," Odd said. "I can't have your blood and the blood of the others on my hands."

"See here," Ragi said, "You won't save anyone by going out. Skorri will burn my hall and drag me to Halfdan no matter what you do. Or what I do."

Odd pressed his lips together but said nothing. Ragi was right, of course. There was no way out for any of them, save going out together through the door and fighting to the last man.

"We can't stay here and burn," Amundi said. "At some point, we have to go."

"Yes," Ragi said. "At some point." He turned to Odd. "But this is my hall, and we go when I say. Trust me."

Suddenly Odd felt foolish, standing there with his sword in his hand. He nodded and slid the blade back into the sheath.

It was then that they heard the crackling. It was not obvious at first, not over the sound of the fire in the hearth and the soft talk of the men. But soon it grew louder, too loud to miss, and there was no question as to what it was: burning thatch.

They looked up just as the first of the flames ate their way through the roof. It was dark, high up in the rafters, but suddenly there was light, brilliant and orange, and it spread and turned more yellow as the open flame worked its way up through the dried reeds.

"He told the truth. He's not a patient man," Ragi said.

Odd put his hand on Blood-letter's pommel. "We should go. Soon," he said.

"Soon," Ragi said. "But not yet."

There was more crackling, more spreading light at the far end of the hall, and they looked up to see that the thatched roof there was starting to burn as well. Near where they stood flaming clumps of thatch were dropping onto the dirt floor, making an archipelago of little fires. A pile of blankets stacked by the wall burst into flames and the fire reached up and ignited a tapestry hanging there, and suddenly the dark hall was flooded with brilliant light.

The flames moved to a pile of fresh straw and that, too, erupted into an impressive conflagration. A few men stared at the spreading fire, but no one moved to put it out. There was no point in trying. It would not be long before the entire hall was engulfed, and there was nothing that anyone could do to stop it now.

"Very well," Ragi said at last. "Let's go. Odd, you can unhand your sword. You won't need it anytime soon."

Odd frowned, but he did as he was told, taking his hand off Blood-letter's hilt.

"You recall, of course, Odd, when Halfdan burned your hall?" Ragi said. "And you recall how surprised we all were when it turned out you had dug a tunnel out of it? Well, I have to tell you, when I saw that, I thought, now here's a very clever idea! I thought, men like Halfdan and Skorri, they so enjoy burning people out of their halls…what a smart thing to make ready for it! So as soon as I returned to my farm, I did just that. Broddi, go ahead!"

All heads turned to Broddi, who stood near the far wall beside a great oak chest. Broddi nodded and two men grabbed onto the chest and with some effort shoved it clear. Then Broddi jammed an iron bar into the floor and levered it down. A short section of wooden planks, covered with dirt, was lifted free and the men who had moved the chest grabbed it and tossed it aside.

"Lead the way, Broddi, and the women will go behind you," Ragi said. "I'll let Odd go last, because if I don't, he'll argue with me, and we don't have time. Now let's go!"

Broddi nodded. He pulled a flaming torch from its holder and stepped down onto what Odd guessed was a ladder hidden in the entrance to the tunnel. The big man disappeared into the hole just as a section of roof at the far end of the hall fell in a great welter of flame.

Chapter Twenty-Three

Tall ships, beyond a number that could reckon them—
In vulgar tongue the custom is to call them "barques,"
The Seine's deep surge was packed so full with ships like these—
That you could wonder where the river'd gone...

Abbo of Saint-Germain

How many years? Louis de Roumois watched the river's shore pass in front of him, like something familiar only from a dream. *How many years?*

He could figure it out if he traced the time back, ticked off the many thrusts and parries he had endured since his father had died and his brother, Eberhard, had assumed the dukedom. The dissolution of the horse guard, the exile to Glendalough, the miserable years during which the abbot and the brothers tried to make a monk out of him. His time with the Northmen. Failend. Thorgrim.

He could figure it out if he tried, standing against *Sea Hammer*'s mast, watching the green fields of Frankia slip by, the smattering of villages, the steeples of the little parish churches standing proud, the fishing boats pulled up on the shores. But his mind was too full to organize his thoughts in such a way.

It had been a long time, a very long time; he knew that much at least. The profound ache for this land, a longing such as he had never longed for anything else in life, had been his constant companion. It was like a ringing in the ears or a pain deep inside: always there, not debilitating, but constant and grinding. It seemed as if his years in exile had lasted longer than his years in Roumois, when he had been the reckless second son of a duke, before redeeming himself in early manhood as leader of the horse guard, protector of the common folk.

Now he was back, living a moment that had been playing out in his mind since the last time he stood on a ship's deck and watched those shores pass by. That vessel had not been a Northman's longship, of course, but a plodding Frankish merchant vessel, carried by wind and tide down the Seine out to open water, and then across the narrow seas to Ireland.

Louis was a markedly different creature now from the man he was then. Louis, pre-exile, had never been farther from his home than Paris, had rarely known anyone who was not a fellow Frank. His life had been fighting and drinking and whoring, the life of a soldier, and he loved it. When it was taken from him, as he watched that life and all of Frankia disappear in the merchant ship's wake, he had been consumed with rage, a boiling, steaming rage, so that he thought he might burst.

Now he shook his head in confusion as all those thoughts tumbled over each other. He had spent countless hours envisioning his return, but in his mind, it had never played out like this. He had imagined triumph. He had imagined great throngs of people rallying to his side, the thrill of the conqueror, Caesar returning to Rome. He had imagined with delicious anticipation the feel of his sword passing through Eberhard's guts.

But this reality was none of those things, and thoughts of triumph or vengeance seemed to have fled. All he wanted to do was to fling himself down on the rich, green fields and weep.

"Louis!" Thorgrim called, jerking him out of his reverie. He looked aft and realized that he had indeed been weeping. He cheeks were wet with tears and his eyes ached and he was sure they were red as a sunset.

"Come back here," Thorgrim said

Louis nodded and started making his way aft, walking with care between the rows of men seated at the oars. His steps were unsteady. Thorgrim was looking out toward the riverbank and Louis took that moment to wipe the tears from his face with the sleeve of his tunic, but he knew he could not hide the fact that he had been crying.

Oh, damn him and damn all of them, Louis thought. He was too far gone in his feelings to care about any of that.

"Louis, the tide's turned. We'll stop for the night," Thorgrim said.

Louis could see the surprise on Thorgrim's face at the sight of him: wet cheeks, red eyes. He wondered if the heathen would make some comment, some jibe, but Thorgrim said nothing more.

"Of course," Louis said, not sure why Thorgrim was bothering to tell him this. Thorgrim did not often solicit other men's opinions on how to manage his fleet. In fact, he never did.

"We'll need some place to beach the ships," Thorgrim went on. "Some place we can defend, if need be. Is there such a place nearby?"

Louis frowned and looked forward, past the bow, at the river ahead of them. His patrols had often taken them this far east, and he knew the roads and the towns as if they were his ancestral home, but he had paid less attention to the river itself.

"Yes, I know of one," Louis said, remembering in just that moment. "A mile upstream, maybe less. There's a great sandbar on the south side of the river. Once, it extended out from the shore, but when last I was here the current had scoured a channel so the sandbar was cut off from the riverbank. The only way onto the sandbar then was by boat."

"Perfect," Thorgrim said.

"Perfect, if the sandbar is still there," Louis added the caveat, "and the channel."

Many things had changed in the years that Louis had been away, but not, as it happened, the shape of the sandbar. They found it right where Louis had suggested, and it still consisted of a stretch of yellow sand jutting up from the current and surrounded by water on all sides, an island in the river. It was a bit of a tight fit for all five ships, but they managed to run their bows up onto the dry ground and set anchors at the end of long ropes to keep them there.

Along with the ships, a considerable amount of driftwood had lodged on the sand, and soon it was turned into a massive fire. A couple of oxen, butchered in Engla-land and stowed down aboard *Blood Hawk*, were cooking over the flames, and casks of ale and mead were rolled out and stove in. There was an exuberance in the air that Louis had not seen among the heathens for some time, and he guessed it was due to their successfully crossing the narrow seas, and their not having to sleep over deep water again, with all the pagan worries that came with that.

Louis, too, was pleased to sleep on dry land. He did not like sleeping at sea any more than the heathens did. But his concern was not the goblins and spirits that the Northmen feared, but rather drowning, which he considered an altogether more reasonable worry.

Thorgrim had around three hundred warriors under his command, and soon the sandbar was a loud and raucous place, strewn with empty casks. Louis found one and stood it up as close to the fire as was comfortable and sat, looking into the flames, letting his mind wander away.

He smiled at the irony of his being there, and in that company. The sandbar was often used by the heathen raiders who rowed their longships up the Seine. That was why Louis knew about it. He had witnessed bacchanals just such as this, watching them from the cover of the trees on shore, him and his fellow horse soldiers. He and Ranulf would discuss where the heathens might land, and how the chevaliers would drive them back into the sea. And more often than not, they did just that.

If there was one thing he would never have imagined, it was that he would be on the sandbar, among the heathens, looking for a way to launch an attack on Roumois.

*So many ghosts…*he thought. Everywhere he looked, every mile of that river, he saw the spirits of a life past.

He sat for some time staring into the flames and his reverie was not disturbed. It rarely was. He had lived and fought for nearly two years with these men, but still they largely ignored him. He suspected that most did not know what to make of him, how they should feel toward this odd young man. A Frank. A Christian. Someone quite out of keeping with who they were and what they understood of the world.

Even more to the point, Louis imagined, they did not know what Thorgrim Night Wolf felt about him. There were times when he and Thorgrim appeared to be friends and times when Thorgrim had tried to kill him. Those who had been a long time in their company knew that Failend had once been Louis's lover, and then she had been Thorgrim's. That would make men wonder how Thorgrim felt about his former prisoner. It certainly made Louis wonder. Thorgrim was not an easy man to read.

Louis was still pondering that when Thorgrim came walking up the sandbar, two cups of ale in his hands. He handed them to Louis, turned another barrel on end and sat, and then took one cup back. He took a long drink and joined Louis in staring into the fire.

"Will we reach this home of yours tomorrow?" Thorgrim asked.

"We should. It's maybe fifteen miles upriver. Can we travel fifteen miles in a day?"

"If the tide runs as I think it will, we'll be there before midday," Thorgrim said. They were silent again for a moment and then he said, "Grifo says there'll likely be no men-at-arms there. Do you think he's right? Is he telling the truth?"

"I don't know," Louis said. "He's certainly right that my brother will have gone to Paris. He would not miss the arrival of the king of Wessex. And Grifo's right that he'll take a company of his men-at-arms with him. Whether or not he'll leave warriors behind for defense, I can't say. I don't know what sort of army my brother has."

Thorgrim nodded. "This must be very strange for you."

"It is," Louis agreed. "It is that."

"My people, we don't suffer wrongs," Thorgrim said. "We seek vengeance. It's who we are. It's part of our laws. So I understand your need to do this thing. But I thought you Christians were not like that."

Louis smiled. "Good Christians are not like that."

"If there's fighting, then you'll be fighting on the side of Northmen. Which you've done many times. But this time you'll be fighting against Franks. Is that something you can do?"

"I don't know," Louis said. "I don't know anything. Two weeks ago, in Engla-land, this was all as clear as water from a spring. Now it's like mud."

To Louis's surprise, Thorgrim reached over and patted him on the knee. "It'll be clear again," he said. "When it's time to act, it'll be clear what you must do, and you'll do it."

He left Louis there, and Louis remained on his barrel for some time longer, staring into the slowly dying flames, looking at his past as if it were a great fresco on a cathedral wall, and trying to peer into his future. Finally, with only the hardiest of the Northmen still pouring ale down their throats, he stumbled off to where he had made his bed on the ground.

He stretched out on the blanket he had laid on the sand and pulled another over him and let the exhaustion drain away. He was grateful to be on solid ground and not trying to sleep on the rolling deck of a ship, but when he closed his eyes, it seemed as if the entire sandbar was heaving and pitching as much as *Sea Hammer* ever did.

"That's damned unfair," he said out loud. He wondered if he would be able to sleep. He wondered if he would puke right there in his bed. He was still wondering that as he fell off into a deep and dreamless slumber.

He woke the next morning to the familiar sound of men preparing what the Northmen called dagmál, and loading gear and supplies back aboard the ships. He stood and stretched and wandered off to the water's edge to relieve himself, and then he found a bowl of porridge and a chunk of bread to break his fast.

He was still eating when Thorgrim came over, a comb in his hand, which he ran through his long salt and pepper hair. This habit of washing and combing was something that the Northmen seemed to do more than any other people Louis had ever known.

"Grifo says we should arm ourselves before we get underway. Be ready for an attack at any time," Thorgrim said.

"That seems wise," Louis said. "I don't think we'll be attacked on the river. The Franks aren't much for doing battle aboard ships, at least not where Northmen are concerned. But any place we go ashore, there's no telling where soldiers might be lying in wait. It's not as if they don't know we're here."

"Very good," Thorgrim said. He began barking orders and soon the crews of the five ships were outfitting themselves with mail or leather or whatever sort of armor they boasted, hanging weapons from belts, settling helmets on heads. The ships were pushed out into the river and the men took their places at the oars and soon the fleet was underway again. Happily the tide was flooding now, and the rowing was not so hard.

Louis stood near the break of the afterdeck in case Thorgrim had need of his local knowledge. He leaned against the side of the ship and stared at the shoreline crawling past. Each mile brought them closer to le Château de Roumois, and the closer they drew to his home, the more populated the land became with the ghosts of his past.

But the ghosts seemed to be the only creatures wandering the shore. He could see no people, and had not seen any for the entire morning in any of the little villages they passed. There were not even signs of people: no smoke from chimneys, no sounds of work, no animals.

"Where is everyone?" Thorgrim asked, noticing what Louis had just noticed. "Has there been a plague?"

Yes, a plague of Northmen, Louis thought, but he kept that thought to himself.

"They're probably ten miles from the river by now," Louis said. "They've been watching us for a day and a half. Everyone's fled as far from the water as they can get."

"That's fine with me," Grifo offered. "We don't need a welcoming party. And for Thorgrim and our friends from the north, if they intend to plunder Roumois, it will make things that much easier."

Louis looked at Thorgrim. It had not occurred to him that the Northmen might sack the town and the château, but Thorgrim was shaking his head.

"We're not here for plunder," he said. "We're here to collect what was promised us."

Louis turned and looked forward, past the tall figurehead that graced *Sea Hammer*'s bow, and the sight made him suck in his breath. Above the oaks and maples rose the spires that marked le Château de Roumois, the tall steeple of the church and the tops of the four towers at the corners of the walls surrounding the great house. It was a sight as familiar to him as anything in life. He felt the tears welling up again and he fought them down.

"There it is," Grifo said, nodding. "Le Château de Roumois," and Louis was grateful that Grifo had said it because he did not trust himself to speak.

Thorgrim made a grunting noise as he looked at the spires. "There's a place where we can land our ships here?"

This time Grifo did not speak, because he could not answer such a question. Louis swallowed hard. "Yes," he said, and he was pleased to hear that his voice sounded reasonably normal. "There's a dock extending out into the river that will accommodate three of your ships, I should think. At least there was the last time I was here. The other ships can run up onto the shore. It's soft mud. I've seen many ships do it."

Thorgrim nodded and pushed the tiller over a bit as *Sea Hammer* swept into the last bend in the river before they would reach the château. He looked over his shoulder to see that the others were still following in his wake.

Louis's eyes were fixed on the shore now. He pressed his lips together and tightened his grip on the sheer strake until his hand ached with the effort. Every inch of that river, every tree and rock and open space, was perfectly familiar to him. He was living out the moment that he had been dreaming of for such a long time, and it all seemed both completely normal and completely unreal.

The ship rounded the bend in the river and the shoreline seemed to open up as if a curtain had been drawn back and there, across a quarter mile of flawlessly tended grass, stood the great stone walls of le Château de Roumois, thirty feet high, and behind them, rising much higher still, the great house. Stone-built, three stories, with three lines of windows in perfect symmetry and columns like giant sentinels around the massive front door. It looked as if it had been standing there since creation.

Louis's head was spinning, his stomach turning over. He felt a cold sweat on his forehead and his back and he knew his hands would tremble if he let go of the sheer strake. He took a deep gulp of air and held it, then let it out slowly.

"There's the dock, there," Thorgrim said. "There's water enough for us?" Louis started at Thorgrim's voice and looked aft.

"There's water enough for us at the dock?" Thorgrim asked again.

Louis turned the other way. *Sea Hammer*'s bow was aimed at the heavy-built wooden dock that jutted out into the river from the grassy bank, unchanged from what he remembered.

"There always was," Louis said.

Thorgrim nodded. "Listen here!" he called forward to the men at the oars. "We're going alongside that dock. I don't see anyone ashore, but it doesn't mean they aren't waiting for us. Tie the ship up quick and get ashore, weapons in hand! Make a line, be ready!"

Thorgrim's words, his preparations were a welcome distraction. Louis climbed onto the sheer strake and balanced himself with one hand on the backstay, as he had seen Thorgrim do many times. From that slightly elevated perch, he could see over the heads of the rowers, could take in the great stretch of open land that surrounded the château.

The grounds were kept that way both for the beauty of it and to deprive an approaching enemy of cover. But now, if the château's defenders hoped to attack the Northmen as they were getting off their ships, they would have to run over hundreds of yards of open ground, fully exposed, just to get to the fight.

Louis looked down, and it seemed to him as if Thorgrim was going to miss the dock entirely, but Thorgrim pushed the tiller hard over and *Sea Hammer* swung to larboard, her bow heading for the riverbank.

"Oars in!" Thorgrim cried and the two banks of oars came sliding in through the row ports as the ship's momentum carried it toward shore.

He turned too soon, Louis thought. On that heading it seemed *Sea Hammer* would hit the riverbank before she came alongside the dock. But the current pushed the ship sideways as fast as her momentum carried her forward, and her starboard side touched the pilings that supported the dock as gently as a woman's touch.

The ship had not yet come to a stop when the first of her crew were over the side, vaulting onto the dock with shields on arms. They hurried down the wooden boards to the shore while others made the ship fast and then raced after them. Thorgrim let go of the tiller and grabbed his shield. He nodded to Louis and Grifo and the three of them clambered over the side and hurried down the dock after the others.

The Northmen advanced up the lawn, a hundred feet or so, and formed into a line. It was not exactly a shield wall, but could become one in an instant if need be. Behind them, Louis heard the sounds of the other ships coming alongside the dock, more footsteps on the wooden planks, and splashing as the smaller ships went up onto the muddy banks.

The air was filled with shouting and the stamp of feet and the clash of weapons and mail as the Northmen stormed ashore and braced for a possible enemy assault. And then it was quiet as the raiders stood ready, but no enemy came. A few moments of that, then shields were lowered, postures became more relaxed, and a soft buzz of talk spread among the men.

"Not much of a greeting for the prodigal son," Grifo said.

"No," Louis agreed. In truth, he had had no idea what to expect. A joyous welcome, perhaps, or a violent attack. Neither would have surprised him. But he had not imagined that his return would bring nothing at all.

He and Thorgrim and Grifo stood at the center of the line, swords in hand. Thorgrim straightened, slid Iron-tooth back into its scabbard, and looked at Louis with an expression that said, *Now what?*

"I guess we had better go in," Louis said, nodding toward the château. "There must be some food and drink left. They couldn't have taken it all."

They formed up in a swine array, a human arrowhead with more than a hundred men on either side and Thorgrim and Louis as the point, because Thorgrim was still wary of being caught off guard. They moved across the trimmed grass toward the big oak doors, one of only four entrances through the stone walls. They were alert as they moved, straining to hear over their own soft footfalls for any sign of attack, but they heard nothing beyond the call of the birds in the distant woods.

They paused when they reached the door, which was fifteen feet high and ten feet wide, made of massive oak planks bound together with iron straps. It was a formidable piece of work that had stood for decades and held up to at least three assaults by Northmen that Louis knew of. He was not sure how they would batter it down now.

He gestured for Thorgrim and the others to stand fast and walked carefully toward the door, his eyes on the wall above, shield ready to raise if archers were to suddenly appear over the parapet. But none did and he reached the door unscathed. He studied it for a moment, and, for the sake of due diligence, leaned against it and pushed.

To Louis's great surprise it moved, swinging ponderously half a foot on well-greased hinges. "Huh," Louis said. He put his shoulder against the oak planks and pushed harder still and the door swung farther open, revealing the familiar and deserted courtyard beyond.

"That was damned considerate of your brother, to leave it unbarred," Grifo said as he and Thorgrim stepped up beside him. They, too, ran their eyes around the courtyard, but there was nothing moving within.

"Unless they're luring us into a trap," Grifo added. "If so, this would be the place for it."

"Maybe," Louis said. "If it was me, I would not have let us get past the walls."

They moved across the courtyard, Louis leading the way, the rest of the Northmen following behind, still moving with caution, still wary, eyes searching. But they saw no living thing within the walls.

At the main entrance of the château, Louis stopped and stared at the familiar door with its elaborate ironwork and massive ring for a handle. Until that moment, he had been too occupied with the threat of attack to really consider where he was, what he was doing. But now, staring at that entranceway, smelling the scents of the courtyard and the stables and the woods and the river, the scents that had been a part of him since he was born, he felt the rush of emotions come over him once again.

Before he had a chance to think any more about it, he stepped forward, lifted the iron handle, and pushed. The door swung open with barely a sound, just as the big gate in the wall had done, and there before him he saw the marbled floor, the massive staircase, the tapestries, the chandeliers, the statuary. All of it. His home.

He stepped through the doorway and walked slowly across the floor as if stepping onto hallowed ground. His gaze moved around the massive foyer but he could see not one thing that had been changed in his absence, and he took an odd comfort from that.

Behind him he heard the soft shuffle of the Northmen's leather shoes on the marble floor as they followed him inside. He wondered if now the frenzy would begin, if now, surrounded by such opulence and facing no resistance, the heathens would begin their wanton pillaging. Louis had been with them for years and he still could not predict what they might do, how they might react.

He turned and looked behind him, and a bit of a smile crept over his lips. Thorgrim's men were staring with expressions that Louis had never seen on their faces, and he could only guess what was going through their minds. Awe, certainly. Unless they had been to Frankia before, none of them would have ever seen a building to rival le Château de Roumois. Even Thorgrim looked impressed, and that was not something Louis had often seen.

To the best of Louis's knowledge, even the most splendid of kings' halls in Thorgrim's country were still just timber and sod-built longhouses, with wooden floors if the lord was particularly wealthy. Even Winchester, the seat of the king of Wessex, was a hovel compared to Louis's ancestral home. And this was just Roumois. To these men, Paris would seem like the realm of God.

But it was not just the splendor, he suspected, that was working on their minds. The place was deserted. They had seen no one: not a man, a woman, a child, not a horse, cat or dog. There was something unsettling about that, as if all living things had been whisked away by some malevolent spirit. Louis knew the minds of the Northmen well enough to know that such unearthly silence was unnerving to them, even if they themselves did not entirely realize it.

"Harald!" Thorgrim broke the silence, his voice sounding even louder than usual as it bounced off the marble floors and the smooth stone walls. "Take some men and go around the west side of the courtyard, see if there's anything living there. Anyone or anything. Asmund, you take a look to the east. Gudrid, get some men out by the gate in the wall."

The men moved instantly, happy, no doubt, to have something to do, some action to take in that strange place. Thorgrim turned to Louis. "Is there any place in here we should search? Anything that should worry us?"

Louis frowned and shook his head. "No, it's mostly sleeping chambers, and the kitchens and such. But we could check the Great Room. Come."

He led the way across the foyer and around to the big doors to the right of the stairs. He felt as if he fit into le Château de Roumois the way a dagger fits into a well-worn sheath. Every step he made he had made a thousand times before, everything that fell under his gaze had fallen under his gaze on nearly every day of his life.

He grabbed the handles of the Great Room doors and pushed them open; they, too, swung inward with little effort. Again, it was just as he remembered: the black-and-white marble floors with inlaid mosaics around the perimeter, the ceiling thirty feet high and painted with frescoes of Biblical scenes, and portraits of ancestors Louis had never known. He ran his eyes around the cavernous space and was so taken with the sight of it that he did not immediately notice the old man sitting at the table in the center of the room. But he did at last, and he nearly jumped in surprise.

It took him a moment, staring at the man's face, but it was only because he had been caught off guard that he did not recognize him instantly.

"Hildirik?" he said, though he did not have to ask.

"Louis," the old man said. There was no hint of emotion in his voice. Not pleasure, not disdain, nothing.

Louis stepped farther into the room, his eyes on Hildirik, who sat erect in his chair with hands folded on the table. He didn't move, save for his eyes, which shifted between Louis and Thorgrim and Grifo.

"Where's my brother?" Louis asked.

"Paris," Hildirik said. "At the summons of the king. But I think you know that."

Louis nodded. Hildirik was something of a mystery. The old man seemed as much a part of le Château de Roumois as the stone walls or the pillars by the entrance. Not a servant of the old duke or Eberhard, but of Roumois itself.

"Did he take everyone in Roumois with him?" Louis asked. "You seem to be the only living thing here."

"They all went with the duke, or went off by his orders. Or fled. Every one of them," Hildirik said. "Duke Eberhard brought the best of the house guard with him to Paris, and sent others to the villages about, looking for you. There was a small garrison left here, and of course, the folk of the village and the château. But word came that you'd return leading an army of heathens, and when the heathen fleet was spotted, the garrison and the other folk collected their valuables and the livestock and fled inland." His tone remained neutral, save for the word *heathen*, which was spoken with an unmistakable note of disdain.

Louis glanced at Thorgrim to see if he had taken offense, and then realized that Hildirik, of course, was speaking Frankish, which Thorgrim could not understand. He glanced at Grifo and saw he was smiling.

"They fled so fast they left the doors unbarred," Louis said.

"No," Hildirik said. "I unbarred them. I figured you would batter them down anyway, and that seemed a hard end for doors that have been standing for a hundred years."

"When does my brother return?" Louis asked.

"I don't know," Hildirik said. "The duke does not tell me much. He doesn't trust me, not like your father did. But I should think he will be back soon."

"With the house guard?"

"With the house guard," Hildirik agreed. "And many of the king's men-at-arms too, I imagine. It's well known that you're here, of course. And I don't think you...any of you" — he gestured to include Thorgrim, Grifo, and the men outside the door — "will long be suffered to live."

Chapter Twenty-Four

This realm should not, because of Paris, be destroyed
But preserved by it and ever be in peace.
If these walls had been granted you as now they are
To us, and you'd fulfilled what you say now is just,
What would you pledge?

Abbo of Saint-Germain

The banquet hall at le Château de Roumois, like every other part of Louis's ancestral home, was unlike anything Harald had ever seen in life.

He had visited the great halls of a few of the minor kings in his home country, buildings that included sleeping chambers and store rooms and kitchens. Louis's banquet hall alone was larger than any of those. And that, of course, was but one room in the château.

The peak of the ceiling was fifty feet above their heads, topping stone walls as smooth as new-formed ice and supported by intricately carved dark wooden beams. The walls were hung with tapestries embroidered with hunting scenes and with images of ships and fish and various animals, real and mythical (or at least Harald thought they were mythical). The floor was not the worn wooden planks he was accustom to but rather polished marble punctuated here and there by mosaics, just like all the other floors he had seen in that grand home.

This must be what the All-Father's feast hall in Valhalla looks like, Harald thought, staring around with wonder while trying to seem unimpressed.

They were all there in the banquet hall, all three hundred of Thorgrim's men, and they fit easily at the long tables that ran down the center of the room. They had mostly eaten their fill. They had had to cook the meat themselves, as well as serve the wine and ale, since all the servants had fled. But that was no great hardship, and there was a vast amount of food and drink in the storerooms and kitchen.

A dais occupied the far end of the room, and Harald and Thorgrim and the other ship masters were sitting there, along with Louis and Grifo and, of course, Starri Deathless, who had invited himself. They had eaten at the table that fronted the raised platform, and then shifted their seats into a semicircle around the fire burning in the big fireplace in the wall.

"Well," said Hardbein, "I tell you, Louis, if I'd known you were master of all this, I would have been much nicer to you."

"I'm fairly sure I said it," Louis said, "and no one believed me. But the truth is, I'm master of nothing. This is all my brother's. I just get to pretend it's mine until he comes back with the king's army to take it from me."

"Was it worth coming back just for that?" Grifo asked.

"It was," Louis said. "I'd rather die on this land trying to put a sword through my traitorous brother than live on, running from him."

The Northmen all nodded. It was a sentiment they could understand and respect.

"But that's not your concern," Louis went on. "You just need to get your silver and you can go."

"Right," Gudrid said. "And how do we do that?"

Louis shrugged. "Ask for it, I suppose."

"Exactly!" Harald piped up, and all heads turned his way. His reply was louder and more enthusiastic than intended, but he had been waiting for a moment such as this to present itself, and he did not want to miss the chance.

"We must ask for it." He tried to sound more casual, as if these thoughts were just coming to him. "That son of a bitch Felix won't go out of his way to pay us. He might not even know we're here. Someone has to go to Paris and demand the silver. And honestly, I think they'll be happy to pay what they owe us, if it means we leave this country."

The others nodded. Harald spoke the truth, and no one raised any objections.

"Do you have any thoughts about who should go to Paris?" Thorgrim asked. The question was clearly rhetorical, but Harald chose to regard it as genuine.

"Well, I think I should go," Harald said. "It can't be you, Father, or any of the other ships' masters, who are obviously men of importance. The Franks would be too tempted to take you prisoner. I'm of no consequence, and I speak these foreign tongues better than any of you."

"But you don't speak Frankish," Louis said. "That will be a problem."

"I'm sure I can get by," Harald said. "Or find someone who speaks the Saxon tongue, or Irish."

"I'll go with him," Grifo said, and even Harald was surprised at that offer, which, in turn, seemed to surprise Grifo. "I have nothing to fear," he said. "I didn't betray anyone. It was Felix who told me to sail with you Northmen. I'm doing his bidding. And when I fought with you, it was to defend the West Saxon fleet. It's not as if I've joined in with you heathens. Besides, Felix owes me money as well."

"You actually think Felix will pay you what he owes you?" Thorgrim asked. "And what he owes us?"

"He might," Grifo said, "just to be rid of you. If Harald goes alone, they'll simply cut his throat. I told you, they never meant to pay. But Felix trusts me. I'm still his man, in good standing. If I'm there to ask, he might see reason."

"Why would you offer to help us?" Thorgrim asked.

Grifo shrugged. "I'm a warrior before I'm anything else. I don't like to see brave men cheated."

They were underway the next morning, with the first hint of dawn. Paris, it turned out, was a bit more than a hundred miles away, and the river was the most practical means of getting there. But there was never a thought that they would make the trip in *Dragon* or any of the longships. They needed something more innocuous than a Northman's warship to make their way unmolested up the Seine.

On the bank of the village just downstream of the château, Harald found several fishing boats to choose from. He picked one that was around twenty feet in length with places for four men at the oars and a single mast with a standing lug rig for when the breeze was favorable. It was a well-used craft, but not as battered as some of the others, and would be utterly unremarkable on the river.

Harald chose four men from the many on *Dragon*'s crew who were eager to go — Brand, of course, and a young man named Erik, another named Sten and a forth named Toke — all of whom had proven themselves to be smart and bold. They loaded supplies aboard and stashed their weapons where they were out of sight but easily had if needed. Harald hoped that his father would not tell him, again, what he should and should not do, but he knew that Thorgrim would not be able to resist, and he was right.

"Your job is to tell Felix that we're in Frankia and we want the silver that's owed to us, and then we leave," Thorgrim said. "That's all." They were standing on the riverbank, the boat crew already at the oars, Grifo standing at Harald's side.

"Yes, Father," Harald said.

"Keep your eyes open," Thorgrim continued. "The Franks might well be putting together a fleet, or an army, to come for us. We know they'll be coming for Louis. See if you can learn anything about that."

"Yes, Father."

"Listen to Grifo. These are his people. And don't do anything heroic."

"No, of course not," Harald said. They embraced and Grifo and Harald climbed down into the boat. Harald made his way aft and took the tiller and Brand, in the bow, shoved off, and a moment later they were pulling against the current, heading east. The tide was against them at first, and the going was slow, but soon a breeze sprang up and they were able to set the sail and let the wind drive them along the twisting waterway.

But that did not last. After a few miles, the river took a turn to the north at such an angle that the sail would not fill, so they took it in and turned to the oars once more. But after a while, the river's course came easterly again, and then south, and they were able to sail once more.

And so it went through the day, as the green fields and stands of woods and the little villages and tall churches passed down either side of the boat, and the quarter-mile-wide river twisted and turned and the men strained at the oars or took their ease as the gray canvas sail pushed them along.

As night came on, they ran the boat up on the riverbank where a wide pasture came down to the water, and they built a small fire on shore and cooked their evening meal. They bedded down on the shore and, having seen no one for the last three miles of river they traveled, Harald did not bother setting a watch.

He woke sometime in the predawn hours and lay motionless, listening, but he could hear nothing beyond the sounds of the country at night and his sleeping companions. He sat up and looked around. Nothing. He climbed quietly out of his bed and over to where Brand lay in deep sleep. It took a bit of doing to wake him, and happily he was too groggy to make a sound when he did.

"Are you awake?" Harald asked in a whisper, barely audible. Brand nodded his head and he seemed alert enough that Harald figured he was. "Listen, we should be in Paris on the morrow, and I have some plans for that, but I need you with me. Do you understand?"

Again, Brand nodded and, again, Harald felt reasonably certain he was awake. He outlined his thoughts quickly. He did not have to think about his words because he had already thought them through, many times. As he spoke, Brand's eyes grew wider, but he nodded along.

"That's it," Harald said when he finished. "Are you with me?"

Brand nodded again, and this time added, "Most certainly."

They were off the next morning with a favorable tide and a fair wind that pushed them upriver at a respectable speed, and once again, they spent the day alternately rowing and sailing. The shores became more populated, the villages more frequent as they made their way deeper into Frankia. They had met few boats on the water the day before, but now they crossed wakes with vessels of every sort, from boats even more humble than their own to large merchant ships bound downstream for open water.

"Not too far now, I think," Grifo said as they passed yet another village, one boasting the most impressive church they had yet seen since leaving Roumois.

Harald looked at the sun. It was late afternoon, but they could count on having light for some time to come. "Will we have time this day to do what we need to do?" he asked.

"Depends," Grifo said. "What do we need to do?"

"Talk to Felix, I suppose," Harald said. "Get him to see reason."

"We have time to talk to him," Grifo said. "If he's available. There will never be enough time to get him to see reason, unless it's in his own interest to do so."

"We'll make sure he understands it is," Harald said. "It's always in everyone's best interest to not make my father angry. Felix knows that already."

They rowed on, and the signs of population—traffic on the river and on the shore, houses and other buildings, livestock, columns of smoke rising from farther inland—grew more numerous. The river which had been running northeast turned east again for a ways, then swung southeast and, suddenly, there in front of them, was Paris.

The city sat on an island in the middle of the wide river, an island ringed by a massive stone wall with parapets along its whole length. Behind the wall Harald could see towered churches and other magnificent buildings rising higher even than le Château de Roumois, higher than any building Harald had ever seen. Between those great structures, the rooftops of lesser buildings crowded together so it looked as if there could be no room for streets to run between them.

To the north and south of the island, low bridges spanned the Seine, connecting the island to the mainland, which was also dense with all manner of structures. A few dozen ships were anchored in the river, and as their boat drew closer, Harald recognized some of the ships that had come with them from Engla-land, ships he had last seen when they sailed off and left him and his fellow Northmen to fight the Frisian raiders alone.

"Well," Grifo said, "what do you think?"

Harald shook his head. He was not finding the words. He had never imagined that there were cities such as this. He had been to Hedeby; he had been to Dubh-lin and Winchester. He had thought that those places were impossibly large, impossibly crowded with buildings and streets and people, but they were mere villages compared to this.

They pulled on toward the city, Harald and Brand and Erik and Sten and Toke staring open-mouthed around them. Grifo watched the banks of the island as they approached, directing Harald where to steer the boat. They pulled around to the south side, where docks jutted out from the shore and ships and boats of every size were made fast. Harald could see tied up among the crowd of vessels the large, ornate ship that had carried the king of Wessex across the narrow seas, and a few others of that fleet, but there was little activity aboard any of them. Harald had no doubt that the king and his court had retired immediately to more comfortable quarters ashore.

He considered going aboard, rummaging around, but he guessed anything of value had long been removed.

"Wherever you can find space to squeeze in there," Grifo said, nodding toward the dock. "This is as good a place as any."

Harald nodded and pushed the tiller over. He scanned the docks and spotted a gap where their innocuous little fishing boat might fit in and swung the bow in that direction. He called for the men to unship their oars and, with the last bit of way, he eased the boat alongside the dock.

"Get your weapons," Harald said as he made the stern line fast to the head of a piling, but Grifo spoke before they could obey.

"I don't think that's a good idea," he said.

"You expect us to go into the city with no weapons?" Harald asked. To him, that was akin to going into the city naked. Worse, in fact. He'd rather be naked with a sword in hand than clothed and unarmed.

"Felix's chambers are in the royal palace, and you most certainly won't be allowed to bring weapons in there," Grifo said. "They'll take them from you at the door, and there's every chance you won't get them back."

Harald looked at Grifo, trying to plumb the man's motives, to make a decision as to whether or not to trust him. And he thought about his sword, Oak Clever, his grandfather's blade, wrapped in oiled canvas and stored in the bottom of the boat. He most certainly did not care to risk losing that weapon.

"Very well," Harald said at last. "Leave your weapons. I'm sure we can take some if we need them. Brand, Grifo, and I will go to see Felix. You others, take the boat a ways out in the river. Not far, just far enough that no one who means you harm can surprise you. Keep an eye out for us returning, and come get us when we do. And stay alert."

The men in the boat looked at him and nodded and Harald was satisfied that they understood. They were smart men, and able, which was why he had chosen them.

"Give us until this time tomorrow," Harald said. "If we're not back, go back downriver and tell my father what happened." He turned to Grifo. "Very well, lead on."

Grifo turned and headed inland. The wood-planked dock ran to the shore, where it merged with a wood-plank road that led to the city's gate.

"That was smart, what you did," Grifo said as they walked.

"What?" Harald asked.

"Having the boat row clear of the dock, wait in the river for you. That was smart."

Harald grunted and did not reply, but he was pleased by the words.

They approached the door to the city, one of several ways in, Harald imagined. He looked up at the walls, looming high above, like the faces of cliffs. He shook his head in wonder at the effort it must have taken to build such a thing. And on an island, no less.

The door itself rose twenty-five feet in height, oak, like that of le Château de Roumois, and bound in iron as well. But this door had a smaller door cut into it, large enough to allow people and animals to pass through, though considerably easier than the full door to open and close. Soldiers in mail, with helmets and spears, flanked the door. They seemed to take no notice of the people going in and out, at least until Harald, Brand and Grifo approached. On seeing them, the guards took a step forward and their spears came down, their points aimed at the three men.

Grifo stepped up and spoke sharply to the Frankish guards. Harald could not understand the words, but he understood the tone, which was one of command and assumed superiority. And whatever words he spoke, they were clearly the right ones, because the spears went up again and the guards stood aside and Grifo led the way through the smaller door and into the crowded city within.

Once more Harald was presented with a site he had never seen before. The streets were narrow and paved in stone and ran between buildings three and four stories tall, so they looked like riverbeds running through banks of high cliffs. There were people of all ages and sizes and conditions moving with apparent urgency, weaving around horses and carts and sundry other obstacles. Dogs rooted through the garbage that was scattered around. Signs depicting various wares — shoes, hats, barrels, bread — hung in front of shops that had doors and windows flung open to invite customers in.

"By all the gods, have you ever seen the like?" Brand asked, speaking in a low voice, with a tone that suggested awe.

"No," Harald admitted. He had never seen any city greater than Hedeby, and Hedeby would have fit in a quarter of the area that Paris covered. Hedeby's city wall was made of wooden palisades, its streets were dirt, or more often mud, and there were no buildings there that boasted more than two stories, and few of those.

"Come along, you farmers," Grifo said. "And try not to trip over your mouths as they hang open."

He led the way down the nearest street, weaving with expert ease through the crowds. He turned onto another street and then another until Harald had lost all sense of the direction in which they were going, and could only hope that Grifo was as sure of his way as he seemed to be.

Apparently he was, because soon a second wall was before them, not quite as imposing as the city wall, but close. Harald could see roofs and spires behind this wall, and more guards at the door, which was open.

Grifo stopped and turned toward them. "This is the king's palace," he said. "With the king of Wessex here, and his court, and all of Charles's nobles, I have no idea what to expect. Madness, I imagine. But we'll see."

They stepped up to the door and this time the guards did not lower their spears, but Grifo paused to speak with them anyway. Words went back and forth, but there seemed to be no difficulty, and a moment later the three men were waved through.

This door led not to more crowded streets but to an open space, the courtyard surrounding the palace. It stretched for several hundred yards in every direction, and within the walls that surrounded it, there were gardens and stables and buildings that Harald guessed were barracks of some sort. He heard a smith's hammer ringing out somewhere, and the familiar clash of steel on steel, steel on wooden shields, men-at-arms practicing their trade.

"This way," Grifo said, leading them across the open ground to the looming palace building on the other side. Harald followed but his gaze was everywhere, taking in all the activity. At the far end of the courtyard stood a train of ox carts, and men were rolling barrels over the ground and hefting them up onto the beds. Spears were standing like sheaves of wheat with their heads interlocked. Men sat at grindstones sharpening swords as others waited their turn.

And then they were at the door to the palace where they were once again stopped, once again questioned by the soldiers there. Grifo gave them a few words, less commanding now, more cooperative in tone. The guards stepped forward and looked the three of them up and down, back and front, and, apparently satisfied, let them pass.

The palace interior reminded Harald of le Château de Roumois, only much grander, a thing he would not have thought possible even a few days before. In fact, Louis's château was so like the palace that Harald suspected it had been built that way on purpose, though the builder of the château could not afford to make it more impressive than the king's own home, or perhaps he did not dare.

Grifo led the way through the palace, and he moved with the same confident familiarity he had shown on the streets outside. They crossed the foyer, climbed a grand staircase, and walked down a long hall on the second floor, past bright-painted doors and elaborate tapestries.

"Here's Felix's secretary," Grifo said, nodding toward a man who was walking in their direction, staring at a scroll he held in his hands. Grifo called to him and the secretary paused and looked up and he and Grifo exchanged words. The man with the scroll nodded and motioned for them to wait, then hurried off in the direction from which he had come.

"Felix is in his chambers, it seems," Grifo said. "We're in luck. This fellow has gone off to see if he'll speak with us now."

Harald and Brand nodded and the three of them stood easy, waiting for the secretary's return. And they continued to wait, for what seemed to Harald more time than was quite necessary for a simple yes or no. He let his gaze wander around, up at the ceiling, down at the smooth stone floors and at the bright threads of the tapestries.

Then Felix's secretary reappeared at last, and behind him, two men-at-arms, swords on their belts, helmets on their heads. Harald felt a jolt at the sight of them, a reflex to fight, and he looked around for a weapon of some sort. But even as part of him readied for combat, another part called for calm, and it prevailed.

"Men-at-arms?" he asked. "Why are they necessary?"

Grifo spoke to the secretary and the secretary replied. "Felix's orders," Grifo said. "Apparently he does not care to meet with Northmen unless soldiers are present."

Probably a smart thing, Harald thought. *Not that it will do him any good.*

They continued on, the secretary leading the way, Grifo following, Harald and Brand following behind him, and the soldiers forming a rearguard. The secretary knocked on a door at the end of the hall and a voice answered from within and the secretary swung open the door.

The room inside was bigger than any jarl's sleeping chamber or throne room that Harald had ever seen, though he guessed it was only middling size compared to others in the palace. Nor was it as lavish or elaborately decorated as the other spaces he'd seen; it was, by those standards, downright spartan. There were several long, wide tables covered with scrolls and various other papers. Tall candleholders stood near the walls, lighting up the room brighter than Harald was accustomed to. A few chairs scattered haphazardly, a big bed like an afterthought in the far corner.

Felix was sitting at one of the tables, reading a scroll rolled out in front of him, as if he had not been expecting anyone to come through the door, as if their presence was an unwelcome, but ultimately brief, annoyance. He looked up, rolled up the scroll, and stood as the six men entered. The door closed behind them and the men-at-arms took their places just behind and to the sides of Harald and Brand.

Harald's eyes were on Felix as the man stepped around the big table and stopped ten feet away. It had only been a week or so since he had seen him in Engla-land, but he looked quite changed. His hair and beard had been neatened up, and the tunic he wore, a fine, deep-blue linen trimmed with silk and embroidery, was finer than anything Harald had seen him wearing on the other side of the narrow seas. His leggings were silk rather than rough wool, and he wore no weapons on his belt.

Felix spoke, and opened his hands in a welcoming gesture. When he was done, Grifo translated.

"Felix says he welcomes you to the palace of King Charles of West Frankia. He thanks you for the good service you did in escorting the fleet across the water and he's glad to see you are safe."

Harald smiled a hint of a smile. Even in translation Felix's words were dripping with insincerity.

"Tell Felix we're happy to be here, particularly after such a hard fight with the Frisian raiders," Harald said. "Tell him he might recall seeing it as he sailed away."

Grifo translated, and Harald wondered how much he softened the words as he did. Then Felix replied.

"Felix is wondering why you're here, what he can do for you now," Grifo said.

"Tell him we've come for the silver that's owed to us, and once we have it, we'll sail for home."

Grifo translated, and as he did, Felix's face took on an expression of unhappy regret that looked just as sincere as his words sounded. Then he spoke, and Harald heard the feigned note of disappointment in his voice.

"Felix says he's very sorry, particularly after your bold action against the Frisians, but it seems that King Charles has declined to participate in the deal Felix struck with your father, and so there is no more silver to be had."

Harald nodded. He was angry, but not as angry as he would have been had he not expected this answer. "The deal was not with Charles," Harald said. "It was with King Æthelwulf. Based on Felix's assurance."

Grifo related that to Felix and Felix replied. "He says he's sorry if there was a misunderstanding, but the second payment was to come from Charles, and Charles has declined to participate, and there is nothing more he can do."

Harald remained silent for a moment, and he and Felix looked one another in the eyes, neither man blinking or looking away.

"In the courtyard," Harald said at last, "I saw an army getting ready for a campaign of some sort. Who, exactly, will they be marching against?"

Grifo translated, but Felix did not answer at first. Instead, he continued to hold Harald's gaze. And then he let out a long breath, as if he had reached a difficult decision.

"Felix says the affairs of Frankia are not your concern," Grifo translated after Felix had spoken. "And he gives you some advice. He says all you Northmen should leave now, while you are able. He says you will not get a second chance."

"That army in the courtyard," Harald said, speaking to Grifo now, "they'll be coming for us?"

"They'll be coming for Louis," Grifo said. "And if you're standing with Louis, then yes, for you as well. Though I suspect Felix would prefer that you just leave rather than fight."

"If he wants us to leave, why doesn't he pay us what he owes?"

"He never meant to pay," Grifo said. "And now that Æthelwulf has arrived safe here, neither he nor Charles is likely to part with another ounce of silver. They have no need of your friendship any more. They have an army. They don't fear your father's fifteen score warriors."

"So what should we do?" Harald asked.

"My advice is the same as Felix's. You should leave while you can."

Felix spoke next, his voice clipped. Grifo answered.

"What does he say?" Harald asked.

"He wants to know what we were talking about, you and me."

Harald looked at Felix again, and he saw a change on the man's face: anger, suspicion. Subtle, but it was there.

"Tell Felix that if he won't give us silver, then we'll agree to leave if he gives us something else," Harald said. "And what I have in mind, it's something he can give us right now."

Grifo translated, and Felix answered with just a few words. "Felix asks, 'What is it you want?'" Grifo said.

"The map," Harald said.

"The map?"

"In Engla-land Felix showed us a map he had, a map of the whole world, or nearly," Harald said. "If he gives us that, we'll leave."

As he spoke, he tried to keep a note of determination in his voice, but he knew he was getting far out on a shaky limb here. His father had certainly not authorized such a deal, and it was not likely he would have. Neither Thorgrim nor most of the Northmen appreciated the true value of that map, a parchment that could show anyone who understood it what was over the next horizon, and the next and the next.

Grifo spoke to Felix. Felix spoke to Grifo. Grifo said, "Felix says he will not give you the map, or the silver. He says you had best leave now. He says he would hate to have to take you prisoner." Harald was sure he heard a note of disgust in Grifo's voice, as if he felt sullied just by translating such a dishonorable threat.

Harald said nothing. He had expected no less. He glanced back over his right shoulder and caught a glimpse of the guard standing there, ready, four feet away. He looked to his left. Brand was standing on the other side of Grifo, who was between them, and Brand's guard was behind him. He and Brand's eyes met and Harald nodded and said, "Ready…with me…"

Grifo looked over at Harald and frowned. "What does that mean?" he asked, his voice suspicious and alarmed, but by the time he spoke, Harald was already in motion.

Chapter Twenty-Five

The city quakes, its people terrified, and trumpets blare,
That all without delay should aid the trembling tower.
The Christians do their best to stand and fight.

Abbo of Saint-Germain

Harald pivoted fast to his right, his eyes on the surprised face of the guard behind him. The man was just starting to react when Harald grabbed the top of his helmet and pulled, pushing the iron rim over the man's eyes and jerking his entire head forward and down.

The guard gave a muffled cry of surprise, but it was cut short as Harald's knee met the man's face with a solid blow. Harald released the helmet and the guard staggered back a step, then another. Harald closed the distance, grabbed the hilt of the guard's sword and pulled it free.

The guard found his footing and pushed his helmet back up onto his head. His nose was skewed at an odd angle and his face and beard were awash in blood. His eyes were on Harald as he reached for the short sword hanging from his belt, but before he could even draw the weapon Harald hit him hard on the temple with the flat of his own sword. The guard's knees buckled and he collapsed where he stood.

Harald stepped back, the sword held ready. He looked to his left. Grifo stood motionless, eyes and mouth wide with surprise. The guard who had been standing behind Brand was now lying in a heap on the floor, his sword in Brand's hand. The secretary had managed to flee to a corner of the room and was crouching there, arms held up to shield his head. He did not seem to be much of a threat.

Harald looked at Felix. Like Grifo, Felix's mouth was open in dumb surprise. For a moment no one moved, then Felix whirled around and lunged across the table behind him, and Harald charged forward as he did.

Papers flew as Felix sprawled over the table and grabbed for a seax which lay buried there. He turned back, pushing himself up, swinging the weapon as Harald came at him. The point of the blade was heading for Harald's neck when Harald caught Felix's wrist in his left hand and held it. Felix jerked his hand back and forth, trying to break free, trying just to move his arm, but his strength was like a child to Harald's.

Harald let the sword in his right hand fall and he reached over and plucked the seax from Felix's grip. Felix opened his mouth to shout, but Harald grabbed a fistful of his tunic and shoved him back down against the table, hard enough to knock the voice out of him. Harald saw no fear in Felix's face, just fury. Felix tried again to shout, but Harald touched the point of the seax to the underside of Felix's chin, which encouraged him to shut his mouth.

For a moment the two just glared at one another. Then Felix tilted his head away from the point of the seax and spoke.

"He says you've made a great mistake, and if you want to live you had best release him now," Grifo said.

Harald was surprised. He would have expected a man such as Felix to come up with a threat that was more original, more intimidating.

He's more scared than he looks, Harald thought.

"Tell him I'm going to let him up, and when I do, he will get the map for us," Harald said, and when Grifo had translated Harald let go of Felix's tunic and stepped back. Felix pushed himself up, glaring at Harald as he spoke.

"He says the map is not here, it's back in the library," Grifo said.

"Is it?" Harald snatched up Felix's right hand and pressed the blade of the seax in the notch between Felix's thumb and hand, then closed the fingers around it. "Tell Felix I'm going to take his thumb off and then I'll let him think about where the map is." He pressed down a bit on the blade. A small trickle of blood ran down Felix's palm. And then Felix was talking again.

"He says let go of his hand and he'll get the map."

Harald released Felix's hand and stepped back again, the seax held low but clearly ready to strike. Felix straightened and pushed past Harald and crossed to a wooden stand that held various scrolls, sheathed in silk and mounted on hooks. He lifted the top one, turned, and handed it to Harald.

"Tell him to roll it out on the table, in case he's made a mistake," Harald said and Grifo translated. Felix frowned deeper still and took the scroll from Harald's hands, replaced it on the rack, and handed Harald the one below it.

Harald pulled the silk sheath off the scroll, set the scroll on the table, and unrolled it. It was all but exactly as he remembered: the blue shapes and the white shapes, the words in what he guessed were Frankish runes, the curved lines, the pictures of men and beasts. It was smaller than he recalled, but other than that, it was the very map that had so occupied his thoughts since first he saw it.

He rolled it up again, slipped it back into its sheath, and set it down on the table. There was a window at the far end of the room and Harald crossed over and looked out. The courtyard where the soldiers had been drilling with sword and spear and the carts loaded with the supplies was below, but it was mostly empty now as the day was getting late. Just a handful of the soldiers were still milling about, a few of the *chevaliers* tending to their horses.

Heavy curtains hung on either side of the window, and Harald stabbed the seax into one of them and sliced it into a series of long strips, then cut the strips free. He crossed back to where Felix stood near the rack of scrolls, grabbed him by the shoulder, and spun him around. He shoved one of the strips into Felix's mouth and bound it behind his head, then bound his arms behind his back. That done, he hefted the man onto the table and tied his legs as well and left him there.

Next, he did the same to the secretary, who made whimpering noises but did not protest beyond that. The guards were not likely to move any time soon, if ever, but Harald had been surprised by such things in the past, so he tied the unconscious men as well. Finally, he turned to Grifo.

"I'm sorry, but I'll have to tie you up, too," he said. "Just to be safe. And it won't look good for you if I don't."

"How do you plan to get out of here without me?" Grifo asked.

Harald shrugged. "I'll find some way."

"No need," Grifo said. "I'll come with you."

"Come with us?" Harald asked. "Why?"

"Felix will have my head whether you tie me up or not. I'd never convince him that I had nothing to do with this. I wouldn't even bother trying."

This was something Harald had not seen coming, and he was not sure how to react. It was true that he would have a hard time getting out of the city without Grifo's help. On the other hand, Grifo might be looking for a chance to betray him and return to Felix's good graces.

"Very well," Harald said. "Let's go." He took the seax and thrust it in his belt.

"Not a good idea," Grifo said, nodding at the weapon.

"Why's that?" Harald asked, and felt his suspicions flair.

"You had no weapons coming in. They might wonder why you have one going out."

"Right." Harald could see the truth of that. He took the seax out of his belt and slipped it carefully into his tunic. Brand relieved the guard at his feet of his short sword and hid it likewise.

"Might I take a weapon?" Grifo asked.

"No," Harald said. "I don't trust you enough."

Grifo nodded. "Probably a good choice. But you had best let me carry the map. That would certainly raise fewer questions."

"All right," Harald said, nodding toward the scroll. Grifo retrieved it and Harald opened the door and peeked into the hall. No one there, and nothing to be heard except the distant sounds from the courtyard. He nodded to the others, and Brand and Grifo stepped out behind him. Grifo closed the door and Harald heard the latch fall.

"Very well," Harald said, speaking softly. "How do we get out of here?"

"Same way we got in," Grifo said. "We walk out, and we look as innocent as babes when we do." He headed off down the hall, Harald and Brand following close behind.

"How long do you reckon before someone finds those bastards we tied up?" Brand asked as they walked.

"Tomorrow morning, if we're lucky," Grifo said. "Or a few moments from now, if we're not. Or something in between."

They reached the head of the big staircase and started down. There were people below moving around the foyer, hurrying one way or another, servants and minor officials and guards. A few passed them on the steps, going up as they went down, but no one paid the three men any attention. They reached the first floor and headed for the main door. There were guards there, but they were on the outside, because no one worried about who was leaving, only who was coming in.

Grifo pushed open the door and the three of them stepped out into the evening. The sun was still up, but it was low in the west, casting long shadows around the courtyard. Much of the activity there had ended, the men-at-arms had given up their training, the ox carts had been rolled off to somewhere for the night. A few soldiers still stood around the grindstones; a few mounted warriors were putting their horses through their paces.

Harald, Brand, and Grifo headed toward the gate through which they had come, a few hundred yards away. They kept up a brisk pace, not a stroll but not moving suspiciously quick either. Harald looked around as much as he dared, and listened intently for any sounds out of the ordinary. But there was nothing that he could hear.

We might just pull this thing off, he thought. He even opened his mouth to say as much, but then shut it quickly. The gods would not look kindly on that sort of hubris. They might well punish him just for thinking it.

He felt a touch of panic as he considered that, a brief terror about what he might have unleashed with his thoughts, but he kept his face fixed and his head down and he marched on in Grifo's wake. He was starting to relax again, just a bit, when the shouting began.

The first cry came from somewhere behind them, and there was no mistaking the urgency in the tone, even if Harald could not understand what was said. The three men stopped and looked back. The palace was a good hundred yards behind them now, but they saw a figure in one of the upper windows and he was shouting loud enough for his voice to echo around the courtyard. And worse, he was pointing directly at the three of them.

"What's he saying?" Brand asked, which Harald thought was a silly question, as it seemed fairly obvious.

"He's calling for the guards to stop us," Grifo said. "Seems they might have found Felix quicker than we hoped."

"We should probably move along, then," Harald said. "Maybe a little faster now."

"Yes, we should," Grifo agreed, and with that the three of them turned and started running flat out toward the front gate. Harald reached into his tunic and pulled the seax free. No point in trying to hide the weapon now.

There were any number of people in the courtyard, but none were terribly close to the three armed and fleeing men, and none were the sort who would be inclined to try and stop them anyway. They were mostly servants, and of those, most were women or children, the rest laborers of various sorts, not folk to get in the way of three warriors in flight.

Harald looked over his shoulder as he ran, back toward where the men-at-arms had been training. Happily, they had mostly retired for the evening, and only a few were now standing and looking in their direction.

And among them, unfortunately, were a handful of the *chevaliers*. Mounted and armed, able to close quickly, and turning in their direction.

"Here's trouble!" Grifo shouted.

Harald thought he meant the mounted warriors, but he realized Grifo was speaking of something else. Harald looked forward and saw the door in the big gate open and a clutch of guards come charging through, alerted by the shouting. They might not have known what was going on, but it was clear enough who the fugitives were.

Harald and the others did not slow and the guards did not slow as they charged at each other. There were four guards, Harald was happy to see: not enough to overwhelm the three of them, but enough to get in each other's way.

"This is good," he said, difficult as it was to speak and run. "They're bringing us weapons."

"I could use a weapon now," Grifo said in a gasping voice.

"You mind the map," Harald gasped back. "Let me and Brand do for these bastards."

The guards had sense enough, at least, to not charge headlong into the fight. A hundred feet ahead of Harald and Brand, they stopped and formed a loose line, shields up, spears held high.

"Get ready!" Harald shouted to Brand. "Go low!" He saw Brand nod as he ran. They covered the distance with lungs burning. Forty feet from the guards, they saw arms go back, spears ready to launch, all four preparing to throw at the same time, a mistake Harald knew they would regret.

Harald's eyes were on the arm of the man directly in his path. Twenty feet away, a distance from which the guard no doubt thought he could not miss, and the arm came forward, the spear flew. In the same instant Harald went down, dropping as he ran, tucking the seax tight against him, hitting the ground with his shoulder and rolling forward. He heard the buzz of spears passing overhead as he careened like a one-man avalanche into the guard in front of him, knocking him off his feet. He felt his shoulder hit the man's legs, heard the man hit the ground, as Harald rolled over and then up onto his feet again.

Brand's guard was down as well, bowled over in the same way, and Brand was just getting back up. The two guards who were still standing held shields in their left hands and nothing in their right, having thrown away their spears. They looked at the men on the ground with mouths open in surprise. The one closest to Harald was just recovering his wits and reaching for his sword when Harald drove the seax into his gut.

He heard a clang and a grunt and turned in time to see the guard closest to Brand dropping where he stood. The guard that Harald had first knocked down was pushing himself to his feet, pulling his sword as he did. But Grifo was there, scroll in hand, and he gave the man a kick in the head that put him down again. Brand stepped up and did the same for the other man on the ground.

Harald heard hoof beats now and looked toward the far end of the courtyard. The mounted warriors were underway, charging across the open space, spears held low. Harald looked at the main gate. Fifty yards to go. He looked back at the chevaliers.

This will be close, he thought.

Brand and Grifo were also staring at the charging warriors when Harald shouted, "Grab the spears! Grab the spears and let's go!" He ran forward, shoving his seax in his belt, and scooped up two of the spears that the guards had thrown. Brand grabbed another and Grifo the fourth, then they turned and once more began to run.

It was all getting louder: the hoof beats, their breath, the shouting from the palace behind them. Like most sailors, Harald was powerfully strong but not so good when it came to running, and that was starting to tell. He imagined Brand was feeling it as well. Grifo was doing better than the younger men were, but he, too, was breathing hard.

The gate was still fifty feet away when the sound of the hooves could no longer be ignored. With no word spoken, all three men stopped in their flight, turned, and brought their spears level. The riders were at a full gallop as they charged down on their prey, spears horizontal, dirt flying behind, five mounted warriors, the leader ten feet in front of the rest.

Harald shifted one of his spears to his left hand, drew back the spear in his right hand, ran forward and let it fly, straight and true. The iron point met the oncoming horse and struck the animal's breast a glancing blow, enough to make a visible gash, enough to make the horse check its charge, let out a loud whinny, and rear back on its hind legs as its rider struggled to stay in the saddle.

Behind the lead horse, the other riders broke right and left, swerving to avoid the rearing animal.

"Come on!" Harald shouted. He ran straight at the wounded horse as the riders behind, unable to turn back in time, charged straight past. The horse in front of him came down on all four feet, the panic ebbing, and Harald grabbed the rider and dragged him from the saddle.

The man hit the ground hard and the breath was knocked clean out of him. He was gasping and kicking as Harald poked the horse with the tip of his second spear, sending the animal charging off. Then Harald turned back to the other riders, who had wheeled now and were ready to charge again.

"More guards coming," Grifo said, his tone matter-of-fact as he nodded toward the palace. Harald saw them too, a dozen at least, racing out from someplace to the west of the building. But they were a couple hundred yards away, on foot and clear across the courtyard, which meant Harald and the others had a few moments, at least, to deal with the more immediate threat.

One of the mounted warriors shouted something, and together the four of them spurred their mounts and charged again. Harald and Brand and Grifo stood their ground, spears level.

"Not much time," Harald shouted as the coming charge built momentum over the fifty feet separating them. "We best finish this quick."

"Good plan," Grifo said as he adjusted his footing on the dry ground. "Excellent plan."

The riders were in line abreast now, four spear points leveled and charging down on them, no chance of pulling the trick Harald had just pulled a second time.

"You two go right, I'll go left." Harald could only hope they understood what he meant as there was no time to explain, only time to move. With the riders just a few horse-lengths short of skewering him, he raced off to his left. Now the rider on the flank was between him and the two riders in the middle, and the two in the middle were deprived of a target.

The chevalier on the flank was not thrown off by the move, however. He adjusted his aim and leaned a bit to his right and brought the tip of his spear in line with Harald's chest. But Harald held his own spear like a staff, and as the point came at him, he swept the shaft of the spear up, knocking the rider's weapon away and driving his own spear's butt into the man's face.

The chevalier was thrown back in the saddle, but he did not fall, and the horse did not slow as it charged past. Harald turned with the horse, flipped his spear around and drove the point into the horse's rear end. Like the first mount, this one whinnied loud in pain and surprise and charged off in a burst of outraged speed, leaving its rider to cling on as best he could.

The other three horses had also thundered past, their riders struggling to stop them, to turn them, to charge again. Grifo and Brand were still standing, though Brand had a rent in his sleeve, through which Harald saw blood starting to flow.

"Come on!" he shouted. There was nothing blocking the way between them and the front gate, at least for that moment, and the three men turned and ran for it, ignoring the riders at their backs.

They were ten feet from the door, the pounding of the hooves loud behind them, and they knew it was time to turn again. They whirled around, spears up, but to Harald surprise the riders were pulling their horse to a stop, yanking back on the reins as the horses twirled and pranced.

The wall! Harald realized. They were too close. If the riders came on at full gallop, they would not be able to stop their charge before slamming into the unforgiving stone. Instead, they reined their horses back and vaulted from their saddles to the ground, ready to meet the fugitives on their level.

But Harald was done with meeting anyone. "Let's go!" he shouted and he and Brand and Grifo raced for the door. Now they heard footsteps, not hoof beats, behind as the chevaliers chased after, but

Harald could see they would reach the door before the others caught up with them.

Grifo was first out, spear in his right hand, the map under his left arm, and Brand was behind him. Harald stopped long enough to grab the handle of the door and pull it closed as he went out. He had no way to secure it—the bar was on the inside, of course—but there was an iron ring for a handle on the outside, and Harald thrust his spear through it so the shaft would fetch up on the wall when someone tried to open the door. It would not hold up the chevaliers for long, but it would buy a moment or two, and for that, it was well worth losing the spear.

"This way!" Grifo shouted, waving, and Harald knew the Frank was in charge now, because the city was as bewildering to him as a strange and trackless forest. He followed behind the tall man as Grifo led him and Brand across the crowded street to a smaller cross street fifty feet away. The people in their path scattered like chickens, wanting no part of whatever business they were running from.

At the cross street, Grifo turned and raced down the center of the narrow, cobbled way, dodging those who could not move quick enough, and still Harald and Brand kept right behind. He turned at an alley, jogged down, then turned at another, into what Harald thought certainly had to be a dead end. Just when it seemed they had run out of room, the alley took a hard turn and they were on yet another street.

Grifo continued to run, down that street for a hundred yards, then into another alley, coming out on yet another street, each looking to Harald exactly like every other. He had no idea where they were going, but he knew for certain it was not the way they had come. He thought of the seax thrust in his belt. Much more of this and he would stop Grifo and determine, with the point of the weapon, whether he was actually taking them where they wanted to go.

Down another alley, and then Grifo stopped and leaned against a wall and tilted his head back and gasped for air. Brand bent over where he stood and likewise sucked in deep breathes. Harald tried to stay upright and mostly succeeded as he, too, labored to breathe.

Finally, their breathing returned to normal and Harald turned to Brand.

"How bad is your arm?" he asked, nodding toward the rent sleeve. The cloth around the tear was pretty well soaked with blood.

Brand looked down at his arm as if just noticing it. "Not so bad," he said. "Nothing to worry about."

They paused again and listened and they could hear the sounds of the city around them, the shouting and bustle of people, the clop of animals' hoofs on cobble stones, the rumbling of iron-rimmed cart wheels. And something else: shouting, horses moving fast, commotion, but far off. Or at least it seemed far off, coming through the densely packed buildings of Paris.

"I guess they got past the spear you put through the handle," Grifo observed.

"Looks like it," Harald agreed. He looked around. "So, where are we?"

"A place those bastards won't come looking," Grifo said. "And not so far from the landing." He walked over to the end of the alley, where it met the street, leaned out and looked both ways. There were people there as there were on every street in the city, dozens of people, but they all seemed to be going about their business. A few had stopped to cock their ears to the distant sounds, but none of them seemed alarmed or frightened, as if the commotion was taking place in another country.

"Come on," Grifo said, waving to the others. He stepped out into the street and did not run this time, just walked quickly, with purpose, his spear over his shoulder, the map under his arm, and once again Harald and Brand followed behind. There was another bewildering twist of streets and alleys and then, at last, they came out on a street that looked somewhat familiar to Harald, though he was not sure it was, since all of those streets looked the same.

Grifo turned to his right and Harald followed and when he did, he saw the gate in the outer wall through which they had come and he understood why the street looked familiar. This was the first street he'd seen on entering Paris. He glanced at Brand and Brand gave him a look that mixed relief with surprise and a bit of hope. Harald nodded his agreement.

They had no more than a couple hundred feet to go, so they pushed through the crowd, walking as swiftly as they could without looking as if they were fleeing. Once again, Harald began to think that they might indeed get away with this reckless adventure. And once again, he heard the pounding of hooves, coming closer.

"By all the gods!" Harald cried. "Don't these people ever give up?"

"Well, they sure didn't follow us," Grifo said, "but it seems they guessed where we were going." He picked up his pace and Harald and Brand did likewise, until they were all but running. Behind them the sound of the horses grew louder, and with it came screams and shouts of the alarmed folk who were likely getting trampled, or near to it, in the charge. The people through whom Grifo was trying to push were stopping now, and looking around in fear and confusion.

And then Grifo stopped as well, so abruptly that Harald nearly collided with him. He turned and started shouting in Frankish, shouting loud and frantically and pointing his spear toward the gate behind him. The folk on the street looked at him and he continued to shout and to point with the spear and to wave.

Then someone, a young woman holding a baby in her arms, panic on her face, began to run, up the street, away from the gate. And when she did, it was as if a dam had let go, and all the people on the streets began racing away from the gate, shouting and pushing and tumbling over any obstacles in the way.

"What did you say?" Harald asked.

"I told them there were filthy heathen Northmen at the gate, coming to kill them all," Grifo said.

At that moment, the horsemen came into view, rounding a bend a hundred yards up the street and riding right into the impenetrable mass of fleeing people. The riders reined back hard, the horses reared and turned, and the horsemen behind tried to stop their animals in time.

"Let's go," Grifo said. "And pray your miserable boat is still there."

"It is," Harald assured him, and wished he felt as certain as he tried to sound.

They ran the last hundred feet to the gate, which, to Harald's surprise, was gaping open. He recalled the bored guards on the other side, and he imagined they were not bored now. They could not have missed hearing the frantic noise on the other side of the wall, and he was certain they would be bracing for whatever came at them.

He drew his seax as they came closer and called to Grifo, "Hold up there! Let me go first!" Grifo stopped, looked at the seax in Harald's hand and nodded. Harald stepped past and over the last ten feet to the gate, looking through the door as he did, trying to see the guards or anything that might pose a threat, but he could see nothing.

He moved closer, quietly, cautiously, then leapt through the door to the other side, weapon held ready. The guards were there, in the same place they had been, but now they were lying on the ground in spreading pools of blood, and Erik and Sten and Toke were standing over them, swords dripping.

Harald looked at the three Northmen. Sten spoke first. "We heard the shouting, and the horses and such," he explained. "Even from out in the river. Figured it had to be something to do with you, and those guards were going to be a problem. So we took care of it."

"Good," Harald said, regaining his wits. "Good."

Brand and Grifo came through the door and the five men raced down the dock to where the fishing boat lay tied alongside. They dropped down into the boat and Erik and Toke and Sten and Brand grabbed the oars, and Harald took up the tiller. They cast off and Grifo pushed them clear of the dock and with a few strokes, they were leaving the city behind.

Harald looked over his shoulder to see the first of the mounted warriors, now on foot, come racing out of the door. But it was too late; they would not catch them now, even if they could pick them out from all the other fishing boats and sundry vessels crowding the waterfront.

Ten more strokes and they were well away from the shore and it was clear that no one was coming after them. Grifo picked up the silk-encased map and set it on the thwart beside Harald.

"Here you are, Harald Broad-arm," he said. "I hope it was worth all that."

Harald looked down at the cylinder and he thought of what was in it, and all the possibilities it unlocked. "Oh, yes," he said. "Oh yes, it most certainly was."

Chapter Twenty-Six

*By land and water
the king's fleet is safe,
and the chief's men also.*

The Poetic Edda

One hundred yards south of Ragi's hall, the ground dropped away in a short cliff that tumbled down to a long, narrow cove forty feet below. It was just below the edge of that cliff that the tunnel emerged.

Odd was the last man out of the tunnel, since he had been the last man to leave the burning hall, just as Ragi had promised. Odd had almost laughed when Ragi suggested, correctly, that he would argue about any other arrangement. In any other circumstance he would certainly have laughed.

Odd did not know Ragi well. They had met only a few times before Ragi joined the fight against Halfdan the Black, and he was a man of few words, at least in the company of his fellow landowners. Odd never doubted Ragi's courage and his loyalty—loyalty to all his compatriots in that fight—but he would not have guessed that Ragi Oleifsson the host, sitting by his own hearth, would have been so gracious and voluble. Odd had always respected Ragi; now he was coming to like him as well.

Ragi's hall had been comfortable and welcoming, but the tunnel left a lot to be desired. Odd found he could only negotiate it on hands and knees, and even that seemed tight. He wondered if the oversized Broddi, leading the way, would get stuck and doom them all. But the progress did not falter, and just as Odd was wondering if he might pass out for want of air he caught a whiff of a breeze and saw the hint of light ahead. And then he was pulling himself free of the earth and climbing to his feet.

He was not sure where he was at first. There were about thirty people in all who had come out of the tunnel: Ragi and his men and the servants, Odd and his party, Bragi Shipslayer and Huginn and Muninn. They stood on a shelf of ground about ten feet wide that seemed to drop off into nothing at the far end. Farther below Odd saw moonlight glittering on the water. The people were swallowed up in deep shadows, but there seemed to be an undercurrent of ambient light as well.

Odd turned and saw there was a ridge of ground fifteen feet high running along the other side of the shelf on which they stood, the edge of which stood out sharply against the sky, illuminated by the massive fire devouring Ragi's hall. The tunnel, he realized, came out through the side of a short cliff and onto this flat section, which might have been a natural feature or might have been dug by Ragi and his men for just this purpose. Which it was, Odd could not tell, but either way it was very clever, a place that was hidden from view where the fugitives could safely gather.

"There's a trail that leads down the side of this cliff and along the shore," Ragi's voice came from somewhere near the head of the crowd, speaking just loud enough to be heard. "We'll take that, make our way north. But we have to move, now. Skorri's probably figured out already that we're not in the hall. The lack of screaming will tell him that."

"What, you expect us to walk like a bunch of beggars?" Bragi Shipslayer's voice came next, and he took less care to remain quiet. "When I see a perfectly fine ship down there?"

Odd took a step toward the far edge of the cliff and looked down. In the diffused light of the burning hall he saw a narrow dock jutting out over the water and the vague but unmistakable shape of a ship tied to it.

"It's a ship, Bragi," Ragi called back, "but it's far from fine. I think the dock's the only thing keeping it afloat. Come." Ragi led the way down the trail, or so Odd assumed, since he could not see him, though he could make out the dark outlines of the others filing off as well.

"We have men enough here to bail!" Bragi called back. "By Thor's ass, we probably have enough to swim alongside with the ship on their shoulders!"

This whore's son really does not like to walk, does he? Odd thought, recalling Bragi's earlier negotiations for a ride in the wagon. The others were shuffling forward now, the crowd on the ledge thinning as more and more of them followed Ragi down the trail. Odd moved ahead, one or two steps, still at the back of the line. Broddi had extinguished his torch, apparently, so as not to give them away, and Odd wondered how well they could see where they were going, and how treacherous the trail was.

Guess I'll find out. His chief concern was for Amundi and Alfdis, the oldest of the crowd, and for Signy, though he knew his wife to be nimble and strong.

"Here!"

Odd heard the voice call out from somewhere behind him, loud and emphatic, and it made him jump. He turned and looked up. The man was standing on the edge of the cliff, maybe fifteen feet above him, sword in hand. The fire from the burning hall was glinting off his mail and his helmet. He held a sword in his hand and he was pointing it down at the people on the ledge. At Odd.

"Here!" he shouted again. His voice was deep and loud, which meant it stood a chance of cutting through the roar of the burning building. He was looking back toward the hall, and with his left hand, he began waving to someone, and though Odd could not see who, he could well imagine.

Son of a bitch! Odd looked at the wall of the cliff facing him, wondered if he could climb it. In the deep shadows he could make out no details at all, but he had the sense that it was loose, crumbling earth, impossible to scramble up.

There was a rock at his feet about the size of a pigeon and he snatched it up and flung it at the man on the cliff. It was a good throw, well-aimed and strong. It hit the man in the chest and bounced off and made him stagger back a step, but it had no effect beyond that. Odd drew his sword and gestured to the man.

"Come on, you bastard! Come get me! Coward!" Odd shouted. The man looked down at him, then back in the direction in which he had been waving. Odd saw the uncertainty on his face, the fight between doing what he wanted to do, which was climb down and fight Odd, and what he knew he should do, which was keep yelling for the others.

Odd half turned toward the people making for the trail. "We're discovered! We're discovered! Hurry! Hurry!" he shouted. He looked up again. The man was still waving, but then he hopped down over the edge of the cliff and half climbed, half slid down to where Odd stood. And that told Odd two things: the man wanted to fight, and Skorri and the others had seen him waving and were on their way.

The man hit the ground and pushed himself up just as Odd was on him, slashing with Blood-letter. In the dark Odd could not see what he was swinging at, save for a glint of light off the man's blade as he raised it, and he and Odd both misjudged, missing one another entirely.

Blood-letter swung past the man's blade, finding only air, and Odd grunted as he twisted with the momentum. He had expected the swing to be checked as his blade struck the man's sword or his body, and when it wasn't, it threw him off balance. He half stumbled and heard the man step closer, so he let himself keep stumbling the rest of the way, falling clear as the man's blade came hacking down.

The sword whistled past and Odd actually felt the slight tremor in the ground as the man's point hit. Odd might have finished it there, but he was still falling, hands out. He came down on the palm of his left hand and the knuckles of his right, his fingers still wrapped around Blood-letter's grip. The pain exploded in his hand and up his arm, and he rolled over, shoulder down, bringing the sword up as he did, expecting to see the man's blade arching down at him.

Instead, he saw the man yank the point of his blade out of the ground and then turn left and right, searching, and Odd realized that the whore's son had been staring at the burning hall and now he was all but blind in the dark. Odd pushed himself to his knees and scrambled away. He felt the wall of dirt and half stood, half pulled himself up. He pressed his back to the loose earth and looked at Skorri's man who was whirling side to side, trying to see where his opponent had gone.

Odd loosened his grip on Blood-letter, flexed his fingers. They hurt, but they were not broken, as far as he could tell, so he took a firm grip on the hilt once more. The man had a shield on his arm, but Odd did not; none of them had even tried to get through that narrow tunnel while carrying shields. They had not intended to fight Skorri's men, but it seemed they would have no choice.

The man was turning toward him now, so Odd leapt forward, pushing off from the wall. At the sound, Skorri's man spun around and took a wild, panicked swing, but Odd paused in his advance and let the point whip on past. Then he took a step forward, and another, and as the man was starting his backstroke, Odd slashed at him, hard.

Odd's blade struck the edge of the man's shield, but the point slashed through his mail shirt and the flesh beneath. Both parted under Blood-letter's stroke and the man dropped his sword and staggered back.

Odd leapt forward and drove his shoulder into the man's shield, held chest-high, and shoved. The man lost his balance, stumbling, flailing, going down. Before he hit the ground, his feet reached the edge of the cliff and he tumbled over, arms waving, mouth open in a scream that faded as he fell and then was cut short as Odd heard a thumping sound in the dark.

He turned and raced for the head of the trail, where all but a few of the folk who had come from the tunnel had disappeared into the dark. There was something happening there, some commotion, people pushing, and Odd was suddenly afraid that they had panicked, that they would fall to their deaths as they tried to get away from Skorri's men.

But that was not it. As he reached the last of the people, he saw Ragi pushing his way back up the trail, Broddi behind him, and a few other of Ragi's men behind Broddi.

"Odd, what is it? We heard you shout," Ragi said.

"Skorri's men, they found us," Odd said. "One man, anyway...I killed him...but there'll be more coming."

Ragi nodded. "It'll be a hard fight on this trail. And Skorri with greater numbers."

"Here!" Broddi pointed up with his sword. The men turned and looked. Outlined by the light from the burning hall, they saw Skorri and more than a dozen men around him, standing at the edge of the cliff, looking down, swords in hands, shields on arms. They were thirty or forty feet away and they seemed not to see the men below them.

"They're blinded," Odd said, speaking softly. "They were staring into the burning hall. Their eyes can't yet see in the dark."

"Good," Ragi said, also speaking in a low voice. "Let's make some distance." He turned to go when suddenly Bragi Shipslayer pushed his way through the last of the people on the ledge.

"Where are they?" Bragi bellowed, his voice like a thunderclap. "Where are these whore's son bastards? I'll rip their lungs out!"

If Skorri had not seen or heard them before, he did then. At the sound of Bragi's voice, all the men on the cliff edge turned as one and looked in their direction. Arms came up and fingers pointed.

"There you are, you sons of bitches!" Skorri roared and he climbed down onto the edge of the cliff and slid down the fifteen feet to the ledge on which they stood.

"Come on, back on the trail!" Ragi shouted, gesturing to the others. "Go! Go!"

"What, we're running away?" Bragi shouted.

"Stay if you wish, but I'll fight them on the trail where they can't surround us," Ragi said, all but shoving Broddi and the others to get them moving.

"Good thinking," Bragi said, and with a nimble leap, he headed back the way he had come, making for the head of the path that lead down the side of the cliff.

Ragi and Odd were last. They looked back to see Skorri and his men advancing quickly: not running, but stepping fast, careful with their footing in the dark.

"Come!" Ragi slapped Odd on the shoulder and nodded toward the trail. He hurried off and Odd followed behind. The ledge on which they were standing narrowed, until finally it was, as far as Odd could see, no more than a shelf a couple feet wide and sloping downhill. Ragi moved quickly, sure of his way, but Odd was a little more hesitant, peering down at the ground beneath his feet, trying to see where he was stepping.

The trail bent around an outcropping, and as Odd maneuvered around it, he nearly collided with Ragi who had stopped on the other side.

"We'll wait for them, give them a surprise," Ragi said in a low voice, nodding up the trail in the direction they had come.

Odd nodded, refreshed his grip on his sword and stood still, staring into the dark.

They heard the crunch of Skorri's men's shoes on the ground and the gentle clinking of their mail as they moved cautiously forward.

Ragi stepped up behind Odd, pressed close, so the two of them were as nearly side by side as they could get on the narrow trail. They stood with swords held ready as the first of Skorri's men appeared around the outcropping, a dark shape, stepping with care. He did not see Odd and Ragi until it was too late, at least for him.

Odd took a half step and thrust with his sword. He felt the tip hit something and heard the man shout, more a cry of surprise than pain. The man lifted his shield and raised his weapon. Ragi swung the sword in his hand and hit him a solid blow on the man's shoulder. The man staggered as Odd shifted Blood-letter to his left hand, grabbed the edge of the man's shield with his right, and jerked hard.

With a cry the man stumbled sideways and then he was gone, a blur of flailing limbs and sword and shield, barely visible as he tumbled off the edge of the cliff. Ragi slapped Odd's arm again and turned and hurried further down the trail. Odd followed behind. Skorri's men, cautious from the start, would be even more cautious now.

They had covered perhaps a dozen yards when Odd heard Ragi make a grunting sound and saw him stopping short as he collided with something on the trail. Two more steps and he saw it was Bragi Shipslayer, who was apparently making his way back up.

"You're having all the fun!" he complained. "Let me have a few of these whore's sons!"

He started to push past Ragi, but Odd called, "Hold up!" Odd had been thinking about their situation, as best as he could in the frenzy of the moment, and it did not look good. They were trying to get to the open ground near the bottom of the cliff, but once they did, Skorri would be on them, his skilled and trained men free to move while Odd and Ragi's men, outnumbered, were trying to protect the women and the servants. They were just asking to be slaughtered.

"Listen, Bragi," Odd said, taking another step forward. "You were right. We need to get on the ship. It's the only way we'll get clear."

"The ship's a wreck, I told you," Ragi said, "barely floating."

"It doesn't have to float long, just long enough for us to get clear," Odd said. "Will you get the people on the ship, Bragi?"

Bragi looked up the trail to where Skorri's men were advancing through the dark, and then down toward the cove below and the ship tied to the wharf.

"Very well, I'll go," he said. He sounded reluctant, but Odd had guessed that the words *you were right* would be irresistible to the man, and apparently, he was correct. With that, Bragi turned and headed off downhill.

They heard Skorri's men coming now, the cautious steps, the rustle of mail. "Let's go, a little farther," Ragi said, turning and hurrying off with Odd on his heels.

"I'm sorry, Ragi, about sending Bragi to your ship, even when you said it would sink," Odd said as they moved. "I just didn't reckon we had much choice."

"We'll see," Ragi said. "I'd rather die by a sword than by swallowing sea water, but maybe we can avoid them both."

Another dozen feet and more dark shapes appeared ahead of them and Broddi and some of Ragi's other men materialized out of the night. "That sailor fellow, he's telling the others to get on the ship," Broddi said. "Not being too quiet about it."

"Yes," Ragi said. "We won't get clear any other way. But hold, we need to slow these sons of bitches down a bit."

"Twenty feet down that way the trail widens some," Broddi said, nodding downhill. "We can make a stand there."

"Good," Ragi said. "Let's go."

They hurried on, and just as Broddi had said the trail widened until it was perhaps six feet across, still not much but wider than it had been, enough for about five of Ragi's warriors to gather. Odd stepped closer to the edge and peered down. There seemed to be a drop of about twenty or thirty feet to the rocky shoreline below, not a distance he would care to fall.

He started to draw back when he felt the ground give below him. He heard himself gasp, felt a shot of panic as he leapt away from the edge, and the place where he had been standing crumbled away as he did.

*We'll keep clear of the edge...*he thought. He looked around the narrow space on which they were standing. The moon was rising now, casting a bit of light around, but the cliff wall was still lost in shadow. Odd recalled how he had hidden himself against that cliff wall earlier, and launched his surprise attack against Skorri's warrior.

"You men, press yourselves against the cliff! Against the cliff!" Odd said in as loud a whisper as he dared. He reached out with his left hand and gently pushed anyone within reach. "You'll be hidden by the shadows!"

Ragi's men understood. With a few quick steps they moved against the wall, pushing themselves close to the side of the cliff. Even with his eyes adjusted as they were, Odd could barely see them there.

He and Ragi stood alone on the trail, a few feet separating them, facing uphill. They heard Skorri's men coming now. They would be moving single file down the narrower part of the trail, moving with great caution, Odd did not doubt.

And then the first was there, seeming to materialize out of the dark, the hints of moonlight that reached that part of the cliff making him just stand out from the blackness. He moved ahead, stepping onto the wider part of the trail. Odd could see enough to know the man's shield was held low, his sword at waist height.

Skorri's man took two steps closer and then he gasped, loud, and his shield jerked up and his sword came back as he must have seen the two men facing him on the trail. Odd shouted and leapt forward and slashed down with Blood-letter. The blade hit the flat of the man's shield and stopped dead, but Ragi was there, coming in low, the point of his sword reaching up under the man's shield and driving in below his mail shirt.

The man shouted and swung his shield down, knocking Ragi's sword away, and as he did Odd thrust, straight and true. Blood-letter's point found its target. Where it struck, Odd could not see, but he felt it, felt the point pierce the mail shirt, felt the tug of the blade as the man twisted away and the point came free.

More of Skorri's men were rushing down the trail, spreading out as they realized the ground widened at that point and they had an enemy in front of them. Odd thought of the men pressed against the cliff wall, unseen.

Wait…steady… he thought, wishing he could speak the words out loud.

Ragi took a step back and Odd did too, and then they took another, yielding ground, letting Skorri's men approach, swords and shields up, all attention on the men in front of them. Odd looked down. They were coming to the end of the wider part and the trail was narrowing again. Another step back and he and Ragi would have no room to move.

Then from out of the dark came a wild shriek, a howl of animal fury, and even Odd, who knew the men were there, jumped in surprise. He saw movement, shields swinging, men turning, shouts of shock and confusion as Broddi and the others launched themselves off the wall and drove into Skorri's men. Odd could see little beyond dark shapes flailing and stumbling, could hear the thumping of bodies against bodies and shoulders hitting shields, the bellowing of the attackers, the uncertain cries of the attacked.

Skorri's men were in a column two or three deep, and Broddi and his men slammed into their flank, pushing them sideways. Their shields were a liability now, wide encumbrances for Broddi's men to shove against. Skorri's warriors stumbled off-balance toward the edge of the cliff. Odd saw arms waving, heard the high-pitched screams as one and then another of Skorri's men went over the edge.

And then the whole side of the trail seemed to give way. The ground below Skorri's men just collapsed, the outer three feet of cliff simply crumbling as Skorri's men dropped straight down or tumbled sideways and disappeared, screaming into the abyss. It was a beautiful sight, but there was no time to watch.

"Broddi! You men, come on! Down the trail!" Odd shouted, and as he did, he wondered how many of Broddi's men had gone over the side with Skorri. They would find out in time, but not now. Now was the time for the men still standing to run.

Ragi led the way, moving downhill, Odd right on his heels. He heard men behind them and he assumed they were Broddi and the others and figured if they were not, then he would know when he got a sword thrust through the back. But he did not think he would. He did not think whoever was left of Skorri's men would be too eager to follow quickly behind.

Odd held Blood-letter in his left hand and he ran his right hand along the cliff edge at his side as he raced down the trail, keeping as close to it, and as far from the uncertain edge, as he could. He looked to his left. The moonlight was touching the water of the cove below, and he could make out Ragi's ship, still tied to the dock a quarter mile ahead and thirty feet below. He thought he saw movement on the deck, but he was not certain.

The trail started leveling out and widening as they made their way down and as it did Odd took his hand away from the cliff edge. Soon the trail was not a trail at all, but a wider expanse of ground, and he knew they had reached the bottom of the cliff, with the water of the cove lapping the shore twenty feet away. He breathed deep and made a sound that sounded very much like a sigh of relief.

He stopped and turned and saw Broddi and the rest of them come streaming past. If there were any men missing, he could not tell, but it did not seem as if there were. He looked back up the trail to see if any of Skorri's men were still in pursuit, but he could see no one.

"This way, Odd," Ragi said. "This way to the ship. Let's see if the Shipslayer is ready to put to sea."

Odd followed behind as Ragi led the men at a jog along the shoreline. He saw the dock just a hundred feet away and the ship tied alongside. They raced over the loose gravel along the shore and then out along the wooden dock, which creaked under their weight. Odd felt one of the planks starting to give under his foot, but he hurried on before it could break clean through.

He reached the ship's side and looked down. It was nearly full, the rowers sitting on the benches with oars raised and the women and the rest of the men crowded down the centerline. Bragi stood on the small deck aft and Huginn and Muninn stood ready to cast off the lines holding the ship to the dock.

"Get aboard, get aboard, what are you waiting for?" Bragi shouted, waving to the men still on the dock. One by one they slipped down over the side and found their footing and stepped onto the ship. Odd was the last to go. He reached down with his foot and found the edge of one of the rowing benches and stepped aboard, then from there stepped down onto the deck. His foot came down in water up to his ankle.

That's not good, he thought.

"Cast off! Cast off!" Bragi shouted and Huginn and Muninn untied the dock lines and tossed them onto the dock. "Oars down! Give way!"

The oars, starboard and larboard, came down and the rowers gave an awkward and uncoordinated pull.

"Together, you sorry bastards!" Bragi shouted. "Now... down... pull!" The oars came down again in far greater unison and pulled as one and the ship began to gather way.

Odd felt the water sloshing against his legs as the ship moved.

"All you whore's sons not rowing, you best find something to bail with, and get to it!" Bragi called. "Ragi wasn't lying…this bastard ship's going down faster than it's going forward!"

Odd could not miss the hint of delight in Bragi's voice.

Chapter Twenty-Seven

Lo, Satan's raging offspring suddenly burst out
From camp, weighed greatly down by weapons flashing bright.

Abbo of Saint-Germain

Felix was pleased with what he saw, and it helped mitigate his fury. Not entirely, but somewhat.

The royal courtyard was filled with men-at-arms: spearmen and archers and mounted warriors, men with shields and helmets and mail and swords. Well-appointed and experienced men. Just the men to crush underfoot Thorgrim and Louis de Roumois, as he was known to the common folk, who viewed him as some sort of hero, and the rest of them.

There were a bit more than six hundred armed men gathered, standing in their little clusters, waiting, preparing weapons, listening to the orders their captains were giving. Carts filled with the supplies that would sustain them in the field rolled out from the storehouses beyond the palace and formed into a line that would follow behind the column. Horses pranced and whinnied and shook their heads, eager, it seemed, to be at it.

It gave Felix a sense of calm, vengeance in the offing, though he still felt the sting of humiliation and defeat. It hurt more than the pain from the dagger cut across his cheek, now covered with a bandage. The wound had not been delivered by Harald, of course— the Northmen had done him no physical harm—but by his own hand. He needed some evidence that he had fought back, so he provided it himself.

It was a servant who found them, a boy sent to empty the chamber pots, of all things. Found them trussed up like swine at the butcher's, but at least the boy had sense enough to cut Felix free before running off in terror. Felix took him by the arm and made him swear to tell no one about what he had seen, the way they had been bound, and assured him that his throat would be cut if he did. Then he sent the boy off to raise the alarm, found his dagger and delivered the wound to his cheek.

The secretary was the only witness to that deception, and he would not say a word, and, indeed, through his blind terror, he might not even have noticed. The guards saw nothing, and likely never would again.

Not that Felix, consumed with rage, cared much about who saw what. He raced out of his chambers, blood streaming down his cheek, and began shouting even as he ran down the hall.

"Guards! Guards! The three men who just left, stop them, damn you all, stop them!"

At first his shouts were met with dumb surprise, but soon people started moving, running here and there, echoing his calls. Someone had the good sense to shout out one of the windows at the front of the palace, down to the ground below, where Grifo and the Northmen were trying to make their escape.

Felix flew down the big stairs and out the front door. He could see them at the far end of the courtyard, making for the gate. He watched with satisfaction as the guards from outside the wall came charging at them from one direction, and the chevaliers came from another. He hoped the men would be taken alive so he could see about killing them slowly. It was not about fear of losing the map; much as he did not want to lose it, he had copies. Rather, it was the humiliation that he could not endure. And nothing would ease that quite like watching Grifo and Harald and the other Northman screaming their lives away.

And so, for Felix, it was a terrible, terrible thing to watch as the fugitives took down first two, then all four of the guards, and then dispatched or eluded the powerful mounted warriors. He stared, open-mouthed and helpless, as Grifo and the others reached the main gate and disappeared into the streets.

There were more men-at-arms running to the sound of the fight and Felix called on them to go in pursuit. He sent them to the bridges and all the landings in the city, figuring that the Northmen would have come by water and would try to get back to their boat. But in his heart he knew it was pointless. Grifo, in his capacity as

Felix's eyes and ears, knew all the hidden streets and alleys of Paris. If he wanted to avoid capture, he was certainly capable of doing so.

The men-at-arms returned some time later, exhausted, frightened to report that two more guards had been killed and the fugitives had escaped. But Felix had expected no less. He was already thinking about what had to be done next.

The south wing of the palace held the chambers for the king's more important guests, including Duc Eberhard of Roumois. It was there that Felix sought him out, rapping on the door with an emphatic knock that suggested he would not be put off. A moment later, a voice called, "Come!"

Felix flung open the door and strode in. Eberhard was seated at a small table, the remains of a meal spread over the surface, a cup in his hand. A few of Eberhard's men were arranged at various other places in the chambers. A servant girl stood off to one side, and Felix had the impression she would be serving the duke more than food and drink that evening.

After I'm done with him, he won't be in the mood, Felix thought.

"Duc Eberhard," Felix said, giving a barely perceptible bow. "You know what's happened just now?"

"Ahh…" Eberhard said, as if he was trying to see what trap Felix might be laying. "I heard you were viciously attacked in your chambers."

"Yes," Felix said, and his fingers brushed the bandage on his cheek. "That traitor Grifo was part of it. The others were Northmen. The Northmen that your brother commands."

"Commands?" Eberhard said. "Does he? I thought you had taken care of all that."

"He is your brother," Felix said sharply. "He is in your dukedom of Roumois. He is very much your problem to deal with."

"Yes, well, I had meant to talk to the king about that very thing," Eberhard started in.

"I speak for the king in this matter," Felix said. And that was mostly true. He had certainly discussed the affair with Charles. But the king had seemed uninterested, even bored by it all, and said only that he was sure Felix could handle the situation. Which he intended to do.

"We'll need men, supplies," Eberhard protested. "I know you were starting to organize something, but I'm sure it will take us some time to get it all together."

"The time is now," Felix said. "You march on the morrow."

"I...I march, you say?" Eberhard asked. "I'm to command?"

Eberhard was many things: a duke, a not-so-close friend to the king, a coward, a failed fratricide, and a man of exceptionally weak will. He was terrified of leading soldiers into battle and terrified of what might happen if he refused to do so. Felix was not sure which of those fears would prove most influential.

"The Northmen are at Roumois," Felix explained. "Louis is with them. They must not come any farther up the Seine. The king will not be pleased if they do. Not pleased at all. Particularly not if the folk rally to Louis's banner. This is your responsibility."

"Well, it's not as if I've done nothing to stop that," Eberhard protested. "I sent my best men to all the towns and villages so they might seek out spies and traitors."

"And did they find any?" Louis asked.

"Yes, a few," Eberhard said, but his defensive tone only reinforced what Louis already knew. Eberhard's house guard had found only a handful of men still loyal to Louis, and might well have hanged several who were not.

There was no way to judge just how much support Louis enjoyed in Roumois, but Felix knew that Eberhard had done little to endear himself to the people. It did not really matter, of course, whether or not the lower sort liked their duke, or, indeed, anyone who ruled over them. But Charles would not be pleased if he had to deal with a rebellion in his kingdom.

If it came to that, then choices would have to be made.

"Your efforts so far, they're neither here nor there," Felix said. "It's time for a bold stroke. For this past week you've been playing at getting your men-at-arms ready. Now it's time to march. On the morrow."

"On the..." Eberhard spluttered. "But I have only my house guard, a couple hundred men at best. I hear the Northmen number in the thousands."

"Three hundred, give or take," Felix said. "And along with your foot soldiers you have your horse guard. They were once the most respected men-at-arms in the kingdom." It was a merciless dig: under

Louis's command the horse guard had indeed earned that degree of respect, but Felix had not heard much good about them since Louis's banishment.

"See here," Felix continued, his tone more conciliatory now. "The king has agreed to lend you four hundred of his best men. With those and your house guard and the mounted warriors you should certainly be able to defeat an undisciplined rabble of heathens."

"Yes...yes..."

"And you have Mariwig to help with the men. He's a good soldier, a seasoned soldier. He fought with Louis and he'll know how to counter him."

"Yes...yes..." Eberhard said again.

Felix crossed his arms and waited to see which fear would win out: Eberhard's fear of battle or his fear of the king's disfavor.

It was the latter, in the end.

"Very well," Eberhard said with an elaborate sigh. "I have a world of things to do here, in court, but I suppose I can ride out and deal with my traitorous brother and these heathens. If that's the king's wish."

"It is," Felix said, making a note that he would have to inform the king about all this as soon as he could. If the king actually seemed at all interested in hearing about it.

And so, the next day, at first light, the courtyard became a scramble of activity as Eberhard's men-at-arms and those of the king who had been named to join them made ready to march, cooking their breakfasts and seeing to their weapons and armor and horses as the last of the supplies were loaded onto the carts.

"Mariwig!" Felix called to the tall man in chainmail who had just finished shouting at a handful of archers, lounging about.

"Lord?" Mariwig said, turning. He was an ugly man, but somehow Felix found encouragement in that. Mariwig was no dandy. He had the look of a fighting man, a man not too refined to shrink from doing what must be done.

"Where's Eberhard?" Felix asked.

"Don't know, lord," Mariwig said. "Ain't seen him. But he'll be along, I don't doubt."

Felix nodded. He had an image of Eberhard puking into his chamber pot, terrified to the point of nausea by the thought of riding into battle. He nodded toward the men-at-arms in the courtyard.

"You have what you need here? To drive Louis and the heathens into the ground?"

"Should do," Mariwig said. "If we can come to grips with them. But that Louis, he's a slippery one, and he knows every inch of Roumois. And the people like him."

"I see," Felix said. "And you? Do you like him?"

Mariwig frowned. "I don't like anyone, lord. But I'm loyal to my duke and my king."

"Glad to hear it," Felix said. "Because you'll be in command here. Eberhard might ride at the head of these men, but you'll command. You understand?"

"Yes, lord."

"I want Louis and the heathens crushed, and crushed quickly," Felix continued. "Understand, the king does not give a damn who rules in Roumois. He cares only that there is no unrest in his kingdom. This cannot spread."

"I understand, Lord," Mariwig said with a shallow bow. He looked off to his right. "Ah, here comes Duke Eberhard at last."

"Very well," Felix said. He did not have the stomach to deal with Eberhard, not at that moment. "I'll leave you, then. You know what I expect."

"Yes, Lord," Mariwig said.

"Louis, and the leader of the heathens, a man named Thorgrim," Felix added. "When you return, pray, return with their heads on pikes. On my honor, you'll be amply rewarded."

There's something he's afraid to say, Thorgrim Night Wolf thought as he listened to Harald's tale. He could hear it in Harald's words: the hesitancy, the meandering.

No, not afraid, Thorgrim corrected himself. *He just doesn't know how I'll react.*

He and Louis and the other captains were in the great room of le Château de Roumois, listening as Harald, Brand, and Grifo recounted their journey. They had arrived back at Roumois only a short while before, four days after first setting out for Paris.

As the story unfolded, Thorgrim nodded his approval. The men's boldness and initiative were very much to his liking. He frowned on hearing of Felix's reneging on the promised payment, though he was not at all surprised.

"So, when I realized that Felix wouldn't pay, I thought we can still get something of value from this bastard, besides silver!'" Harald said.

Here it is, Thorgrim thought. "And what is that?"

"This!" Harald took the scroll in his hand and rolled it out on the table. Thorgrim looked at it. It was vaguely familiar, but he could not quite place it.

"Don't you recall?" Harald asked. "This is the map that Felix showed us, back in Engla-land. The map of the whole world. Or most of it, anyway."

Thorgrim nodded. He recalled now, though he was still not entirely clear as to what he was seeing, or why Harald thought it was of such value.

"And this…" Thorgrim said. "You think this is worth as much as silver?"

"Well, maybe not as much as silver," Harald said. "But think…a map that shows a man all the places he can go. In the whole world."

"And Felix just gave this to you?" Thorgrim asked.

"Just like that," Grifo said. "After Harald and Brand killed the guards and Harald held a knife to Felix's throat."

"Hmm…" Thorgrim said. If Felix would only give the map up on threat of death, then he, too, must consider it to be of great value. Thorgrim wondered what it was about this strange parchment that he was not understanding.

"If you had a knife to Felix's throat," Thorgrim said, "I'm guessing you didn't just walk out of there, map in hand."

"No," Harald admitted. "No, it took a little more than that." He went on to describe in broad strokes the fight in the courtyard, the run through the alleys, Grifo's creating a stampede in the face of the mounted warriors.

Harald did not exaggerate his exploits, or puff himself up in the telling, and he gave his companions ample credit, all of which Thorgrim was happy to hear. But he could picture the truth of the thing as Harald spoke, the hard fighting, the clash of weapons, the desperate feeling of being overwhelmed.

Harald concluded with their rowing clear of the Paris docks and a mention of the two days it took them to pull downriver to where they had set out. Around him, Thorgrim heard whistles of surprise and grunts of admiration from the others, but he was not so sure.

"So," he said, "you risked your life, and the lives of your men, for...that?" He gestured toward the map laid out on the table.

"Yes," Harald said, and Thorgrim heard the defensiveness creeping into his voice. The boy seemed surprised that he, Thorgrim, did not see that it was worth taking such risk for such a reward. "This map is...I've never seen the like. And neither have you, Father."

Thorgrim's eyebrows came together, but before he could speak, Grifo jumped into the conversation. "There was another thing Harald seems to have forgotten about," he said.

"And that is?" Thorgrim asked.

"There was an army making ready to move. Mounted warriors, spearmen, archers. Looks like they were putting together a supply train. I can well guess where they're bound."

Thorgrim looked at Harald and then back at Grifo. That was indeed a pretty important detail to leave out, more important than this strange map that seemed to have captured Harald's imagination.

"Were they close to marching?" Thorgrim asked.

"Not when we saw," Grifo said. "But I suspect Harald's exploits have inspired them to greater speed."

"I see," Thorgrim said. "Will they come by boat?"

"No. They'll march. Three, four days. So, assuming they left the day after we made our escape, they'll be here...soon."

"If I had my mounted warriors as scouts, then we'd know exactly where they are," Louis said. "But I have no one."

"It seems that way," Thorgrim said. "And it seems this army may appear any time. Which means we had best sail on the next tide. You can come with us, Louis, or you can go hide in the woods, as you wish."

Louis frowned. He looked around the room at the other men and then back at Thorgrim. "There's still silver to be had," he said. "Silver in my brother's vaults. I can pay you, if you stay and fight."

Thorgrim smiled. "More Frankish promises? How about we just take that silver now, and then sail? What stops us from doing that?"

Louis paused again. "Nothing," he admitted.

"No harm to you," Thorgrim continued. "It's your brother's silver we're taking, not yours, isn't that right?"

"Yes," Louis admitted. "Yes, that's right."

Thorgrim nodded. In truth he was just toying with Louis de Roumois. He had no intention of sailing off. If the Franks, Felix, and his lot, would not pay in silver, they would pay in blood. And they would pay with whatever plunder or ransom could be had from the defeated army.

Besides, Thorgrim did not care to abandon Louis. He had come to respect the man, even like him, at least during those time when he did not wish to cut his throat.

"No, I've changed my mind," Thorgrim said to Louis. "Me and my crew, we'll stay and fight with you, and we'll take whatever blood and treasure we're owed. But I won't tell anyone else here what to do." He turned to the other captains. "You decide for yourselves, each man on his own. Anyone who wants to sail off, that's fine with me. It's not our fight, I get that. You can take some time to think on it, if you wish. But not too long."

The other captains looked surprised by this, having not realized, apparently, that Thorgrim was just needling Louis. But they did not need long to consider their choice.

"I'll stay and fight, me and the Dragons," Harald said, which was hardly a surprise, but Asmund of *Oak Heart* was just behind him, grunting and saying, "Me and my men, we'll fight." And then each in turn; Gudrid of *Blood Hawk*, Halldor, who commanded *Black Wing*, Hardbein of *Fox*, all nodded and affirmed that they, too, would join Louis in the fight.

"Well," Louis said, then paused, struggling for what to say next. "Thank you."

"You can thank us with silver, once we've butchered your brother and his men," Asmund said and the others nodded.

"And that I will," Louis said. "But first, let us consider how we'll bring that great slaughter about."

Chapter Twenty-Eight

*Our enemy is a foreigner, begirt with the arms
and the wealth of almost all the West.*

Saxo Grammaticus
The Danish History

The evening was getting on, the shadows deep, which was very much to the men's liking. They were crouched at the edge of the tree line, looking out over the open ground, and confident that they could not be seen. They watched in silence. They were not encouraged by what they saw.

"Five hundred men, I should think," said the younger man. He spoke in a soft voice, nearly a whisper, though there was little chance of their being overheard. The others were a hundred yards away, and the air was filled with the sounds of shouting and hammers falling and horses whinnying and barrels rolling off carts: the clamor of an army making camp.

"Five hundred, for certain," the old man said. He nodded to the middle of the open ground. "Here goes Eberhard's tent." A round pavilion, sixteen feet in diameter, a striking white canvas with crimson fringe around the upper edge of the wall, was being raised by a dozen men.

"A wonder he can endure such hardship," the younger man said.

"He doesn't reckon to be in the field long."

The army had marched from Paris two days earlier, but Ranulf and Gunthar had only just received word of its presence. Not that they were terribly surprised. Once word reached West Frankia that Louis de Roumois had returned, they knew there would be a response from the duke, and a forceful one at that. Now, here it was.

"Another two days and they'll reach le Château de Roumois," Gunthar said. "If that's where they're heading."

"That's where they're heading," Ranulf said with certainty. "Secrets are not easily kept. Besides, if you and I know that Louis and his heathens are at the château, then Eberhard certainly knows it as well. So that's where he'll go."

Gunthar grunted his agreement. "He has men enough for the job at hand, it seems," he added.

"He does," Ranulf said. "The archers, and the foot soldiers, over there." He pointed to the west end of the field where a series of small tents were going up. "Those are the king's men, not the duke's."

"So the king will get his hand in this?" Gunthar asked. He sounded worried.

"He has to," Ranulf said. "He has to be seen to support the sitting duke. But the force he's sent, it's not so impressive. He could have sent a thousand men if he wanted to."

"So why didn't he?"

"I don't know," Ranulf said. In fact, he had been wondering just that thing.

"Maybe he has trouble elsewhere," he suggested. "Or maybe he wants all his men-at-arms at home while the king of Wessex is at court. Or maybe he just doesn't care that much about le duc de Roumois."

"Let us pray it's the last one," Gunthar said.

They watched for a few moments more as the men-at-arms settled into camp and the darkness spread over the field. Then, in a half-crouch, they shuffled back until the trees hid them entirely and they dared to stand upright again. They found the trail they had taken and made their way, in the fading light, a quarter mile to where they had left their horses tied to saplings. They mounted and rode in silence, listening over the soft clomp of the horses' hooves for any worrisome sounds, but there was nothing but the insects in the grass and the call of the nightjars.

It was two miles or so along a road that was barely discernable, but soon they smelled the faint tang of wood smoke and, occasionally, that of roasting meat and they knew they were getting close. Suddenly, a dark shape moved in front of them, a shade in the night, and a voice.

"Hold! Who's there?"

"Ranulf and Gunthar," Ranulf said. "Is all well?"

"Aye, yes, sir," the shade replied and they saw him move aside and they rode on. A hundred yards farther, they emerged from the trees and saw the smattering of cook fires spread over the field, people moving in and out of the light, and the silhouette of the tree line against the last of the evening's sky, but it was nearly full dark by then, and they could see little else.

They made their way through the camp, and Ranulf nodded and greeted the men they passed, and spoke words of encouragement, though he was not particularly encouraged himself. These were the men who had rallied when word spread of Louis's return, the men who had been waiting for three years and more for this moment. Some of them were men-at-arms who had set aside their swords some time ago. Some were farmers armed with axes and scythes. Some were smiths or coopers or butchers and they came to fight with whatever weapons they could lay hands on.

They numbered around three hundred. Ranulf thought of the five hundred trained and experienced warriors bedding down a few miles away, the men-at-arms against who this sorry lot would be fighting, and he sighed, despite himself.

"More will come," Gunthar said, divining the meaning of Ranulf's sigh. "Word is getting around the country. Hundreds more are on their way, you'll see."

"More farmers?" Ranulf said. "More coopers?"

"Get enough farmers with axes and coopers with spears and they'll overrun legions," Gunthar said, and Ranulf smiled.

"You're right, of course," Ranulf said, though he did not add that they meant to attack on the morrow, or the next day at the latest, and they would not gather enough men by then to overrun legions. But they didn't have to overrun legions. They had only to overrun Eberhard's men. That would be enough.

"Besides," Gunthar added, "we have Mariwig. And I have to think that Louis will bring his Northmen."

"Yes…" Ranulf said. "The Northmen."

He had to marvel at that odd twist. He and Louis had spent years fighting Northmen, driving the vermin from the shores of the Seine. They had become legendary for their skill and daring. Every man now rallying to Louis's banner was there because of their gratitude for the way that they—Louis and Ranulf and Mariwig and the rest of the chevaliers—had protected Roumois from the Northmen. It was not just their hatred of Eberhard that drove them, though that was palpable. It was their love for Louis.

And now, they were counting on Northmen to help defeat their rightful duke and to put Louis in his place.

The two riders reached the pavilion tent near the center of the camp, a round affair, the poverty-stricken cousin of the one that Eberhard was currently occupying. They reined the horses to a stop and slid to the ground as a couple of boys stepped up to take the horses away, then the men ducked through the flap of the pavilion and stepped inside.

A few lanterns hung from hooks, casting the interior in light and shadow. There were five pallets for beds around the perimeter, and a table in the center, strew with bottles, cups, papers and a platter with bread and cheese. A man of middling age, the one other person in the tent, was sitting on a bench at the table and studying the papers spread out before him, but he looked up as Ranulf and Gunthar stepped in.

"Ah, good sirs, you're back," he said, matter-of-factly.

"Good evening, Adalman. Yes, we're back," Ranulf said as he and Gunthar unbuckled their sword belts and laid down their weapons.

"And what did you find?" Adalman asked.

"Pretty much what the scouts reported, though Eberhard has more men than they thought he did. About five hundred, I would say. Archers, spearmen. The chevaliers. Eberhard's house guard and king's men as well."

"Well, the king would have to involve himself, wouldn't he?" Adalman said. "He couldn't simply leave one of his nobles out to dry. Not the example he would wish to send."

"No, indeed," Ranulf said. "But his majesty was not overly generous with the men he sent. I get comfort from that."

"As do I," Gunthar said. "Has Childric returned?"

"No," Adalman said.

Ranulf was disappointed to hear it, but not surprised. These men—Childric, Adalman, Gunthar—were the ones who had long been part of the planning begun by Ranulf, preparations for the day when Louis would return from across the narrow seas.

There had been no word from Louis during his exile. He had had no part in these schemes, was not even aware that they were taking place. Ranulf, in truth, did not actually know if Louis really would return, or if he was even still alive. But he had had faith, and that faith had driven him, and now it would be rewarded.

He hoped.

"I wouldn't expect Childric to be back yet," Gunthar said. "It's a long ride to le Château de Roumois and back. And there's much for him to discuss when he's there."

Ranulf nodded. *Time*, he thought. *If only we had more time.*

The irony did not escape him. This uprising had been years in the making. Hiding out from Eberhard's men, moving from village to village, struggling to make something—anything—happen, Ranulf had felt as if there was nothing but time. And then, suddenly, like a thunderclap, came word of Louis's return, and with it a feeling that there was no time left at all, and so much to put into motion.

The Northmen were something Ranulf had not foreseen, and how could he have? In his imagination, Louis returned in secret to Roumois, and the two of them spent months gathering their forces, planning their strike, amassing weapons and training their ad hoc army. But it had not worked out that way. Instead, Louis had come in company with a host of Northmen and the king of Wessex, of all things. His presence, far from being secret, was well known in court and to Eberhard. Ranulf was prepared for none of that.

But that was all right. Ranulf was a warrior, and a warrior learned early that things rarely played out the way one envisioned. And so, in battle, you improvised. And he was doing that now. He had sent Childric, that trusted man, off to le Château de Roumois to meet with Louis. And they would improvise.

Gunthar picked up a knife from the table and cut a slice of cheese, then set it on a hunk of bread and handed it to Ranulf.

"Thank you," Ranulf said, taking the food gratefully and biting off a piece.

"You think these Northmen will fight with us?" Gunthar asked. "Childric isn't just wasting his time?"

Ranulf swallowed. "I have no idea. I can't begin to guess what their connection to Louis might be. But it seems they brought him here, and from what we've heard, they've stayed with him, so I have to imagine they're allies, of a sort."

Gunthar and Adalman both nodded. "Strange," Adalman said.

"It is that," Ranulf agreed. "But I'll be happy for any help. Despite young Gunthar's optimism, we don't have time to gather enough men to fight Eberhard. But with the Northmen on our side, we stand a chance. Three hundred of them, or so I'm given to understand. And the heathens, I can tell you, they fight like demons."

"They *are* demons," Adalman said and crossed himself. "I just hope we're not making a mistake, making friends with the devil."

"I'll take the devil over Eberhard," Gunthar said. "I'll warrant the devil ain't so greedy and cruel as that one."

"I'll warrant you're right." Ranulf sat down on the bench nearest him, suddenly weary to the bone. He reached down and pulled off one boot, and then the other.

"Pray God the Northmen are with us," Ranulf said. "We can't delay. The high ground south of Rouen, that's where we want to fight, and Eberhard will be there tomorrow."

Gunthar and Adalman nodded. They had scouted the road from the border of Roumois to the château looking for the best place to strike. They found it south of Rouen, at a place where the road ran through a pass between steep hills and was lined with deep forest on either side. An army could hide in those woods, unseen, and launch its attack as the enemy marched out from the pass. The confines of hills and trees would make maneuvering difficult, and flanking impossible. It would give Ranulf's inferior force an advantage they would never enjoy on open ground.

"It will be a race to get there," Adalman said. "Get there and get our men in place before Eberhard comes blundering along."

"That won't be a problem," Ranulf assured him. "With all their field equipment, their baggage train, the oxen, Eberhard's damned pavilion…we could crawl to Rouen and still beat them there. And Louis and the Northmen, they have half the distance to cover that we do. It will be a hard fight, but we have good reason for hope."

Ranulf's words were meant to reassure his younger friends, but as it happened, they were also true. A well-set ambush, Mariwig in place, the help of the Northmen, it was not a dream that they might crush Eberhard underfoot; it was a very real possibility. A likelihood, even.

Ranulf opened his mouth to say more and then shut it as he heard hoofbeats beyond the tent, a rider coming fast. He stood and Adalman stood and the three of them ducked through the flap and out into the night.

The rider was just reining up as they emerged, the light from the few lanterns by the door glinting off the horse's sweat-streaked flanks. It was Childric, as the men expected it would be, and he dropped from the saddle even as the horse was just coming to a stop.

"Childric!" Ranulf said. "Do tell, what news? Did you speak with Louis? Are the Northmen with us?"

Childric was breathing hard, his eyes wide, his expression not one that Ranulf found particularly comforting. He took a deep breath and wiped his brow with his sleeve and said, "They're gone, Ranulf. The lot of them, they're gone."

This was met with silence. Ranulf was the first to speak. "Who's gone? The Northmen?"

"The Northmen," Childric said. "And Louis. Everyone. The only soul at the château was some ancient named Hildirik and he told me they had all sailed off."

"Where? Sailed off to where?" Gunthar asked, a desperate note in his voice.

"He didn't know with any certainty, but Louis told him something about sailing for Frisia and gathering more warriors there. This Hildirik thought Louis reckoned he didn't have enough men to take on his brother, and so he left to gather more."

"And you saw no ships there? No men?" Ranulf asked.

"I met some farmers on the road, and they said they had seen the Northmen's ships sail away. But at the château there was not a one, save for Hildirik, like I said."

Hildirik, Ranulf thought. He had known the man for many years. Hildirik had been entirely loyal to the old duke, and devoted to Roumois, though Ranulf had always thought his loyalty to Eberhard was something less than complete. But he had no reason to think that Hildirik was playing them false.

Ranulf's head was swimming with this new revelation. It was too terrible to believe, and yet, it made complete sense. Louis knew nothing of the army gathering in his support. He would hardly think that he had men enough to defeat Eberhard, who he would know was backed by the king. Perhaps the Northmen had no intention of fighting with him. That would have left Louis completely alone. Of course he would sail off in search of fighting men.

"Is that it, then?" Adalman asked. "Do we call off the attack, wait on another day?"

That was the question, of course, to fight or not to fight. Ranulf knew he should think about it, should consult with the others. There were valid arguments to be made either way. But Ranulf was not in the mood for arguments, valid or otherwise.

"No," he said. "We fight. Eberhard must be stopped before he reaches le Château de Roumois. Once he's behind those walls, there will be no getting at him. We've put this all in place. We have the men gathered and ready. We spoke with Amsind yesterday and he assures us Mariwig and the others are ready as well. Nothing has changed."

"Except that Louis is not here. And the Northmen are not here," Adalman said.

"We never counted on the Northmen anyway," Gunthar pointed out.

"And Louis will not be gone for long, I wouldn't think," Ranulf said. "He knows that the moment is now, now that word has spread of his return." He hoped the others could not hear the lack of conviction in his voice. With each new bit of bad news their position seemed to grow more tenuous. But it did not change the fact that they were ready to strike on the morrow, and so strike they must.

"We're agreed, then?" Ranulf asked, looking at the faces of each of the silent, worried rebels. "We attack as we planned? We have surprise, we have our men-at-arms assembled. We have Mariwig in place. And we have God, who sides with the righteous in fights such as this."

Slowly, one by one, the others nodded. But they did not look terribly certain. Not certain at all.

Chapter Twenty-Nine

Great shouts and uproar grow, and fear is greater yet,
These fight, and those fight back, with clashing arms.

Abbo of Saint Germain

It was dawn, first light, and Eberhard heard the sounds of the camp stirring to life: the clang of cooking pots, the muted call of orders, the shuffle of men over the dew-covered grass. He smelled the wood smoke creeping in through the canvas door of his pavilion, and the odors of horses and porridge and roasting meat.

He was awake, and had been for some time. Indeed, he had been awake through a good part of the night, staring up at the canvas roof of his tent, illuminated by the various lanterns he kept burning all through the dark hours. He did not like the dark. Darkness meant cover for those who would do him harm.

Darkness, of course, was not the only cover for the treacherous. Mendacity was a cover. False loyalty was a cover. Pretended obedience was a cover. Lanterns could not hold those things at bay, but other forces could. A core of trusted men, men who could truly be trusted, could do that. Having eyes and ears everywhere could do that. And Eberhard had both those things.

"Otker!" Eberhard shouted. He had been waiting a torturously long time to get things going. He had meant to wait even longer, until after the men had broken their fasts, but he could not stand it for a moment more. This had been so long in the making. The men and their stomachs could wait now. It was time to act.

"Otker!" he called again, but as he did, the door to the pavilion was drawn back and Otker stepped in. He was dressed in a mail shirt, sword and short sword on his belt, crimson-and-white sash around his waist. He was a burly, ruddy-faced man, probably twenty years

Eberhard's senior. He had been charged with protecting Eberhard ever since the young heir to Roumois had first left the nursery.

Eberhard had never felt the need to replace him. Rather, he paid him handsomely and lavished him with silver and land and women. In exchange, Eberhard received loyalty. Complete loyalty. Otker and his men, twenty in all, formed Eberhard's personal bodyguard, and they were the only men he trusted completely, the only ones whose loyalty he had not felt it necessary to test. It was their presence alone that allowed him to sleep at night, at least on those occasions when he was able to sleep.

"Lord Eberhard?" Otker asked. Otker was smart enough, but not too smart, and that was another reason that Eberhard trusted him. Eberhard did not like clever men.

"I think it's time," Eberhard said. "Bring Mariwig to me."

"Yes, lord." Otker nodded and ducked back out of the tent. Eberhard had told him they would do this after the men broke their fast, and now he was changing his mind, but Otker knew better than to question.

Eberhard called for his servant next, and as he waited on Otker, he donned his padded tunic and mail shirt and strapped on his sword belt. He felt a little twist in his stomach as he made ready. He would very likely be drawing his sword in battle this day, which was not a thing he was much used to doing, or very eager to do.

He would be surrounded by Otker's men, of course, and ranks of the king's men would stand between him and the enemy, an enemy that would likely be a rabble of outnumbered farmers. He was not likely to be in much danger. He reminded himself of that fact, and tried to take comfort from it.

But of course, there was Louis.

His brother was out there, somewhere. From what Eberhard had heard, Louis was ensconced at le Château de Roumois in the company of three hundred Northmen. And that was Eberhard's real concern. Louis was a fighter, a skilled warrior, and even though Eberhard would never say as much out loud, he knew that it was true. And now it seemed his brother was commanding not chevaliers but barbaric heathens who knew no sort of Christian mercy. That was a situation to be feared.

"Your Grace?" Otker's voice came from outside the canvas door.

Eberhard moved behind a table that stood in the middle of the pavilion and called for him to enter. Otker pushed aside the door and stepped through, with Mariwig behind him and two of Otker's men behind Mariwig. They stopped at the opposite side of the table and gave shallow bows.

"My lord?" Mariwig said. He did not look frightened or suspicious, necessarily, but he did not look entirely at ease, either.

Nor would Eberhard have expected him to be. This was a very odd situation. He was accustomed to speaking with his duke in private, not with three of Eberhard's bodyguards surrounding him. If nothing else, it should be clear that something was out of the ordinary.

"Mariwig," Eberhard said. "Have you seen Amsind this morrow?"

"Ahh...no, my lord..." Mariwig said the words slowly, as if looking for a trap as he spoke.

"And last evening? Did you see him then?"

"Not sure I recall, my lord," Mariwig said. "He has his duties; I have mine. Sometimes we're called to different places."

"Ah, I see," Eberhard said. He was the cat now, playing with the mouse. "But Amsind is your second-in-command. Your trusted friend. I would think you would have much to discuss, here on the eve of battle."

"We do, mostly," Mariwig said. "But sometimes we have no need of speaking. With this campaign, we know our duties." Despite the calm on the man's face, Eberhard could hear the growing concern in Mariwig's voice.

"Actually, Amsind has no duties," Eberhard said. "I've had him arrested."

"Arrested?" Mariwig said, and his surprise sounded genuine, but then Mariwig had a talent for hiding his disloyalty. Eberhard could see that now. It was what had allowed Mariwig to live and to resume his duties even as his brother died under the ax. Eberhard had been fooled, and he did not like to be fooled. And now it was time for someone to pay.

"If it please your lord, why was Amsind arrested?" Mariwig continued.

"Let's go find out, shall we?" Eberhard stepped around the table and out the pavilion door. Otker, he found, had followed his orders precisely, as he usually did. Amsind, hands bound, was standing to one side, flanked by two of Otker's men. One of his eyes was black and bloody and swollen shut, and a wide streak of dried blood ran down from the corner of his mouth. His hair was in wild disarray and his clothes were torn and caked with mud.

The rest of the camp were assembling, forming a half-circle around the entrance to Eberhard's pavilion. Mariwig's horse guard, dismounted and unarmed, were in the front ranks, Eberhard's spearmen behind them, and the king's men farther back. In the middle of the half-circle, as conspicuous as possible, stood a chopping block.

Eberhard moved to one side and let Otker and the two guards lead Mariwig to the center of the open space, stopping a few feet from the block.

"Amsind," Eberhard said, speaking loud enough that the assembled men could hear. "You were arrested last night. Please tell the men why you were arrested."

For a moment Amsind just glared at Eberhard, an amazing show of defiance, really, given what he had been through during the night. Eberhard nodded to the guard at Amsind's side and the man wound up and hit Amsind hard in the back of the head, sending him sprawling to the ground. The other guard stepped up and grabbed a fistful of his hair and pulled him back to his feet.

"Why were you arrested?" Eberhard asked again.

"Meeting with an enemy," Amsind said, his voice barely audible. The guard at his side grabbed his hair once again and jerked his head back.

"Meeting with the enemy!" Amsind repeated, considerably louder this time.

"Meeting with the enemy," Eberhard said. "Like some thieving whore's son you snuck out of camp and met with the enemies of the king and Roumois, isn't that right? Or are Otker's men who followed you lying to me?"

Again, Amsind paused, until the guard at his side lifted his clenched fist once more.

"I did it, lord," Amsind shouted before the man could strike him. "Yes, I did it!"

"And who was this enemy you met with?"

"Don't know, lord, I…"

"Yes, yes," Eberhard interrupted. "I don't care who you met with. Who commands this enemy? The enemy you're so friendly with?"

Amsind looked from Eberhard to Mariwig and then back at Eberhard. "Ranulf," he said. "It's Ranulf!"

"Shut your mouth, you damned fool!" Mariwig roared. "Do you think you can save yourself?"

Otker spun half around and hit Mariwig hard on the face with his open hand, making him stagger sideways. Mariwig looked up at him, glaring, blood running from his nose and down his beard.

"You talk when you're asked a question, you traitorous bastard!" Otker ordered.

"Ranulf?" Eberhard said, turning to Mariwig. "But I thought Ranulf was dead. Don't you recall, Mariwig, you brought me his head yourself?"

There were any number of excuses that Mariwig might have presented, any number of tales the man might have told, and Eberhard was ready to counter any of them. But none came. Mariwig did not speak. He only glared at Eberhard, blood flowing down his face.

"Tell us, why were you meeting Ranulf's men?" Eberhard asked, turning back to Amsind. He himself had heard it all last night, after Otker and his men had applied sufficient threats and punishment, and now it was time for the others to hear. "Ranulf, who seems to have risen from the grave. What were you planning?"

Amsind was silent. He frowned and stiffened, bracing for another blow. He looked to Mariwig as if waiting for orders, but Mariwig said nothing.

The guard hit Amsind hard on the back of the head, snapping his head forward, and Amsind shouted at Mariwig, "He says he'll take my wife! My wife and my children! Feed them to his dogs!"

Mariwig nodded. "And nothing you say now will stop him."

"Speak!" Eberhard shouted and the guard hit Amsind again.

"We were going to turn on you!" Amsind said, the last vestige of hope gone, the words spilling out. "When Ranulf and the others attacked, Mariwig would give the word and the horse guard would turn on you and fight with Ranulf! It was Mariwig's plan all along!"

Eberhard looked at Mariwig, expecting some protest from the man, but Mariwig just slowly shook his head. He seemed to have more pity and disgust than anger.

"Well?" Eberhard said. "What say you?"

Mariwig met his eyes, and his face, as usual, was hard to read, but there was nothing good to be seen there. Then, in one swift motion, Mariwig reached down and ripped off the crimson-and-white sash from around his waist, threw it on the ground, and drove his foot into it.

"I say you're a coward and a miserable pile of shit!" Mariwig growled. "I say Louis will rip your lungs out with his bare hands!" He spit at Eberhard, even as Otker hit him once again, hard enough to drive him down on one knee.

There was growling now, an undercurrent of angry noise. Eberhard turned to the gathered men. The horse guard were stirring, speaking in voices too low for him to make out the words, but he knew what they were saying. He nodded to the spearmen behind them and said, "Now!" Forty spears came down level, points aimed at the horsemen's backs, some even poking into the flesh of those bold enough to take a step in Eberhard's direction.

The horse guard fell silent and did not move.

Mariwig was standing again, the blood flowing faster than before. Eberhard pointed at him and shouted, "This man is a traitor! You heard it, heard if from his own lips! And now we see what becomes of traitors!"

The two guards flanking Mariwig grabbed his arms and pulled them back behind him and lashed his wrists together. They shoved him forward three steps to the chopping block then pushed him to his knees, his head on the scarred wood. Mariwig made no sound, and he did not resist.

Otker stepped up to Mariwig's side, drawing his sword as he did. He brought the weapon up over his head, holding the hilt with two hands.

"God save Louis and Roumois!" Mariwig shouted and the sword came down, a fast, powerful stroke with a sharp blade, and it did not pause as it took Mariwig's head clean off. Blood gushed from the stump of the neck. Mariwig's body seemed to deflate and sink in on itself as his head hit the ground and rolled.

Otker held the sword aside, grabbed Mariwig's head by the hair, and lifted it up, face toward the crowd. "This is an end to traitors!" he shouted. The guards who had pushed Mariwig to the ground now dragged his headless corpse clear of the block. Eberhard clenched his teeth and looked away and willed himself not to vomit in front of the men.

He turned to Amsind and gestured for the men standing guard over him to bring him forward. Unlike Mariwig, Amsind twisted and struggled as the guards dragged him over to the chopping block.

"No!" Amsind shouted. "Faith, I did what you wanted, I told the truth! You gave your word, Eberhard!"

Eberhard leaned a bit closer, but he did not look Amsind in the eyes. Rather, he looked down at the bloody ground at their feet as he said, "You're a treasonous bastard, Amsind, with no honor. I've no call to keep my word to such filth as you. But as you go to your death, know this. I won't feed your family to my dogs. Your children will be sold at the slave markets. Your wife will be given to my personal guard for their amusement. And when they're done with her, if there's anything left, then that will be fed to my dogs."

Amsind started to shout, but the guard at his left hit him in the head and the one to his right pushed him to his knees and forced his head down on the block. Eberhard looked at Otker who had tossed Mariwig's head aside and was taking his place for the second stroke.

"When you're done here, let the men break their fast and then get ready to move out," he said. "We have a long day ahead, I think." With that he turned and retreated to his pavilion, certain that his stomach could not endure another beheading.

Chapter Thirty

Not e'er have I found, in the bosom on one
More learning of olden lore;
But with wiles art thou duped, thus dallying here
While dawn is upon thee, dwarf!
Behold! Sun shines in the hall.

The Wisdom of All-Wise
The Poetic Edda

Ragi's men, seated on the rowing benches larboard and starboard, fell into a rhythm. The ship moved out into deeper water and the dock soon disappeared into the night. Odd was not sure what he should do. He felt the water swirling around his ankles, and he knew enough about seafaring to know that their first concern would be getting the water that was inside the ship back out of the ship. But he was not sure how.

Between the benches he saw a dozen men with buckets scooping water and throwing it overboard. He wondered where the buckets had come from, then decided that, given the condition of the ship, Ragi must have put extra ones on board. Some of Ragi's warriors had worn their helmets during the escape from the hall, and now those too were being employed in bailing.

Odd looked around him, as best as he could in the dark, but could see nothing with which he might bail, so he knelt and began scooping water with his hands and tossing it over the side. He did this twenty times at least before concluding that it was pointless and stood up again. The best thing for him would be to relieve one of the men with a bucket when they began to tire.

He was up by the bow, so he made his way aft, which was like walking on the beach at the edge of the surf. Amundi and Alfdis and

Signy were seated on a big coil of rope just forward of the mast, and
Signy leapt to her feet when she saw him. She took two steps through
the water and wrapped her arms around his neck and pulled him
tight.

"Thank the gods you're all right, husband," she whispered in his
ear.

"And you, my love," he said. He pushed her back a few inches
and looked her up and down. "You're not hurt?"

"No," she said. "A few bruises, nothing more. But I lost sight of
you after we went in the tunnel. I didn't know…"

"I'm a little bruised as well," Odd said. "But fit enough to swim if
we have to. Which we might."

He saw Signy smile, which made him happier than he had been in
some time. He pulled her close and turned to Amundi and Alfdis.
"And you, my friends? How are you faring?"

Amundi grunted. "Too old for this sort of thing," he said. "But
I'm still breathing, it seems."

"Me as well," Alfdis said. "Though I tell you, I'll let myself roast
before I ever crawl through another tunnel."

"I understand that," Odd said. "Though your husband and I seem
to be getting pretty well used to it."

They fell silent, and Odd strained his ears to hear any sound from
the shore, any shouts or the sound of horses moving along the
water's edge. He heard the creaking of the oars in the tholes and the
occasional grunt of the men pulling at them. He heard the slosh of
water in the bottom of the ship and the splash of the bucketfulls
going over the side, but he could hear nothing beyond that.

"So, what now?" Signy asked.

"I don't know," Odd said. "It's Ragi's ship, and his home waters. I
should go see what he has in mind. Amundi, will you join me?"

With a groan Amundi stood and arched his back to work out the
kinks. "Too old," he said again.

Odd squeezed Signy, kissed the top of her head, then let her go,
and he and Amundi started splashing aft. They walked down the
centerline of the ship, around the mast, past the men on the rowing
benches and the men between them with buckets and helmets,
scooping water. In the dark, Odd could not tell if they were winning
the battle with the leaking seams, losing, or fighting to a draw. It was
close, whichever it was.

There was a short, raised deck aft, and Odd found Ragi there on the larboard side and Bragi Shipslayer to starboard, the tiller in his hand. They were the only people on board with dry feet.

"Ragi, how are you faring?" Odd asked. "Did you get through that unhurt?"

Ragi patted his chest and stomach, as if checking for wounds. "I seem to have. How's your lady? Amundi, you and Alfdis are all right?"

"Signy's unhurt," Odd said.

"And Alfdis," Amundi said. "Thanks to your foresight, Ragi. Otherwise, we'd be piles of ash, like your hall."

"Ha!" Ragi said. "Not foresight, just an idea I happily pilfered from Odd. And now, I reckon it's time for more ideas. What do you say, Odd? What do we do next?"

Odd frowned. He had not really thought about what they would do next. It had not occurred to him that it might be his decision to make. He had been running from Halfdan for so long, and had been the most helpless of prisoners before that, that he had all but forgotten that he had once been the leader of this nascent rebellion. And now it seemed they were once again looking to him to lead.

"Better that we don't go ashore, unless we have to," Odd said, thinking out loud. "Skorri and his men, they must have horses. If they ride south along the shore, they might run us down."

"You think Skorri's alive?" Ragi asked. "When the cliff gave way, it took him with it."

"It did," Odd agreed. "And if the gods are with us, they dropped the whole hillside on top of that bastard. But we have to assume he lives. Or that whoever was his second will take up the chase."

"Agreed," Ragi said.

"So, better if we can escape by sea," Odd said. "But can we? Or will this poor boat sink under us, like you warned us it would?"

"It won't sink!" Bragi spoke, and his voice held all its usual brash confidence. "It's a fine ship! A bit damp, sure, but a fine ship!"

"So, those poor bastards with the buckets, they can stop bailing?" Amundi asked.

"Well, I wouldn't recommend that," Bragi allowed. "But mark my words, the ship won't sink!"

"Still, hadn't we best put her up on a beach, at least until dawn?" Odd asked. "You can't steer in the dark, Bragi."

"Of course I can steer in the dark!" Bragi said. "Are you sure you're not really a sheepherder? You talk like a sheepherder. The stars show me how to steer. And the way the waves hit the side of the ship, and the breeze on my cheek, which was southwest when we set off, and has held steady. That's all I need."

"Hmm…" Odd was dubious. Certainly the stars and the breeze and the waves would allow Bragi to steer a straight course, but he knew that those waters were littered with rocks and ledges and islands, and all the stars in the sky would not tell Bragi where those were. But there was a bit of a moon, and dawn was not too far off, so Odd figured that Bragi's self-assurance would not necessarily doom them all.

"Well, if we must go ashore, we can land on the western side of the bay," Odd said. "Skorri can't reach us there."

"We might be better off running into a ledge," Ragi said. He paused and looked to larboard and starboard, but there was nothing to see but blackness. "I'm not sure where we are, but wherever it is, Halfdan's hall at Grømstad is on the western side of the bay, and we're not far from it."

Odd shook his head. *Stupid…how do you forget such a thing?* he thought. He knew as much, of course, knew that Ragi's farm was on the eastern shore of the long bay down which they were pulling, and King Halfdan's hall, the seat of his power, was on the western side. Which made the western side the last place that they wanted to land.

And then another thought occurred to Odd.

"If we mean to sail out of this bay," he said, "then we'll have to pass close by Halfdan's hall. The water's narrow there, if I'm remembering right. Less than half a mile from the western shore to the eastern."

"That's right," Bragi said. "Tricky going, but it'll be daylight by the time we get there. Not that it matters to me. I might drive us through with my eyes closed, just to make it a challenge. But it does mean passing close by the king's hall."

Odd ignored him, turned to Ragi. "What do you think?" he asked. "Halfdan's hall is at the head of that small harbor and set back some. From there they can't see the water, as we well know. But will Halfdan have ships out patrolling?"

"He might," Ragi said. "Halfdan has eyes everywhere. But I don't see as we have any choice but to sail past. We don't dare land anywhere. Anyway, if they give chase they won't catch us. There's no one who can catch Bragi Shipslayer at sea; he's the best ship handler alive. And if you doubt that, just ask him. He'll tell you. Isn't that right, Bragi?"

"You're learning fast, Ragi One-hand!" Bragi said.

They continued to pull south through the dark, and Odd closed his eyes and listened, but he heard nothing beyond the sounds of the ship. He looked to the east and thought he saw the sky growing lighter, but he was not certain. Still, it could not be that much longer, he thought. Dawn had to be close. And then, on reflection, he realized that he had no sense at all for how much of the night had passed. It seemed like a week ago that they had crawled through Ragi's tunnel.

"Now, here's the question," Ragi said, eventually breaking the silence. "Once we are clear of Grømstad, where do we go?"

"Fevik." Odd said it with a certainty that surprised even him. He had not come to any decision in his own mind, had only been mulling over the question, but the idea of Fevik had been appearing sharper and sharper, like a headland coming out of a fog. He was tired of running. Tired of hiding. He was ready to be done with this, one way or another.

It was that moment in Ragi's hall that decided it for him, though he had not understood it at the time. That moment when he drew Blood-letter and told Ragi to open the door and let him go out fighting. Relief had swept over him like a warm breeze, relief that the running and hiding were over and now it was time to act.

He had not gone out fighting, of course. He was not afraid to die, but neither would he throw away his life, not when Ragi and his tunnel offered a chance to escape. But he did not intend to keep running, not any longer.

"Fevik?" Ragi said, and there was a note of surprise in his voice. "If there's one place Halfdan or Skorri will look for you, it'll be Fevik."

"Then they should find me there," Odd said.

"In Fevik, the people will join with you? You'll raise your army?" Bragi asked.

"I don't know," Odd said. "They're my neighbors. They joined me in the fight before, just like Amundi and Ragi here did. They all saw what I saw, that Halfdan has no respect for the rights of freemen. Whether or not they'll join me again…I don't know."

"Well, I'm with you," Ragi said. "If I didn't have reason enough to hate Halfdan before, now he's gone and burned down my hall. Besides, he'll kill me whether I'm with you or not, just because I helped you. Or Skorri will." There was no resentment in his voice, or even anger. He was just stating a fact.

"Same for me," Amundi said. "Halfdan will never leave me in peace, so I might as well join the war."

"Count me in as well!" Bragi said.

"Thank you, Bragi," Odd said. "I didn't know how you felt about all this, if you looked on Halfdan as an enemy or not."

"I don't give a rat's ass for Halfdan or any of that," Bragi said. "I just like to fight."

"That'll do," Ragi said.

Odd looked over the larboard side, out toward the eastern shore where Skorri and his men might even now be scouting for them, and he was startled to see the edge of the land standing out in a dim line against the sky.

"Sun's rising," he said, and the others turned and looked and made grunting sounds of agreement. They rowed on in silence, gazing outboard as the gray light behind the eastern hills turned slowly orange, and the water around them and the men on the rowing benches began to resolve out of the dark.

Odd stepped over to the starboard side and stared out toward the west, toward where he guessed Halfdan's hall would be. That part of the bay was slowly coming visible in the gathering dawn, but there was not much to see: a long, low stretch of shoreline, with hilly country set a bit further back, dark forest unbroken by any sort of village or clearing.

He leaned over the side and looked forward, past the high prow. Just ahead, less than half a mile or so, the bay narrowed down into a narrow stretch, maybe five hundred feet across, before growing wider again. There was a half-moon-shaped harbor around the point of land that made up the western side of that narrow stretch, and just inland from there was Halfdan's great hall. As they rowed past, they would be less than half a mile away.

"Here, what did I tell you?" Bragi said, gesturing toward the land all around. "We're right in the middle of the bay! I don't need light to drive a ship, I can smell the way to go!"

Odd looked back at the narrow strait leading out of the bay. *You're a lucky man, Bragi, that the sun came up when it did*, he thought. Bragi might have found his way down the wider part of the bay, but treading that needle in the dark would not have been so simple.

A lucky man… Odd thought again. He could use lucky men around him. For that matter, he could stand to have a bit of his own luck. They were bound off for Fevik and he had no idea what awaited them there. He only knew that the running was over. It was time to make a stand.

Perhaps he would find an army to stand with him. Perhaps it would be just himself and the men in the ship. Perhaps he would be alone. It did not matter. In Fevik, he would make a stand. If Halfdan wanted him, he would be there.

Chapter Thirty-One

The very shields, struck by the stones, sing their laments
And helmets vomit bloody sounds as they come out
Beneath the air; the breastplate's pierced by cruel sword.

Abbo of Saint-Germain

Eberhard's column was south of Rouen when the rebels struck. It was a spot where the road was hemmed in by steep hills before opening up to a stretch with woods crowded along either side. The place was well chosen, good ground on which to launch a surprise attack. Eberhard would have expected no less from Louis and Ranulf. And it might have been effective, if it had indeed been a surprise. Which it was not.

It might likewise have been a win for the rebels if Mariwig's horse soldiers had changed sides in the middle of the fight, as planned. But, of course, that did not happen either.

The rebels had lost any chance at surprise when Eberhard's men discovered Amsind in his clandestine meeting. Because of that, Eberhard knew an attack was coming, knew that the rebels would strike his column somewhere. Amsind had revealed that much, after the threats and the beatings. But Eberhard did not know just where the attack would take place because Amsind did not know.

Mariwig most certainly knew, but no amount of violence would have dragged it out of him, so Eberhard did not waste his time trying.

Still, Mariwig did provide some useful information, despite himself. On their first day marching from Paris, he told Eberhard that if the rebels attacked, they would likely do so within a few miles of le Château de Roumois. He reckoned, or so he said, that if Louis was defeated, he would hope to retreat behind the walls of the château, and so would not want to get too far afield.

It made sense. And now, having uncovered Mariwig's treason, Eberhard knew one thing for certain: the attack would most definitely come long before they were within a few miles of the château.

That alone was a great advantage, but there were others to be gleaned from Mariwig's treachery.

Following the beheadings and the men's breakfast, when the army was finally ready to move, Eberhard ordered Otker to round up Mariwig's treasonous hoard, the former horse guard, and have them kneel on the ground. He left them there for some time, letting them think about what fate might await them. Letting them conjure up images of Mariwig's severed head, held aloft.

Finally, Eberhard left his pavilion and crossed the ground to where the men were gathered. He was wearing a mail shirt that gleamed in the morning sun, with a crimson and white cape over one shoulder, and from his belt a sword worth more than any of those sorry bastards could earn in half a lifetime. He made a notable contrast to those men who had been stripped of all armor and weapons, even shoes, and wore only their tunics and leggings.

Eberhard stood in front of the former mounted warriors, sixty or so in all, and looked over their faces as they looked unflinchingly at him. He did not see fear, but then he had not imagined he would. These were not the sort of men to fear the near proximity of death. He did see anger, however, and defiance.

"You men are traitors, every one of you," Eberhard announced. "And you saw this morrow what becomes of traitors. But I will give you each a choice. If you wish, you may join the ranks of my army once again. You'll march at the head of the column. I'll give each man a spear and a helmet. If the enemy attacks, you will be first in the fight.

"The king's spear warriors will be behind you. If any man runs in any direction, the king's men will kill him. If any man even begins to turn away from the fight, the king's men will kill him. Any man who proves himself, I will consider reinstating as a foot soldier. That is my offer. Any man who accepts, stand. Any man who does not accept, remain on your knees and you will have your turn at the headsman's block directly."

He folded his arms and looked out over the kneeling men. It took a moment, but finally one stood, and then another, and then another, until soon all of the former horse soldiers were standing and staring their fury at him.

And Eberhard now had a phalanx of fighting men to take the brunt of the attack: well-trained, experienced, and completely disposable.

The horses, weapons, armor, and equipment that had once belonged to Mariwig's men were given out to others of known loyalty and ability, a new horse guard that was faithful to Eberhard alone. Patrols were sent out in advance of the column to scout the road ahead, and if they were seen at all by Louis's men, they were left unmolested. Louis, after all, would think they were still secretly on his side.

The mounted patrols did not discover any men lying in wait, no traps ready to spring. They did not see any Northmen or any of the lowly sort who were rumored to have taken up arms in Louis's support. But they did come upon several places that would be ideal spots for ambush, if such a thing was forthcoming. One was a place where the road ran between steep hills and opened onto a wooded stretch.

They were still half a mile away when Otker rode up to Eberhard's side. With Mariwig's death, Otker had taken over command of the men-at-arms, and he had spent the morning going up and down the column, keeping it moving quickly and in good order.

"Your Grace, up ahead, it's one of the spots that looks likely for an ambush, if such might happen, lord," he said.

"Very well," Eberhard said. He felt his stomach tighten a bit and he gripped his reins hard to stop his hands from trembling. He looked forward, over the heads of the marching men. He saw the former horse guard, his traitorous forlorn hope, in the van, the king's men behind them. That was good.

"Spread the word for the men to stand ready," Eberhard continued. "Remind those in the front that they fight or they die, the choice is theirs. And remind the king's spearmen of their duty to kill any man who flinches."

"Very well, my lord," Otker said and headed off toward the front of the column. On either side of the road, the hills rose up higher, steep banks hemming them in, which would make it impossible for Eberhard's men to spread out to meet an assault. Eberhard felt his stomach twist up even more. He felt sweat on his palms, and knew his hands would certainly shake if he let go of the reins.

This is ridiculous, he thought.

He glanced around. He was surrounded by his personal bodyguard, Otker's men, who were loyal and skilled with their swords. They would fight to the last man for him, and if the unthinkable happened and his army was defeated, he could certainly ride away to safety while those men kept the enemy at bay. There was no chance that anyone among Louis's men or the Northmen had a horse that could match his for speed.

Northmen...Eberhard thought next. With all the considerations weighing on him, he had all but forgotten about the Northmen. Of course, they were the unknown, the real danger. He could well scoff at whatever local folk Louis or Ranulf might have scraped up to throw into the fight, but the Northmen were undeniably a threat.

There are but three hundred of them, by the best reports, Eberhard though. *While I have five hundred or more fighting men.*

He rested his hand on the hilt of his sword, a gesture he found comforting, and kept his eyes forward as he rode. Otker was up near the front of the column, just behind where the king's spearmen were marching. Ahead of them, the former horse guards were leading the way, spears held diagonally across their chests. They were past the place where the road was hemmed in by the hills and were well into the wooded part of the road. And still no attack.

Maybe that bastard Louis thought better of this, Eberhard thought. It was certainly possible. Louis most certainly had men watching the road. He must have seen how powerful a force he, Eberhard, commanded.

But Eberhard did not really believe that. Louis would not shrink from a fight. Eberhard knew it was coming. But still he startled and cursed when the first scream of battle came ringing out.

"Damn it!" he yelled out loud as the battle cry came rolling down the line. He half stood in his stirrups and looked ahead. Men were pouring out of the woods on either side of the road, spears leveled, axes held over their heads, screaming like the damned on their way to hell.

"Bastards!" Eberhard shouted. He whirled his horse around. Why, he did not know. Then he realized that he was checking the road behind them, making sure the enemy was not in their rear, making sure he had a clear route of escape if need be. But he saw nothing there, save for his own men, alert to the sound of battle, holding weapons at the ready, fighting the urge to surge ahead and get jammed up on the road even as Eberhard was fighting the urge to run.

He spun his horse back the other way. Louis's men had come out of the trees on either side of the road and hit both flanks of the column, hit the king's spear men, who had turned right and left and were fighting with fierce skill. But that left the forlorn hope, Mariwig's traitors, cut off and unguarded.

For a moment they seemed stunned by the sudden attack, unsure what to do. Then Eberhard heard a shout and saw spears raised high and Mariwig's men surged into the fight. But they did not drive into Louis's men, attacking from the trees. Rather, they charged into the king's men, slaughtering them with their iron-tipped weapons, screaming a cry of vengeance.

"Bastards! Bastards!" Eberhard shrieked. Those men, those villainous scum, had betrayed him again. Any fear he might have felt at the king's men being overwhelmed was lost in the rush of fury. Otker was deep into the fight, still mounted and slashing with his sword. Eberhard turned his horse half around. The new horse guard was positioned just behind his own personal guard in the line of march, and they were watching the fighting with grim and angry faces.

"Get in there!" Eberhard screamed, pointing at the mounting battle. "Get in there, you sorry bastards, and cut them down!"

"Can't get through, lord!" the lead man shouted, gesturing toward the road. Narrow and hemmed in, it was packed with Eberhard's column, most of whom were struggling to get through and into the fight, just as Louis no doubt had intended. But none of those men would be as effective as the mounted warriors, riding the enemy down with sword and spear.

"Get in there, I said!" Eberhard shouted. "Ride right over them if you must, I don't care, just get in there and kill those whore's sons!"

The horse guardsman looked uncertain, but he also looked like a man who knew better than to question the raging Duke of Roumois. He flicked his reins and pushed his horse forward—not charging, as Eberhard would have had him do—but pushing through the men, giving them time enough, if just barely, to get clear of horse and rider. The rest of the new-made horse guard followed behind.

Eberhard looked down at his bodyguard, still gathered around his mount, swords drawn, shields on arms. "You men stay put, don't you dare leave my side!" he shouted, then looked back up at the fight.

More of Louis's men were coming out of the trees and others were charging down the road, hitting the head of the column. But they did not realize that the men at the head of the column were Mariwig's men, their own secret allies, and so they were tearing into them, cutting them down even as the former horsemen were trying to cut down the king's men. It was a bloody, confused, chaotic mess, and it was then that Eberhard's horse guard came charging in.

A shout went up from Louis's men as Eberhard's column parted like the Red Sea to let the riders through. Eberhard smiled as he heard it. It was a cry of triumph, a cry of victory. Louis's men thought this was Mariwig, switching sides and coming to fight with them.

"Now you get the surprise of a lifetime, you traitorous bastards!" Eberhard shouted, and he watched with delight as the first of the horsemen reached the head of the column and brought his long, straight sword down on Louis and Ranulf's men.

Otker was yelling, whirling, pointing, and slashing, driving the mounted warriors forward, directing their assault at the three directions from which Louis's men were coming. The cries of victory died on the rebels' lips as the horse guard plunged into them, swords flashing, and they realized something had gone terribly wrong, that whatever thing they had expected to happen was not coming to pass.

Eberhard watched with satisfaction, and felt the first sense of calm he had known that day. He saw the confusion sweeping through the ranks of Louis's men, the cheers turning to shouts of distress and panic. Eberhard saw men backing away, men looking left and right for orders, for affirmation. He saw them trying to fight off the mounted warriors with whatever crude weapons they had, and dying where they stood.

And then they began to run. First the men on the edge of the fight turned and raced for the trees, and then those closer in, and then more and more as panic took hold. Men threw shields and spears and axes aside in their flight for the cover of the woods. The men still engaged tried backing off, realizing they had been abandoned, and one by one they too turned and ran, though few made it far

A moment later, it was over, the rebels disappearing into the trees, the riders and the king's men who were still standing chasing them to the edge of the road. Otker called for them to stop, to pursue no farther, but he need not have bothered. The riders could not get through the tree line, and the men on foot had little desire to go racing into the arms of an unseen enemy. Nor was there any reason to do so. The fight was over. The victory was complete.

Eberhard realized that he was clenching every muscle in his body and he forced himself to relax as Otker came riding up to report.

"I congratulate you on your victory, your Grace," Otker said, reining to a halt.

"Thank you, Otker," Eberhard said, nodding slightly.

"Your brother's men, they made a bloody mess of the king's spear warriors, your Grace," Otker went on. "And they butchered most of Mariwig's old horse guard as well. But the rebels got worse than they gave, I'd say. Damned lot of dead."

"Any of Mariwig's men who still live will be drawn and quartered on the morrow," Eberhard said.

"Yes, your Grace," Otker said. "But...I don't think there's any still alive, lord. Or, those that did live, they run off."

"Hmm," Eberhard said. He was disappointed. On the other hand, even as he gave the order he realized that he probably could not stomach a drawing and quartering, so he was relieved to be spared that spectacle.

"What shall I tell the men, lord?" Otker asked.

"Yes..." Eberhard said, recalling he had to give directions for his men-at-arms. "We have wounded....must attend to them...." he said, speaking even as the thoughts were coming to him. "We'll get them in wagons, move down the road until we find some open ground where we can make camp. The dead in wagons, too. Just our dead. And not the same wagon as the wounded. We'll set up camp, organize what defense we can. But I don't think the rebels will bother us again, not for some time."

"No, your Grace," Otker agreed.

"Any of the rebel dead, just toss them into the woods. But any wounded who can still talk, you bring them with us, and make sure you keep them alive. At least for now. There are questions to be answered."

"Yes, your Grace," Otker said, and then he turned and walked his horse back along the column, calling orders to the captains as he did.

Chapter Thirty-Two

Far have I fared, much have I ventured
Oft have I proven the powers
Whence comes a new Sun, in the clear heaven again
When the Wolf has swallowed the old.

The Words of the Mighty Weaver
The Poetic Edda

The sky was growing light with dawn, and men were calling his name, and that was all that Skorri Thorbrandsson knew when he opened his eyes. His head was pounding and there was a profound ache in his left thigh and he was not certain that he could move. He had no idea of where he was, or how he came to be there.

He shifted a little, as much to test his ability to do so as for any other reason. His arms seemed to work as they should, and he could flex his fingers.

"Skorri?" the voice called again. It was not particularly close by, and Skorri did not yet have the wherewithal to respond, so he didn't. Instead, he tried his left leg, the one that hurt so badly, and found he could move that as well. He heard the sound of gravel scraping under his heel.

He was lying on the ground, on rocky ground. His right foot was numb, and for a moment he thought it was dead, but how his foot could be dead and the rest of him not he did not know. And then he realized his foot was sitting in water, very cold water. He lifted it and pulled it back and set it down again. The gravel crunched once more, and he remembered the cliff.

Bastards, he thought.

It came back suddenly, like shutters thrown open to reveal the world outside a dark room. The trail down the cliff, the traitors

311

fleeing along that narrow ledge. They had run them down, come face to face with them. It had been dark, terribly dark, but still Skorri felt certain it was Ragi and Odd who had confronted them. So close. A sword thrust away.

And then what?

Skorri tried to remember. The traitors were in their grasp, and he was already entertaining visions of dragging them into Halfdan's great hall and tossing them down at the king's feet. And then…nothing. Until that moment, on the ground, waking with his body wracked in pain.

"Skorri?"

It was growing brighter, Skorri saw, the dawn slowly revealing the water in front of him. He twisted his head and looked behind him. He saw he was lying on a narrow, broken, rocky shoreline at the edge of a cove near the bottom of a steep cliff. There was fresh dirt strewn over the rocks, the result, clearly, of part of that cliff having given way.

It came back to him then. Facing off with Odd and Ragi. An attack from the dark by men they had not seen. He remembered the sensation of the ground collapsing under him, of his body suddenly dropping, turning, and twisting as he fell. He shuddered at the memory. He could feel it again: falling, falling, and then nothing.

He put his hands down on the gravel and tried to push himself up and found that he could. His head spun and he paused and let it settle, then pushed once again, forcing himself into an upright position. It was still not clear if his legs would function, but he managed to get himself to his knees and stayed like that, swaying a bit, trying to determine whether he could stand.

"Skorri!"

He looked to his right and saw Osvif thirty feet away, just visible in the gray light of predawn, moving toward him along the edge of the water, seemingly unhurt. Osvif smiled and broke into a jog as he caught sight of Skorri. He shouted back over his shoulder, "Here! I found him! Here!"

When Osvif reached Skorri he held out his arms and hesitated, unsure what to do. "Are you hurt?" he asked.

Of course I'm hurt, you idiot, I fell down a cliff! Skorri thought, but he bit off that scathing reply and instead growled, "Give me a hand up, come on, you fool."

Osvif grabbed Skorri under the arms and lifted and Skorri pushed with his feet and between them they managed to get him upright and standing. His head was whirling as if he was ready to pass out drunk, and his thigh pulsed with pain. He looked down and saw that his leggings were torn, but there seemed to be no blood so he guessed he was only bruised.

He stood for a moment, his arm around Osvif's shoulder, gasping for breath and easing more and more weight onto his battered leg. Soon the whirling in his head subsided and he found he could stand on both legs, so he removed his arm from Osvif's shoulder and looked around.

Farther up the shore he saw more of his men hurrying toward him, and he realized there were at least three others lying nearby, but unlike him, they were not moving. One, whom Skorri recognized as a warrior named Thorvard, was face down in the water, arms spread at his sides, one leg twisted at an unnatural angle.

"How many are dead?" Skorri asked.

"We don't know for certain," Osvif said. "We've been looking...looking for you, mostly...but it's been too dark to see."

"Odd? Ragi? And the others?"

"Ah...in truth...I don't know where they got off to," Osvif stammered, then added with a forced note of optimism, "Can't have got too far."

Skorri pressed his lips together to keep himself from cursing out loud or lashing out at Osvif. *I had them, by all the gods! Right there, right in my hands!*

He heard the sound of soft leather shoes on gravel and looked up to see more of his men making their way toward him along the shoreline. He saw Hrolf and a man named Ingolf. Kolbein was leading them.

Kolbein jogged the last dozen feet. "Skorri, are you hurt?"

"Of course I'm hurt, you great festering idiot!" Skorri snapped, then, forcing calm into his voice, said, "But I'll be all right. How many others are hurt? Or dead?"

Kolbein looked around. "Not sure. Just getting light enough to look. That looks like Thorvard, there." Kolbein nodded toward the corpse floating a few feet away.

"Found this," Hrolf said, holding out Skorri's sword. "Somewhere over there." He gestured back over his shoulder.

Skorri grunted, took the sword, and returned it to its scabbard. He looked Kolbein up and down, and Osvif as well. "How do you come to be unhurt?" he asked.

"We were farther up the trail," Kolbein said. "Trying to get in the fight, but there was no room. And then the edge of the trail collapsed, and you and the others went down."

"Then what?" Skorri demanded. "Did you go after Odd and the rest? What became of them?"

"Well…" Kolbein said, glancing at Osvif and then back at Skorri. "We chased them down the trail, to be sure. Hard to see where they were going. Dark night. But we thought we saw a ship… underway…"

Skorri frowned, and suddenly, he felt as if he was falling all over again. There *had* been a ship. He recalled seeing it, barely visible from the high trail. He took a step toward the water. His thigh throbbed with pain but his legs were supporting him. He looked along the shoreline. It was light enough that he could see the dock, a hundred yards away. There was no ship tied to it now.

"Son of a bitch!" Skorri shouted. So close to success, only to have it snatched away. His fury broke like a thunderclap—fury, but not despair. His resolve did not waver. The anger refreshed him and drove him harder. It was what made him the man he was.

He took a deep breath, and then another. "Very well," he said. "We'll gather up those who are still alive, and then we go after the traitors and we run the whores' sons down." He turned and made his way along the shore, stepping over the mounds of loose dirt that had slid down from the ledge and around the rocks strewn along the shoreline.

They found a warrior named Geir half-buried in the dirt, his head turned sideways on a broken neck. They found another man named Vandrad whom they thought to be dead, but who revived on shaking and seemed not too badly hurt. They reached the end of the landslide then turned and made their way back.

Twenty feet beyond where Skorri had landed, and fifteen feet up the side of the cliff, they found Valgard Arason, Skorri's second-in-command. He had been at Skorri's side when the trail gave way. He was inverted now, his feet higher than his head, his arms splayed out. The side of his skull had hit a rock on the way down the cliff, or so it seemed; it was caved in, a bloody ruin, his one remaining eye open and staring at the sky.

Well, you're done for, you son of a bitch, Skorri thought. Valgard had been a good second—loyal, smart, brutal. His service would be missed, if nothing else about him would be.

Osvif called from a little farther along the shore, from where he had climbed up on the loose dirt. "Here!" he called, waving, and Skorri and the others made their way up to where he stood.

A man named Bjorn was sprawled out on the dirt, his head moving side to side, his right thigh broken, the bone protruding through flesh and leggings. He opened his eyes and looked up. "Skorri…" he said. "My leg…"

"Doesn't look good," Skorri said. "Too bad for you." He turned and started back down the earth slide and Bjorn called after him.

"Skorri! Don't leave me like this!"

Skorri turned back. "We have no time, and you're a dead man, Bjorn, no matter what we do," he said, but then Kolbein came up to him, standing close by.

"We can't leave him, Skorri," he said in a low voice. "He's a dead man, sure, but the others… they won't like it." Skorri looked around. The other men who were there were watching, waiting.

"Do I give a rat's ass what the others will like?" Skorri asked, speaking louder than Kolbein had. "They do what I say."

"They do," Kolbein said. "But they…we all…have become Halfdan's enemies, following you. Don't forget that, I beg you. Don't give them cause to resent it."

Skorri stared at Kolbein as if he were looking at some strange new creature he had never seen before. He frowned and his eyebrows came together, then he pushed past Kolbein and walked back up the slope. He stood over Bjorn, looking down at him, and Bjorn met his eyes.

"I've been your man, Skorri," Bjorn said, and his voice was pleading and strangled with pain.

"Yes, you have," Skorri agreed. "Followed me to the end."

In one swift motion he pulled his sword and brought it back over his head. Bjorn's eyes went wide and his mouth opened to speak, but before he made a sound the sword hacked down on his neck, cutting it halfway through until the point buried itself in the dirt.

Bjorn's eyes rolled back and the blood gushed out around Skorri's blade as he jerked it free. A tremor ran through Bjorn's body, and when it stopped, Skorri wiped his blade on Bjorn's tunic and slid it back into the scabbard.

"There," Skorri said, turning to the others. "Now, you probably think I'm some monster. Well, Bjorn was going to die a painful death and there was nothing we could do about it. You all know that's true. Letting him live on would have been weakness, not mercy. So I've done Bjorn a great mercy. Anyone else care to question me, I'll show them the same mercy." He looked around. Some of the men were staring at him in surprise, some in what he guessed was anger. Some in fear, no doubt, though they hid it well. He gave them a moment, but no one spoke.

"Very well," Skorri said. He turned and walked inland, toward the dock, where the shoreline widened out. He looked back toward the cliff. He could see the narrow trail cut into its side, leading up the way they had come, and he headed off in that direction.

His thigh was in agony, his body ached, and his head was still pounding. He felt like one might expect after plunging down a cliff in a landslide. But he did not slow and he did not allow any of the pain to show on his face or in the way he moved. He found the bottom of the trail and started making his way back up to the top. He did not bother to see if his men were with him. He knew they were.

In the daylight the trail did not seem as narrow or uncertain as it had been in the dark, and Skorri moved quickly despite the pain. He came to the place where the cliff edge had given way under him. The trail was still three feet wide at that point, but the outer edge was all fresh, raw dirt. Someone's sword was still lying on the ground where he had dropped it.

Skorri gave the place no more than a quick glace as he continued up. Soon he reached the top of the trail, the wide shelf fifteen feet below the cliff edge, and there, sure enough, he saw what he thought he would see.

"Son of a bitch," he muttered. It was the mouth of a tunnel, a tunnel that no doubt led right to Ragi's hall. Or the charred remains of Ragi's hall. It was the same trick Odd had played on Halfdan. And once again, it had worked. Skorri felt like a fool, having been tricked that way. And Skorri did not care to feel like a fool.

He turned as the last of his men came up the trail and onto the flat ground. He did not bother to count them, but it seemed he had a good two dozen warriors still with him, more than enough to crush Odd and his band.

"Come along," he said. He looked over the steep bank of dirt that rose from the ground on which they stood to the ground above until he found a place where they could climb, and then he led his men up the bank and onto the open field. One hundred yards away stood a few small buildings surrounding a great blackened heap of timber, all that was left of Ragi's hall. Wisps of smoke were still rising from the burned debris.

Skorri led the way back over the ground they had covered the night before, past the remains of Ragi's farm and toward the stand of trees where they had left their horses tied. He did not speak; his mind was a whirl as he forced himself to think despite the pounding in his head.

*Where will they go? Where, where…*he toyed with the question. There were few villages near, but if the traitors were on a ship, they would have no need to seek out a village. They could go anywhere. And if they were on a ship, then he would need a ship to go after them.

He considered the country thereabouts. He did not know it well, but he knew it well enough. The cove that Ragi's farm abutted was part of a long, narrow bay. Near the head of the bay sat Vik, the home of Thorgrim Night Wolf, Odd's father. It was Thorgrim's farm, or rather Halfdan's ambitions to own Thorgrim's farm, that had started all this.

Would he go to Vik? Skorri wondered. If there was any place Odd might be recognized, it was Vik, where he was born and raised. Or Fevik, where he made his home now. Neither one was a smart place for him to hide.

But perhaps he was done with hiding. Perhaps his plan now was to inflame the people once again, to try and raise another rebellion. Then Fevik made the most sense. It was his home, the most likely place to find people who would protect him, who would rally to his banner. Fevik would be exactly the right place to go.

By the time they reached the patch of woods, Skorri's head was starting to clear, the various aches were subsiding, and he had made up his mind. He led his men down the trail to the small clearing where they had left the horses, and he was pleased to see that the beasts were still there, contentedly chewing the grass within reach.

"Mount up," Skorri said, taking the reins of his horse and untying them from the sapling to which they were made fast.

"Where are we going?" Kolbein asked, but Skorri ignored him, putting his foot in the stirrup and swinging himself up into his saddle. He twisted around until he was looking Kolbein in the eyes. He held the man's gaze a moment, making him wait for a reply, making certain he knew that Skorri was doing him a great honor in answering his question.

"Fevik," Skorri said.

Kolbein's eyebrows came together and he and a few of the men around him exchanged glances. "Fevik's where Odd's from," Kolbein said. "They know him there. He's well-loved in Fevik."

"What does that matter to us?" Skorri asked.

"We'll find little welcome there," Hrolf said.

"We don't care about being welcome," Skorri said. "We care about finding Odd and Ragi and taking them or their bloody corpses to Halfdan. Now get on your horses, all of you. If I must tell you again I'll do it with my blade."

One by one the men found their horses and mounted, and the horses that no longer had riders were tied to the saddles of those that did. Skorri flicked the reins, nudged his horse's flanks, and led the way out of the copse and onto the wide path that passed for a road from Ragi's farm to the world beyond.

They made their way roughly north with the narrow bay off to their left. Skorri rode by himself at the head of the warrior band. He was never very keen to engage in pointless chatter, but that morning he was even less inclined to be sociable, or what he considered sociable, which by most standards would have been considered barely civil. He had a great deal to consider.

He had been hunting Odd for months now, a single-minded quest that had grown into something far greater than just a means to clear his name and get back in the king's good graces. This was his life now. He had lost a third of the men he had started out with; they had either run off or been killed or been dispatched with messages for Halfdan and never heard from again. The rest had stuck by him, but there was grumbling going on. He could feel it. He sensed it in the many hesitations and hints of disrespect he was getting.

He looked back over his shoulder. The men were mostly spread out along the road, riding by themselves or in pairs. But Kolbein and Hrolf and Osvif were riding together, near the back of the group. Kolbein was now second-in-command, after Valgard's death. He should have been at the head of the band. He should have been riding on Skorri's flank. The only reason that Skorri could think of for Kolbein to be back there was so that he could have a discussion that Skorri could not hear.

Your luck has just about run dry, Kolbein, Skorri thought. It was time for a lesson, one that all those disloyal bastards would understand.

A mile farther and Skorri saw a small farm in the distance, a modest house surrounded by a wattle fence, a trail of smoke rising from the end of a steep thatched roof, fields spreading out beyond it. He tugged the reins to one side and directed his horse toward the place. He did not bother to speak or look back to see if the others were following behind.

They were still a hundred yards away when Skorri saw people in the yard outside the house: a woman, it seemed. Two women. And smaller figures. Children. He saw the woman send the others hurrying off. They would have no real cause for concern—the king's peace reigned over East Agder, and raiding parties would be rare indeed—but still the sight of two dozen mounted warriors approaching was bound to give them pause.

Skorri reached the farm at last and stopped his horse at the closed gate in the wattle fence. On the other side stood the woman, an attractive woman with long, blond hair. She had the look of the lady of the house, her clean, simple dress held up by two broaches with a string of beads between them, keys and scissors hanging from a leather belt around her waist.

"Good day," she said, a friendly note in her voice that sounded more than a little forced.

"Good day," Skorri said. "We're on the king's business. We need to water our horses, and we need food and drink." He nodded toward the gate that stood between them.

The woman hesitated, just a heartbeat, and then stepped forward and unlatched the gate and swung it open. Skorri rode through and the rest followed behind, and once they were all in the yard, they dismounted and stretched weary limbs, then led their horses off to a water trough to drink.

"Where's your husband?" Skorri asked the woman.

"In the field," the woman said. If she was frightened, she was hiding it well. "I sent my children to fetch him."

Skorri nodded. He looked around. There were a few cows grazing outside the wattle fence and a sty with some impressive pigs sitting in a pool of mud. He turned back to the woman. "Food and ale," he said.

The woman nodded and retreated to the house, and soon returned with food that she laid out on a trestle table in the yard. She took multiple trips in and out, and hams and cold beef, carrots and course bread and a pitcher of ale all appeared. What cups she had she put out as well.

Skorri was pleased with what he saw. There was food enough for his men to eat well, and even enough that they could take some for later. It would be a great hardship for the farmer and his family, cutting deep into their stores, but that was not Skorri's concern. His mission was far more important than the discomfort of one family.

The men were just sitting down on the benches alongside the table, digging in, when the farmer appeared, his tunic dirt-smeared and wet with perspiration, his shoes caked with mud. Behind him was a girl of sixteen, perhaps, with long, blond hair like her mother's, a strikingly pretty girl, and behind her a boy of thirteen or so and another of eight.

The farmer paused, looked over the crowd at the table. He met his wife's eyes. She nodded toward Skorri, and the farmer crossed over to where Skorri was standing and watching all that was going on.

"I'm Serk Thorgilsson," the man said. "This is my farm."

Skorri nodded. He did not speak. He did not really have anything to say to the man.

"If you're on the king's business, then you may eat your fill," Serk continued. "But do not leave us with nothing." He was trying to sound commanding, ruler of his domain, but he could not quite manage it.

"I'll do as I wish," Skorri said. "Now gather your family and take them in the house and do not leave." He held the man's gaze for a moment and neither of them moved. Finally, the man gave a nod, just a tiny gesture, and waved for his family to follow him inside. Skorri took his seat on the short bench at the head of the table and reached for the bread and ham.

There were a few murmured conversations around the table, but mostly the men ate in silence. Skorri took big bites of food and washed them down with ale. He did not speak and did not make eye contact with the other men as he brooded on the disloyalty that was starting to show itself. Perhaps he had been too lenient, he thought, or perhaps these men were just weak and feckless.

Either way, he could not have it. He needed men who would do as he commanded, with no hesitation and no questions. He certainly needed that in a second-in-command, and he did not believe he had it in Kolbein. But he would find out. He would put the man to the test, and make an example of him if he failed.

"Kolbein!" he called down the table. Kolbein had chosen not to sit near Skorri, and that in itself was a bad sign.

"Yes, Skorri?"

"Take some men and bring that farmer and his family out here," Skorri said, nodding toward the farmhouse. "Bring all of them out here."

Kolbein nodded, and Skorri saw the hesitation and concern on the man's face. But he stood and called to three of the others and led them across the yard and into the dark interior of the house. A moment later they returned with the farmer and his wife and children following behind. They crossed the yard and stopped a few feet from where Skorri sat.

For a moment no one moved or spoke. Skorri saw the uncertainty on the farmer's face. He was trying to guess what Skorri was about, trying to figure if his speaking up would make things better or worse. But Skorri did not give him a chance.

"Kolbein," Skorri said, and his voice was calm and even. "Kill the men. The farmer and his sons. We'll take our pleasure with the women, and then we'll be on our way."

The farmer's face lost its color. He opened his mouth to speak, but Skorri glared at him and he shut it again. His wife and the children seemed too stunned by fright to make a sound.

Kolbein at least found his voice. "What?" he stammered. "You want me to…" He shook his head but did not continue.

Skorri stood slowly, the pitcher in his hand. "I said kill the farmer and the boys. Do it. Now. By your own hand."

"I…" Kolbein stammered again. "I…we're not raiding some Frankish village, by all the gods, Skorri! This is the king's land, you can't just…"

"Do as I say. I command it." Skorri looked Kolbein in the eyes, wondered what the man would do. He had a pretty good idea, but it was possible that Kolbein would surprise him.

Kolbein hesitated for a moment more, then seemed to come to a decision. He nodded and slowly drew his sword and turned to the farmer. "Skorri commands here," he said, "and I have no say in this mattered."

The farmer's mouth dropped open and he made some sounds as if he was trying to speak. Skorri took a deep drink from the pitcher and rested his left hand on the hilt of his seax, which he wore strapped horizontally across the front of his belt. Kolbein raised his sword over his head. No one spoke.

Then Kolbein slashed down with his sword, turning as he did, bringing the blade down not at the farmer's head but at Skorri's. In a flash Skorri had his seax out and up and the two weapons hit. Kolbein's blade slid along the edge of Skorri's seax and stopped dead as it caught on the cross guard. Skorri pushed the sword away, swung the pitcher around and smashed it into the side of Kolbein's head. The pitcher shattered into a hundred pieces and a wave of ale washed over Kolbein and he was knocked sideways and down.

Skorri grabbed the hilt of his sword with his right hand and pulled it free. He turned to the others, sword and seax at the ready.

"Who's next? You sons of whores! Who'll try me next?"

Skorri had expected one or two would join in with Kolbein—Hjolf and Osvif certainly—but he was surprised to see a dozen swords leave their scabbards, a dozen furious looks directed at him, and not one man he could see who was coming to fight at his side.

So be it…I'll kill the lot of you! he thought. Vandrad was the closest, five steps away, and Skorri leapt at him, point first. Vandrad slashed and missed and Skorri drove the point of his sword into Vandrad's shoulder, but Vandrad twisted free before the sword could do any great hurt.

Skorri twisted and slashed at the man to his left. He knocked his blade away, lunged and missed, then swept his sword backhand to the right, driving back another one of the traitorous bastards. He knew he had better start wounding or killing quick if he meant to live through the day. He thrust left with the seax, right with the sword. Iron rang on iron, men grunted and shouted and moved for advantage.

Vandrad was back, sword raised, moving to Skorri's right. Skorri shifted his stance, following, and just as he was ready to attack he realized there was movement behind him. He was starting to turn when something smashed into his back and shoulders, something solid, something with real weight behind it. Skorri pitched forward and the sword and seax flew from his hands and the next thing he knew he was down.

He rolled over and saw Kolbein standing above him, the short bench on which he had been sitting clutched in his hands. Skorri twisted around, looking for his sword, and someone kicked him hard in the gut, driving the air out of him. He felt his eyes go wide and he gasped for breath. Hands grabbed his shoulders and rolled him over and he was powerless to resist.

He felt knees in his back, hands on his arms, pulling them back behind him, and then the sharp feel of a cord digging into his flesh as his wrists were bound together. He was rolled over again, onto his back, looking up at Kolbein and Vandrad and the others, who were looking down at him.

"We're done with this, Skorri," Kolbein said. "Time for us to get back in Halfdan's good graces. And we figure that bringing you in will help."

Chapter Thirty-Three

What man is here, who dares in my hall
To throw his word at me thus
Thou shalt ne'er come forth, again from our courts
If thou be not the wiser of twain.

The Words of the Mighty Weaver
The Poetic Edda

It took some time, and a considerable amount of pointing and yelling, to get Eberhard's column moving again. There was a great deal to do: the prisoners gathered up, the injured attended to, the wagons brought forward. Eberhard's wounded were laid in the wagon beds, the rebel wounded (those too far gone to live long) were tossed to the side of the road, and the dead sorted out in a similar manner.

Otker sent riders ahead to scout the road and look for a suitable place to stop. They returned with reports of no rebels in sight and an open field on the crest of a small hill that would make an ideal encampment.

Eberhard tried to remain patient, detached from it all, but he could not shake his fear that his brother and the Northmen would strike again, while the cries and pleadings of the wounded put his nerves on edge. He climbed down from his horse, stretched weary muscles, yawned, and hoped the others would take that to mean he was so calm as to be bored by the situation.

Finally, Otker came riding up. "Column is ready to move now, you Grace."

"Good," Eberhard said. "Put half the mounted troops leading the way, then let us go."

"Yes, your Grace, very good," Otker said and he turned his horse and rode off.

Eberhard mounted again, and from horseback could see that Otker had already put half the mounted troops leading the way. Then Otker shouted an order and the surviving army, still close to five hundred men strong, rolled out.

The day was not too far advanced by the time they made camp again. The wounded were laid out on the ground where they could be tended to, fires stoked up in makeshift pits across the hilltop. Eberhard was in his pavilion, always one of the first structures to be erected, when Otker appeared.

"Guards posted on the perimeters, your Grace," he reported. "And riders sent out in every direction, but they haven't seen anything, and I don't reckon they will."

"Good," Eberhard said, though he was not really listening. He had other considerations foremost on his mind. "You have the prisoners under guard? How many do we have?"

"Ten, lord, I think, still alive, last time I looked. They're all wounded, which is why I reckon they didn't run off. Some are so badly wounded that if they're not dead now, they will be soon."

"They'll all be dead soon," Eberhard corrected. "But I would speak with them now. Find the most likely looking one and bring him to me."

Otker gave a bow and disappeared through the pavilion door. A few moments later he was back. Behind him came two of Eberhard's bodyguards, men under Otker's command. Between them, hands bound behind his back, was a man of about twenty years, hair long and wild, a scruffy beard, dressed in the manner of a farmhand or a cooper's apprentice of some such. The guards jerked him to a stop ten feet from where Eberhard sat.

Eberhard looked at the guards and nodded toward the ground, and the two men forced the prisoner to his knees as Eberhard stood up from his chair and approached. The man glaring up at Eberhard, but all his hatred could not entirely mask the fear.

A foot away Eberhard stopped, and the prisoner craned his neck to meet Eberhard's eyes. Then Eberhard hit the man hard across his face with the back of his hand, snapping his head around and drawing blood from his lips. The man looked back up at Eberhard and spit blood at Eberhard's feet. Eberhard nodded to the guard on the man's right. The guard grabbed a handful of the man's hair and jerked his head back hard, then drew his short sword and held the blade to the man's neck.

"Who do you serve?" Eberhard asked. For a moment the prisoner remained silent, until the guard put a bit more pressure on the blade across his throat.

"Ranulf," he said. "Ranulf of Roumois."

"Ranulf," Eberhard said. "And my brother Louis, isn't that right?"

"On his return…" the prisoner said. "Ranulf said Louis'd be made le duc de Roumois on his return, and we'd serve him then."

Eberhard frowned. This made no sense, as if they were having two different conversations. He nodded to the guard and the guard moved the short sword aside and let go of the man's hair. The prisoner was talking. He had taken the threat seriously, it seemed, as intended.

"What do you mean 'on his return'?" Eberhard asked. "Louis was leading you in the attack."

Now the prisoner frowned and seemed confused. "No, lord. Louis wasn't there."

"I've had it on good authority that my brother has returned," Eberhard said.

"I heard that, too, lord. We heard Louis had come back with an army of Northmen. And then we heard they all sailed off again. But those were just rumors, lord, that the others were saying. I don't know the truth of it. I just know Louis weren't there, lord."

"And the Northmen? What of them?"

"No Northmen, lord," the prisoner said. "It was just those what rallied to Ranulf's banner."

Eberhard slowly shook his head. This was not at all what he had expected. Felix himself had said Louis had returned, leading a small heathen army. But certainly, in the course of the fight, Eberhard had seen no sign of Louis or any Northmen, though he knew that did not mean much, since he had not exactly been at the forefront of the battle.

He asked the prisoner a few more questions about Ranulf's intentions, but it was clear that the man knew nothing, so he ordered him taken away. As the guards half dragged him from the tent, Eberhard turned to Otker.

"What do you think of what that man said?" he asked. "Did you catch sight of Louis during the fight?"

"Well, lord," Otker said, and he seemed to be trying to form an image in his mind. "It was confused, lord, like battle can be, as you well know. I did think I saw Ranulf once in the fighting, but I wasn't sure. The fellow I saw had a helmet on, makes it hard to know who it is. But I never saw anyone I thought was your brother, lord."

"And the Northmen?"

"Never saw one who looked like a Northman, lord. Not during the fight. And none of the dead or wounded, either."

Were you going to mention this, you damned idiot? Eberhard thought, but he held his tongue and said, "This is very strange. Go get another of the prisoners and we'll see what we get from him."

One by one the prisoners were brought into the pavilion and forced to their knees, and one by one each told his story, and each story was remarkably similar to the last. They had been led by Ranulf and a few others whose names meant nothing to Eberhard. Louis had not been with them. The Northmen had not been with them. The word was that Louis had returned at the head of an army of Northmen (whose numbers varied from two hundred to a thousand) and that they had taken le Château de Roumois, but then they had sailed off again.

When the last of the prisoners was dragged away, Eberhard once again turned to Otker. "Well?" he demanded.

"Don't know, lord," Otker said. "Mayhaps I should…question them further? Be a bit more demanding?"

"Yes. Good idea. But take them away from the camp," Eberhard said. "Not good for the men to hear," he explained, though in truth he did not wish to hear the screams of the men as they were subjected to Otker's more thorough scrutiny.

"Of course, you Grace," Otker said, bowed, and ducked out of the tent.

Otker's questioning lasted through sunset and Eberhard's supper, until much of the camp had wandered off to bed. Eberhard wondered if Otker was taking so long because he was enjoying himself. On a few occasions he heard high-pitched, terrible sounds in the distance, which might have been the result of Otker's work, but might also have been some bird or animal off in the trees.

Finally, the guard announced Otker's return and Eberhard called for him to enter. Otker stepped into the pavilion and bowed slightly.

In the lantern light Eberhard saw there was still blood on the man's imperfectly washed hands.

"Well?" Eberhard asked.

"I never got a different story from any of them," Otker said. "It was all the same. They heard Louis and these Northmen were here, and then they sailed off. They most certainly were not in the fighting today."

"Hmm," Eberhard said, considering the implications of this. "And you think that's true?"

"Don't know if it's true, lord," Otker said. "But I'm sure them prisoners thought it was true. And so that means it most likely is."

"Very good." Eberhard felt his confidence reasserting itself at long last. "Then tomorrow I reckon we'll break camp and march on le Château de Roumois. And it seems there's not one damned thing to stop us."

Despite the profound relief that this latest intelligence brought, Eberhard slept fitfully, and was already awake when he sensed the first easing of the darkness and heard the first sounds of the men moving about and making ready to break camp. He remained in his field bed for some time longer, then finally with a groan swung his legs over the edge and stood and called for his servant.

When at last he stepped out through the canvas door, dressed, armed, having relieved himself and broken his fast, he discovered that the pavilion was the only thing still standing; the tents and flies and such had all been struck and loaded on the wagons, the fires put out, the iron pots stowed away, and the men were in their order of march, ready to move out.

Otker rode up as Eberhard was mounting his horse. "Beg pardon, lord, but I took the liberty of sending patrols out in each direction. Been gone since first light, no word yet."

"Very good," Eberhard said, nodding his approval. "The men are ready to move?"

"Yes, lord."

"Good. Then let us be off."

With shouted orders the foot soldiers, the mounted troops, the oxen and wagons all rolled forward, finding their rhythm as they moved down the worn road. Eberhard took his place near the center of the column, his bodyguard surrounding him as they moved. The day was clear and cool, good marching weather. They were about eight miles shy of the château, and even the ponderous column, Eberhard was sure, would be able to close that distance by midday, or just past.

It will be good to be in my home again, Eberhard thought. *Good to be behind the walls of the château.* He felt very exposed, marching through open country this way.

The land around was familiar now, the fields and woods he had known all his life, the road he had traveled many times, and that familiarity brought with it more comfort, more security. As they marched, riders from Otker's patrols came in with word of what they had seen, which was blessedly nothing of importance. No sign of the rebels who had attacked them. No sign, really, of much at all. The countryside, it seemed, was all but deserted.

And so, apparently, was le Château de Roumois. One of the riders whom Otker had sent on ahead while the column was still a few miles away returned with news. There were no heathen longships in the river. No sign of anyone at the château. No smoke from fires, no sign of horses, no servants. It seemed le Château de Roumois had been abandoned.

"We found some of the local folk," the rider said. "And they said they been watching the château, and the heathens lit out two days ago. Just loaded their ships and left, heading downriver. Last anyone seen of them."

Eberhard nodded as he listened, and thought, *Louis, you coward.* All those years his brother had had this reputation as a fearless warrior, the man who kept the Northmen at bay, the savior of Roumois. And now, when it came to a real fight, he and his craven heathen allies fled before they even crossed swords.

Eberhard turned to Otker, who was riding beside him. "It seems the way is clear," he said. "We should be behind the walls of the château directly."

"Yes, lord," Otker said. "But, as we approach the walls, lord, should I get the men into a battle formation, weapons at the ready? Just in case of a surprise, lord?"

"Yes…just what I was going to say," Eberhard said, though it was not actually what he was about to say. He had stopped thinking about the possibility of trouble, confident as he was that they would soon reach the safety of the château. But that was a mistake, and he knew it.

Dear God, I can't wait to be behind those walls! he thought. There he would be secure. Once he and his men were ensconced in the château there would be no getting them out. Louis could return with all the Northmen he wished; it would take more than a heathens mob to get past those defenses.

The roofline of le Château de Roumois was in sight over the trees when Otker suggested that they stop and get the men into a battle formation, and Eberhard agreed. The spearmen were brought to the front, with archers behind them and mounted warriors on the flanks. Shields were placed on arms, swords and axes and spears held ready, and with Otker in the lead and Eberhard toward the middle, his bodyguard around him, the army advanced once again.

The road ran up over a small hill and once they crested it the château came into view: the long expanse of open, grass-covered ground, the stone walls with their parapets and great oak doors, the massive house within, half hidden by the walls; it was just as Eberhard had seen a thousand or more times before. To the west the lawn ran down to the wide River Seine, which moved lazily past its banks and was blessedly devoid of longships or vessels of any kind.

As the army moved across the open ground, Eberhard studied the walls and the house beyond. No smoke. No people. No movement. No sign that there was anyone at all within those walls or without.

Word of the Northmen must have reached them…they would have seen the ships, Eberhard thought. *Everyone ran for the hills.*

News of longships coming up the Seine would certainly have reached Roumois and the people would have been in a panic. Worse, with half of Eberhard's house guard with him in Paris and the rest spread out over the countryside looking for Louis, there would have been no one here to defend the folk who lived in or near the château.

Little wonder they all fled….

He heard Otker call for a halt and then slowly the men stopped in their advance. Eberhard was about to demand an explanation when he saw six men break off from the rest and jog across the open ground toward the château's main gate. When they reached the gate, three of the men held up shields to defend against any possible archers on the walls and the other three grabbed onto the great iron rings and pulled.

To Eberhard's surprise, the massive doors swung open. They were not even barred. But then, there was little reason why they should be.

If someone was intent of sacking the château, then barred gates would not have slowed them down for long, not without men-at-arms on the walls to defend them.

The six men came jogging back and took their place in line and once again the column moved forward, Otker leading at a slow and cautious pace. Eberhard's gaze was everywhere, but still there was nothing to see, no threat to observe.

The spearmen at the head of the column, with Otker leading the way, reached the open gate and moved through, and the archers came behind them. Eberhard was still in the middle of the pack, still surrounded by his bodyguard, and he felt his sense of relief growing as the men moved into the courtyard ahead. It seemed they had run the gauntlet and come out the far end barely scathed.

He reached the wall a moment later and did not pause as he rode through the gate, like Caesar returning triumphant to Rome, and into the courtyard. From his vantage point on horseback he saw that nothing had been disturbed, nothing was out of place. If the heathens had indeed been there then they had left without doing any visible damage. It would not be until he had inspected the treasury and the library and the storehouses that he would know for certain, but thus far it seemed le Château de Roumois had been left unmolested.

Eberhard smiled to himself. *Home...home,* he thought. And safe within stone walls, thirty feet high.

And then he heard the cry—piercing, a barely human sound—and from the main door of the château and from the stables and from the guardhouse hundreds of screaming Northmen came bursting out, shields and weapons in hand, charging across the open ground.

Chapter Thirty-Four

They hurl their cruel battles at the faithful fold
From here and there fly spears, and through the air falls blood
And mixed with these are slings and battered catapults:
Between the earth and sky that's all that fills the air.

Abbo of Saint-Germain

When Starri Deathless came bursting out of the stable door, screaming as he ran, and Thorgrim watched the Frankish men-at-arms stop short, heads turning, weapons raised quickly, all he could think was, *You're surprised, I'll wager.*

It seemed a safe bet, as the front ranks of the Frankish army whirled left and right in confusion. It was a surprise that was well planned, put in place by Thorgrim and the rest since they first decided to stay and fight.

They had talked it through, he and his captains and Louis and Grifo, sitting in that massive, ornate room in Louis's childhood home. Whatever force the king and Felix and Louis's brother sent against them, it would certainly be well-trained and experienced and would likely outnumber them two to one at least. They would not defeat such an enemy through brute force alone.

Surprise. It could be their one, powerful advantage, if they were able to achieve it. But that would not be easy, not when the entire countryside knew they were there. Not when word of their coming and reports of their strength would most certainly have reached the king and his men in Paris, and would have done so even if Harald had not pulled the foolish and ill-advised stunt that he did.

Since their arrival was well-known, Thorgrim figured the best thing for them to do was to leave again, so visibly and ostentatiously that that, too, would be widely reported. He did not doubt their

332

movements were being observed, and that everything they did would be relayed to their enemies, and Louis felt the same, so they decided to give the watchers something to see.

They spent the next morning loading supplies on board the ships, a parade of Northmen streaming from the storehouses to the wharf and back again, rolling barrels, carrying bales and sacks. When the ships were fully laden, they went aboard and broke out the oars and headed off downriver, retracing their course there, sweeping past the smattering of villages along the banks where curious eyes were no doubt watching from hidden places.

They rowed through all the daylight hours and then, as evening came on, Louis directed them into a small tributary, just deep and wide enough to get their ships a mile or so upstream. They stopped at a place where the trees came down to the edge of the water and even overhung the river at their tops, as well-hidden a spot as they might hope to find. They tied the ships to the riverbanks and left half a dozen protesting men behind to guard them and headed out overland.

None of this would have been possible were it not for Louis de Roumois, who knew every road and track and path and open field across every square foot of that country. He led them back along hidden trails and darkened roads and across pastures where a few somnambulant cows stood motionless in the moonlight.

The first hints of dawn were showing when they emerged from a stand of trees to see the now familiar walls of le Château de Roumois across the open ground, not the front of the château, facing the river, but rather the back that looked inland toward the countryside. They crossed the wet grass and entered through a small sally port that had been left unbarred, and once again they were safe behind the walls, safe in Frankish luxury.

They spent the day hidden away, eating le duc de Roumois's food, drinking his ale, keeping their presence a secret. Louis led a half dozen men, the most skilled hunters, out beyond the walls to scout around, ranging as far as a mile from the château. They saw nothing. Louis posted scouts to stand watch over the approaches to the château, and they maintained that lookout through the night and over the course of the following day, but still nothing.

On the morning of the third day, when once again the scouts reported seeing nothing overnight, Thorgrim told Louis, "I don't think your brother is coming. Maybe he figures there's no need, since he thinks we sailed off."

"No," Louis said, "that's not right. My brother will come. He'll still fear for his château and his treasury. And he's more likely to come if he thinks we've left. If he thinks he won't have to fight."

Thorgrim nodded. Louis did not sound as certain as his words would imply. *You have one more day*, he thought, *and then we'll decide if we sack your fine home, or if we sail to Paris and take our revenge, or just leave Frankia astern.*

But Louis did not need a full day to be proven right. He did not even need until midday before the scouts returned with word of a powerful column of men approaching, and not so far away. Thorgrim's men left off their feasting, which had been pretty much continuous since their return, and donned mail and helmets and took up weapons and shields.

They spread out between the stables and the guardhouse the main house itself, which would allow them to attack from three directions. Thorgrim hoped they were not too stuffed with beef, pork, and bread and butter to stand in a shield wall. He gave strict orders. They would attack when half the column had passed through the main gate, which would let them do serious hurt to the vanguard while the back of the column was still trying to get through the relatively narrow entrance. No one was to make a move until he did.

That last, he knew, would not be obeyed, at least not by Starri. He would not be able to keep the berserker in check. But he would keep the man at his side, and try to hold him back as long as he was able.

They were standing in the twilight of the stable, looking out through the chinks in the wall at the big oak doors a hundred yards away, when they swung open. They had heard nothing; the sound of the approaching column had been completely muffled by the thick stone walls. Thorgrim readjusted his grip on Iron-tooth, settled his shield on his arm and waited, but no one came through.

"They're taking care," Louis said in a low voice. "Probably sent some poor bastards to pull the door open and see if someone would kill them if they tried. Wait for it."

And so they waited. But not for long. Soon the first of the column, men with shields held high and spears leveled, moved through the big doors. Thorgrim heard Starri starting to make the guttural noises he made just before the insanity took complete hold, heard his feet shuffling in the straw on the ground as he whirled, as if the berserker energy shooting through him was spinning him around.

"Wait, Starri, hold fast," Thorgrim said. The spearmen were only the first of them, streaming in through the gate, but they kept coming, rank on rank. The scouts had estimated the column at five or six hundred men, twice his own strength. The advantage of surprise was going to have to do a lot of lifting that day.

And still the spearmen came on through the gate, one hundred, two hundred at least. And behind them the archers, bows up, arrows nocked. They all moved with an admirable degree of discipline, keeping in good order, looking around, searching for threats, but not wavering in their line. It was a sign of men trained to that sort of thing. Thorgrim wondered if they had discipline enough to stand up to the wild attack that was about to fall on them, seemingly out of nowhere.

They would find out soon enough.

That must be half of them at least, Thorgrim thought, watching the Frankish men-at-arms come through the gate.

"There," Louis said. He was standing at Thorgrim's side, looking out through the wall. "The one on horseback. That's Eberhard. My brother."

Thorgrim nodded. The man Louis had indicated, Eberhard, apparently, seemed to be surrounded by a personal guard, and he rode with the air of one in command. Thorgrim wondered if he had left it too long, if he had let too many of the enemy get into the courtyard, onto the killing ground. He opened his mouth to shout for his men to move, but a heartbeat before he could speak, Starri broke.

Thorgrim had heard the battle cry a hundred times, but it still chilled him as it ripped from Starri's lungs and filled the dim-lit, dusty stable. Some of the men cursed in surprise, and then Starri was bursting out the door and racing across the open ground, axes in each hand, the muscles in his bare back flexing, his gait more like a deer than a man.

"Go! Go! Shields up, mind the archers!" Thorgrim shouted and he raced through the door on Starri's heels, though he knew he had no chance of keeping up with the man.

He looked to his left as he ran. The door to the main house was open and men were pouring out, and beyond that they were rushing out from around the sides of the guardhouse and through the door.

Asmund was leading the men from the château, Gudrid those from the guardhouse. They were coming on fast but in good order, rushing forward in wedge-shaped formations, shields up. It was an attack that even the most disciplined troops would be hard pressed to fend off.

Starri Deathless had halved the distance to the Frankish spearmen when the archers let fly. "Arrows! Shields up!!" Thorgrim shouted, though not as loud as he intended. The run was already stealing his breath.

He raised his shield just as the first flight of arrows was loosed. He saw Starri lurch left, the arrows tearing up the ground around him and whipping past as they streaked toward Thorgrim's line. He thought Starri had been hit, but then the berserker lurched right and left again, looking like nothing so much as a rabbit bounding one way and another to elude the dog on his heels.

Thorgrim felt his arm jolt as an arrow drove into his shield and he felt the weight of it pulling the shield down, just enough to throw it off the balance. He reached around and grabbed the shaft, snapping it in two and tossing the arrow aside as he ran.

Someone at the head of the Frankish line was shouting orders, directing the spearmen to fan out, to meet the threat coming at them from three directions. Shields went up, spears were leveled, and then Starri was on them. His axes came down, sweeping side to side, knocking spears aside, making a hole in the line of iron points through which he charged. He leapt off the ground, airborne, at the wall of spearmen, but as he jumped a shield came up and slammed into his legs, knocking him sideways. He dropped to the ground in a whirl of axes and limbs and the spearmen were on him, points thrusting, shields hammering down, and Starri was lost from sight in the frenzy.

Thorgrim was breathing hard and he was looking at the thrashing tangle of men who were piling on Starri and he thought, *No, no, no...*

It was not possible that Starri could meet his end here. It did not seem possible that Starri Deathless could meet his end anywhere, as desperately as he longed for it.

Then Thorgrim was up with the struggling mass of men, Iron-tooth slashing down on helmeted heads, thrusting at the gaps between shields. But the Frankish men-at-arms were ready for him and met his attack as it came. He felt Iron-tooth bounce off the flat of a shield, saw a spear point thrusting out at him. He moved to block the point with his shield as Louis stepped up at his side, sword darting in, finding its target as the spear dropped to the ground, the spearman's shriek loud in their ears.

Thorgrim slammed his shield sideways, knocking the man in front of him off balance, brought Iron-tooth down again, and this time he felt the blade strike. To his right and left his men were driving into the Frankish line, screaming in their feral way, hacking with swords and axes. It was not disciplined in the Frankish manner, but rather another sort of discipline, the discipline of the raiders from the North: wild and brutal and relentless.

Thorgrim was shouting now as Iron-tooth thrust right and left, looking for the openings, knocking spearpoints aside, smashing shields with powerful strokes. He saw a spear thrust out from the line and he twisted away. He saw the point pierce his mail and felt the heat of it ripping though the flesh of his shoulder as it glanced off. But he felt nothing beyond that, and he pushed the point aside and thrust the tip of his sword into the wide-eyed man who had wounded him.

Red rage, Thorgrim thought. Just a few years past, a fight like this would have sent him into the red rage, a wild fighting madness that would overtake him in battle, not a berserker's madness but something close. The madness of the Night Wolf. But he had not felt that in some time, like a sharp edge grown dull.

He shouted again, louder, from deeper in his gut, as if to prove to himself that he could still summon the madness and the fury. He hacked down again and again, pushing forward, delivering blows so fast and relentless that the spearmen could do nothing but hold their shields between themselves and the wild, gore-soaked blade.

Louis was still there, right beside him, fighting a very different fight, shield moving, his quick blade finding the places to sneak in for the kill. He was a cat, subtle and quick, and Thorgrim was a wolf, tearing into the fight with body and soul.

Through the close-packed line Thorgrim caught glimpses of Gudrid's men hitting the Franks on the other flank, and he felt the Frankish line bending under the pressure of the multiple attacks. He felt the spearmen stepping back, unable to stand up much longer against the fury of the Northmen.

"Push them! Push them!" Thorgrim shouted as he hacked with his sword and slammed his shield forward. The more confusion they could create the better. If they could get the spearmen running so they collided with the rest of the Frankish column trying to get through the gate, then they could turn this into a slaughter. Shatter the front half, then shatter the back, it was as much of a plan as he had.

Thorgrim caught a glimpse of Grifo, a sword in each hand, slashing and thrusting in every direction, and Harald, clearing a path with his shield and lunging and hacking in the space he opened up. He felt the shredded line of Frankish men-at-arms folding back on itself and he knew they were ready to break and run.

Then Thorgrim became aware of more shouting from back toward the gate—someone bellowing orders, others shouting in surprise or protest—and he guessed that the men outside the walls were trying to push through, trying to get in where they could join in the battle.

"Push them! Push them! Break them!" Thorgrim felt his own men surge forward again, pushing against the foe, cutting down the men in front, rolling over them, heaving them back. If they could get the spearmen running in panic, then it would be chaos among the Frankish men-at-arms.

Run you bastards, run! Thorgrim thought. And then he heard a new sound: shouts of encouragement. Cheers. He felt a shift in the line in front of him. He looked up and over the heads of the spearmen and the archers and he saw mounted warriors riding into the fight. They came charging around the flanks on armored horses, fifty or sixty strong, shields and spears and long swords in hand.

"Riders!" Thorgrim shouted. "Look to your sides! Harald, look to your side!"

The horsemen must have driven right through the press of men in the main gate to get into the courtyard, probably trampling any number of their own soldiers to get past. But now they had broken free of the crowd and were coming around the sides of the battle lines, driving to get in behind the Northmen, to trap them between their horses and swords and shields and the spearmen in their front, who were rallying at the sight of them.

"Bastards!" Thorgrim shouted in frustration. The spearmen had been on the verge of breaking, and now, heartened by the riders, they were finding more fight in them. He stepped back from the battle line and stepped back again, getting clear of the spears so he would have room to engage the mounted warriors as they came.

A spear flew from the crowd ahead and Thorgrim ducked and felt the shaft glance off his mail-clad shoulder. He saw another catch one of Harald's crew in the belly and drop him screaming and writhing to the ground. And then the first of the riders was there, driving directly at Thorgrim with sword raised, and Thorgrim just had time enough to get his shield up and block the powerful downward slash. He felt the impact in his arm, saw a section of his shield shatter. A few more blows like that and it would be nothing but splinters.

The riders charged past, and as they did the spearmen surged forward with a cheer, weapons leveled, driving Thorgrim and his men back. The Northmen slashed at the points of the spears and knocked them aside with their shields, while behind them they heard the tramp and pounding of hooves, the whinnying of horses as the riders whirled and made ready for another charge.

"Forward! Into them!" Thorgrim shouted and pushed toward the spearmen, hacking and driving with his damaged shield. Perhaps they could still send the foot soldiers into panicked flight, still create chaos. It might help, or it might not, but it seemed the only chance they had.

He looked to his left and right. Harald and Louis and Grifo and the others were also driving into the spearmen, attacking the line with all the fury they could conjure up. And behind them, the hoofbeats were getting louder.

"Behind you! Riders are coming!" Thorgrim shouted, but he was not the only one who had heard the horsemen. His men were trying to disengage from the spearmen, trying to turn to meet this new threat, but they were pressed on both sides now, an enemy at their backs no matter which way they turned.

"Harald!" Thorgrim shouted. "Look to the spearmen, I'll see to the riders!" and Harald nodded his understanding. Thorgrim turned, facing the riders, his back to the spears, and he wondered if Harald could actually hold the line off of him while he, in turn, held the riders off Harald.

The nearest horseman was almost on top of him, his sword raised high. Thorgrim's eyes were on the man's blade as he readied to counter the stroke, but suddenly, unexpectedly, the rider reined up hard and the horse's head shot out, teeth bared, snapping at

Thorgrim's face. Thorgrim, in his surprise, was slow to react. The horse's mouth was mere inches away, so close Thorgrim felt the animal's breath on his skin, before he got his shield up and slammed its rim into the horse's jaw. The horse reared back, screaming in shock and pain, and Thorgrim raced forward, three quick steps, around behind the rider and mount.

The horse came back down on four feet, the rider pulling on the reins, fighting to regain control, when Thorgrim delivered a slashing cut across the horse's rump. The animal bolted forward and Harald leapt aside as it charged into the spearmen, knocking some to the ground, making others leap aside where, off guard, they were cut down by the Northmen.

That was luck, no more, Thorgrim thought. He had created a moment of confusion, used the mounted warrior against the Frankish spearmen, but he would not pull that trick twice. Time to think of something else.

Thorgrim looked to his left. He saw Gellir, twenty feet away, knocked to the ground by a lashing hoof. He saw him try to stand, saw the horse come down on him with both feet, crushing him in a spray of blood. There were wounded and dead sprawled out in the dirt, his own men and the Frankish soldiers. The spearmen were pressing the Northmen hard, and the riders were hacking and thrusting from their vantage point on horseback.

Another horseman whirled up between Thorgrim and the others, cutting him off from Harald and his men. Thorgrim tried to duck under the animal's head, but the rider was too fast, pushing his horse forward and slashing down with his sword so that Thorgrim just had time enough to raise his shield and take the blow. The sword hit in a powerful down stroke and the wooden planks collapsed into so many splinters. Thorgrim threw the shield aside and moved back a few steps, looking for room to fight.

Another rider charged down on him, this one on the other side, so that he was hemmed in front and back by the snapping, kicking beasts, their riders thrusting and slashing at him. Thorgrim parried a blade, lunged for the rider's thigh, but the rider jerked the reins over, dancing his mount sideways, clear of the blow, and Iron-tooth found only air.

Thorgrim felt movement behind him. The hair on his neck stood up and he whirled around as the second rider brought his sword down like an ax. There was no getting Iron-tooth up in time for the parry so Thorgrim swung his left arm sideways, hitting the blade with his mail-clad forearm, knocking the sword aside, then reaching up and grabbing the rider by the arm and pulling him down.

The first rider was back, lunging straight out for Thorgrim's chest. Thorgrim twisted as he pulled the second rider down from his horse, making a shield of the man, and the sword passed through the Frankish horseman's throat. Thorgrim let go and drove Iron-tooth up under the first rider's chin and kept going until he felt the tip break through his skull and hit the inside of the man's helmet.

He pulled Iron-tooth free and jumped clear as the horses bolted off in different directions. He looked around. The fight had devolved into a formless melee. Numbers, the sheer weight of men, would make a big difference in such a battle, and Louis's brother had the advantage there.

Thorgrim shook his head in wonder. Was he really going to die defending the very sort of place he had spent a lifetime raiding?

But even as he thought that, he realized that something more was happening back toward the gate, something was rippling through the fighting men. He saw looks of confusion on their faces at the changed sounds of the battle. He saw the mounted warriors, whose height of eye gave them a better view of what was taking place at the far end of the field, frowning and staring at whatever it was.

"Harald! Do you see what's happening?" Thorgrim called and Harald looked at him and shook his head.

Then, twenty feet in front of where Thorgrim stood, Starri Deathless erupted out of the dense press of Frankish warriors like a partridge bursting from the tall grass into noisy flight. He seemed to come straight up from the ground and he kept coming, driving his axes down on the men closest at hand and stepping up on them as they went down.

Starri! Thorgrim had seen him lost under a pile of spearmen and that was the last of it. In the fury of the battle, he had forgotten all about the man and now he wondered where he had been all that time. Unconscious on the ground? Maybe. He was wounded in a half dozen places that Thorgrim could see and coated in blood, though with Starri it was hard to know whose blood it was. A good portion of it, certainly, seemed to be his.

Starri's emergence from the depths brought something new to the increasingly chaotic fight in the courtyard. He whirled right and left with his axes and the spearmen fell over one another trying to get away, which created greater confusion, and more opportunity for the Northmen to cut them down.

Thorgrim turned, ready to face the mounted warriors as they resumed the fight, but to his great surprise the horsemen were gone. They had spurred their horses on, charging back toward the main gate, as if trying to escape, but Thorgrim doubted they were doing that. What they were doing he could not guess.

One of Gudrid's men was lying dead nearby, his blood dark and wet on the dry ground, and one of the spearmen was flung across him, dead as well. Or near enough. Thorgrim put his foot on the spearman's back and stood and the two feet of height that the bodies provided allowed him to see over the heads of the fighting men, over the whirling bedlam of Starri Deathless, and off toward the main gate beyond. He could see now with perfect clarity what was happening. But he did not understand it at all.

There was more fighting taking place by the wall, but he knew it was not his men doing the fighting. His men had hit the Franks from the opposite direction and had not pushed through nearly that far. This was some other band of warriors who had joined in, who had most likely come in through the gate and hit Eberhard's men from behind. And if that was true, it did not bode well for Eberhard's men.

Thorgrim leapt down from his makeshift perch. "Push them! Push them!" he shouted, realizing that once again they had the Franks on the edge of a panicked route. He snatched a shield up off the ground and slipped it on his arm as he raced forward. He slammed into the nearest of the spearmen who looked up just as Thorgrim hit him with the shield and bowled him over. Thorgrim did not waste the effort to drive Iron-tooth into the man. He would not be getting up again soon, and would likely be trampled by his compatriots as he tried.

"Harald! Gudrid! Asmund! Rally your men, push these bastards back! They'll break soon!" he shouted as he wielded his sword and his shield and applied all the pressure he could to the Frankish line. On either side his men were rushing up to join him, forming a loose shield wall, pressing forward. But their effort was nothing compared to Starri Deathless, who was tearing around like a rabid animal, whirling and slashing. A few of the Frankish soldiers tried to bring him down and they died for their efforts, but most were shoving the others aside in their attempt to get away.

More and more of the Northmen stepped up to the line, once again presenting a disciplined attack, and the Frankish men-at-arms fell back and were cut down or knocked to the ground. But they stood their ground, good soldiers that they were, holding back the press with spears and shields and short swords.

And then they broke.

It happened the way Thorgrim had seen it happen many times. One moment an army is fighting, hard-pressed, and then suddenly a spirit of panic and defeat sweeps through it, and as if on some powerful but unspoken command, they turn and flee. Spears were tossed aside—not hurled at the enemy, just tossed aside—and shields were thrown off as the fighting men raced off toward the main gate, running in the only direction that seemed to offer safety.

But it no longer did. Thorgrim saw for certain now what was happening. Some new column of men had come in through open doors to fall on the rear of Eberhard's army. The living were fighting on; the dead were scattered all over the courtyard. But Thorgrim saw men on their knees as well, hands up in surrender, and more and more were joining them.

It was this new fight that the fleeing, largely weaponless spearmen ran into, but there was no fight left in them. One by one they, too, dropped to their knees, raised their hands, and begged for mercy. And mercy they were shown. Thorgrim had seen plenty of instances where surrendering men were cut down like rye, but these newly arrived warriors seemed more inclined toward prisoners than corpses.

Louis de Roumois stood nearby, his mail shirt rent, his legging torn. There was blood on his face and his hands and on the blade of his sword, which was resting point-down on the ground. He was staring off across the courtyard, toward the main gate where the last of the Frankish men-at-arms were taking a knee. His mouth was half-open and he looked dazed, as if he had been hit on the side of the head.

Thorgrim stepped toward him. If anyone would know who these new arrivals were, it would probably be Louis, and Thorgrim figured he had better find out if they were friends or yet another enemy to fight.

"Louis," Thorgrim said, but Louis continued staring off across the open space. He squinted and then he spoke, one word, and it was more to himself than to Thorgrim.

"Ranulf?"

Chapter Thirty-Five

Life loves my righteous folk and hates the sinister;
Death loves the enemy; our friends are steered by life;
Then sleep gives rest to citizens, while wretches flee.

Abbo of Saint-Germain

Dear God, do you still live? Louis thought, looking out across the courtyard.

Thorgrim stepped up beside him, following his gaze. "You know this fellow, who led these men in through the gate?"

"I think so," Louis said. "It's been a long time. He's changed. Come."

They walked across the open ground, past the dead men and the wounded men, some of whom were twisting and groaning, some who were all but motionless. They walked past the king's men on their knees, hands up, who had surrendered and were being looted by the Northmen of anything of value they held, then pulled to their feet and shoved off to stand dejected under guard.

The man Louis had been staring at was lean and tough-looking, his head shaved, a moustache and goatee hiding the lower part of his face. He did not look much like the man Louis remembered, but the shape of him, the way he moved, the way he carried himself, seemed utterly familiar. He had apparently received a notable wound on his forearm and was standing patiently while one of his fellows bound it with a bandage torn from a white and crimson sash. He looked up as Louis and Thorgrim approached. He squinted and his mouth came partway open.

"Louis?" he said.

"Ranulf?"

They just stared at one another, briefly, and then Ranulf pulled his arm free from the fellow bandaging him, took three long strides and grabbed Louis up in a hug, which Louis returned enthusiastically. Louis felt his head swimming from the onslaught of emotion, the crush of sensations all piling in. This was a moment, exactly like this, that he had seen in his mind over and over while huddled half-frozen in his little monk's cell in Glendalough.

They remained like that for some moments, the old campaigner and his protégée, then finally they released one another.

"I wasn't sure it was you," Louis said. "I heard that my brother had you killed. You've grown old, but you still look pretty hale for a dead man."

"Your brother tried to have me killed, to be sure. We found someone more worthy of the honor to take my place," Ranulf said. "But I didn't think to see you here. We heard you and your heathens had sailed off."

"We did," Louis said. "But we came back. So we could surprise Eberhard. And it seems we did." He looked around at the various groups of prisoners, the men guarding them, and he felt a sudden tinge of panic. "Please tell me Eberhard has been taken prisoner."

Ranulf shook his head. "I fear not. I saw it myself. He was in the middle of it, surrounded by his body guard. They were fighting like demons to keep us back. And dying for their efforts. But they couldn't hold, and once Eberhard saw that, he bolted. Rode right over his own men to get out the gate and he was gone."

"Damn!" Louis said. That was going to complicate things. "Is there no chance we can catch him?"

Ranulf shook his head. "He's been gone some time, and his horse looked like a fast one. Probably halfway to Paris by now." He nodded toward Thorgrim. "Is this one of your heathens I've heard tell of?"

"Yes, yes," Louis said. "This is Thorgrim Ulfsson, known as Thorgrim Night Wolf. He commands these men. And he's a surprisingly good man himself, for a Northman. Took me some time to realize that."

He turned to Thorgrim and said in Thorgrim's tongue, "This is Ranulf, a chevalier of the horse guard. A great fighting man. He taught me everything I know."

Thorgrim nodded and shook Ranulf's hand. Having seen Ranulf fight, having heard that description, Thorgrim was inclined to respect the man.

"You speak the heathen tongue?" Ranulf asked.

"I do," Louis said. "I've been in their company...longer than I care to think. A thousand confessions won't wash me clean of the sins I've committed."

"Ha!" Ranulf said. "I don't recall you ever being worried about your sinful ways. I guess your time in the monastery did you some good."

Louis smiled. Ranulf, his old friend, his fellow campaigner, had seen Louis take part in plenty of reproachful behaviors. Much of it Ranulf had led him into. The life of a soldier.

"But how in the world do you come to be here?" Louis asked. It was the obvious question, but in all the confusion and joyful reunion he had forgotten to ask it.

"Ah! Well, there's a tale that could be days in the telling," Ranulf said. "But I'll shorten it some."

In a few broad strokes he painted the picture of life in Roumois since Eberhard had ascended to the dukedom and sent Louis packing to Ireland. He told of Eberhard's increasing paranoia, and the way he purged the ranks of any man he thought might still be loyal to his brother. About how he had ordered his, Ranulf's, execution, and how Mariwig had duped him into thinking it had been carried out. Of the years of quietly building up a secret rebel force, waiting on the day that Louis would return.

As Louis listened, he translated the words for Thorgrim, who seemed to find it fascinating, if a bit amusing.

"When word reached us that you were on your way back to Roumois, leading an army of Northmen, we figured our moment had come," Ranulf continued. "We called up what men we could. I sent Childric...you remember Childric?"

"Certainly," Louis said.

"I sent Childric to the château to speak with you, to tell you our plans, but when he got here you were gone. Folks around said they had seen you and the Northmen sail off. Still, we had the army, we had our fighting ground picked out. Mariwig had put it in place that the chevaliers would turn on Eberhard in the midst of battle. We prayed that would be enough. The bold stroke, as you know, is often the best. So we attacked. Two days back."

"And?" Louis asked.

Ranulf shook his head. "Mariwig was found out. Eberhard beheaded him in front of the rest and stripped the chevaliers of their horses and gear. Put his own men in their stead. He knew we were lying in wait for him. It was…not good. Not for us."

"I see," Louis said. *Mariwig…* He remembered the tough, ugly warrior very well, one of his most trusted men back when he commanded the horse guard. He wondered how Mariwig had avoided Eberhard's axe for as long as he had.

"But more and more men kept coming in, despite our defeat," Ranulf continued. "Men who had been waiting years to get back at Eberhard. The whole countryside, they all rose up and flocked to our banner.

"We had our scouts shadowing Eberhard's army, hoping for another chance. Never found one, and when Eberhard reached the château, we reckoned that was it. With such a force as we had, untrained men and so few of them, there would be no fighting him behind these walls. Then, glory be to God, the scouts come riding back to report there's some sort of battle going on!"

"Who did you think was fighting?" Louis asked.

"I had no idea," Ranulf said. "Some other band of rebels? Bandits? I had no notion, but I figured anyone who was doing battle with Eberhard couldn't be all bad, and we had best go to their aid."

Louis smiled. And then, because he could not help himself, he hugged the old man again.

It was late in the day before the aftermath of the battle was attended to, the prisoners and their wounded confined in the stables, Thorgrim's wounded brought into the château and made comfortable. The dead were wrapped in cloth and laid out in two lines, Norsemen and Franks. Heathens and Christians.

Riders were sent out to round up the servants who had fled, and by nightfall there were dozens of men and women swarming over the main house and the grounds. The kitchens produced roasted meat and bread and greens, the cellars a seemingly unlimited supply of ale and wine and even mead, and the victors, crowded into the château's great hall, enjoyed it all.

Louis and Thorgrim and Thorgrim's captains sat at the big table on the dais, along with Ranulf and his captains and Hildirik, who had emerged from the place where he had unapologetically hidden himself. They, too, feasted on the great stores of food that Eberhard had laid in. And from his place at the center of the table, Louis took it all in.

There was an unreality about this situation, and the tighter Louis tried to grasp it, the more it seemed to slip from his fingers. It seemed dream-like in some ways, but after the bloody work of that afternoon,it was, as well, all too real. Here was the culmination of all the plans he had made all those years. Plans to take his brother's place as le duc de Roumois. His brother's worst fear and, ironically, something that Louis never would have wanted if his brother had not turned on him.

They were plans that he had made by himself, during his miserable exile in Glendalough, with no notion of how he could ever bring them off. And now, here he was.

"Gentlemen!" Louis called down the table, left and right. The Northmen had finished singing a particularly loud song and now Louis was forcing himself to confront the reality of the moment. "We must talk. Now. In some place where we need not shout."

Heads nodded. Grifo had taken it upon himself to translate for Thorgrim and the other Northmen, and they nodded as well. Louis led the way off the dais and out the door of the hall, and if any of the men engaged in the bacchanal noticed, no one said a thing. From there, Louis escorted them into the great room and they took their places around the big table.

"Hildirik," Louis said, turning to the old man at his right hand. "It would seem my brother escaped. I have to assume he's back in Paris. So, what will happen now?"

Hildirik let out a long sigh. "This is a frightfully complicated situation. Frightfully complicated." He paused, collecting his thoughts, collecting them for so long that Louis began to think he was done, when he started in again.

"The king will not be happy about this, none of it," Hildirik said. "He's no great supporter of the people rising up in arms, as you can imagine."

"I'd think not," Ranulf said.

"No, indeed," Louis said. "We've not set an example the king will much care for. I'd have liked to have Eberhard as a hostage, but we don't. Now, I don't see as the king'll do anything but send a strong force out to put us down."

"That would seem his most likely move," Hildirik said. "But…as I said, it's complicated. If this were just an uprising among the common sort, the king would certainly crush it under foot. But this is a fight amongst the nobility, brothers at war for rule. That's something the king understands well, having gone to war with his own brothers. Nor will the king wish to acknowledge unrest in the country. He would be loath to do so in any circumstance, but he certainly will not care to do so while Æthelwulf is at court."

Louis was quiet for a moment as he considered that. He was not entirely sure what Hildirik was suggesting. "The king will see this as an embarrassment? Something he'd rather ignore?" he asked. "Are you saying…what are you saying?"

"I'm saying there is a good chance the king will send a real army, not just the column he gave to Eberhard, here to Roumois to put this down and hang us all. But today certainly proved that that will be no simple task. So there is also a good chance that he'll tell Eberhard to just make peace somehow. Tell him he doesn't care a fig who the duke is, but he won't stand for war in Roumois."

This again was greeted with silence. "So, how should we prepare?" Ranulf asked.

"If you wish to fight, make ready to fight," Hildirik said. "But honestly, I don't think you'll know which way the king is going to jump until you see who shows up outside the gates; a lone messenger from Paris or three thousand men-at-arms."

Felix sat behind the big, cluttered table in his room, making a tent of his fingers and listening to the tale told by the man who stood opposite him, one of the soldiers who had come straggling back to Paris from Roumois. There had been ten of them, just ten, who managed to return from the fight, and Felix had made a point of interviewing each personally. This was the last of them.

The first back from Roumois, of course, had been Eberhard, pounding in through the gates on a mount that Felix felt sure would fall over dead, so hard had the poor beast been ridden. Eberhard was just as lathered up, a volcanic and demanding mixture of fear and rage, insisting on an audience with the king. Which he most certainly was not going to get. He would not even get an audience with Felix, at least not until he had calmed down and Felix had spoken to any other man who came straggling in from the fight.

Felix wanted to know the truth for himself before he had to listen to Eberhard's version of it.

"So you were...?"

"With the spearmen, at the back of the column, lord," the soldier before him said. He was picking his words as carefully as his limited imagination would allow. "The rear guard, if you will."

"And?"

"Well, on the whole march to le Château de Roumois we never saw the enemy, not after we sent them running a few days before, like I said. Never a one. And then half the column goes in through the gate, and next thing we know, they're attacked, lord. We couldn't see nothing, those of us to the rear, but we could hear it."

"Who did you think was attacking?"

"We weren't sure, lord," the spearman said. He was clearly frightened, as well he might be, and probably wondering if he had made a mistake returning to Paris. But he was conducting himself well, for all that.

"We'd heard that Louis...he was leading an army of Northmen...but we'd heard they'd sailed off," the man continued. "Just stories, of course. Simple fighting men, they don't tell us nothing. But we thought maybe it was them. The Northmen. Or the rebels."

"I see," Felix said. "And when you heard the fighting, what did you do?"

"Well, lord, the captains, they ordered us forward, and of course, we obeyed," the soldier said, and Felix had to admire the man's subtly shifting blame to his officers for any wrong decision that might have been made. "But we were all trying to get in through the gate, and it was just madness, lord. Then the mounted warriors were ordered forward, and they just ran down anyone who couldn't get out of the way. Charged right through and into the courtyard."

"And what was Duke Eberhard doing at this point?"

"Don't know, lord. He was inside the gate, see, and I was outside. But after the chevaliers cleared the way, those of us in the rear were able to get in. And then I saw Duke Eberhard and he was with his bodyguard and they were in a bloody fight with the heathens, lord. Bloody. Never saw a man fight as bravely as Duke Eberhard.

I can just imagine, Felix thought. This man was lying, most assuredly, thinking that Felix would want to hear tales of Eberhard's bravery, but it didn't matter.

"And then?" Felix asked.

"Well, the chevaliers and Eberhard, they were really doing slaughter to the heathens, lord. Bloody butchery. Then just as it seemed victory was ours, these others come charging in through the gate, right into our rear. Same rebels who attacked us the day before, I'll warrant. But more of them. A lot more."

"And things fell apart then?"

"Yes, lord," the spearman said. "We were taken by surprised, and had enemy front and back. We all fought, as best we could. Eberhard was like the devil himself with sword and shield, but even he couldn't hold them off any longer, so he made his retreat."

"And you?"

"I...I don't even much recall what happened to me. Somehow I found myself outside the walls, and the fighting all but over, so I made my retreat as well. Hoping to find Duke Eberhard and serve in his bodyguard as he made his way back here."

You're a lying cur, Felix thought. *You ran like a rabbit when you saw how things would go.* He considered having the man drawn and quartered for his cowardice, but decided that it would not help in the present situation. He wished to bring as little attention as possible to the debacle at Roumois.

"Very well," Felix said, standing and stepping around the table. He saw the heightened apprehension on the man's face, but he dug into his purse and pulled out a gold coin. "Take this for your bold action on the field. And...let me emphasize this...say nothing of this to anyone. Understood?"

"Yes, lord." The spearman took the coin the way an earnest novitiate might take Holy Communion.

"I'm quite serious," Felix said, looking the man hard in the eyes. "There will be consequences for careless talk. Dire consequences. Do I make myself clear?"

The eagerness was gone from the man's face, and in its place was fear, and when he said. "I understand, lord," Felix knew that the man did indeed understand.

The guards escorted the spearman from the room and Felix stared unseeing at the carpet as he considered the interviews he had heard thus far. Some of the men had been at the front of the column, some in the middle or near the rear, but all of their stories had been similar enough. They had thought Louis and his heathens had fled, and thought as much right up until the surprise attack had been launched.

Louis and his band must have sailed off, and then beached their ships and marched back unseen.

Damned clever...

And still they had nearly been beaten. Would have been, it seemed, if the other rebels had not arrived when they did.

But more of them. A lot more. That was what the spearman had said. And that meshed with other reports that Felix had heard from around Roumois. Despite the beating that the rebels had taken from Eberhard's column, and the beheading of the traitor Mariwig, the folk had flocked to join the uprising in support of the pretender, Louis.

Felix had been aware for some time that the people of Roumois did not look kindly on Eberhard, that they felt no love or loyalty to the young duke. But he had not realized the discontent ran that deep.

"Oh, damn his soul," Felix muttered. Eberhard had put him in a difficult situation. And as he looked at the various ways out of the trap he was in, there was only one that seemed to lead where he wanted to go. It was the least pretty of all his options, but it was likely the most effective.

He looked up at the remaining guard who was standing near the door and staring dutifully off into space. "Go fetch Eberhard, please," Felix said.

"Yes, lord." The guard ducked out the door. A moment later the first guard returned, having escorted the spearman to the barracks, and Felix was able to have a quick word with the man before the other arrived with Eberhard on his heels.

Eberhard seemed much deflated by the time he had spent waiting alone for this audience, and Felix was pleased to see it. A combination of fear and exhaustion had taken him down considerably since he had first come charging in a mad panic through the gates of Paris.

"Ah, Eberhard, there you are," Felix said, sounding almost glad to see the man.

"Felix," Eberhard said. "Have you seen the king? I must speak to the king. This...this must be crushed. Now. Quickly. Before it spreads."

"Before it spreads..." Felix repeated. "But it has spread, my dear Eberhard. I've heard from any number of people. All of Roumois has rallied to your brother's banner."

"Then all of Roumois must be crushed," Eberhard said, some of the fire returning to his voice. "And my traitorous brother must be crushed."

Felix wanted to sigh, but he held it in. It was all so tedious. Every one of these petty dukes thought his own situation was so critical, the intrigue on which the entire kingdom hinged. The king did not give a damn who was le duc de Roumois, as long as there was peace in the region and the duke and his people paid their taxes.

"You know, Eberhard, we all must exit this *vallis lacrimarum* at some time or other," Felix said. "And what better way than a hero's death? Fighting the invading Northmen who came to sack Roumois?"

Eberhard frowned and his eyebrows came together in confusion. "What do you mean?"

"I mean if a man died in battle, and it was understood abroad that he died protecting his home and people from heathens, that would be a grand legacy. As good as any of us might hope for."

Eberhard shook his head. "Are you talking about Louis? Or...I don't follow you."

"No, indeed." Felix nodded to the guard who stood just behind Eberhard, and in one quick move the man stepped up and looped a thin cord around Eberhard's neck and drew it tight, so tight it bit deep into the skin. So tight that Eberhard could not get his clawing fingers under it, try as he might.

Eberhard's eyes went wide and his face turned red and he twisted side to side but he was no match for the guard's strength. The duke's gaze met Felix's but it was not clear to Felix if Eberhard could really see him, or if he was blinded in his pain and terror. He was grateful that Eberhard could make no sounds; he was in no mood to listen to any pathetic pleading or arguments.

The twisting and pushing and kicking went on for a surprising length of time, then it grew weaker and Eberhard's legs failed him at last. He sank to his knees and the clawing at the garrote ceased and Eberhard's arms fell to his sides. But the guard, a thorough fellow, still did not release him, holding Eberhard's body up by the cord around his neck. Then finally, after Eberhard had ceased moving for a moment or two and showed no inclination to ever move again, the guard let him go.

Eberhard fell face first onto the carpet and his body twitched a few times and then lay still. The three men in the room stared at the corpse for some time as Felix let the guard catch his breath.

"Very well," Felix said at last. "There's an empty trunk by the south window which should serve to get this out of here."

"Yes, lord," the guard said.

"He'll need some noble wounds, see to that. And do it soon or he won't bleed in any believable way."

"Yes, lord."

"The sort of wounds that might allow a man to ride for an hour or so before falling dead," Felix continued. "Then see him wrapped in a blanket or some such. Have some men bring the body to Roumois. They're to tell Louis that Eberhard was found by the road, after having bravely fought the heathens who were sacking the place. Do you understand?"

"Yes, lord," the guards said together and hurried off to the south window to fetch the trunk.

It was all absurd, of course. Plenty of people had seen Eberhard arrive in Paris. But Felix knew that no one would give it more than a moment's curious thought. If the king did not care—and he most certainly did not—then no one else of importance would care either.

Louis was smart enough to pick up on the deceit, Felix felt certain of that, and was not likely to raise any objections. Not with his brother dead and him the new duc de Roumois, the very thing for which he had wished all those years. The winds had shifted; they had blown Louis into his brother's place, and that was really no concern of Felix's.

The guards brought over the trunk, set it down beside Eberhard's body and opened the lid. They lifted the corpse and dropped it inside, grabbing the legs which were draped over the edge and tucking them in. They did not touch the purse or the bejeweled dagger that hung from Eberhard's belt, but Felix knew those would be gone as soon as the body was out of his sight.

"You know what to do?" Felix asked.

"Yes, lord," the guards said in unison. Felix nodded. He trusted these men. They were smart and loyal and well paid, which was why they served as his personal guard.

The two men shut the lid, grabbed the handles on either end of the trunk and hefted it up. They maneuvered it out the door, then shut the door behind them.

Felix stared at the closed door, then turned and took his seat again behind his table. A letter he had begun earlier that day was laying there and he considered finishing it, but instead pushed it aside and pulled out a fresh parchment. He would write a brief letter to Louis, expressing his sympathy concerning his brother's death and his certainty that Eberhard's heroism would not be forgotten. He would assure Louis of the king's support, and remind him of his majesty's expectations concerning loyalty and payment of taxes.

That should take care of it, Felix thought as he reached for his quill. A brief letter, the business would be finished, and none of them need ever think of it again.

He wished every problem could be solved so easily.

Epilogue

All the Chosen Warriors are waging war
In the dwellings of Odin that day
They choose the slain, ride home from the strife,
Then at peace sit again together.

The Words of the Mighty Weaver
The Poetic Edda

Halfdan the Black drummed his fingers on the armrest of his throne, a massive oak affair, carved with wild, intricate motifs of mythical beasts and scenes from the lives of the gods. Nearby, standing on its perch, his gyrfalcon shifted side to side, it's hooded head swiveling side to side.

Halfdan looked down at the man kneeling in front of him, hands bound behind his back. Two guards stood motionless behind him.

He does not look well, Halfdan thought. He had lost weight since last Halfdan had seen him. His hair and beard were unkempt and there was an ugly bruise around one eye and dried blood on his face. His tunic was torn and filthy.

But for all that, the man was not looking down in shame, or staring off in the distance, or looking at Halfdan with a supplicant's pleading eyes. No, he was meeting Halfdan's gaze and holding it, bold and unflinching.

Defiant bastard, Halfdan thought. Most men would be withering under the king's gaze by now, but not him. Finally, Halfdan spoke.

"Skorri Thorbrandsson…"

"My lord," Skorri said, his tone flat, neutral. Defiant.

No, not defiant, Halfdan thought. It was something else. Halfdan would have sensed defiance immediately, like biting into bitter fruit. This attitude did not have the same flavor, but what it was, Halfdan could not tell.

"You're a coward, Skorri. A traitor. You deserted me."

"No, lord," Skorri said, his voice still even. "I did not desert you. I failed you."

Halfdan felt his eyebrows raise at this statement. *I failed you…* That was not a thing other men ever dared say, even when it was true.

"How did you fail me?"

"You sent me to run the traitors Odd and Amundi and Onund to ground, and I failed. And I could not bear the thought of failing my king, so I vowed I would not return until I achieved the task you set for me. I sent men to you with word of my efforts. Whether or not they reached you, I don't know."

Halfdan continued to drum his fingers as he considered those words. One man had indeed come in to report just what Skorri had said, but Halfdan had not believed him, not entirely. Had he been certain the man was lying he would have had him beheaded immediately, but the truth of the matter was not entirely clear, so he had him locked up instead.

I guess I'll let that one go free, Halfdan thought. *Lucky bastard.*

"So where have you been all this time, when I thought you had run off?"

"I was hunting the traitors, lord. Me and the men who were with me. We had them, the very day they escaped, but that bastard Helgason and his warriors arrived in time to free them, and me with just a handful of my men. So once I had all my men together, we looked for them at Vifil's farm, but they had fled, so we hunted them through the high country and along the coast. We asked questions, heard rumors, but found nothing. Until just a few days past."

Halfdan frowned. The story told by Kolbein and the other men who had brought Skorri in was not quite the same as this. In the broad outline it was, and it did not appear as if they lied, but they made it seem as if Skorri had lost his wits, and was no longer working on his king's behalf, but simply for his own enrichment and vengeance. They had said nothing about finding Odd and Amundi.

"What do you mean, a few days past?" Halfdan said.

Skorri looked confused for a brief moment, and then he nodded and gave a rueful smile. "Of course, the traitor Kolbein and the rest didn't tell you that," he said. "We found them at last. Odd and Amundi. They had taken refuge at Ragi Oleifsson's farm, across the bay. We burned Ragi's hall to the ground, but the sons of bitches had a tunnel, just like Odd had. Still, we caught them coming out the other end and we fought them. We were fighting on a cliff edge, and the cliff collapsed under me and my men. That's how they got away."

Halfdan frowned deeper still. "And you're certain it was them? Odd and Amundi? You saw them?"

Skorri held Halfdan's eyes, but he did not answer right away. Instead he seemed to consider the question. "No…" he said at last. "No, I did not see them. At least I can't say with absolute certainty. It was very dark, where we were fighting. But I would gladly wager my life that it was them."

Halfdan nodded. It was lucky for Kolbein and the others that Skorri was willing to admit this. If it had turned out that they knew for certain Odd and Amundi had been within their grasp, and they had failed to mention it, then it would have been the chopping block for all of them. He looked up at the guard behind Skorri.

"Cut his wrists free," he said. The guard pulled a knife and bent over and cut the thongs that bound Skorri's wrists.

"You may stand," Halfdan said, and Skorri nodded and struggled to his feet. He was clearly in pain from various wounds and bruises, but he managed to get up unaided and stand fairly straight.

"So, you found Odd and Amundi. For the second time, as you tell it. And for the second time, they escaped. How did that happen?"

"As I said, lord, we chased them to Ragi's farm, and when they would not come out we set the hall on fire. But Ragi had dug out a tunnel, the way Odd had. The tunnel led to a cliff side with a trail down to the water. We discovered they had escaped and chased them on the trail. It was night, lord, very dark.

"Anyway, we fought with them on the trail, and I'm all but certain Odd was among them, but the trail collapsed under me and my men. I was knocked out cold. There was a ship, and when I came to, at dawn, the ship was gone. Didn't find Odd's body, or Amundi's or Ragi's, so I reckon they didn't go down like me and my men. Reckon they got away on the ship."

"So what did you do?"

"I collected my men and we were heading for Grefstad, where I meant to find a ship to go after them. That's when Kolbein and the others betrayed me."

Halfdan stared at Skorri and did not reply. *Tenacious son of a bitch, aren't you?* he thought. He had always known as much, but he had never understood quite how tenacious the man was. Skorri had spent all this time, taken all this risk, just so he would not fail his king.

Kolbein and the men who had brought Skorri in had claimed Skorri was off on his own, and no longer working in the king's interest, and to them that probably seemed true. But they did not see what Halfdan saw—loyalty almost to the point of madness. That's what Halfdan saw. And he liked it.

"You were heading for Grefstad to find a ship to go after them," Halfdan said. "That would suggest that you know where Odd and the others are going."

"Yes, lord," Skorri said. "They're going to Fevik."

"Fevik? How do you know that?"

"Odd has only two ways to stop you from killing him," Skorri said. "Either he can hide, or he can rally the people around him and hope they will be enough to protect him. He's been hiding all this time, but he's back now, and that tells me he'll need the people to side with him. There are two places where he might make that happen. One is Vik, where he grew up, but that's too close to your hall for safety. The other is Fevik, where he's lived for years now, and where he's known and admired."

Silence again, and then Halfdan said, "I should have your head off, for deserting my service."

"Yes, lord," Skorri said.

"You would not object?"

"Since entering your service I've done nothing but try to obey your wishes, whatever it took. That's still true, since I consider myself still in your service. So, if you wish to have my head, I won't protest."

Halfdan studied the man for a long moment. He looked for any sign of duplicity, any indication that Skorri Thorbrandsson was lying to save his neck, but he could see none.

"How many men would it take to crush Odd Thorgrimson and his followers once and for all?" Halfdan asked.

"Five hundred good warriors by land, and a half dozen ships so the bastards cannot escape by sea," Skorri answered without hesitation.

"Good," Halfdan said. "I'll assemble those men. And you will lead them."

Skorri's eyebrows came together and he frowned. "Lord?"

"You will lead them," Halfdan said again. He had made the decision just moments before, but it was the right one, he was certain. Skorri's loyalty was well beyond the general sort; it was bordering on madness, and that meant the man would not hesitate to do what needed to be done, whatever that was, no matter how brutal.

"You'll lead the five hundred to Fevik. You'll find Odd and any who are rallying to his banner. And you'll crush them like the vermin they are."

Thorgrim Night Wolf dreamed he was running. Deep woods. Dark night. He sensed the trees and the bracken and the rotting limbs lying across the path. He twisted and ducked and leapt over the things that blocked his way. He was moving, moving fast, but still he seemed to be getting nowhere.

He was accustomed to the taste of blood in his mouth, but now all he tasted was fear. It was strange and ill-defined; not fear for himself or anything remotely like that. But fear nonetheless, a pervasive sense of dread. It drove his legs and made him push through the aching in his lungs. It was fear that was making him run, but he was not running away from anything. He was running toward it. Or trying. But he did not know what it was.

He heard a sound far off, sharp and quick, and then it was gone, but it brought him skidding to a halt on the carpet of damp leaves. The murmur of the woods—the breeze, the creaking of limbs, the scurrying in the undergrowth—those things passed unnoticed, but this new sound was not one of those.

Thorgrim lifted his head a bit and craned his neck left and right trying to hear the sound again. He heard breeze...creaking...nothing else. He took a silent, tentative step forward. And then he heard it again. Howling. Plaintive, high-pitched, and far off. Calling to him. The sound of it was like a spear point rammed into his gut. He felt the fear redouble, and with it, desperation. He had to get to the source of that cry.

He turned in the direction of the sound and was off again, bursting into a run, weaving his way through the gauntlet in his path. He still heard the howling, but it seemed no closer. His breath was coming harder, the rasping loud in his ears. Up and over a fallen trunk, splashing through a shallow stream, eyes piercing the dark.

Then he heard it again, the same sorrowful note, calling to him, pleading for him to come. But it was no closer than it had been, and it was not in front of him anymore. He stopped and listened. Now it was coming from someplace behind, back in the direction from which he had just come. And with that realization came an overwhelming sense of despair, of hopelessness. Every fiber of him demanded that he save this unseen creature, and yet there was nothing he could do, nothing, because he was not there to help.

He gasped, a sudden intake of breath, choking on his sorrow, and then he was awake. He sat up quick, eyes and mouth open wide. He was in a grassy field near the crest of a hill. Spread out below him, just visible in the dawn light—or the evening light, he did not know which—was a town of some note, with dozens and dozens of buildings, their thatched roofs just visible, the streets that cut between them illuminated here and there by the lanterns of people going about their business.

The edge of the town lay snug against a harbor, where dozens of ships and boats were tied up to wharves or riding at anchors a little ways out. Thorgrim smelled the tang of the sea mixed up with the smell of the grass and the soft dirt on which he sat.

He looked back over his right shoulder. He was sitting at the base of a high stone wall, old and worn, but skillfully built. That much was still obvious despite the years. It reminded Thorgrim of the sort of walls and buildings and such he had seen scattered around Engla-land, the ones built by the Romans, whoever the Romans were. Some ancient people, long gone, he had been led to believe. Gods of a lesser sort, perhaps.

Thorgrim looked over his left shoulder. Starri Deathless was sitting there, his knees drawn up against his chest, his arms wrapped around his legs. For a moment the two men just looked at one another.

"Wolf dream?" Starri asked.

Thorgrim nodded. He looked out over the town and was about to ask if it was morning or night when he realized the light was starting to spread and he could see more and more of the buildings and the harbor and the ships. So, dawn, then. He looked back at Starri.

"You were starting to get...the way you get, Night Wolf," Starri said. "I brought you up here. It seemed a good place."

Thorgrim nodded again. During those times when the black mood—harbinger of the wolf dreams—came on him at day's end, he was not fit for the company of men. Ugly, morose, and violent, he had learned long ago that it was best if he went away by himself. But sometimes his temper was too foul, his mind too confused, for him to do so. That was when Starri Deathless would step in.

The wolf dreams had been part of him since he was a young man, and in all those many years, Starri Deathless was the only one whose company he could tolerate when they came. Starri would sit silently by, awake and alert through the night, while Thorgrim was off running in whatever dream world the gods spun for him. Sometimes Thorgrim would tell Starri what he had seen in the dreamworld, but Starri never asked.

Thorgrim shut his eyes and lowered his head and rubbed his face and his eyes with the palms of his hand. He ran his fingers through his hair and scratched his scalp, trying to drive away the sleep. He had no notion of how long he had been gone from this world, but he did not feel in the least bit rested. He felt, in fact, exhausted.

He looked at Starri again and shook his head. "Sometimes, in the wolf dreams, the gods show me things," he said. "But now they're toying with me. That, or maybe I'm growing as blind in the dreamworld as I am in this one. They told me of danger. They told me of someone needing me. Someone I love. But they would tell me no more."

"Hmm…" Starri said. "Hardly the first time the gods have toyed with you, Night Wolf. You're favored by them, that's why they test you."

Thorgrim was not at all sure that was true, or if it was, it seemed a very odd way to show favor, but he knew better than to argue with Starri Deathless. Instead, with considerable effort and under protest from assorted joints and muscles, Thorgrim pushed himself to his feet. He looked out over the town and the harbor, now clearly visible in the sun that was rising behind him.

Frisia, he thought, as it started coming back to him. He was in Frisia, a place the Frisians called Dorestad. His fleet had arrived two days before, as best as he could recall. He ran his eyes along the waterfront. It was close to a mile away, but he could make out *Sea Hammer* tied to a wharf, with *Blood Hawk* tied alongside, just where he remembered them having been.

They had left Frankia, and le Château de Roumois, the week before, two weeks after the battle with the king's men. When the fighting was done, they had retrieved their ships and brought them back to Louis's magnificent home. The vessels were already loaded and ready for sea, and had been when they made their faux departure, but Thorgrim decided to stick around a bit longer. He was still waiting on his fifty pounds of silver per ship, and was curious as to what would happen next.

The old man, Hildirik, had said they should expect one of two things: a lone messenger from Paris or three thousand men-at-arms. In the end it was neither, but rather something none of them had foreseen: a half-dozen men-at-arms escorting the bloody corpse of Louis's brother, Eberhard, who they claimed had died of the wounds he received fighting. Eberhard, whom a hundred men had seen fleeing unscathed from the field of battle.

But according to the men-at-arms escorting the body he had not been unscathed at all. They vowed that Eberhard had been found dead by the side of the road, a mile or so from the château, and that he had not been fleeing but rather trying to rally more men to the fight.

Louis ordered the corpse lifted out of the rough wooden casket in which it had been laid and the bloody canvas shroud peeled back. And there, undeniably, was Eberhard. And just as undeniable were the vicious wounds across his chest, legs, and neck.

For a long moment they stared at the body: black, bloated, and grotesque. Then Thorgrim looked up and saw tears running down Louis's face. And, as if sensing he was being watched, Louis looked up as well and met his eyes.

"My brother," Louis said. "All these years I thought I would rejoice to see him dead."

They wrapped the body up again and put it back in the coffin and brought it inside the walls of the château. Hildirik felt certain that someone in Charles's court had murdered Eberhard and arranged for it to seem a noble death in hopes of making the uprising in Roumois go away.

That seemed an absurd and unlikely idea until a letter from Felix arrived two days later. The letter expressed sympathy for Eberhard's noble death, congratulated Louis on his accession to the dukedom, and reminded Louis of his and Roumois's obligations regarding taxes to be paid to the king, with the bulk of the emphasis on that latter part. Only then was Louis willing to admit that Hildirik was, apparently, correct.

"So you are le duc de Roumois," Hildirik said after reading the letter aloud to the group. "I congratulate you, lord, and advise that this whole affair be buried with your late brother, the last duc de Roumois."

And Louis agreed. He arranged for an elaborate funereal mass in the château's ornate church, a ceremony to which the heathen Northmen were not invited, to their great relief. After that, Eberhard was interred in the family cemetery that bordered the church. The funeral itself was attended by all the servants of the household, many of Eberhard's—now Louis's—tenants, and Thorgrim's three hundred. As far as Thorgrim could tell, no one even acted as if they were in mourning.

A feast followed the funeral, and that at least was met with great enthusiasm. In the midst of the bacchanal, Thorgrim pointed out to Louis that the Northmen had still not received their silver, and since honor would not allow them to sail without it, he feared he would have to take it one way or another.

"I'll pay you the silver," Louis told him. "I'll pay it out of my brother's treasury."

"Your brother is dead," Thorgrim said. "It's your treasury."

"Then I'll pay it out of my treasury," Louis said. "Anything to be rid of you plague of Northmen." And the next day he did just that; his servants carrying out six small caskets filled with silver in various forms: coins, ingots, arm rings, brooches.

"Just past midday you'll have the tide in your favor," he informed Thorgrim.

Thorgrim smiled. "You're eager for us to be gone? Now that you have no more use for us?"

"It does my reputation harm, being seen with your sort," Louis said. "I am, after all, le duc de Roumois."

But Thorgrim had no desire to remain in Frankia, no more than the Franks wished for him and his heathens to remain. So the Northmen piled on board their longships and brought the oars down from the gallows and sat waiting on their sea chests for Thorgrim's order to get underway.

Thorgrim was last aboard, standing on the wharf where *Sea Hammer* was tied up, looking up at the magnificent house that was now in Louis's possession. It was how long ago…two years?…that Louis had first mentioned that he was a very wealthy man, a nobleman in Frankia. None of Thorgrim's men had really believed him, or much cared.

But Thorgrim, at least, had thought he was telling the truth, or some version of it. Louis did not fight like some farmhand or tradesman. He certainly did not fight like the Christ priest he had purported to be.

A puff of breeze lifted a strand of Thorgrim's hair, as if the gods were gently reminding him that the tide was in his favor now. He took his eyes from the grand house and its high walls and looked at Louis, standing a few feet in front of him, the only other man on the dock. He thought back over the years, the meeting in Glendalough when he had taken Louis and Failend prisoner, the times Louis had escaped, the times the gods had thrown them back together again, the times he had nearly killed Louis, the times they had fought side by side. So much water under the keel.

Thorgrim took a step closer. He held out his hand. "Goodbye, Louis."

Louis took his hand and gripped it hard. "Goodbye, Thorgrim."

They held each other's eyes for a heartbeat, and then another, and then they released their grips. Thorgrim turned and climbed aboard *Sea Hammer*. He ordered the lines cast off, the oars down. He did not look back.

It had been an easy passage to Frisia, with fair winds and only the occasional sail to be seen on the horizon. They had landed in Dorestad to repair a persistent leak in *Blood Hawk*'s garboards and to spend some of the considerable wealth they had accumulated. Even Thorgrim found the visit tolerably enjoyable. Until the wolf dream.

"I need ale," he said to Starri.

Starri nodded and stood in that unique way he had, which seemed more like unfolding himself than getting to his feet. The two of them staggered down a worn path that led to the town below. Just off the crest of the hill Thorgrim saw three men lying dead in the grass, their clothes and flesh rent with wide, fresh wounds. He looked at them with vague curiosity, but did not bother to ask Starri what had happened.

By the time they reached the edge of the town Thorgrim's head was a little clearer, his gait a bit more steady. They walked down streets crowded with Frisians and Franks and Danes and Northmen and men from strange lands to the east. They made their way through the cattle, horses, pigs, barrows, wagons, all trying to maneuver down the hard-packed dirt roads. They walked past the shops of smiths and carpenters and coopers, and lean-tos under which venders were selling all manner of goods.

They came at last to a stall where a fat merchant and his wife stood by a barrel of ale, with rough, earthenware cups stacked on the side of a trestle table. "Here," Thorgrim said, nudging Starri and nodding toward the stall. They stepped up and Thorgrim pointed to the cups and held up two fingers. He had no notion what languages the man spoke, but he figured his communication was clear enough.

The fat man nodded, picked up two cups, dipped them into the barrel and set them down on the table. Thorgrim and Starri each took one up and drained it in a few quick gulps, then set them down again. Thorgrim nodded toward the barrel and the fat man nodded again, and refilled them. Once again Thorgrim and Starri drained them and set them down, and once again Thorgrim nodded toward the barrel.

He saw the fat man was looking worried now. He was wondering no doubt if the wild-looking Northmen intended to pay, but he seemed to understand it was not in his best interest to challenge them. He picked up the cups and refilled them with less enthusiasm this time.

Thorgrim dug into the purse that hung from his belt and extracted the first thing his fingers fell on, which turned out to be a silver ingot of respectable size and weight. It was an absurd amount for six cups of mediocre ale, but he was not in the mood for haggling or even putting any thought into the transaction. He set down the ingot and the ale merchant's eyes went wide and before he could move his hand, his wife's shot out and snatched up the silver.

"Come," Thorgrim said, picking up the cup and handing it to Starri, then heading down the road once more. The silver ingot, he reckoned, entitled him to at least walk off with the earthen cups, and indeed the merchant raised no objection.

They strolled along, drinking their ale, looking with vague interest at the crowds of people and goods, but Thorgrim could not rid himself of the lingering effects of the wolf dream, of the fear and desperation that clung to him the way the smell of wood smoke clung to one's clothing. He wanted to ask Starri what he thought it meant, but he felt sure Starri would just consider it a blessing from the gods. It was certainly from the gods, of that Thorgrim was certain. But he did not think it was a blessing.

"Thorgrim?"

The street was filled with noise, but the voice cut through all of it, a voice filled with surprise, almost incredulous. Thorgrim turned. A man was standing twenty feet away, a youngish man, a Northman by his clothing and weapons. His eyes were wide and his mouth was open and there was something about him that was familiar, but Thorgrim was not certain.

"Thorgrim Ulfsson?" the man said. "Thorgrim Night Wolf?" In a few long strides, he closed the distance between them and to Thorgrim's surprise he grabbed him by the shoulders and looked into his face and smiled wide, shaking his head. "By the gods, you live! After all these years, you still live!"

And then Thorgrim remembered. Hakon Styrsson. He owned a small farm about a league from Thorgrim's own. They had met many times at various gatherings, had once, in company with some other neighbors, hunted down a troublesome pack of wolves. Hakon was just a few years older than Thorgrim's son Odd. A good man. A reliable man.

"Hakon Styrsson, yes, I still live," Thorgrim said.

Hakon shook his head. "It's been so long, Thorgrim. And never a word. We had all despaired of you, thought sure you had taken your place in the corpse hall."

"No such luck," Thorgrim said. "The gods still suffer me to live. And you, too. How do you happen to be here?"

"I'm going a'viking," Hakon said. "I've gathered a crew and we're off to make our fortune."

"Really?" Thorgrim said. "Winter will be on us soon enough. Most men would wait for springtime to go off raiding."

With that Hakon's expression changed, so fast and so completely it took Thorgrim by surprise, as if the young man had suddenly recalled some terrible thing.

"Thorgrim..." he said. "Of course, you wouldn't know..."

"What?" Thorgrim asked, and he felt the fear come back again, the fear and the hints of desperation.

"Your son, Odd...." Hakon said. "Oh, he lives, don't worry about that. He was alive when last I saw him, at least. But...King Halfdan...there's been a war..."

Thorgrim felt his stomach twist. He felt the fear and the desperation come piling on again. He heard the sound once more, the howling, far off and plaintive, and he understood the wolf dream now, what the gods were whispering to him.

He held up his hand, stopping Hakon in mid-sentence. He turned to Starri. "Go find the men. Whoever you find, tell them to find the others and get back to the ships as fast as we can. We sail on the tide, and whoever is not with us gets left behind.

Starri nodded. He did not ask, he just raced off and Thorgrim watched him go. He would hear Hakon's story now, hear what troubles were plaguing Agder, what danger had befallen his son. He would hear it all, though he had already heard enough. His home was calling. His son was calling. And he would return, or he would draw his last breath in the attempt.

Acknowledgements

My thanks as ever, to the crew: Steve Cromwell for his excellent work on the cover, and Chris Boyle for the maps. Once again, bringing the production to another level. And thanks much to Cindy Vallar for her insightful editing and her sharp eye. Thanks to Nat Sobel and Judith Weber and all the great folks at Sobel Weber who make this whole production so much more than it might have been otherwise.

And, as always, I am blessed by the support of my family: Elizabeth Lockard, Nathaniel Nelson, Jonathan Nelson, Abigail Nelson, and Stephanie Nelson. And of course, my shipmate, my wife of thirty years, Lisa Nelson.

Fair winds and deep water to all.

Would you like a heads-up about new titles in The Norsemen Saga, as well as preview sample chapters and other good stuff cheap (actually free)?

Visit our web site to sign up for our (occasional) e-mail newsletter:

www.jameslnelson.com

Other Fiction by
James L. Nelson:

The Brethren of the Coast:
Piracy in Colonial America
The Guardship
The Blackbirder
The Pirate Round

The Samuel Bowater Novels:
Naval action of the American Civil War
Glory in the Name
Thieves of Mercy

The Isaac Biddlecomb Novels:
Naval action of the American Revolution
By Force of Arms
The Mddest Idea
The Continental Risque
Lords of the Ocean
All the Brave Fellows
The Falmout Frigate

The Only Life that Mattered:
The Story of Ann Bonny, Mary Read and Calico Jack Rackham

Glossary

adze – a tool much like an ax but with the blade set at a right angle to the handle.

Ægir – Norse god of the sea. In Norse mythology he was also the host of great feasts for the gods.

Asgard - the dwelling place of the Norse gods and goddesses, essentially the Norse heaven.

athwartships – at a right angle to the centerline of a vessel.

beitass - a wooden pole, or spar, secured to the side of a ship on the after end and leading forward to which the corner, or clew, of a sail could be secured.

berserker - a Viking warrior able to work himself up into a frenzy of blood-lust before a battle. The berserkers, near psychopathic killers in battle, were the fiercest of the Viking soldiers. The word *berserker* comes from the Norse for "bear shirt" and is the origin of the modern English "berserk".

block – nautical term for a pulley.

boss - the round, iron centerpiece of a wooden shield. The boss formed an iron cup protruding from the front of the shield, providing a hollow in the back across which ran the hand grip.

bothach – Gaelic term for poor tenant farmers, serfs.

brace - line used for hauling a **yard** side to side on a horizontal plane. Used to adjust the angle of the sail to the wind.

brat – a rectangular cloth worn in various configurations as an outer garment over a *léine*.

bride-price - money paid by the family of the groom to the family of the bride.

byrdingr - a smaller ocean-going cargo vessel used by the Norsemen for trade and transportation. Generally about 40 feet in length, the byrdingr was a smaller version of the more well-known **knarr**.

cable – a measure of approximately 600 feet.

clench nail – a type of nail that, after being driven through a board, has a type of washer called a rove placed over the end and is then bent over to secure it in place.

clew – one of the lower corners of a square sail, to which the **sheet** is attached.

ceorl – a commoner in early Medieval England, a peasant, but also a small-time landowner with rights. Members of the ceorl class served in the **fyrd**.

curach - a boat, unique to Ireland, made of a wood frame covered in hide.

They ranged in size, the largest propelled by sail and capable of carrying several tons. The most common seagoing craft of medieval Ireland. **Curach** was the Gaelic word for boat which later became the word *curragh.*

dagmál – breakfast time

danegeld - tribute paid by the English to the Vikings to secure peace.

derbfine – In Irish law, a family of four generations, including a man, his sons, grandsons and great-grandsons.

dragon ship - the largest of the Viking warships, upwards of 160 feet long and able to carry as many as 300 men. Dragon ships were the flagships of the fleet, the ships of kings.

dubh gall - Gaelic term for Vikings of Danish descent. It means Black Strangers, a reference to the mail armor they wore, made dark by the oil used to preserve it. *See* *fin gall.*

ell – a unit of length, a little more than a yard.

eyrir – Scandinavian unit of measurement, approximately an ounce.

félag – a fellowship of men who owed each other a mutual obligation, such as multiple owners of a ship, or a band or warriors who had sworn allegiance to one another.

figurehead – ornamental carving on the bow of a ship.

fin gall - Gaelic term for Vikings of Norwegian descent. It means White Strangers. *See* *dubh gall.*

forestay – a rope running from the top of a ship's mast to the bow used to support the mast.

Frisia – a region in the northern part of the modern-day Netherlands.

Freya - Norse goddess of beauty and love, she was also associated with warriors, as many of the Norse deity were. Freya often led the **Valkyries** to the battlefield.

fyrd – in Medieval England, a levy of commoners called up for military service when needed.

gallows – tall, T-shaped posts on the ship's centerline, forward of the mast, on which the oars and yard were stored when not in use.

hack silver – pieces of silver from larger units cut up for distribution.

hall – the central building on a Viking-age farm. It served as dining hall, sleeping quarters and storage. Also known as a **longhouse**.

halyard - a line by which a sail or a yard is raised.

Haustmánudur – early autumn. Literally, harvest-month.

Hel - in Norse mythology, the daughter of Loki and the ruler of the underworld where those who are not raised up to Valhalla are sent to suffer. The same name, Hel, is given to the realm over which she rules, the Norse hell.

hersir – in medieval Norway, a magistrate who served to oversee a region under the rule of a king.

hide – a unit of land considered sufficient to support a single family.

hird - an elite corps of Viking warriors hired and maintained by a king or powerful **jarl**. Unlike most Viking warrior groups, which would assemble and disperse at will, the hird was retained as a semi-permanent force which formed the core of a Viking army.

hirdsman - a warrior who is a member of the **hird**.

hólmganga – a formal, organized duel fought in a marked off area between two men.

jarl - title given to a man of high rank. A jarl might be an independent ruler or subordinate to a king. Jarl is the origin of the English word *earl*.

Jörmungandr – in Norse mythology, a vast sea serpent that surrounds the earth, grasping its own tail.

knarr - a Norse merchant vessel. Smaller, wider and sturdier than the longship, knarrs were the workhorse of Norse trade, carrying cargo and settlers wherever the Norsemen traveled.

Laigin – Medieval name for the modern-day county of Leinster in the south-east corner of Ireland.

league – a distance of three miles.

lee shore – land that is downwind of a ship, on which a ship is in danger of being driven.

leeward – down wind.

leech – either one of the two vertical edges of a square sail.

leine – a long, loose-fitting smock worn by men and women under other clothing. Similar to the shift of a later period.

levies - conscripted soldiers of ninth century warfare.

Loki - Norse god of fire and free spirits. Loki was mischievous and his tricks caused great trouble for the gods, for which he was punished.

longphort - literally, a ship fortress. A small, fortified port to protect shipping and serve as a center of commerce and a launching off point for raiding.

luchrupán – Middle Irish word that became the modern-day Leprechaun.

luff – the shivering of a sail when its edge is pointed into the wind and the wind strikes it on both sides.

Midgard – one of nine worlds in Norse mythology, it is the earth, the world known and visible to humans.

Niflheim – the World of Fog. One of the nine worlds in Norse mythology, somewhat analogous to Hell, the afterlife for people who do not die honorable deaths.

Njord – Norse god of the sea and seafaring.

Norns – in Norse mythology, women who sit at the center of the world and hold the fate of each person by spinning the thread of each person's life.

Odin - foremost of the Norse gods. Odin was the god of wisdom and war, protector of both chieftains and poets.

oénach –a major fair, often held on a feast day in an area bordered by two territories.

perch - a unit of measure equal to 16½ feet. The same as a rod.

Ragnarok - the mythical final battle when most humans and gods would be killed by the forces of evil and the earth destroyed, only to rise again, purified.

rath – Gaelic word for a **ringfort**. Many Irish place names still contain the word Rath.

rod – a unit of measure equal to 16½ feet. The same as a perch

rove – a square washer used to fasten the planks of a longship. A nail is driven through the plank and the hole in the washer and then bent over.

ringfort - common Irish homestead, consisting of houses protected by circular earthwork and palisade walls.

rí túaithe – Gaelic term for a minor king, who would owe allegiance to nobles higher in rank.

rí tuath – a minor king who is lord over several **rí túaithe.**

rí ruirech –a supreme or provincial king, to whom the **rí tuath** owe allegiance.

sceattas – small, thick silver coins minted in England and Frisia in the early Middle Ages.

seax – any of a variety of edged weapons longer than a knife but shorter and lighter than a typical sword.

sheer strake – the uppermost plank, or strake, of a boat or ship's hull. On a Viking ship the sheer strake would form the upper edge of the ship's hull.

sheet – a rope that controls a sail. In the case of a square sail the sheets pull the **clews** down to hold the sail so the wind can fill it.

shieldwall - a defensive wall formed by soldiers standing in line with shields overlapping.

shire reeve – a magistrate who served a king or ealdorman and carried out various official functions within his district. One of the highest ranking officials, under whom other, more minor reeves served. The term shire reeve is the basis of the modern-day *sheriff.*

shroud – a heavy rope stretching from the top of the mast to the ship's side that prevents the mast from falling sideways.

skald - a Viking-era poet, generally one attached to a royal court. The skalds wrote a very stylized type of verse particular to the medieval Scandinavians. Poetry was an important part of Viking culture and the ability to write it a highly regarded skill.

sling - the center portion of the **yard.**

sœslumadr – official appointed by the king to administer royal holdings. Similar to the English **shire reeve.**

spar – generic term used for any of the masts or yards that are part of a ship's rig.

stem – the curved timber that forms the bow of the ship. On Viking ships the stem extended well above the upper edge of the ship and the figurehead was mounted there.

strake – one of the wooden planks that make up the hull of a ship. The construction technique, used by the Norsemen, in which one strake overlaps the one below it is called *lapstrake construction*.

swine array - a Viking battle formation consisting of a wedge-shaped arrangement of men used to attack a shieldwall or other defensive position.

tánaise ríg – Gaelic term for heir apparent, the man assumed to be next in line for a kingship.

thegn – a minor noble or a land-holder above the peasant class who also served the king in a military capacity.

thing - a communal assembly.

Thor - Norse god of storms and wind, but also the protector of humans and the other gods. Thor's chosen weapon was a hammer. Hammer amulets were popular with Norsemen in the same way that crosses are popular with Christians.

thrall - Norse term for a slave. Origin of the English word "enthrall".

thwart - a rower's seat in a boat. From the old Norse term meaning "across".

tuath – a minor kingdom in medieval Ireland that consisted of several **túaithe**.

túaithe – a further subdivision of a kingdom, ruled by a **rí túaithe**

Ulfberht – a particular make of sword crafted in the Germanic countries and inscribed with the name Ulfberht or some variant. Though it is not clear who Ulfberht was, the swords that bore his name were of the highest quality and much prized.

unstep – to take a mast down. To put a mast in place is to step the mast.

Valhalla - a great hall in **Asgard** where slain warriors would go to feast, drink and fight until the coming of **Ragnarok**.

Valkyries - female spirits of Norse mythology who gathered the spirits of the dead from the battle field and escorted them to **Valhalla**. They were the Choosers of the Slain, and though later romantically portrayed as Odin's warrior handmaidens, they were originally viewed more demonically, as spirits who devoured the corpses of the dead.

vantnale – a wooden lever attached to the lower end of a shroud and used to make the shroud fast and to tension it.

Varonn – springtime. Literally "spring work" in Old Norse.

Vik - An area of Norway south of modern-day Oslo. The name is possibly the origin of the term *Viking*.

wattle and daub - common medieval technique for building walls. Small sticks were woven through larger uprights to form the wattle, and the structure was plastered with mud or plaster, the daub.

weather – closest to the direction from which the wind is blowing, when used to indicate the position of something relative to the wind.

wergild - the fine imposed for taking a man's life. The amount of the wergild was dependent on the victim's social standing.

witan - a council of the greater nobles and bishops of a region, generally assembled to advise the king.

yard - a long, tapered timber from which a sail was suspended. When a Viking ship was not under sail, the yard was turned lengthwise and lowered to near the deck with the sail lashed to it.

Printed in Great Britain
by Amazon

23264527R00219